Antisemitism: Its History and Causes

Bernard Lazare

Contents

ANTISEMITISM:
ITS HISTORY AND CAUSES

BY

Bernard Lazare

ANTISEMITISM.

CHAPTER I
GENERAL CAUSES OF ANTISEMITISM.

Exclusiveness.—The Political and Religious Cult.—Jehovah and the .Law.—Civil and Religious Regulations.—Jewish Colonies.—The Talmud.—The Chosen People Doctrine.—Jewish Pride.—Separation from the Nations.—Pollution.—The Pharisees and the Rabbinites.—The Faith, Tradition and Secular Science.—The Triumph of the Talmudists.— Jewish Patriotism.—The Mystic Fatherland.—The Restoration of the Kingdom of Israel.—The Isolation of the Jew.

To make the history of antisemitism complete, omitting none of the manifestations of this sentiment and following its divers phases and modifications, it is necessary to go into the history of Israel since its dispersion, or, more properly speaking, since the beginning of its expansion beyond the boundaries of Palestine.

Wherever the Jews settled after ceasing to be a nation ready to defend its liberty a Wldependencft. one observes the development .of antisemitism, or rather anti-Judaism; for antisemitism is an ill-chosen word, which has its raison *d'etre* only in our day, when it is sought to broaden this strife between the Jew and the Christians by supplying it with a philosophy and a metaphysical, rather than a material reason. If this hostility, this repugnance had been shown towards the Jews at one time or in one country only, it would be I easy to account for the local causes of this sentiment. ; But this race has been the object of hatred with all the : nations amidst whom it ever settled. Inasmuch as the , enemies of the Jews belonged to divers races; as they dwelled far apart from one another, were ruled by different laws and governed by opposite principles; as they had not the same customs and differed in spirit from one another, so that they could not possibly judge alike of any subject, it must needs be that the general causes of antisemitism have always resided in Israel itself, and not in those who antagonized it.

This does not mean that justice was always on the side of Israel's persecutors, or that they did not indulge in all the extremes born of hatred; it is merely asserted that the Jews were themselves, in part, at least, the cause of their own ills.

Considering the unanimity of antisemitic manifestations, it can hardly be admitted, as had too willingly been done, that they were merely due to a religious war, and one must not view the strife against the Jews as a struggle of polytheism against monotheism, or that of the Trinity against Jehovah. The polytheistic, as well as the Christian nations combatted not the doctrine of one sole God, but the Jew.

Which virtues or which vices have earned for the Jew this universal enmity? Why was he ill-treated and hated alike and in turn by the Alexandrians and the Romans, by the Persians and the Arabs, by the Turks and the Christian nations? Because, everywhere up to *our own days the jew* was an unsociable being.

Why was he unsociable? Because he was exclusive, and his exclusiveness was both political and religious, or rather he held fast to his political and religious cult, to his law.

All through history we see the conquered peoples submit to the laws of the conqueror, though they may guard their own faith and beliefs. It was easy for them to do so, for with them a line was drawn between their religious teachings which had come from the gods, and their civil laws which emanated from legislation and could be modified according to circumstances, without inviting upon the reformers the theological anathema or execration; what had been done by man could be undone by man. Thus, if the conquered rose up against the conquerors, it was through patriotism along, and they were actuated by no other motive but the desire to regain their land and their liberty. Aside from these national uprisings, they seldom took exception to being subjected to the general laws; if they protested, it was against particular enactments which placed them into a position of inferiority towards the dominant people; in the history of the Roman conquests we see the conquered bow to Rome when she extended to them the laws which governed the empire.

Not so with the Jewish people. In fact, as was observed by Spinoza, [1] "the laws revealed by God to Moses were nothing but laws for the special government of the Hebrews." Moses, [2] the prophet and legislator, assigned the same authority for his judicial and governmental enactments, as for his religious precepts, i. e., revelation, Not only did Yahweh say to the Jews, "Ye shall believe in the one God and ye shall worship no idols," he also prescribed for them rules of hygiene and morality not only did he designate the territory where sacrifices were to be offered, he also determined the manner in which that territory was to be governed. Each of the given laws, whether agrarian, civil, prophylactic, theological, or moral, proceeded from the same authority, so that all these codes formed a whole, a rigorous system of which naught could be taken away for fear of sacrilege. In reality, the Jew lived under the rule of a lord, Yahweh, who could neither be conquered, nor even assailed, and he knew but one thing, the law, i. e., the collection of rules and decrees which it had once pleased Yahweh to give to Moses,—a law divine and excellent, made to lead its followers to eternal bliss; a perfect law which the Jewish people alone had received.

With such an idea of his Torah, the Jew could not

[1] Tractatus theologico-politieus.

[2] 'When I say "Moses assigned,:" it is not to maintain that Moses himself elaborated all the laws which pass under his name, but merely because he is credited with having revised them.

accept the laws of strange nations; nor could he think of submitting to them; he could not abandon the divine laws eternal, good and just, to follow human laws, necessarily imperfect and subject to decay. If only he had been allowed to make one part of this Torah; to put on one side all civil ordinances, on the other all religious decrees! But had they not all a sacred character, and did not the welfare of the Jewish people depend upon their full observance?

These civil laws which attached to the people, not to municipalities, the Jews would not abandon upon settling among other nations, for though these laws no longer had any justification beyond Jerusalem and the Kingdom of Israel, they were none the less religious obligations binding upon all the Jews, who, by an ancient covenant with the Deity, had undertaken to fulfill them.

Thus, wherever colonies were founded by the Jews, to whatever land they were deported, they insisted, not only upon permission to follow their religion, but also upon exemption from the customs of the people amidst whom they were to live, and the privileges to govern them-selves by their own laws.

At Rome, at Alexandria, at Antioch, in Cyrenaica they were allowed full freedom in the matter. They were not required to appear in court on Saturday;[3] they i were even permitted to have their own special tribunals, and were not amenable to the laws of the empire; when the distribution of grains occurred on a Saturday

[3] **Cod. Theod.**, book II, title VIII, §2. **Cod. Just**, book I, title IX, §2.

their share was reserved for them until the next day;[4] they could be decurions, being at the same time exempt from all practices contrary to their religion[5]; they enjoyed complete self-government, as in Alexandria; they had their own chiefs, their own senate, their ethnarch, and were not subject to the general municipal authorities.

Everywhere they wanted to remain Jews, and everywhere they were granted the privilege of establishing a State within the State. By virtue of these privileges and exemptions, and immunity from taxes, they would soon rise above the general condition of the citizens of the municipalities where they resided; they had better opportunities for trade and accumulation of wealth, whereby they excited jealousy and hatred.

Thus, Israel's attachment to its law was one of the first causes of its unpopularity, whether because it de-rived from that law benefits and advantages which were 1 apt to excite envy, or because it prided itself upon the excellence of its Thorah and considered itself above and beyond other peoples.

Still had the Israelites adhered to pure Mosaism, they could, doubtless, at some time in their history, have so modified that Mosaism as to retain none but the religious land metaphysical precepts; possibly, if they had no other sacred book but the Bible they might have merged in
the nascent church, which enlisted its first followers among the Sadducees, the Essenes, and the Jewish prose

[4] Philo, *Legat*. ad Cat.

[5] *Dig* .t book I, title III, §3. (Decisions by Septimius Severus and Caracalla.)

lytes. One thing prevented that fusion and upheld the existence of the Hebrews among the nations; it was the growth of the Talmud, the authority and rule of the doctors who taught a pretended tradition. The policy of the doctors to which we shall return further made of the Jews sullen beings, unsociable and haughty, of whom Spinoza, who knew them well, could say: "It is not at all surprising that after being scattered for so many years they have preserved their identity without a government of their own, for, by their external rites, contrary to those of other nations, as well as by the sign . of circumcision, they have isolated themselves from all other nations, even to the extent of drawing upon themselves the hate of all mankind."[6]

Man's aim on earth, said the doctors, is the knowledge and observance of the law, and one cannot thoroughly observe it without denying allegiance to all but the true law. The Jew who followed these precepts isolated himself from the rest of mankind; he retrenched himself be-hind the fences which had been erected around the Torah by Ezra and the first scribes [7], later by the Pharisees and the Talmudists, the successors of Ezra, refomers of primitive Mosaism and enemies or the prophets. He isolated himself, not merely by declining to submit to the customs which bound together the inhabitants of the countries where he settled, but also by shunning all intercourse with the inhabitants themselves. To his un-sociability the Jew added exlusiveness

With the law, yet without Israel to put it into practice,

[6] Spinoza, *Tractatus theologico-politicus*

[7] The *Dibre Sopherim.*

the world could not exist, God would turn it back into nothing; nor will the world know happiness until it be brought under the universal domination of that law, i. e., under the domination of the Jews. Thus the Jewish people is chosen by God as the trustee of His will; it is the only people with whom the Deity has made a covenant; it is the choice of the Lord. At the time when the serpent tempted Eve, says the Talmud, he corrupted her with his venom. Israel, on receiving the revelation from Sinai, delivered itself from the evil; the rest of mankind could not recover. Thus, if they have each its guardian and its protecting constellation, Israel is placed under the very eye of Jehovah; it is the Eternal's favored son who has the sole right to his love, to his good will, to his special protection, other men are placed beneath the Hebrews; it is by mere mercy that they are entitled to divine munificence, since the souls of the Jews alone are descended from the first man. The wealth which has come to the nations, in truth belongs to Israel, and we hear Jesus Himself reply to the Greek woman: "It is not meet to take the children's bread and so cast it unto the dogs." [8] This faith in their pre-destination, in their election, developed among the Jews an immense gride. It led them to view the Gentiles with contempt, often with hate, when patriotic considerations supervened to religious feeling.

When Jewish nationality was in peril, the Pharisees, under John Hyrcanus, de-clared impure the soil of strange peoples, as well as all intercourse among Jews and Greeks. Later, the Shamaites advocated at a synod

[8] Mark, vii, 27.

complete separation of the Jews from the heathens, and drafted a set of injunc-tions, called *The Eighteen Things*, which ultimately prevailed over the opposition of the Hillelites. As a result Jewish unsociability begins to engage the attention of the councils of Antiochus Sidetes; exception is taken to "their persistence in shut-ting themselves up amidst their own kind and avoiding all intercourse with pa-gans, and to their eagerness to make that intercourse more and more difficult, if not impossible" [9] And the high priest Menelaus accuses the law, before Antiochus Epiphanes, "of teaching hatred of the human race, of prohibiting to sit down at the table of strangers and to show good-will towards them."

If these prescriptions had lost their authority when the cause which had pro-duced and, in a way, justified them, had disappeared, the evil would not have been great. Yet we see them reappear in the Talmud and receive a new sanction from the authority of the doctors. After the controversy between the Sadducees and the Pharisees had terminated in the victory of the latter, these injunctions became part of the law, they were taught with the law and helped to develop and exaggerate the exclusiveness of the Jews.

Another fear, that of contamination, separated the Jews from the world and made their iso-lation still more rigorous. The Pharisees held views of extreme rigor on the subject of contamination ; with them the injunctions and prescriptions of the Bible were insufficient to preserve Man from sin. As the sacrificial vases were contaminated by the least im

[9] Derembonrg, *Geographie de la Palestine.*

pure contact, they came to regard themselves contaminated by contact with strangers. Of this fear were born innumerable rules affecting every-day life: rules relating to clothing, dwelling, nourishment, all of which were promulgated with a view to save the Israelites from contamination and sacrilege; all these rules might properly be observed in an independent state or city, but could not possibly be enforced in foreign lands, for their strict observance would require the Jews to flee the society of Gentiles, and thus to live isolated, hostile to their environment.

The Pharisees. and the Rabbinites went still farther. Not satisfied with preserving the body, they also sought to save the soul. Experience had shown them that Hellenic and Soman importations imperiled what they deemed their faith. The names of the Hellenistic high priests, Jason, Menelaus, &c, reminded the Rabbinites of the times when the genius of Greece, winning over one portion of Israel, came very near conquering it. They knew that the Sadducean party, friendly to the Greeks, had paved the way for Christianity, as much as the Alexandrians and all those who maintained that "none but the legal provisions, clearly enunciated in the Mosaic law, were binding, whereas all other rules growing from local traditions or subsequently issued, could lay no claim to rigorous observance. [10]

It was under Greek influence that the books and oracles originated which prepared the minds for Messiah. The Hellenistic Jews, Philo and Aristobulus, the pseudo-Phocylides and the pseudo-Longinus, authors of the

[10] Graetz, Histoire des Juifa, b. II, p. 409.

Sibylline oracles and of the pseudo-Orphics, all these successors of the prophets who continued their work, led mankind to Christ. And it may be said that true Mo-saism, purified and enlarged by Isaiah, Jeremiah and Ezekiel, broadened and generalized by the Judaeo-Hel-lenists, would have brought Israel to Christianity, but for Ezraism, Pharisaism and Talmudism, which held the mass of the Jews bound to strict observances and narrow ritual practices.

To guard God's people, to keep it safe from evil influences, the doctors exalted their law above all things. They declared that no study but that of the law alone became an Israelite, and as a whole life-time was hardly sufficient to learn and penetrate all the subtleties and all the casuistry of that law, they prohibited the study of profane sciences and foreign languages."Those among us who learn several languages are not held in esteem," said Josephus; [11] contempt alone was soon thought insufficient, they were excommunicated. Nor did these expulsions satisfy the Rabbinites. Though deprived of Plato, had not the Jew still the Bible, could he not listen to the voice of the prophets? As the book could not be proscribed, it was belittled and made subordinate to the Talmud; the doctors declared: "The law is water, the Mishna is wine." And the reading of the Bible was considered less beneficial, less conducive to salvation than the reading of the Mishna.

However, the Rabbinites could not kill Jewish curiosity with one blow; it required centuries. It was as late as the fourteenth century, after Ibn Ezra, Rabbi

[11] *Ant. Jud.,* xx, 9.

Bechai, Maimonides, Bedares, Joseph Caspi, Levi Ben Gerson, Moses of Narbonne, and many others, were gone, all true sons of Philo and the Alexandrians, who strove to verify Judaism by foreign philosophy; after Asher Ben Yechiel had induced the assembly of the rabbis at Barcelona to excommunicate those who would study profane sciences; after Rabbi Shalem, of Mont-pellier had complained to the Dominicans of the *Moreh Nebukhim*, and this book, the highest expression of the ideas of Maimonides, had been burned;—it was only after all this that the rabbis ultimately triumphed. [12]

Their end was attained. They had cut off Israel from the community of nations; they had made of it a sullen recluse, a rebel against all laws, foreign to all feeling fraternity, closed to all beautiful, noble and generous ideas; they had made of it a small and miserable nation, soured by isolation, brutalized by a narrow education, demoralized and corrupted by an unjustifiable pride. [13]

[12] The Jewish thought still had a few lights in the fifteenth and the six-teenth century. But those among the Jews who produced anything mostly took part in the struggle between philosophy and religion, and were with-out influence upon their co-religionists; their existence is therefore no de-nial of the spirit inculcated on the masses by the rabbis. Besides, one meets, throughout that period, none but unimportant commentators, physicians and translators; there appears no great mind among them. One must go as far as Spinoza to find a Jew truly capable of high ideas; it is well known how the Synagogue treated Spinoza.

[13] *"Insolentia Judoeorum"* spoken of by Agobard, Amolon and the polemists of the Middle Ages means nothing but the pride of the Jews, who consider themselves the chosen people. This expression has not the sense forced into it by modem antisem-ites, who, it may be noted, are poor historians.

With this transformation of the Jewish spirit and the victory of sectarian doc-tors, coincides the beginning of official persecution. Until that epoch there had only been outbursts of local hatred, but no systematic vexations. With the triumph of the Rabbinites, the ghettos come into being. The expulsions and massacres commence. The Jews want to live apart,—a line is drawn against them. They detest the spirit of the nations amidst whom they live,—the nations chase them. They burn the Moreh,—their Talmud is burned and they themselves are burned with it.[14]

It would seem that no further agency was needed to render the separation of the Jews from the rest of mankind complete and to make them an object of horror and reprobation. Still another cause must be added to those just mentioned: the indomitable and tenacious patriotism of israel.

Certainly, every people was attached to the land of its birth. Conquered, beaten by the conquerors, driven into exile or forced into slavery, they remained true to the sweet memories of their plundered city or the country they had lost. Still none other knew the patriotic enthusiasm of the Jews. The Greek, whose city was de-stroyed, could elsewhere build anew the hearth upon which his ancestors bestowed their blessings; the Roman

[14] The Roman laws, the Visigothic ordinances and those of the Councils will probably be cited; yet nearly all these measures proceeded principally from Jewish proselytism. It was not until the thirteenth century that the Jews were radically and officially separated from the Christians, by ghettos, by symbols of infamy (the hat, the cape, etc.). See Ulysse Robert, *Les Signes d'infa-mie au moyevage.* (Paris, 1891.)

who went into exile took along with him his penates; Athens or Some had nothing of the mystic fatherland like Jerusalem.

Jerusalem was the guardian of the Tabernacle which received the divine word; it was the city of the only Temple, the only place in the world where God could efficiently be worshipped and sacrifices offered to Him. It was only much later, at a very late day, that prayer houses were erected in other towns of Juda, or Greece, or Italy; still in those houses they confined themselves to the reading of the law and theological discussion; the pomp of Jehovah was known nowhere but at Jerusalem, the chosen sanctuary. When a temple was built at Alexandria, it was considered heretical; indeed; the ceremonies which were celebrated there had no sense, for they ought not to be performed anywhere but in a true temple; so St. Chrysostome, after the dispersion of the Jews and the destruction of their city, was justified in saying: "The Jews offer sacrifices in all parts of the earth except there where the sacrifice is permitted and valid, i. e., at Jerusalem."

With the Hebrews the air of Palestine is the best; it is sufficient to make a man learned [15] its holiness is such that whoever resides beyond its limits is as if he had no God.[16] Therefore one must not live elsewhere, and the Talmud threatens with excommunication those who would eat the passover lamb in a foreign land.

All Jews of the period of dispersion sent to Jerusalem the didrachm tax for the maintenance of the temple;

[15] Talmud, *Bava Bathra*. 158, 2.

[16] Talmud, ***Kethuvoth***

once in their lives they came to the holy city, as later the Mohammedans came to Mecca; after their death they were carried to Palestine, and numerous craft anchored at the coast, loaded with small coffins which were thence forwarded on camel's back.

It was because in Jerusalem only, in the land given by God to their ancestors, their bodies would be resurrected. There those who had believed in Yahweh, who had observed his law and obeyed MB word, would awake at the sound of the last trumpet and appear before their Lord. Nowhere but there could they rise at the appointed hour; every other land but that washed by the yellow Jordan was a vile land, fouled by idolatry, deprived of God.

When the fatherland was dead, when adversity was sweeping Israel all over the world, after the Temple had perished in flames, and when the heathens occupied the holiest ground, mourning over bygone days became everlasting in the soul of the Jew. It was over; they could no longer hope to see on the day of mercy the black buck carry away their sins into the desert, neither could they see the lamb killed for the Passover night, or bring their offerings to the altar; and, deprived of Jerusalem during life, they would not be brought there after death.

God ought not to abandon his children, reasoned the pious; and naive legends came to comfort the exiles. Near the tombs of the Jews who die in exile, they said, Jehovah opens long caverns through which the corpses roll as far as Palestine, whereas the pagan who dies there, near the consecrated hills, is removed from the chosen land, for he is unworthy Of remaining there where the resurrection will take place.

Still that did not satisfy them. They did not resign themselves to visiting Jerusalem merely as pitiable pilgrims, weeping before the ruined walls, many of them so maddened by grief as to let themselves be trampled upon by horses' hoofs, embracing the ground while moaning; they could not believe that God, that the blessed city had abandoned them; with Judah Levita they exclaimed: "Zion, hast thou forgotten thy unfortunate children who groan in slavery ?" .

They expected that their Lord would by his mighty right hand raise the fallen walls; they hoped that a prophet, a chosen one, would bring them back to the promised land; and how many times, in the course of ages, have they left their homes, their fortunes,—they who are reproached of being too much attached to worldly goods,—in order to follow a false Messiah who undertook to lead them and promised them the return so much longed for! Thousands were attracted by Sere-nus, Moses of Crete, Alroi, and massacred in the expectation of the happy day.

With the Talmudists these sentiments of popular enthusiasm, this mystic heroism underwent a transforma-tion. The doctors taught the restoration of the Jewish empire ; in order that Jerusalem might be born anew from its ruins, they wanted to preserve the people of Israel pure, to prevent them from mixing with other people, to inculcate on them the idea that they were everywhere in exile, amidst enemies that held them captive. They said to their disciples: "Do not cultivate strange lands, soon you will cultivate your own; do not attach yourself to any land, for thus will you be unfaithful to the memory of your native land; do not submit to any king,, for you have no master but the Lord of the Holy Land, Jehovah; do not scatter amongst the nations, you will forfeit your salvation and you will not see the light of the day of resurrection; remain such as you left your house; the hour will come and you will see again the hills of your ancestors, and those hills will then be the centre of the world, which will be subject to your power."

Thus all those complex sentiments which had in olden days served to build up the hegemony of Israel, to maintain its character as a nation, to develop a high and powerful originality, all those virtues and vices which gave it the spirit and countenance necessary to preserve a nation; which enabled it to attain greatness and later to defend its independence with desperate valor worthy of admiration; all that, after the Jews had ceased to be a State, combined to shut them up in the most complete, the most absolute isolation.

This isolation has been their strength, in the opinion of some apologists. If they mean to say that owing to it the Jews have survived, so much is true; if the conditions are considered, however, under which the Jews have preserved their identity as a people, it is obvious that this isolation has been their weakness, and that they have survived up to modern times, as a race of pariahs, persecuted, often martyred. Moreover, it is not only to their seclusion that they owe this surprising persistence. Their extraordinary solidarity, due to their misfortunes, and mutual support count for very much; and even in our day, when they take part in public life in Borne countries, having abandoned their sectarian dogmas, this very solidarity prevents them from dissolving and disappearing as a people, by conferring upon them certain benefits to which they are by no means indifferent.

This solicitude for worldly goods, which is a marked feature of the Hebrew character, has not been without effect upon the conduct of the Jews, especially since they left Palestine; by directing them along certain avenues, to the exclusion of all others, this feature of their character has drawn upon them the most violent animosities positive. His mysticism has come down from the theo-phanies of the desert to the metaphysical dreaming of the kabbala; his positivism, or rather his rationalism, manifests itself in the sentences of the Ecclesiastes as well as the legislative enactments of the rabbis and the dogmatic controversies of the theologians. Still if mysticism i leads to a Philo or Spinoza, rationalism leads to the usurer, the weigher of gold; it creates the greedy trader.It is true that at times these two states of the mind are found in just opposition, and the Israelite, as it occurredin the middle ages, can split his life into two ""parts: one devoted to meditation on the Absolute, theother to business.

Of the Jewish love for gold, there can be no question here. Though it may have grown so abnormal with this race as to have become well-nigh the only motive of their actions, though it may have engendered a violent and exasperated antisemitism, yet it cannot be classed among the general causes of antisemitism It was, on the contrary, the effect of those very -causes, and we shall see that it is partly the exclusiveness, the persistent patriotism and pride of Israel, that has driven it to become the hated usurer of the whole world.

In fact, all the causes we have just enumerated, if they be general, are not the only ones. I have called them general, because they depend upon one constant element: the Jew. Still the Jew is only one of the factors of antisemitism; he provokes it by his presence, but he is not the only one that determines it. The nations among whom the Israelites have lived, their manners, their customs, their religion, the philosophy even of the nations in whose midst Israel has developed, determine the particular character of antisemitism, which changes with. time and place.

We shall trace these modifications and variations of antisemitism through the course of ages down to our epoch; and we shall examine whether, in some countries at least, the general causes I have attempted to deduce are still operating, or whether the reasons for modern antisemitism must not be sought elsewhere.

CHAPTER II.

ANTI-JUDAISM IN ANTIQUITY.

The Hykos.—Haman.—Antisemitism in Ancient Society.—In Egypt, Manetho, Chaeremon, Lysimachus. —Antisemitism at Alexandria.—The Stoics: Posi-donius, Apollonius Molo.—Apion, Josephus and Philo.—"Treatise Against the Jews," the "Contra Apionem," and the "Legation to Caius."—The Jew at Rome.—Roman Antisemitism.—Cicero, Disciple of Apion, and *Pro Flacco* .—Persius, Ovid and Petronius.—Pliny, Suetonius and Juvenal.— Seneca and the Stoics.—Government Measures.— Antisemitism at Antioch and in Ionia.—Antisemitism and Antichristianity.

Modern antisemites who are in quest of sires for themselves, unhesitatingly trace the first demonstrations against the Jews back to the days of ancient Egypt. For that purpose they are particularly pleased to refer to Genesis, xliii, 32, where it is said: "The Egyptians might not eat bread with the Hebrews; for that it is an abomination unto the Egyptians." They also rely upon a few verses of the Exodus, among them the following: "Behold, the people of the children of Israel are more and mightier than we; come on, let us deal wisely with them, lest they multiply." (Exodus, i, 9,10.)

It is certain that the sons of Jacob who came to the land of Goshen under the Shepherd Pharaoh Aphobis, were treated by the Egyptians with the same contempt as their brothers, the Hyksos, referred to in hieroglyphic texts as lepers, called also "plague" and "pest" in some inscriptions. [17] They arrived at that very epoch when a very strong national sentiment manifested itself against the Asiatic invaders, hated for their cruelty; this sentiment soon led to the war of independence, which resulted in the final victory of Ahmos I., and the enslavement of the Hebrews. However, unless one is a violent anti-Jew, it is impossible to perceive in those remote disturbances anything beyond a mere incident in a struggle between conquerors and conquered.

There is no antisemitism until the Jews, having abandoned their native land, settle as immigrants in foreign countries and come into contact with natives or older settlers, whose customs, race and religion are different from those of the Hebrews.

Accordingly, the history of Haman and Mordecai may be taken as the beginning of antisemitism and the antisemites have not failed so to do. This view is, perhaps, more correct. Though the historical reality of the book of Esther can scarcely be relied upon, still it is worthy of note that its author puts into the mouth of Haman some of the complaints, which, at a later . period, are uttered by Tacitus and other Latin writers. "And Haman said unto the king, Ahasuerus: there is a certain people scattered abroad and dispersed among the people in all the provinces of thy kingdom; and their

[17] Inscription of Aahmes, chief of the mariners, cited in Le-drain's *Histoire du peuple d'Israel*, I, p. 53.

laws are diverse from all people; neither keep they the king's laws." (Esther, iii, 8.)

The pamphleteers of the middle ages, of the sixteenth and seventeenth centuries, and of our own time, say nothing else; and if the history of Haman is apocryphal, which is highly probable, still it cannot be denied that the author of the Book of Esther has very ably brought out some of the causes, which for many centuries exposed the Jews to the hatred of nations.

Yet we must go to the period of Jewish expansion abroad, to be enabled to observe with certainty that hostility against them, which by a peculiar misuse of terms has in our days been called antisemitism.

Some traditions refer the entrance of the Jews into the ancient world to the epoch of the first captivity. While Nabu-Kudur-Ussur led away to Babylonia a portion of the Jewish people, many of the Israelites, to escape from the conqueror, fled to Egypt, to Tripoli, and reached the Greek colonies. Tradition brings back to the same period the arrival of the Jews in China and India.

Historically, however, the wanderings of the Jews across the globe commence in the fourth century before our era. About 331 B. C. Alexander transported some Jews to Alexandria, Ptolemy sent some of them to Cyrenaica, and about the same time Seleucus led softie of them to Antioch. When Jesus was born Jewish colonies flourished everywhere, and it was among them that Christianity recruited its first adherents. There were Jews in Egypt, in Phoenicia, in Syria, in Coele-Syria, in Pamphylia, in Cilicia, and as far as Bithynia. In Europe they had settled in Thessalia, Boeotia, Macedonia, Attica and Peloponnesus. They were to be found in the Great Isles, on Euboea, on Crete, on Cyprus, and at Rome. "It is not easy to find a place on earth," says Strabo, "which has not received that race."

Why were the Jews hated in all those countries, in all those cities? Because they never entered any city as citizens, but always as a privileged class. Though having left palestine, they wanted above all to remain Jews, and their native country was still Jerusalem, i. e., the only city where God might be worshipped and sacrifices offered in His Temple. They formed everywhere republics, as it were, united with

Judea and Jerusalem, and from every place they remitted monies to the high priest in payment of a special tax for the maintenance of the Temple—the didrachm.

Moreover, they separated themselves from other inhabitants by their rites and their customs; they considered the soil of foreign nations impure and sought to constitute themselves in every city into a sort of a sacred territory. They lived apart, in special quarters, secluded among themselves, isolated, governing themselves by virtue of privileges which were jealously guarded by them, and excited the envy of their neighbors. They intermarried amongst themselves and entertained no strangers, for fear of pollution. The mystery with which they surrounded themselves excited curiosity as well as aversion. Their rites appeared strange and gave occasion for ridicule; being unknown, they were misrepresented and slandered.

At Alexandria they were quite numerous. According to Philo, [18] Alexandria was divided into five wards. Two were inhabited by the Jews. The privileges accorded to them by Caesar were engraved on a column and guarded by them as a precious treasure. They had their own Senate with exclusive jurisdiction in Jewish affairs, and they were judged by an ethnarch. They were ship-owners, traders, farmers, most of them wealthy; the sumptu-ousness of their monuments and synagogues bore witness to it The Ptolemies made them farmers of the reve-nues; this was one of the causes of popular hatred against them. Besides, they had a monopoly of navigation on the Nile, of the grain trade and of provisioning Alexandria, and they extended their trade to all the provinces along the Mediterranean coast. They accumulated great fortunes; this gave rise to the ***invidia auri Judaici.*** The growing resentment against these foreign cornerers, constituting a nation within a nation, led to popular disturbances; the Jews were frequently assaulted, and Germanicu, among others, had great trouble protecting them.

The Egyptians took revenge upon them by deriding their religious customs, their abhorrence of pork. They once paraded in the city a fool, Carabas by name, adorned with a papyrus diadem, decked in a royal gown, and they saluted him as king of the Jews. Under Philadelphus, one of the first Ptolemies, Manetho, the high-priest of the Temple at Heliopolis, lent his au-thority to the popular hatred; he considered the Jews descendants of the Hyksos usurpers, and said that that leprous tribe had been expelled for sacrilege and im-

[18] *In Flaccum*

piousness. Those fables were repeated by Chceremon and Lysimachus. It was not only popular animosity, however that persecuted the Jews; they had also against them the Stoics and the Sophists. The Jews, by their proselytism, interfered with the Stoics; there was a rivalry for for influence between them, and, notwithstanding their common belief in divine unity, there was opposition between them. The Stoics charged the Jews with irreligiousness, judging by the sayings of Posidonius and Apollonius Molo; they had a very scant knowledge of the Jewish religion. The Jews, they said, refuse to worship the gods; they do not consent to bow even before the divinity of the emperor. They have in their sanctuary the head of an ass and render homage to it; they are cannibals; every year they fatten a man and sacrifice him in a grove, after which they divide among themselves his flesh and swear on it to hate strangers. "The Jews, says Apollonius Molo, are enemies of all mankind; they have invented nothing useful, and they are brutal." To this Posidonius adds: "They are the worst of all men."

Not less than the Stoics did the Sophists detest the Jews. But the causes of their hatred were not religious, but, I should say, rather literary. From Ptolemy Philadelphus, until the middle of the third century, the Alexandrian Jews, with the intent of sustaining and strengthening their propaganda, gave themselves to forging all texts which were capable of lending support to their cause. The verses of Aeschylus, of Sophocles, of Euripides, the pretended oracles of Orpheus, preserved in Aristobulus and the *Stromata* of Clement of Alexandria were thus made to glorify the one God and the Sabbath.

Historians were falsified or credited with the authorship of books they had never written. It is thus that a History of the Jews was published under the name of Hecataeus of Abdera. The most important of these inventions was the Sibylline oracles, a fabrication of the Alexandrian Jews, which prophesied the future advent of the reign of the one God. They found imitators, however, for since the Sibyl had begun to speak, in the second century before Christ, the first Christians also made her speak. The Jews would appropriate to themselves even the Greek literature and philosophy. In a commentary on the Pentateuch, which has been preserved for us by Eusebius, [19] Aristobulus attempted to show that Plato and Aristotle had found their metaphysical and ethical ideas in an old Greek translation of the Pentateuch. The Greeks were greatly incensed at such treatment of their literature and philosophy, and out of revenge they circulated the slanderous stories of Manetho, adapting them to those of the Bible, to the great fury of the Jews; thus the confusion of languages was identified with the myth of Zeus robbing the animals of their common language. The Sophists, wounded by. the conduct of the Jews, would speak against them in their teaching. One among them, Apion, wrote a *Treatise against the Jews*. This Apion was a peculiar individual, a liar and babbler, to a degree uncommon even among rhetors, and full of vanity, which earned him from Tiberius the nickname of *"Cymbalum mundi"* His stories were famous; he claimed to have called out,

[19] Preparatio Evangelico.

by means of magic herbs, the shade of Homer, says Pliny:

Apion repeated in his *Treatise against the Jews* the stories of Manetho, which had been previously restated by Chaeremon and Lysimachus, and supplemented them by quoting from Posidonius and Apollo-nius Molo. According to him, Moses was "nothing but a seducer and wizard," and his laws contained "nothing but what is bad and dangerous." [20]

As to the Sabbath, the name was derived, he said, from a disease, a sort of an ulcer, with which the Jews were afflicted, and which the Egyptians called *sabbato-sim*, i. e., disease of the groins.

Philo and Josephus undertook the defense of the Jews and fought the Sophists and Apion. In Contra ***Apionem***, Josephus is very severe on his adversary. "Apion," says he, "is as stupid as an ass and as imprudent as a dog, which is one of the gods of his nation." Philo, on the other hand, prefers to attack the Sophists in general, and if he mentions Apion at all, in his ***Lega-tio ad Caium***, it is merely because Apion was sent to Borne to prefer charges against the Jews before Caligula.

In his Treatise on ***Agriculture*** he draws a very black picture of the Sophists, and insinuates that Moses has compared them to hogs. Nevertheless, in his other writings, he advises his co-religionists not to irritate them, so as to avoid all provocation to disturbances, but to await patiently their chastisement, which will come on the day the Jewish Empire, the empire of salvation, will be established on earth.

[20] Josephus, ***Contra Apionem***, book II, ch. 6.

Philo's injunctions were not heeded; the exasperation on both sides often led to violent riots and massacres of Jews; the latter, however, valiantly defended themselves.[21]

At Rome the Jews had a powerful and wealthy colony as early as the first year of the Christian era. If Valerius Maximus may be trusted, they first came to the city about 139 B. C, during the consulate of Popilius Loenus and Cajus Calpwinius.[22]

Certain it is that, in 160 B. C, an embassy from Judas Maccabee arrived in Borne to negotiate an alliance with the Republic against the Syrians; other embassies followed, in 143 and in 139.[23]

The settlement of the Jews at Borne probably dates from that time. Under Pompey they came in numtant factor in politics. Caesar availed himself of their support during the civil wars and lavished favors upon ers, and as early as 58 B. C, they had quite a settlement Turbulent and formidable, they were an impor-them; he even granted them exemption from military service. Under Augustus the distribution of free bread was postponed for them whenever it fell due on Saturday. The Emperor gave them permission to collect the did-rachm which was sent to Palestine, and he ordered the sacrifice of one or two lambs to be offered in his behalf at the Temple of Jerusalem for all time to come. When

[21] Philo, *In Flaccum*.

[22] Valerius Maximus, I. 3, 2.

[23] *Maccal*. viii., 11, 17-32; xii, 1-3; xiv, 16-19, 24.—Josephus, *Antiqu. Jud.* xii, 110; xiii, 5, 7, 9 *Mai script vet.*, Ill, part 8, p. 998.

Tiberius became emperor, there were at Home 20,000 Jews, who were organized in colleges and *sodalitates.*

Except the Jews of prominent families, like the Herods and the Agrippas, who mixed in public life, the Jewish masses lived in retirement. The majority resided in the dirtiest and busiest quarter of the city, the Transti-berinus. They were to be seen near the Via Portuensis, the Emporium and the great Circus, in the Campus Martius, and in Suburra, beyond the Capenian Gate, on the banks of the Egerian Creek, and near the sacred grove. They were engaged in retail trade and the sale of second-hand goods; those at the Capenian Gate were fortune tellers. The Jew of the Ghetto is already there.

At Rome the same causes were at work as at Alexandria. There, also, the excessive privileges of the Jews, the wealth of some of them, as well as their unheard-of luxury and ostentation, excited popular hatred. This resentment was aggravated by deeper and more important reasons of a religious character; it may even be maintained, strange as it may seem, that the motive of Roman anti-Judaism was religious.

The Roman religion resembled in nothing the admirable and profoundly symbolic polytheism of the Greeks. It was ritual rather than mythical; it consisted of customs closely connected with the doings of everyday life, as well as with all sorts of public acts. Rome was one body with its gods; its greatness was bound, as it were, with the rigorous observance of the practices of their national religion; its glory depended upon the piety of its citizens, and it seems that the Roman must have had, like the Jew, that notion of a covenant between the deities and himself, which was to be scrupulously lived up to by both parties. Somehow or other, the Roman was always in the presence of his gods; he left his hearth, where they abode, only to find them again in the Forum, on the public highways, in the Senate, even in the fields, where they kept watch over the power of Rome. At all times and on ail occasions sacrifices were offered; the warriors and the diplomats were guided by auguries, and all authority, civil as well as military, partook of the priesthood, for the officer could not perform his duties unless he knew the rites and observances of the cult.

It was this cult that for centuries sustained the Republic, and its commandments were faithfully obeyed; when they were changed, when the traditions became adulterated, when the rules were violated, Rome saw its glory fade, and its agony commenced.

Thus the Roman religion preserved itself for a long time without change. True, Rome was familar with foreign cults; she saw the worshippers of Isis and Osiris, those of the great Mother and those of Sabazius; still, though admitting them into her Pantheon, she gave them no place in her national religion. All these Orientals were tolerated; the citizens were allowed to practice their superstitions, provided they were harmless; but when Rome perceived that a new faith was subversive of the Roman spirit, she was pitiless, as in the case of the conspiracy of the Bacchantes, or the expulsion of Egyptian priests. Rome guarded herself against the foreign spirit; she feared affiliation with religious societies; she was afraid even of Greek philosophers, and the Senate, in 161, upon the report of the praetor Marcus Pom-ponius, barred them from entering the city.

From this, one may understand the feeling of the Romans toward the Jews. Greeks, Asiatics, Egyptians, Germans, or Gauls, while bringing with them their rites and beliefs, made no objection to bowing before Mars of the Palatine, or even before Jupiter Latiaris. They conformed, within certain limits, to the rules of the city, to its religious customs; at all events, they showed no opposition. Not so the Jews. They brought with them a religion as rigid, as ritualistic, as intolerant, as the

Soman religion. Their worship of Yahweh excluded all other worship; thus they shocked their fellow citizens by refusing to swear to the eagles, whereas the eagle was the deity of the legion. As their religious faith was blended with the observance of certain social laws, the adoption of this faith was pregnant with a change of the social order. Therefore the Romans were worried by its establishment in their midst, for the Jews were eager to make proselytes.

The proselytic spirit of the Jews is attested by all the historians, and Philo justly says: "Our customs win over and convert the barbarians and the Hellenes, the continent and the isles, the Orient and the Occident, Europe and Asia, the whole world, from end to end."

The ancient nations, at their decline, were deeply attracted by Judaism, by its dogma of divine unity, by its morals; many of the poor people were attracted by the privileges accorded to the Jews. These proselytes were divided into two great classes: those who accepted the circumcision and thereby entered into the Jewish community, thus becoming strangers to their families, and those who, without complying with the requisites for admission to the community, nevertheless gathered around it.

These conversions, generally by suasion and at times by force, as when the rich Jews converted their slaves, were bound to create a reaction. It was this chief cause, together with the secondary causes previously referred to, viz., the wealth of the Jews, their political influence, their privileged condition, that led to anti-Judaic demonstrations at Home. The majority of Roman and Greek writers from Cicero on bear witness to this state of mind.

Cicero, who was a disciple of Apollonius Molo, inherited his teacher's prejudices; he found the Jews in his way: they were with the popular party against the party of the Senate, to which he belonged. He feared them, and we can see from some passages of ***Pro Flacco,*** that he hardly dared to speak of them, so numerous were they around him and in the public place. Nevertheless, one day he burst forth. "Their barbarous superstitions must be fought," says he; he accuses them of being a nation "given to suspicion and slander," and proceeds by saying that they "show contempt for the splendor of the Roman power," [24] They were to be feared, according to him— those men who, detaching themselves from Rome, turned their eyes towards the far away city, that Jerusalem, and supported it by denaries which they drew from the Republic. Moreover, he reproached them for winning citizens over to the Sabbatarian rites.

[24] ***Pro Flacco.***

It is this last charge that recurs most frequently in the writings of the polemists, the poets and the historians. The Jewish religion, which charmed those who had penetrated its essence, was repulsive to others who had a scant knowledge of it and regarded it as a heap of absurd and dismal rites. The Jews are nothing but a superstitious nation, says Persius [25]; their Sabbath is a lugubrious day, adds Ovid [26]; they worship the hog and the ass, affirms Petronius. [27]

Tacitus, well informed as he is, repeats, with regard to Judaism, the fables of Manetho and Posidonius. The Jews, says he, are descended from lepers, they honor the head of an ass, they have infamous rites. He further specifies his charges, which, one would say, are those of modern French Nationalists: "All those who embrace their faith," says he, "undergo circumcision, and the first instruction they receive is to despise the gods, to forswear their country, to forget father, mother and children." And he warms up by saying: "The Jews consider as profane all that is held sacred with us." [28] Suetonius and Juvenal repeat the same thing; the principal charge reads: "They have a particular cult and particular laws; they despise the Roman laws." [29] This is likewise the complaint of Pliny: "They despise the gods." [30]

Seneca has the same grudge, still with the philosopher other motives supervene. There was a rivalry be-

[25] ***Sat.,*** V.

[26] *Art amatoria,* I, 75, 76.

[27] *Fragm. Poet*.

[28] "Tac, *Hist.*, v. 4, 5.

[29] Juvenal, *Sat.*, xiv, 90, 104.

[30] *Hist, not.,* xiii 4.

tween Seneca, the Stoic, and the Jews, the same as there had been between the Stoics and the Jews at Alexandria. He quarrelled less with their contempt of the gods than with their proselytism which thwarted the spread of the doctrine of the Stoics. He thus gives expression to his displeasure: "The Romans," says he regretfully, "have adopted the Sabbath." [31] And, further speaking of the Jews, he says in conclusion: "This abominable nation has succeeded in spreading its usages throughout the whole world; the conquered have given their laws to the conquerors." [32] Seneca's view was in accord with the attitude of both the Republic and the Empire, by which measures were adopted from time to time to check Jewish proselytism. Under Tiberius, in the year 22,a senatus-consult was directed against the Egyptian and Judaic superstitions and four thousand Jews, says Tacitus, were deported to Sardinia. Caligula subjected them to vexatipus persecution; he encouraged the doings of Flaccus in Egypt, and Flaccus, sustained by the Emperor, robbed the Jews of the privileges granted to them by Cæsar; he took away from them their synagogue and directed that they might be treated as inhabitants of a captured city. Domitian imposed a special tax upon Jews and those who led a Judaic life, hoping by the levy of the tax to stop conversions, and Antoninus Pius prohibited the Jews from circumcising others than their sons.

Anti-Judaism manifested itself not only at Rome and Alexandria, but wherever there were Jews: at Antioch, where great massacres occurred; in Lybia, where, under

[31] *Epistle* xv.

[32] *De superstitione,* fragm. xxxvi.

Vespasian, the governor Catullus stirred up the populace against them; in Ionia, where, under Augustus, the Greek cities, by an understanding among themselves, forced the Jews either to renounce their faith or to bear the entire burden of public expenditures.

Yet it is impossible to speak of the persecution of the Jews without speaking of the persecution of the Christians. For a long time Jews and Christians, these hostile brothers, were included in the same contempt, and the same causes which made the Jews hateful made the Christians hateful as well. The disciples of the Nazarene brought into the ancient world the same deadly principles. If the Jews taught the people to leave their gods, to abandon husband, father, child and wife, and to come to Jehovah, Jesus also said: "I have not come to unite, but to separate." The Christians, like the Jews, refused to bow to the eagle; like the Jews they would not lie prostrate before idols. Like the Jews, the Christians knew another country than Rome; like the Jews, they would be oblivious of their civic, rather than their religious duties.

Thus, during the first years of the Christian era, the Synagogue and the ancient Church were despised alike. Simultaneously with the Jews "a certain *chrestus*" [33] and his followers were driven from Rome. Each side endeavored to convince the people that it ought not to be mistaken for the other, and no sooner did Christianity make itself heard than it rejected, in its turn, the descendants of Abraham.

[33] Suetonius, Claud.. 25.

CHAPTER III.

ANTI-JUDAISM IN CHRISTIAN ANTIQUITY FROM THE FOUNDATION OF THE CHURCH OF CONSTANTINE.

The Church and the Synagogue.—Jewish Privileges and the First Christians.—Jewish Hostility.—Judaic Patriotism.—Christian Proselytism and the Rabbis. —Attacks upon Christianity.—The Apostates and Maledictions.—Stephen and James.—Jewish Influence Contested.—Christianity Among the Pagans and Among the Jews.—Peter and Paul.—Judaiz-ing Heresies.—The Ebionites, the Elkasaites, the Nazarenes, the Quartodecimans.—Gnosticism and Jewish Alexandrinism.—Simon the Magician, the Nicolaites and Cerinthus.—First Apostolic Scriptures and the Tendencies of the Judaizing.—The Epistles to the Colossians and Ephesians, the Pastorals, the Second Epistle of Peter, the Epistle of Jude, the Apocalypse.—The Epistle to Barnabas, the Seven Letters of Ignatius of Antioch.—Christian Apologists and Jewish Exegesis.—The letter to Diognetus.—The Testament of the Twelve Patriarchs.—Justin and the Dialogue with Tryphon.— Aristo of Pella and the Dialogue of Jason with Papisus.—Christian Expansion and Jewish Proselytism.—Rivalries and Hatred; Persecutions; The Case of Polycarp.—The Polemics.—The Bible, the Septuagint, Aquila's Version and the Hexapla.—Origen and Rabbi Simlai.—Abbahu of Caesarea and the Physician Jacob the Minaean.—The Contra Cel-sum and Jewish Ridicule.—Theological Anti-Judaism.—Tertullian and De Adversus Iudaeos.— Cyprian and The Three Books Against the Jews.— Minucius Felix.—Commodian and Lactantius.— Constantine and the Triumph of the Church.

The Church is the daughter of the Synagogue; she owes her early development to the Synagogue; she grew in the shade of the Temple, and from her first infant cry she opposed her mother, which was quite natural, for they were divided by a wide divergence of opinion.

In the first centuries of the Christian era, during the apostolic age, Christian communities sprang forth from Jewish communities, like a swarm of bees escaping from a beehive; they settled on the same soil.

Jesus was not yet born when the Jews had built their prayer-houses in the cities of the Orient and the Occident; their expansion to Asia Minor, Egypt, Cyrenaica, Rome, Greece and Spain has already been noted. By their unceasing proselytism, by their preaching, by the moral influence they exercised over the nations amidst whom they lived, they paved the way for Christianity. True, even before them philosophers had arrived at the conception of one God, but the teaching of the philosophers was restricted to the few* it was not accessible to the common people, to those of humble station whom the metaphysicians rather despised. The Jews addressed the little ones, the weak, and planted in their souls germs of new ideas which had theretofore been foreign to them. They brought with them the spirit of the prophets, the spirit of brotherhood, pity and also of revolt, that spirit which begat the pitying and sullen anger of Jeremiah and Isaiah and led to the tender sweetness of Hillel, that spirit which inspired Jesus.

This immense class of proselytes won over by the Jews this God-fearing multitude, was ready to receive the, broader and more humanitarian teachings of Jesus, those teachings which the universal Church, from its very inception, undertook to adulterate and to turn away from their true meaning. These converts whose numbers steadily increased during the first century before Christ, were free from the national prejudices of Israel; they Judaized, but their eyes were not turned toward Jerusa-lem, and, one may say, the fervld patriotism of the Jews rather checked the conversions. The Apostles, or at least some of them, completely separated the precepts of the Jewish faith from the narrow idea of nationality; they built upon the foundation of Jewish work accomplished before and thus won for themselves the souls of those who had received the Jewish seed.

The Apostles preached in the synagogues. In the cities, where they arrived, they went straight to the prayer-houses and there made their propaganda and found their first helpers; later a Christian community was founded, side by side with the Jewish community, and the original Jewish nucleus was increased by all those whom they had convinced among the Gentiles.

Without the existence of Jewish colonies Christianity would have encountered much greater obstacles; it would have had greater difficulties in establishing itself. As has been stated, the Jews in ancient society enjoyed considerable privileges; they had protective charters assuring them an independent political and judicial organization and freedom of worship. These privileges facilitated the development of the Christian churches. For a long time the associations of the Christians were not distinguished by the authorities from Jewish associations, the Roman government taking no cognizance of the division betwen the two religions. Christianity was treated as a Jewish sect, thus benefiting by the same advantages; it was not only tolerated, but, in an indirect way, protected by the imperial governors.

Thus, on the one hand, unwillingly, the Jews were unconscious auxiliaries of Christianity while, on the" other hand, they were its enemies, for which there were numerous reason. It is known that Jesus and his teachings enlisted their first following among the Galilean provincials who were despised by the Jerusalemites for having yielded more than others to foreign influences. "Can there any good thing come out of Nazareth?" they said. These humble folks of Galilee, though much attached to the Judaic rites and customs, in which respect they were, perhaps, stricter than the Jerusalemites, were ignorant of the Law and were therefore despised by the haughty doctors of Judea. This scorn likewise followed the first disciples of Jesus, some of whom, besides, belonged to the disreputable classes, such e. g., as the publicans.

Nevertheless, while the origin of the primitive Chris-tians brought upon them the scorn of the Jews, it was not enough to excite their hatred; graver reasons were required for that, foremost among them was Jewish patriotism.

The birth and early development of Christianity coincided with the time when the Jewish nation attempted to shake off the yoke of Rome.. Offended in their religious feelings, ill-treated by the Roman administration, the Jews felt a yearning for liberty, which grew with their hatred of Borne. Bands of zealots and assassins traversed the mountains of Judea, entering the villages and wreaking vengeance upon Rome by striking those of their brethren who bowed to the imperial authority. Plainly, these zealots and assassins who attacked the Sadducees for mere complacency towards the Roman procurators, could not spare the disciples of Him to whom the words were attributed, "Render unto Cæsar the things which are Cæsar's.")

Absorbed in the expectation of the coming Messianic reign, the Jewish Christians of those days were "men without a country"; the thought of free Judea no longer made their hearts throb, though some, like the seer of the Apocalypse, had a horror of Rome, still they had no passion for captive Jerusalem, which the zealots strove to liberate; they were unpatriotic.

When all Galilee rose in response to the appeal of John of Gischala, they held aloof, and when the Jerusalemites triumphed over Cestius Gallus, the Jewish Christians, indifferent to the outcome of this supreme struggle, fled from Jerusalem, crossed the Jordan and sought refuge at Pella. In the last battles which Bar Giora, John of Gischala and their faithful gave to the Roman power, to the trained legions of Vespasian and Titus, the disciples of Jesus took no part; and when Zion was reduced to ashes, burying under its ruins the nation of Israel, no Christian met his death amidst the destruction.

One may well understand what could have been the treatment accorded, in those days of exaltation, before, during and after the insurrection, to the Jewish and Gentile Christians, who, with St. Paul, counseled submission to the power of Borne. The patriotic indignation roused by the nascent Church was seconded by the wrath of the rabbis against Christian proselytism.

Originally the relations between the Jewish Christians and the Jews were fairly cordial. The followers of the Apostles, as well as the Apostles themselves, recognized the sanctity of the ancient law; they observed the rites of Judaism and as yet had not placed the worship of Jesus side by side with that of the one God. The development of the dogma of the divinity of Christ made a breach between the Church and the

Synagogue. Judaism could not admit Of the deification of a man ; to recognize any one as the son of God was blasphemy; and as the Jewish Christians had not severed their connections with the Jewish community, they were disciplined. This accounts for the flagellation of the Apostles and the new converts, the stoning of Stephen and the beheading of the Apostle James.

After the capture of Jerusalem, after that storm which left Judea depopulated, the best of her sons having perished in battle, or in the circus where they were de- livered to the beasts, or in the lead mines of Egypt, during this third captivity called by the Jews the Roman exile, the relations between the Jews and Jewish Christians became still more strained. Their country being dead, Israel gathered around their doctors. Jabne, where the Sanhedrin reconvened, replaced Zion without extin- guishing its memory, and the conquered attached themselves still more closely to the Law which the sages commented upon.

Thenceforth, those who assailed that Law, which had become the most cher- ished heritage of the Jew, were to be treated as enemies worse than the Romans. The doctors accordingly fought the Christian doctrine which was making pros- elytes amidst their flock, and their attitude explains the severe words against the Pharisees which the evangelists put into the mouth of Jesus. These doctors, the *Ta- naim,* merely defended their religious faith; they acted like all the pillars of religion and constituted authority towards their assailants, and they conducted themselves with as little logic and intelligence. "The Gospels must be burned—says Rabbi Tar- phon—f or paganism is not as dangerous to the Jewish faith as the Jewish Christian sects. I should rather seek refuge in a pagan temple than in an assembly of Jewish Christians." He was not the only one who thought so, and all the rabbis compre- hended the danger threatening Juda-ism from Jewish Christianity. Thus it was not against those who preached to the gentiles that their first wrath was directed, but against those who came to seek sheep in their own fold; and, if measures were taken, it was against their own apostates.

Some modern interpreters of the Talmud have gone to the rabbinical discus- sions and decisions of that epoch for weapons against the Jews, accusing them of blind hatred against anything that did not bear the mark of Israel; they do not seem, however, to have carried into their researches the requisite scientific spirit and good faith.

The Sanhedrin of Jabne regulates the relations between the Jews and the Minaens; the latter are none others but Jewish Christians, Jews deemed apostates, traitors against God and the Law. It is they that are declared inferior to the Samaritans and the Gentiles; it is with them that all intercourse is enjoined. It was at a much later epoch that these injunctions were applied to Christians generally, viz.: when the Christians became persecutors. Thus it was that some, exasperated by suffering and humiliation, applied to them what is said in the Talmud against *Goim,* i. e., those Hellenes of Caesarea and Palestine who were always at war with the Jews.

Originally, all Talmudical inhibitions contemplated the Jewish Christians alone. The *Tanaim* wanted to preserve the faithful from Christian contamination; for this purpose the Gospels were likened to books on witchcraft, and Samuel Junior, by order of the patriarch Gamaliel, inserted in the daily prayers a curse against the Jewish Christians, *Birkat Haminim,* which has furnished the foundation for the charge that the Jews curse Jesus thrice a day. | While the Jews thus sought to separate themselves I from the Christians, the Church, swayed by a great re-ligious movement, was forced to cast away Judaism. To conquer the world, to become a universal creed, Christianity had to rid itself of Jewish particularism, to break the narrow chains of the ancient law, so as to be able to spread the new one. This was the work of St. Paul, the true founder of the Church, who opposed to the exclusiveness of the Jewish-Christian doctrine the principle of catholicity.

As is well known, the struggle between these two tendencies in the nascent Christianity, which were symbolized by Peter and Paul, was long and bitter. The whole apostolic service of Paul was a long battle against the Judaizing., On the day when the Apostle declared that in order to come to Jesus one need not pass through the Synagogue nor accept the sign of the old covenant, the circumcision, on that very day all ties which bound the Christian Church to its mother were torn and the nations of the world were won over by Jesus.

The resistance of the Judaizing who wanted to belong to Jesus and at the same time to observe the Sabbath and the Passover, was in vain; their prejudice against the conversion of the Gentiles was of no avail. After Paul's journey to Asia Minor the cause of Catholicism was won. The Apostle was braced up by an army, and that army arrayed against the Jewish spirit the Hellenic, Antioch against Jerusalem.

The great bulk of the Jewish Christians tore themselves away from the narrow doctrine of the little com- munity of Jerusalem; the ruin of the holy city led them to doubt the efficacy of the ancient law. It was good for the further development of the Church. Ebionism met its death. If Christianity had followed the Jerusalem-ites it would have remained a small Jewish sect. To become the creed of the world, Christianity had to cast off Jewish particularism. Indeed, the new believers, the Gentiles, could not observe the Jewish religion while remaining Greeks or Romans. Having rid itself of the Ebionites and the Jewish Christians and cut loose from its mother, Christianity allowed the nations to come to it without forfeiting their individuality, whereas Peter and the Judaizing would have forced upon them the customs of Israel, thereby compelling them to give up a part of their national individuality and to accept that of their converters.

Thus, what was originally a branch of the orthodox Church, gave birth, towards the end of the first century, to two heresies, Ebionism and Elkasaism. Their formation was quite natural, since the bulk of the Jewish Christians accepted the ideas of Paul and united with the Christian converts from paganism; there remained only the small group of stubborn Judaizing, who originally represented staunch orthodoxy. Since, however, the Church had adopted a new course, they became heretics. Nevertheless their spirit remained, and we shall find it again among the Nazarenes and the Quar-todecimans; but since that time they were enemies of catholicity, and catholicity turned against them, or, rather, it fought Judaism from which they drew their force.

To safeguard its supremacy, the Church had to fight the Jewish spirit in two forms. The first was that noted above, the Judaic positivism, hostile to anthropomorphism and deification of heroes. Nevertheless this positivism has maintained its existence throughout the ages so that a history of the Jewish current in the Christian Church could be written, beginning with early Ebionism down to Protestantism, including among others the Unitarians and Arians.

The second form is the mystic form represented by the Alexandrian and Asiatic gnosis. The Alexandrian Jews, as known, were influenced by Platonism and Pythagorism; Philo himself was the forerunner of Plotinus and Porphyry in this renovation of the metaphysical spirit. Aided by Hellenic doctrines the Jews interpreted the Bible and scrutinized the mysteries contained therein, construing them into allegories and further developing them.

Proceeding from monotheism and the conception of a personal God as their religious point of departure, the Jews of Alexandria were bound to come metaphysically to pantheism, to the idea of a divine substance, to the doctrine of intermediaries between man and the Absolute, i. e., to emanations, to the Eons of Valentinus and the Sephiroths of Kabbala. To this Jewish fund were superadded the contributions of Chaldean, Persian and Egyptian religions, which coexisted at Alexandria; at that time were elaborated those extraordinary Gnostic theogonies, so multifarious, so varied, so madly mystical.

When Christianity was born, the gnosis was already in existence; the Gospels brought new elements into it; it speculated on the life and words of Jesus, as it had speculated on the Old Testament, and when the Apostles, in their early preaching, addressed themselves to the Gentiles, they were confronted with the Gnostics, and primarily the Jewish Gnostics. Peter met them at Samaria in the person of Simon the Magician; Paul faced them at Colosse, at Ephesus, at Antioch, wherever he came with his Gospel, and possibly he fought Cerinthus; [34] John himself fought them, [35] and, in the Epistles of the Apocalypse he opposed the Nicolaites who were "of the Synagogue of Satan."

After having escaped the danger of crystallizing into a barren Jewish community, the Church was thus exposed to the new danger of Gnosticism, which, if triumphant, would have resulted in splitting it up into small sects and breaking its unity.

Though at a later date Christianity witnessed the birth of the Hellenic gnosis, originally it had found only the Jewish gnosis, i. e., that of the Nicolaites and of Cerinthus, or similar systems built upon a Judaic basis.

All preachers of the Christian religion had to contend against this gnosis; traces of that fight are found in the Epistles of Paul to the Colossians and Ephesians, in the pastoral letters, in the second Epistle of Peter, in the Epistle of Jude and in the Apocalypse. They did not confine themselves to persecuting the Jewish spirit in the gnosis; as soon as the Pauline spirit had triumphed over Peter, they declared war to the Judaizing tendencies within the Church, as well as to the Jews themselves.

Since 182, after the insurrection of Bar-Cochba, the separation of the Christians from the Jews became final. In 70 the Jewish Christians exhibited indifference to the destinies of the Jewish nation; under Hadrian it was still worse. Five hundred thousand Jews responded to the call of the Son of the Star, and the

[34] St. Irenaeus. II. 26.

[35] Apocalypse, II and III.

Roman legions retreated before them; it required the best general of the Empire to overcome this handful of Judeans who fought for their liberty against Rome, and the last feeble hope of Israel perished with its last citadel, Bethany, and its last liberator, Bar-Cochba; measures of extreme repression were taken against the Jews; they were forbidden to observe their religion; the spot where Jerusalem had stood was levelled with the plow, and the very name of Jerusalem disappeared; at that hour the Jewish Christians would report to the provincial gov-ernors the Jews who clandestinely observed their rites and devoted themselves to the study of the Law.

On the other hand, to prevent treason, Bar-Cochba and his soldiers executed a great many Jewish Christians and measures were taken to distinguish the Christians from the Jews. On both sides the enmity was very bitter, and since the Church of Jerusalem had, after 131, become Helleno-Christian, the rupture was complete: Jews and Christians became enemies for ages to come.

On the one hand the Gentiles, who joined the Chris-tian community, brought with them all the hatred and prejudices of the Greeks and Romans against the Jews. On the other hand, the Jewish Christians, after withdrawing from the Jewish community, became still more embittered against their brethren in Israel than the Gentiles.

We find all these sentiments reflected in the writings of the Apostle Fathers, with a growing desire to separate Christianity from Judaism; and with the development of the dogma of the divinity of Jesus, the Jews became the abominable people of Deicides, which they had not been originally. The Synagogue is now "the erstwhile fruitful wife," in the words of the *II Clementine Homily,* and it is thought that "the law of Moses was not made for the Jews, who never comprehended it." This expression is found in the Epistle of Barnabas, dating from the time of Nerva (A. D. 96) and for the most part reproducing the ideas contained in the oldest of the apostolic writings, viz., the Doctrine of the Twelve Apostles, which can be traced to the year 90. [36] The Pauline traditions resound in the beginning of the second century in the seven letters of Ignatius of Antioch addressed to the churches of Rome, Magnesia, Philadelphia, Ephesus, Smyrna and Tralles and to the Bishop Poly-carp. These seven letters attack very strongly the Judaizing Docetae and try to guard the faithful against those doctrines.

Still in face of these hostile demonstrations the Jews were not inactive and proved very dangerous adversaries. It was under the fire of their criticism that the dogma was constructed; it was they who, by their subtle ex-egetics, by their firm logic, forced the teachers of Chris-tianity to give precision to their arguments. Their hostility worried the theologians; though having severed themselves from Judaism, they wanted to win over the Jews to their side; they believed that the triumph of Jesus would only be assured on the day when Israel would recognize the power of the Son of God; indeed, this belief has survived under different forms throughout the ages. It

[36] ***Doctrina duodecim apostolorum.*** Ed. Funk. 1887.

would seem as though the Church were not satisfied of the legitimacy of its faith until the day when the people of whom its God had come were converted to the Galilean. This sentiment was far stronger in the hearts of the first Fathers than it could have been with Bossuet and the Figurists of the seventeenth century. It was, therefore, necessary to defeat the Jewish exegesis, and to borrow from them for this purpose their own arms, i. e., the Bible. Efforts were made to demonstrate to the Jews that the prophecies had been fulfilled; that Jesus was he whose coming Isaiah and David had announced; it was even sought to prove to them that the Christian doctrines were found in the Old Testament; proofs in support of the Trinity were drawn from the opening words of Genesis or from the meeting of Abraham with the three angels. For centuries the defenders of Christ and the enemies of the Jews employed no other method.

This work was taken up by the apologists of Christianity, and their apologetic prepossession was mixed with violent enmity. Thus the ***Letter to Diognetus,*** which has been preserved for us in the work of St. Justin, and was written to refute the errors of the adversaries of the Christians, may be considered as one of the first anti-Jewish writings. The unknown author of this brief epistle, in his vigorous attack upon the Millenarian ideas, speaks of the Jewish rites as superstitions. The motives are not the same as those which actuated the unknown author of the ***Testament of the Twelve Patriarchs,*** for he wanted, and so he declared, to convert the Jews and convince them of the excellence of the word of Christ.

The most thorough of the apologists of that epoch is assuredly Justin, the philosopher. His ***Dialogue with Tryphon*** will remain a model of this kind of dialogical polemics, of which we have another sample from the same epoch in the ***Altercation of Jason and Papiscus,*** from the pen of the Greek Ariston of Pella; the latter dialogue was reproduced in the fifth century by Evagrius, in his ***Altercation of Simon and Theophilus.*** Justin, a native of Samaria, and well acquainted with the Judeans, puts all the objections of the Jewish exegetes into the mouth of Tryphon, meant to represent Rabbi Tarphon, who vigorously fought against the apostolic evangeliza-tion. The author attempts to persuade him that the New Testament is in accord with the Old, and to reconcile monotheism with the theory of Messiah as the Word incarnate. At the same time, replying to Tryphon's reproach that the Christians have abandoned the Mosaic law, he maintains that it was merely a preparatory law. Justin attacked the Judaizing tendencies in both forms, viz., Jewish Christian-ity on the one hand, and, on the other, Alexandrinism, which would admit the Word only as a temporary irradiation of the One Being. He closes . with the warn-ing: "Blaspheme not the Son of God; listen not to the Pharisees; ridicule not the King of Israel, as you are doing daily." The irony of the Jews he met with sarcasm directed against the rabbis: 'Instead of expounding the meaning of the prophecies your teachers indulge in tomfoolery; they are anxious to ascertain why male camels are referred to in this or that passage, or why a certain quantity of flour is required for your oblations. They are worried to know why an alpha is added to the original name of Abraham. This is the subject of their studies. As to things essential, worthy of meditation, they dare not speak of them to you, they do not attempt to explain them, and they prohibit you from listening to our interpretation."

The last complaint is important, it indicates the character of the struggle for the conquest of souls in which Judaism was defeated. The second century is one of the most momentous epochs in the history of the Church. The dogma, still uncertain in the first century, is then formulated and defined; Jesus advances toward divin-ity and attains it, and his metaphysics, his worship, his conception, are blended with Judeo-Alexandrian doctrines, with Philo's theories of the Word of God, the Chaldean ***memra*** and the Greek ***logos.*** The Word is born, it becomes identified with the Galilean; in Justin's apologetics and the fourth Gospel, we see the work completed. Christianity has become Alexandrian, and its most ardent upholders, its defenders, even its orators, are at that hour the Christian philosophers of the Alex-andrian school: Justin, the author of the fourth Gospel, and Clement.

While this dogmatic transformation was going on, the idea of a universal church gained strength. Bonds of union were formed between the small Christian communities, detached from Jewish congregations; the more their numbers increased the stronger became the ties, and this conception of unity and catholicity kept pace with the growing expansion of Christianity.

This expansion could not proceed undisturbed. Christian preaching addressed itself to all the Jewries of Asia Minor, Egypt, Cyrenaica and Italy, wherever there was an unorthodox element among them, the Hellenized Jews whom the Christian teachers sought to win over to their side. The propagandists likewise spoke to the anxious masses who had already lent their ears to the Jewish word. The Jews witnessed the failure of their influence and, perhaps, of their hopes; at all events, they saw their beliefs, their faith, attacked by the neophytes; the feeling of the Jews against the Christians was as bitter as that of the Christians when they saw the obstacles which the Jewish preachers put in their way. Furious hatred was mutual, and the parties were not content with Platonic hatred. Originally the Jews had a better official standing than the Christians. The Christian congregations, unlike the Jewish communities, were not recognized by the law; they were considered enemies of law and a danger to the Empire. From this there was but one step to violence; this accounts for the periods of suffering the Church had to go through. The Church, in those evil days, could not count upon its rival, the Synagogue, for assistance; in some places where the struggle between the Jews and the Chirstians had reached an acute stage the Jews, recognized by Roman legislation and possessed of vested rights, would join the citizens of the towns in dragging the Christians before the court. In Antioch, for example, where the enmity between those two sects was most bitter, in all probability, the Jews, like the pagans, demanded the trial and execution of Polycarp. They are said to have fed with great eagerness the stake upon which the bishop was burned.

Still, not everywhere was the strife marked with such bloody manifestations. The controversy was always very lively, yet it must be said it was not conducted with equal weapons. The Bible was their common arsenal, but the Christian teachers had but a scant knowledge of it. They did not know Hebrew and used the Septuagint version, which they interpreted very freely, often relying, in support of their dogma, upon passages interpolated into the Septuagint by falsifiers for the good of the cause. The Greek-speaking Jews did not hesitate to do the same, so that the Septuagint, a bad translation as it was, full of absurdities, became available for any purpose. The Jews undertook first to place in the hands of their faithful a purified text, which gave birth to a scrupulous and literal Greek translation by the proselyte Aquila, friend and disciple of Rabbi Akiba. It was only later that the same need was felt by the Christians, and Origen brought forth his Hexapla, which embodied, however, Aquila's version.

It was a matter of necessity with the Christian apologists who were plainly at a disadvantage, as compared with the Rabbinists, and it was felt by Origen himself in his debate on the Trinity with Rabbi Simlai. These debates between Jewish and Christian teachers were not infrequent; in Caesarea, *e. g.*, Rabbi Abbahu debated with the physician Jacob the Minaean, on the Ascension.

These controversies, which continued through long centuries, were not always courteous. Simultaneously with touching legends concerning Jesus, scandalous stories were invented. To humiliate their enemies, the Jews attacked him of whom the former made their God, and to the deification of Jesus they opposed the stories of the soldier Pantherus, of abandoned Mary; these were taken up by philosophers hostile to Christianity, and Origen refuted them in his **Contra Celsum,** meeting abuse with abuse.

Amidst these battles was born a theological anti-Judaism, purely ideological, which consisted in rejecting as bad or worthless anything coming from Israel. This sentiment is evidenced by Tertullian's **De Adversus In-daeos.** In that work the fiery African attacked circumcision, which, he said, brought no salvation, but was a simple sign for distinguishing Israel; when Messiah would come he would substitute spiritual for bodily circumcision; he attacked the Sabbath, the temporal Sabbath, to which he opposed the eternal Sabbath.

But this special anti-Judaism, which we find again in **Octavius,** by Minucius

Felix; in *De Catholicae Ecclesiae Unitate,* by Cyprian of Carthage; in *Instructiones Ad-versus Gentium Deos,* by the poet Commodian, and in *Divinae Institutiones,* by Lactantius, was mixed with the desire to convince the Jews of the truth of the Christian religion, of the soundness of its beliefs, its dogmas and principles; hence the ambition to make proselytes among them. This anti-Judaism crossed with the efforts which the Church was making to arrive at universality, and during the first three centuries remained purely theoretical. We shall further see how, since Constantine and the triumph of the Church, this anti-Judaism was transformed and more precisely defined.

CHAPTER IV.

ANTISEMITISM FROM CONSTANTINE TO THE EIGHTH CENTURY.

The Church Triumphant.—The Decadence of Judaism. —The Passover and the Judaizing Heresies.—The Council of Nicaea.—Transformation of Theological Anti-Judaism.—Conclusion of Apologetics.—The Anti-Judaism of the Fathers and Clergy.—Abuse. —Hosius, Pope Sylvester, Eusebius of Caesarea, Gregory of Nyssa and St. Augustine.—St. Ambrose, St. Jerome, and St. Cyril of Jerusalem.—St. John Chrysostom.—Ecclesiastical Writers.—The Edict of Milan and the Jews.—Jewish and Christian Pros-elytism.—The Jews, the Church, and the Christian Emperors.— Influence of the Church upon Imperial Legislation.—Koman Laws.—Vexatious Treatment of the Jews.—Popular Movements.—The Defense of the Jews, Their Revolts.—Isaac of Sepphoris and Natrona.—Benjamin of Tiberias and the Conquest of Palestine.—Julian the Apostate and the Jewish Nationality.—The Jews among the Nations.—Anti-Judaism Becomes General.—In Persia.—The Magi, the Jewish Teachers and Jewish Academies.—In Arabia.—Influence of the Jews in Yemen.— Vic-tory of Mohammedanism and Persecution of the Jews.—Spain and the Visig-othic Laws.—The Bur-gundians.—The Pranks and Roman Legislation.—Canon Law, the Councils, and Judaism.—The Condition and Attitude of the Jews.—Catholicism.

For three centuries the Church had to contend against those with whom the greatness of Some was inseparable from the secular worship of the Gods. Still, the resistance of the civil authorities, of the priests and philosophers, could not arrest the march of the Church; perse-cutions, hatred, hostility enhanced its power of propaganda; it addressed itself to those whose spirit was troubled, whose conscience was vacillating, and to them it brought an ideal and that moral satisfaction which they lacked. Moreover, at that hour when the Roman Empire was rending all over, when Rome, having abdicated all power and authority, received its Caesars from the hands of the legions, and competitors for the purple bobbed up , in every nook of the provinces, the Catholic Church offered to that expiring world the unity it was seeking.

Yet, while offering intellectual unity to the world, the Church at the same time was ruining its institutions, customs and manners. In fact, at Borne, as well as in the Empire, all public functions were at once civil and religious, the magistrate, the procurator, the dux being invested with priestly functions; no public act was per-formed without rites; the government was, in a manner, theocratic; this ultimately came to be symbolized in the worship of the Emperor. All those who wanted to withdraw from that worship were held to be enemies of Caesar and the Empire; they were considered bad citizens. This sentiment explains the Roman dislike of Oriental religions and of the Jews; it explains the measures adopted against the wor-shippers of Yahweh, and still more the severity shown towards the worshippers of Mithra, of Sabazius and particularly towards the Christians, for the latter were not foreigners like the Jews, but rebel citizens.

The triumph of Christianity was brought about by political considerations, and so, to make its victory and domination lasting, it was obliged to adopt many of the ceremonial observances of ancient Rome. When the Christians had increased in numbers, and formed a considerable party, they were saved and could see the dawn of victory glimmer, for now a pretender to the throne could find support among them and use their services to solidify his authority. So it happened with

Constantine, and Constantius, perhaps, foresaw it when he commanded the Gallic legions. The victorious church succeeded to Borne. She inherited its haughtiness, its exclusiveness, its pride, and almost without any transition period the persecuted turned persecutrix, wielding the power by which she had been fought, holding the consular fasces and hatchet and commanding the legionaries.

While Jesus was taking possession of the superb city and his universal reign was commencing, Judaism was in agony in Palestine; the teachers of Tiberias were powerless to hold the young Judeans and the "illustrious, most glorious, right reverend" patriarch had but the shadow of authority. The flourishing Jewish schools were in Babylonia; the centre of Israel's intellectual life was transferred thither; still wherever Christianity endeavored to extend its influence it had to reckon and to contend with the influence of Judaism, though since the close of the third century the latter was of little importance, at least directly. Indeed, at that time the Judaizing heresies were nearly extinct. The Nazarenes, those circumcised Christians attached to the old law, who are mentioned by St. Jerome and St. Epiphanius, were reduced to a handful of meek believers, who had found refuge at Berea (Alep), at Kokabe in Batanea, and at Pella, in the Decapolis. They spoke the Syro-Chaldaic language; a remnant of the primitive Church of Jerusa-lem, they no longer exerted any influence, swamped as they were amidst Greek-speaking churches.

Still, though Ebionism was dying out, Judaizing continued; the Christians attended the synagogues, celebrated the Jewish holidays, and the contentions over the Passover were still on. A large faction in the churches of the Orient insisted upon celebrating the Passover at the ! same time as the Jews. It required the action of the Nicaen Council to free Christianity of this last and weak bond by which it had still been tied to its cradle. After the Synod all was over between the Church and the Temple, officially, and from the orthodox standpoint, at least; it required, however, the action of further councils to prevent the faithful from conforming to the old usage, and it was not until 341 A. D., when the Council of An-tioch had excommunicated the Quartodecimans that unity of the celebration of the Easter was effected.

Since the Church had become armed, anti-Judaism underwent a transformation. Purely theological in the beginning, confined to arguments and controversies, it defined itself and became harsher, more severe and aggressive. Beside writings, laws appeared; the enactment of laws resulted in popular manifestations. The writings themselves underwent a change. Throughout the centuries of persecution, apologetics had flourished, and a vast literature had come into being, born of the need felt by the Christians to convince their adversaries. They

addressed themselves now to the Jews, now to the pagans, now to the emperors, and all of them, Justin, Athenagoras, Tatian, Aristo of Pella, Melito, endeavored to prove to Caesar that their doctrines were not dangerous to the public weal; that even without sacrificing to the gods, they could be loyal subjects, as obedient as the pagans and morally superior. They argued with the Jews that it was they, the Christians, that were the only faithful to tradition, for they fulfilled the prophecies and the least details of their dogmas were foreseen and announced by the Scriptures. Triumphant Christianity was no longer in need of apologists; Caesar had been converted and Cyril of Alexandria, the author of a book against Julian the Apostate, was the last of the apologists. As regards Israel, the Christians persisted, even to our own day, in demonstrating to them their stubbornness; it was done in a less insidious and less convincing manner; they spoke as masters, and from the middle of the fifth century, apologetics proper ceased, reappearing only much later considerably modified and transformed.

They no longer tried to win over the Jews to Christ; indeed, a *few years* sufficed to show to the theologians the futility of their efforts, and the effect of their reasoning, based most frequently upon a fantastic exegesis or a few surdities of the Alexandrian translation of the Bible, was lost on these stubborn men, who listened only to their *own* teachers and clung the stronger to their faith the more it was despised. To arguments was added insult; the Jew was regarded less as a possible Christian than as an unrepenting deicide. They denounced those men, whose persistence was so shocking and whose very presence marred the complete triumph of the Church. Pains were taken to forget the Jewish origin of Jesus and the Apostles; to forget that Christianity had grown in the shade of the Synagogue. This oblivion perpetuated it-self, and to-day who in all Christendom would acknowledge that he bows to a poor Jew and a humble Jewess of Galilee?

The Fathers, the bishops, the priests, who had to contend against the Jews, treated them very badly. Hosius in Spain; Pope Sylvester; Paul, bishop of Constantine; Eusebius of Caesarea, [37] call them "a perverse, dangerous and criminal sect."

Some, like Gregory of Nyssa, [38] remain on dogmatic P. G., XLVI.

ground, and merely reproach the Jews for being infidels, who refuse to accept the testimony of Moses and the prophets on the Trinity and Incarnation. St. Augustine [39] is more vehement. Irritated by the objections of the Talmudists he brands them as falsifiers, and declares that one need seek no religion in the blindness of the Jews, and that Judaism may serve only as a term of comparison to demonstrate the beauty of Christianity. St. Ambrose [40] attacked them from another side; he took up anew the charges of the ancient world, those which had been

[37] *Demonstratio Evangelica.*

[38] *Testimonium adversus Judaeos ex Tetere Testamento,* Mlgne,

[39] Oratio adversus Judaeos, Migne, P. L. XLII,

[40] De Tobia. Migne, P. L. XIV.

used against the first Christians, and accused the Jews of despising the laws of Rome. St. Jerome [41] claimed that an impure spirit had seized the Jews. Having learned Hebrew in the schools of the rabbis, he said, referring doubtless to the curses pronounced against the Mineans and distorting their meaning: "The Jews must be hated, for they daily insult Jesus Christ in their synagogues"; and St. Cyril of Jerusalem [42] abused the Jewish patriarchs, claiming that they were a low race.

We find all these theological and polemical attacks combined in the six sermons delivered at Antioch, by St. John Chrysostom [43] against the Jews; an examination of those homilies will give us an understanding of the methods of discussion, as well as the reciprocal attitude of Christians and Jews and their mutual relations.

The Jews, says Chrysostom in the first of his sermons, are ignoramuses, who lack all understanding of their own law, and are consequently impious. They are wretches, dogs, bull-headed; their people are like a herd of brutes, like wild beasts. They have driven Christ away, therefore they are capable of evil only. Their synagogues may be likened to playhouses, they are dens of brigands, the abode of Satan. Being obliged to admit that the Jews are not ignorant of the Father, he adds that this is not enough, since they have crucified the Son and reject the Holy Ghost, and that their souls are the abode of the devil. Therefore they must be mistrusted; the *Jewish disease* must be guarded against. And Chrysos-

[41] Ep. CLI, Quaest. 10, Migne, P. L. XXII.

[42] Ep. CLI, Quaest, 10, Migne, P. G., XXXIII.

[43] Adversus Judaeos, 10, Migne, P. G., XLVIII.

torn thus apostrophizes his faithful: Do not frequent the synagogues, do not observe the Sabbath, the fast-days and other Jewish rites. If you meet the Judaizing, warn them of the peril, for you are the army of Christ; let not yourselves be seduced; it would be sheer folly. What will you gain in this den of men who deny Moses and the prophets? If the Jewish teachings excite your admiration, you must find the Christian teachings false.

In the second sermon these diatribes are resumed; Chrysostom appears in it much worried over the influence exerted by the Jews. "Our sheep," he exclaims, "are surrounded by Jewish wolves," and he reiterates the warning: Avoid them; avoid their impiety; it is not insignificant controversies that separate us from them, but the death of Christ. If you think that Judaism is true, leave the Church; if not, quit Judaism. Do you not know that the Jews offer sacrifices everywhere on earth, except in the only place where sacrifice is valid, i. c., at Jerusalem ? Are you not aware that it is only there that they can celebrate Passover, as the law says (Deuter. xii) ? Therefore do not conform to their delusive Passover.

The other four sermons are chiefly theological. Availing himself of the invectives of the prophets, Chrysostom calls the Jews thieves, impure, debauchees, rapacious, misers, crafty, oppressors of the poor; they have filled the measure of their crimes by immolating Jesus. He does not content himself with all that. He advances arguments upon controversies which must have been very lively at Antioch. He defends the Church; he shows that Israel is dispersed in consequence of the death of Christ; he draws from the prophets and the stories of the Bible proofs of the divinity of Jesus, and he recommends to his flock to stay away from the sermons of those Jews who call the cross an abomination and whose religion is null and useless to those who know the true faith. In short, say3 he in conclusion, it is absurd to consort with men who have treated God with such indignity and at the same time to worship the Crucified.

These homilies of Chrysostom are characteristic and valuable. One finds there already the policy which the Christian preachers were to pursue throughout the ages to follow; that mixture of argument and apostrophizing, of suasion and abuse, which has remained peculiar to anti-Jewish preaching. Especially worthy of notice is the part of the clergy in the development of anti-Judaism—originally religious anti-Judaism, for social anti-Judaism arose much later in Christian society. These sermons portray, in a live picture, the relations between Judaism and Christianity in the fourth century; these relations continued for a long time, until about the ninth century. The Jews had not arrived yet at that exclusive conception of their individuality and their nationality which was the work of the Talmudists. Their mode of life did not differ externally from that of other nations in whose midst they lived; they generally took part in public affairs, in Asia Minor, as well as in Italy; in Gaul, as well as in Spain. Coming into daily contact with the Christians, they exerted an influence upon them, and as they had not as yet shut themselves up in that sullen isolation which their teachers later preached, they attracted to their worship many of those who were undecided and irresolute. Their proselytic ardor was not dead; they were not conscious of the fact that they had forever lost their moral power over the world, and they struggled on. They persuaded pagans and Christians to Judaize, and they found followers; if need be they would make converts by force; they did not hesitate to circumcise their slaves. They were the only foes the Church had to face, for paganism was quietly passing away, leaving in the 60uls but legendary survivals, which have not entirely died out even to this day. If paganism, through its last philosophers and poets, still opposed the diffusion of Christianity, it no longer sought, since the fourth century, to regain those whom Jesus held by his bonds. The Jews, however, had not given up; they deemed themselves in possession of the true religion, upon as good a title as the Christians, and in the eyes of the people their assertion had the attraction flowing from unflinching convictions.

In the morning of its triumph the Church as yet did not hold that universal ascendancy which it gained later; it was still weak, though powerful; but those who directed it aspired to universality, and they could not help considering the Jews as their worst adversaries; they had to strain themselves to the utmost to weaken Jewish propaganda and proselytism. In this the Fathers followed a secular tradition; upon this battle ground they are unanimous, and there are legions of theologians, historians and writers who think and write of the Jews the same as Chrysostom: Epiphanius, Diodorus of Tarsus, Theodore of Mopsuestia, Theodoret of Cyprus, Cosmas Indicopleustes, Athanasius the Sinaite, Synesius, among the Greeks; Hilarius of Poitiers, Prudentius, Paulus Orosius, Sulpicius Severus, Gennadius, Venantius For-tunatus, Isidore of Seville, among the Latins.

However, after the edict of Milan, anti-Judaism could no longer confine itself to oral or written controversies; it was no longer a quarrel between two sects equally detested or despised. Before his conversion, Constantine, who originally declined to grant any exclusive privileges to Christians, accorded, by the edict of tolerance, to every one the right to observe the religion of his choice. The Jews were thus put on an equal footing with the Christians; the pagan pontiffs, the priests of Jesus, the patriarchs and teachers of Israel enjoyed the same favor and were exempt from municipal taxes. But in 323, after the defeat and death of Licinius, who had reigned in the Orient, Constantine, the victor and lord over the Empire, supported by all the Christians of his states, showed them marked preference. He made them his great dignitaries, his councillors, his generals, and thenceforth the Church had the imperial power at its disposal to build up its dominion. The first use it made of this authority was to persecute those who were hostile to the Church; it found

Constantine quite obedient to its wishes. On the one hand, the emperor prohibited divination and sacrifices, closed the temples, ordered the gold and silver statues of the gods to be melted for the embellishment of the churches; on the other hand, he consented to repress Jewish proselytism and revived an ancient Roman law which prohibited the Jews from circumcising their slaves; at the same time he deprived them of many of their former privileges and barred them from Jerusalem, except on the anniversary of the destruction of the Temple, and that upon payment of a special tax in silver. Thus, by aggravating the burdens which were oppressing the Jews, Constantine favored Christian proselytisin, and the preachers were not slow to represent to the Jews the advantages baptism would bring. To encourage the hesitating, who were held back from apostasy by the fear of revenge and ill-treatment from their coreligionists, the emperor promulgated a law which condemned to the stake those Jews who persecuted their apostates by stoning. [44]

Still, in spite of his hostility to the Jews, perhaps factitious, since the authenticity of the letter written in a violent language and attributed to him by Eusebius [45] cannot be vouched for, he took pains to protect them against the attacks of their own renegades. Under his successors, no such reservation was made. The Church was now all-powerful with the emperors. Catholicism became the established religion, the Christian worship was the official worship, the importance of the bishops increased from day to day, as well as their influence. They inculcated upon the minds of the emperors those sentiments with which they were inspired themselves, and while their anti-Judaism manifested itself in writings, imperial anti-Judaism found expression in statutes. These laws, inspired by the clergy, were directed not only against the Jews, but against Christian heretics as well. Indeed, during the fourth century, so fertile in

[44] *Codex Justinianeus,* l. I, tit. viii, 3.

[45] Eusebius, *Vita Constantini,* III, 18, 20.

heresies, the orthodox themselves were at times disturbed when heretical theologians led the emperors.

Of these laws, all of which were enacted from the fourth to the seventh century, the majority are directed against Jewish proselytism. The penal statutes directed against those who circumcise Christians are reaffirmed;[46] the offense is made punishable by exile for life and confiscation of property. The Jews are prohibited from owning Christian slaves; [47] they are not allowed to marry Christians; such unions are treated like criminal fornication. [48] Other laws encourage Christian propaganda and proselytism among the Jews, either directly—by protecting the apostates [49] and enjoining Jews from disinheriting their converted sons and grandsons [50] —or indirectly, by vexatious legislation against Jews. Their privileges were curtailed. It was decreed that the moneys which were sent by the Israelites to Palestine should be paid into the imperial treasury; [51] they were debarred from holding public office; [52] they were assessed with hard and oppressive curial taxes; [53] they were practically deprived of their special tribunals.[54] The vexations were not confined to that; the Jews were harassed even in the observance of their religion; the law undertook to regulate the

[46] *Codex Justinianeus,* l. I, tit. IX, 1G.

[47] *Codex Theodosianus,* l. XVI. tit. VIII, 5.

[48] *Codex Justinianeus.,* l. I., tit. IX, 6.

[49] *Cod. Theod.,* b. XVI. tit. viii. 8.

[50] *Code Theodosien,* l. XVI. iti. VIII.28.

[51] *Codex Justinianeus,* l. 1, tit. IX, 17 and *Cod. Theodos.,* l. XVI, tit. VIII, 14.

[52] *Codex Justinianeus,* I. tit. IX.

[53] *18. Justinianus, Novellae,* 45.

[54] *Codex Justinianeus,* l. I., tit. IX. 15.

manner of observing the Sabbath; [55] they were ordered not to celebrate their Passover before Easter, and Justinian went as far as to prohibit them from reciting the daily prayer, the **Schema,** which proclaimed one God, as against the Trinity.

Still, notwithstanding the favorable disposition of Emperor Constantine, the Church was not given a free hand in everything. While restricting the religious liberties of the pagans and the Jews, he was obliged to act with caution; the worshippers of the gods were still numerous under his reign, and he dared not provoke dangerous disturbances. The Jews benefited to some extent by this hesitation. With Constantius everything changed. Constantine, who was baptized only on his deathbed by Eusebius of Nicomedia, was a skeptic and a politician, who used Christianity as a tool; Constantius was an orthodox, as fanatical and intolerant as the clergy and the monks of his day. With him, the Church became dominant, and wielded its power for revenge; it 6eems the Church was eager to make its erstwhile persecutors pay dearly for all it had suffered at their hands. No sooner was it armed than it forgot its most elementary principles, and directed the secular arm against its adversaries. The pagans and the Jews were persecuted with utmost severity; those who offered sacrifices to Zeus, as well as those who worshipped Jehovah, were maltreated: anti-Judaism went together with anti-paganism.

The Jewish teachers of Judea were exiled, they were

[55] **Codex Justinianeus** l. I., tit. IX, 13, and -Cod.

Theod., l. VIII, tit. IV, 8.

threatened with death if they persisted in giving instruction, they were compelled to flee from Palestine, while in other provinces of the empire they were denied the rights of Roman citizenship. While the Roman legions, on expedition against King Shabur II., of Persia, were camping in Judea, the Jews were treated like inhabitants of a conquered country. They were heavily taxed; they were forced to bake bread for the soldiers on Sabbath and on holidays.

In the cities, monks and bishops denounced pagans and Jews, inciting against them the Christian populace and leading fanatical mobs in assaults upon temples and synagogues. Under Theodosius I., and under Arcadius, ·synagogues were burned at Rome and at Callinicus, in Mesopotamia. Under Theodosius II, at Alexandria, St. Cyril stirred up the mob, hermits invaded the city, massacred all the Jews and pagans they met, assassinated Hypathia, plundered synagogues, set the libraries on fire, defying the efforts of the prefect Orestes whom the emperor later disavowed. At Imnestar, near Antioch, Simon, the ascetic, acts likewise, and under Zeno similar scenes are enacted at Antioch. A fury of destruction takes possession of the Christians; one might say, they wish to destroy all traces of the old world to prepare the sweet reign of Christ.

Still the Jews did not behave passively in the face of their enemies, they had not, as yet, acquired that stubborn and touching resignation which became their characteristic later.

To the vehement discourses of the priests they replied by discourses, to acts they responded by acts; to Christian proselytism they opposed their own proselytism and vowed execration on their apostates. Violent sermons were preached in the synagogues. Jewish preachers thundered against Edom, i. e., against Rome, the Rome of the Caesars which had become the Rome of Jesus, and which was now ravishing the faith of the Jewa after having ravished their nationality. They did not content themselves with rhetorical common-places, they excited their brethren to revolt. While Gallus, Constantius's nephew, governed the Oriental provinces, Isaac of Sep-phoris raised the Judeans, being aided in his under-taking by a fearless man, Natrona, whom the Romans called Patricius. "Natrona," exclaimed Isaac, "will deliver us from Edom, Mordecai and Esther as delivered us from the Medes, the Hasmonaeans as liberated us from the Greeks." The Jews took up arms, but they were severely repressed by Gallus and his general, Ur-8icinus. Women, children and old men were butchered, Tiberias and Lydda were half destroyed, Sepphoris was razed to the ground and the catacombs of Tiberias were filled with fugitives who were hiding for months to escape detection and death.

Under the reign of Phocas the Jews of Antioch, tired of persecutions, outrages and massacres, one day rushed upon the Christians, assassinated the patriarch Anastas-ius the Sinaite, and took possession of the city. Phocas sent against them an army with Kotys in command, the Jews at first repelled the imperial legions, but unable to hold out against large enforcements brought to Antioch, they were subdued and massacred, maimed, or banished. . Their submission, however, was merely apparent; they were awaiting an opportunity to renew the struggle; the opportunity soon presented itself. When Chosru II., king of Persia, marched against the Byzantine empire, to avenge his son-in-law, Mauritius, whose throne had been usurped by Phocas, the Jews joined the king. Sharbarza invaded Asia Minor, disregarding the peace proposals of Heraclius, who had just dethroned Phocas, and he saw the Jewish warriors of Galilee flock under his banners. Benjamin of Tiberias was the soul of the revolt; he armed and led the rebels. The Jews wanted to reconquer Palestine and restore it to that purity which to them had been polluted by the Christian cult. They burned the churches, sacked Jerusalem, destroyed the convents, raising on their way all their co-religionists, and joined by the Israelites of Damascus, Southern Palestine, and the Isle of Cyprus, they besieged Tyre, but were forced to raise the siege. For fourteen years they were masters of Palestine, and the Christians of Palestine were in great numbers converted to Judaism. Heraclius drew them away from the Persians, who had not lived up to their promise to surrender to their allies the holy city of Jerusalem; he reached an understanding with Benjamin of Tiberias, promising to the Jews impunity and other advantages; but when the emperor reconquered his provinces from Chosru, he ordered, at the instigation of monks and the Patriarch Modestus, to massacre those with whom he had treated. As he had pledged his oath to the Jews not to molest them, Modestus released him from his oath and instituted, doubtless in compensation, a fast day which the Maronites and the Copts observed for a long time thereafter. Still the Jews of Judea were but a handful and their history was closed. When Julian the Apostate, after repealing the restrictive laws of Constantine and Constantius against the Jews, wanted to reconstruct the Temple of Jerusalem, the foreign Jewish communities remained deaf to the imperial appeal; they had become estranged from their national cause, at least directly. With all the Jews of that time, the restoration of the Kingdom of Judah was intimately bound with the advent of Messiah and they could not expect it from a crowned philosopher; they had but to await the heavenly king who had been promised them; this sentiment persisted throughout the ages. With the death of the last patriarch Gamaliel VI., the phantom of royalty and of a Jewish nationality passed away and there was left to Israel but the chief of exile, the exilarch of Babylonia, who disappeared in the eleventh century. Still, the Jews, who were spread over the world and organized into powerful and wealthy communities, created for themselves numerous fatherlands to which they were bound by their interests. This attachment, however, was not complete, for their religion kept them in a state of grievous isolation; mixed with all nations, they suffered, whereever precise and dogmatic religions were established, the consequences of their religious non-conformity. Thus we see anti-Judaism flourish not only in Catholic countries, but also in Persia and Arabia.

In Persia and Babylonia, the Jews lived since their captivity; after the ruin of Jerusalem many more sought refuge in that admirable and fertile country, where they were given land to farm on and lived happily under the benevolent rule of the Arsacidae. They founded schools at Sora, Nachardea and Pumbaditha, and made numerous proselytes. But in the middle of the third century the dynasty of the Arsacidae, who were very unpopular, fell with Artaban, and Ardashir founded the dynasty of the Sassanides. It was a national and religious movement. The Neo-Persians or Guebres execrated the Hellenizing Arsacidae who had abandoned the fire worship. The triumph of Ardashir was the triumph of the Magi, who raged against the Hellenizing, the Christians of Edessa and the Jews, for the anti-Judaism of the Magi was combined with anti-Christianity; so the hostile brothers were persecuted simultaneously, still the Jews, more feared for their numbers and their strength, suffered more in consequence, in those troublous days. However, those persecutions were never of long duration. After suffering oppression at the end of the third century from Shabur II., who led away 70,000 Jewish prisoners from Armenia to Ispahan, the Israelites were for many years left undisturbed ;but in the sixth and the seventh century under Tezdigerd II., under Pheroces, and under Kobad, restrictive measures were adopted at the instigation of the Magi. The Jews were prohibited from celebrating the Sabbath; their schools were closed, the Jewish tribunals were abolished. During the reign of Kobad, Mazdak, the Magus, was the originator of these persecutions. Mazdak, the founder of the sect of Zendiks, preached communism and deprived the Jews and Christians of their wives and property. Under the leadership of the Exilarch Mar Zutra II, the Jews rebelled, and, according to Persian chronicles, they defeated the partisans of the Magus and founded a state, whose capital was Mahuza, a city inhabited by Persian converts to Judaism. This state existed for seven years until Mar Zutra was defeated and killed.

Since then the Jews, in Persia, witnessed alternately peace and trouble; happy under Chosroes Nushirvan and Chosru II., oppressed under Hormisdas IV., they ultimately tired of their precarious situation, and, in concert with the Christians of the Sassanide kingdom aided Omar to capture the throne of Persia, thus contributing to the triumph of Mohammed and the Arabs.

Still the Jews had little to rejoice at under the Mussulman yoke. Their first settlement in Arabia, disregarding the legends which trace it as far back as Joshua or Saul, must date from the time of the captivity, or of the destruction of the first Temple. The original nucleus was swelled by fugitives from Judea, who reached Arabia at the time Palestine was conquered by the Romans. In the beginning of the Christian era there were in Arabia four Jewish tribes, whose centre was Medina.

The Jews accomplished a moral and intellectual conquest of the Arabs, whom they converted to Judaism; at least they made them adopt its rites. The kinship between the two peoples made it easy, the more so that, in Yemen, the Jews had in their turn adopted Arabian customs, which differed but little from the early Jewish customs. They were farmers, shepherds and warriors, at times freebooters and poets. Divided into small groups, fighting among themselves and taking part in the quarrels which divided the Arab tribes, they at the same time founded schools at Yathrib, built temples and propagated ·their religion as far as the Himyarites with whom their traders were in regular intercourse. In the sixth century, under the reign of Zorah-Dhu-Nowas, all Yemen was Jewish. With the conversion of one Arab tribe of Nedjran to Christianity, difficulties began; they were, however, of short duration, for Christian propaganda was cut short in Arabia by Mohammed. Mohammed was nursed by the Jewish spirit; fleeing from Mecca, where his preaching had aroused against him the Arabs who were true to old traditions, he sought refuge at Medina, the Jewish city, and as the apostles found their first adherents among the Hellenic proselytes, so he found his first disciples among the Judaizing Arabs. Likewise, the same religious causes embittered Mohammed and Paul to hatred. The Jews rebelled against the preaching of the prophet, they heaped ridicule upon him, and Mohammed who had until then been inclined to compromise with them, violently repudiated them and wrote the celebrated Sura of the Cow, in which he unmercifully inveigled against them. When the prophet had assembled an army of followers he no longer confined himself to abuse, he marched against the Jewish tribes, vanquished them, and decreed that "neither Jews nor Christians" should be accepted as friends. The Jews rose and allied themselves to those Arabs who rejected the new doctrines, but the extension of Mohammedanism triumphed over them. By the time of Mohammed's death they had been reduced to extreme weakness ; Omar completed the work. He drove out of Chai-bar and Wadil Kora the last Jewish tribes, as well as the Christians of Dedjran, for Christians and Jews alike polluted the sacred soil of Islam.

Wherever Omar carried his arms, the Jews, oppressed by reason of that very affinity which united them with the Arabs, favored the second calif, who took possession of Persia and Palestine. Omar enacted severe laws against the Jews, who had assisted his antagonist; he subjected them to restrictive legislation, prohibited the erection of new synagogues, forced them to wear dress of a particular color, enjoined them from riding on horseback, and imposed upon them a personal and a land tax. Christians were treated likewise. Nevertheless the Jews enjoyed greater liberty under Arab rule than under Christian domination. On the one hand, the legislation of Omar was not rigorously enforced; on the other hand, aside from a few manifestations of fanaticism, the Mussulmanic mass, in spite of religious differences, showed a friendly disposition towards them. And later, with the expansion of Islam, the Arabs were hailed as liberators by all the Western Jews.

The condition of the Western Jews since the destruc-tion of the fragile Soman empire and the rush of barbarians upon the old world, was subject to all the vicissitudes of the times. The Caesars, those poor Caesars who bore the names of

Olybrius, Glycerius, Julius Nepos, and Romulus Augustulus, fell, but the Soman laws remained ; and if for short periods they were not enforced against the Jews, they still remained in effect, and the German sovereigns could make use of them at pleasure.

From the fifth to the eighth century the fortunes of the Jews wholly depended upon religious causes which were external to them, and their history among those who were called barbarians is bound with the history of Arianism, its triumph and defeats. So long as the Arian doctrine predominated, the Jews lived in a state of relative welfare, for the clergy and even the heretical government were busy fighting against orthodoxy and little worried about the Israelites, who, to them, were not the enemies to be crushed. Theodoric, however, was an exception. No sooner was the Ostrogoth empire established than the king prohibited the erection of synagogues and endeavored to convert the Jews. [56] He pro-tected them, however, against popular outbreaks, and compelled the Roman Senate to rebuild the synagogues which had been set on fire by the Catholic mobs which rose against the Arian Theodoric.

Still in Italy, under the Byzantine dominion so harassing to them, or under the more indifferent Lombard rule, for the Arian and the pagan Lombards scarcely took notice of the existence of Israel,—the Jews were guarded against the zeal of the lower clergy and their flocks by the benevolence of the pontifical authority, which, from the earliest days of its power, seems to have desired, with rare exceptions, to preserve the synagogue as a living testimony of its victory.

In Spain the condition of the Jews was quite different. From time immemorial they freely settled in the peninsula; their numbers increased under Vespasian, Titus and Hadrian, during the Judean wars and after

> [56] His course was probably influenced by his Minister Cassio-dorus, who seems to have had scant sympathy for the Jews—he characterized them as scorpions, wild asses, dogs and unicorns.

the dispersion; they owned large fortunes, they were wealthy, powerful and respectable and exerted a great influence upon the population among whom they lived. The imprint received by the peoples of Spain from Judaism, endured for centuries, and that land was the last to witness once more the contest, with almost equal weapons, between the Jewish and the Christian spirit. More than once Spain came very near becoming Jewish, and to write the history of that country until the fifteenth century means to write the history of the Jews, for they were intimately connected in a most remarkable way, with its literature and intellectual, national, moral and economic development. The church, from its very establishment in Spain, contended against Jewish tendencies and proselytism, and it was only after a struggle of twelve centuries that it succeeded in completely extirpating them.

Until the sixth century the Spanish Jews lived in perfect happiness. They were as happy as in Babylonia, and they found a new mother country in Spain. The Roman laws did not reach them there and the eccleciastical ordinances of the Council of Elvira, in the fourth century, which enjoined Christians from intercourse with them, remained a dead letter.

The Visigothic conquest did not change their condition and the Arian Visigoths confined themselves to persecuting the Catholics. The Jews enjoyed the same civil and political rights as the conquerors; moreover, the Jews joined their armies and the Pyrenean frontier was guarded by Jewish troops. With the conversion of King Reccared everything changed; the triumphant clergy heaped persecution and vexation upon the Jews, and from that hour (589 A. D.) their existence became precarious. They were gradually brought under severe and meddlesome laws which were drafted by the numerous councils, held during that period in Spain, and were enacted by the Visigoth kings. These successive laws are all combined in the edict promulgated, in 652, by Receswinth; they were re-enacted and aggravated by Erwig, who had them approved by the twelfth council of Toledo (680). [57] The Jews were prohibited from performing the right of circumcision and observing the dietary laws, from marrying relatives until the sixth generation, from reading books condemned by the Chris-tion religion. They were not allowed to testify against Christians or to maintain an action in court against them, or to hold public office.

These laws which had been enacted one by one, were not always enforced by the Visigoth lords, who were independent, in a way, but the clergy doubled their efforts to procure their strict enforcement. The object of the bishops and the dignitaries of the church was to bring about the conversion of the Jews and to kill the spirit of Judaism in Spain and the secular authority lent them its support. Prom time to time the Jews were put to the choice between banishment and baptism; from that epoch dates the origin of the class of **Marranos,** those Judaizing Christians who were later dispersed by the Inquisition. Until the eighth century the Spanish Jews lived in that state of uncertainty and distress, relying only upon the transitory good will of some kings like Swintila and

[57] Leges Visigoth, L. XII, tit. 11, 5.

Wamba, They were liberated only by Tarin, the Mo-hammadean conqueror, who destroyed the Visigothic empire with the aid of the exiled Jews joining his army and with the support of the Jews remaining in Spain. After the battle of Xeres and the defeat of Roderick (711), the Jews breathed again.

About the same epoch a better era dawned for them in Prance. They had established colonies in Gaul in the days of the Roman republic, or of Caesar, and they prospered, benefiting by their privileges of Roman citizenship. The arrival of the Burgundians and Franks did not change their condition, and the invaders accorded them the same treatment as the Gauls. Their history was subject to the same fluctuations and rythms as in Italy and Spain. Free under pagan or Arian dominion, they were persecuted as soon as orthodoxy became dominant. Sigismund, king of the Burgundians, after his conversion to Catholicism enacted laws against them which were confirmed by his successors. [58] The Franks, being ignorant of the very existence of the Jews, were wholly guided by the bishops, and after Clovis they naturally began to apply to the Jews the provisions of the Theo-dosian Code. These provisions were aggravated and complicated by ecclesiastical authority which left to the secular power the duty of enforcing and compelling the observance of its decrees. From the fifth to the eighth century that part of the canon law relating to the Jews was worked out in Gaul. The laws were formulated by the councils and approved by the edicts of the Merovingian kings.

[58] Lex Burgundionum, tit XV, 1, 2, 3.

The chief concern of the church, during those three centuries, seems to have been to separate the Jews from the Christians, to prevent Judaizing among the faithful and to check Israelite proselytism. This legislation which had, towards the eighth century, become extremely severe in dealing with the Jews and the Judaizing, was not enacted at one stroke; beginning with the council of Vannes, of the year 465, the synods first confined themselves to platonic injunctions. The clergy at that epoch had but very scant authority and could inflict no penalties; it was not before the sixth century that the support of the Frank chiefs enabled it to enact penal legislation, which originally applied only to clerical offenders against the decisions of the councils, but later was extended to laymen. These canonical penalties, however, comprising excommunication and, for priests, eventually corporal punishment, contemplated only the faithful; as to the Jews, the synods took no punitive measures against them, which has enabled many writers to claim with apparent justification that the church maintained a benevolent attitude toward the Jews. [59]

This is not so, however. It must not be forgotten that the church had no right to legislate in civil matters; yet the synodical regulations, the ecclesiastical interdictions and prohibitions and the arguments by which they were supported, exerted an enormous influence upon the

[59] The Councils confine themselves to ordering the baptism of the issue of mixed marriages as well as the dissolution of the marriage in case the Jewish consort is not converted. Besides, they decree that any Jew attempting to convert his slaves shall forfeit them to the fisc.

political authorities; furthermore, the episcopate exerted a personal and manifest influence over the Merovingian or Visigothic kings, and it can be shown that Childebert or Clotaire II., e. g., or Receswinth, in giving their sanction to ecclesiastical decrees and in promulgating their own edicts, acted at the instigation of the bishops.

Still the clergy did not confine themselves to influencing legislation; it was ever at work inciting against the Jews the populace whose orthodoxy was not sufficiently intolerant. It was under the leadership of these priests that the mob attacked the synagogues and put the Jews to the alternative of being massacred, banished or baptized.

Nevertheless, one must not imagine the condition of the Jews at that epoch as very miserable. On the Jewish, as well as on the Christian side, one notices a mixture of tolerance and intolerance which is accounted for either by a mutual desire to make converts, or even to some extent by reciprocal religious good-will. The Jews took an interest in public life, the Christians ate at their tables; they shared in their joys and sorrows, as well as in factional fights. Thus they are seen, at Aries, to unite with the Visigothic party against the bishop Caesarius, [60] and later to follow the funeral of the same bishop, crying: *Vae! vac!* They were the clients of great seignors (as witnessed by two letters of Sidonius Apollinaris), [61] and the latter helped them to evade the vexatious ordinances. In many regions the clergy visited them, a great many Christians went to the synagogues,

[60] *Vie de Saint Cesaire,* Migne. *Patrologie latine,* t. LXVII.

[61] *Sidonius Apollinaris,* 1. III, ep. IV, and 1. V. ep. V.

and the Jews likewise attended Catholic services during the mass of the catechumens. They resisted, as far as possible, the numerous efforts to convert them, at times attended with violence, notwithstanding the recommendations of certain Popes; [62] and they boldly engaged in controversies with theologians who endeavored to persuade them by the same means as the Fathers of former ages. We shall return to these controversies and writings when we shall come to study the anti-Jewish literature.

Thus, as shown above, during the first seven centuries of the Christian era, anti-Judaism proceeded exclusively from religious causes and was led only by the clergy. One must not be misled by popular excesses and legisla-lative repression, for they were never spontaneous, but always inspired by bishops, priests, or monks. It was only since the eighth century that social causes super-

[62] Fredegaire (Chronique, XV), ***and Aumoin*** (Chronique Moissiacensis, XLV) relate that, at the instigation of Emperor Heraclius, Dagobert gave to the Jews the choice between death, exile and baptism. (***Gesta Dogoberti,*** XXIV). The same is reported of the Visigothic King Sisebut (see appendix to the Chronicle of Bishop Marius, A. D. 588; Dom Bouquet, t. II, p. 19). Chilperich forced many Jews to be baptized. (Greg-oire de Tours, H. F., 1. VI, ch. XVII). Bishop Avitus compelled the Jews of Clermont to renounce their faith, or leave the city. Gregoire de Tours, H. F., 1. V, ch. XI). Other bishops resorted to force, and it required the interference of Pope St. Greg-ory to stop or at least moderate their zeal. "The Jews must not be baptized by force, but brought over by sweetness," says he in his letters addressed to Virgil bishop of Aries, to Theodore, bishop of Marseilles, and to Pascha-sius, bishop of Naples. (***Regesta Pontificum Romanorum,*** ed. Jafle, nos. 1115 and 1879). But the authority of the Pope was not always effective.

vened to religious causes, and it was only after the coincided with the universal spread of Catholicism, with the development of feudalism and also with the intellectual and moral change of the Jews, which was mostly due to the influence of the Talmudists and the exagger-ated growth of exclusiveness among the Jews. We shall now proceed to examine this new transformation of anti-Judaism.

CHAPTER V.

ANTI-JUDAISM PROM THE EIGHTH CENTURY TO THE REFORMATION.

Expansion and Christianity.—Diffusion of the Jews Among the Nations.—Constitution of the Nation-alities.—The Role of the Jews in Society.—The Jews and Commerce.—Gold and the Jews.—The Love of Gold and Business Acquired by the Jews.— The Jew as Colonist and Emigrant.—The Church and Usury.—The Birth of Patronage and Wage-System.—Transformation of Property.—The Economic Revolution and the Quest of Gold.—The In-stinct of Domination.—Gold and Jewish Exclu-sivism.—Maimonides and Observation.—Solomon of Montpellier.—Ben-Adret, Asher ben Yechiel, and Jacob Tibbon.—The *Moreh Nebukhim.* —Intellec-tual and Moral Abasement of the Jews.—The Tal-mud.—Influence of this Abasement on the Social Position of the Jews.—Transformation of Anti-Judaism.—Social Causes; Religious Causes; Their Combination.—The People and the Jews.—The Pastoureaux, the Jacques and the Armleders.—The Kings and the Jews.—The Monks and Anti-Judaism.—Pierre de Cluny, John of Capistrano, and Bernardinus of Feltre.—The Church and Theological Anti-Judaism.—Christianity and Mohammedanism.—The Albigenses, the Heretics of Orleans, the Pasagians.—Heresies and Judaization. —The Hussites.—The Inquisition.—The Bourgeoisie and the Jews.—Ecclesiastic and Civil Legisla-tion Against the Jews.—Controversies and Condemnation of the Talmud.—Vexations.—Expulsions.—Massacres.—The Condition of the Jews and of the People.—The Relativity of the Jewish Sufferings.—The Reformation and the Renaissance.

The church reaches its final constitution in the eighth century. The period of great doctrinal crises is at an end, dogma is settled and heresies will not cause it any trouble until the Reformation. Pontifical primacy strikes deep root, the organiza-tion of the clergy is henceforth solid, religion and liturgy are unified, discipline and canonic law are settled, ecclesiastic property increases, the tithe is established, the federal constitution of the Church—sub-divided into sufficiently autonomous circuits—disappears, the movement of centralization for the benefit of Rome is clearly outlined. This movement came to an end, when the Carolingians had established the temporal power of the popes, and the Latin church, strongly hierarchical before, became as centralized, in a comparatively short time, as the Roman empire of yore, which the church's universal authority had thus supplanted. Simultaneously Christianity spread further still and conquered the barbarians. The Anglo-Saxon missionaries had set the examples in Saint Boniface and Saint Willibrod; they had followers. The gospel was preached to the Alamans, the Frisians, the Saxons, the Scandinavians, the Bohemians and the Hungarians, the Russians and the Wends, the Pomeranians and the Prussians, the Lithuanians and the Finns. The work was accomplished at the end of the thirteenth century: Europe was christianized.

The Jews settled in the wake of Christianity as it kept spreading by degrees. In the ninth century, they came from France to Germany, got thence into Bohemia, into Hungary and into Poland, where they met another wave of Jews—those coming by way of the Caucasus and converting on their march several Tartar tribes. In the twelfth century they settled in England and Belgium, and everywhere they built their synagogues, they organized their communities at that decisive hour, when the nations were coming out from chaos, when states were being formed and consolidated. They remained outside of these great agitations, amid which conquering and conquered races were amalgamating and uniting one with the other; and in the midst of these tumultuous combinations they remained spectators, strangers and hostile to these fusions: an eternal people witnessing the rise of new nations. However, their role was surely of account at all times; they were one of the active elements of ferment of these societies in the process of formation.

In some countries, as, *e. g.,* in Spain, their history is in so high a degree interlinked with that of the peninsula, that, without them it is impossible to grasp and appreciate the development of the Spanish people. But if they had influenced its constitution by the numbers of their converts in that country, by the support they had given in succession to the various masters in possession of its soil,—they did so by seeking to bring to themselves those among whom they lived and not by letting themselves be absorbed. Still, the history of the Spanish Marranos is exceptional. Everywhere, though, as we shall see, the Jews played a part of economic agents; they did not create a social state, but they assisted after a fashion in establishing it, and yet they could not be treated with favor among the organizations to whose formation they had lent aid. For this there was a seri-our obstacle. All the states of the Middle Ages were moulded by the church; in their essence, in their very being, they were permeated with the ideas and doctrines of Catholicism; the Christian religion gave the unity they lacked to the numerous tribes which had gathered together into nations. As representatives of contrary dogmas, the Jews could not but oppose the general movement, both by their proselytism, and by their very presence as well. As the church led this movement it was from the church that anti-Judaism, theoretical and legislative, proceeded," anti-Judaism which the governments and the peoples shared and which other causes came to aggravate. The social and religious state of affairs and the Jews themselves gave origin to these causes. But they had remained ever subordinated to those essential reasons which may be traced to the opposition, then secular already,—between the Christian spirit and the Jewish spirit, between the universal, and so to say, international Catholic religion, and the particularist and narrow Jewish faith. At bottom, and we keep in mind the changes which had taken place, the situation was the same as in Pagan antiquity. By the very fact of denying the divinity of Christ, the Jews placed themselves as enemies of the social order, since this social order was based on Christianity, just as formerly in Rome, they had been, together with the Christians themselves, enemies of another social order. In the midst of the downfall of the ancient world, amid the radical transformations which had taken place this ubiquitous people of the Jews had not changed. It pretended to preserve as ever before, its manners, its customs, its habits and at the same time to participate in all the advantages which states granted to their members or their subjects. For all these states, very heterogeneous at first, were becoming homogeneous; they were advancing to an ever-increasing unity; from the middle ages on they were aspiring to that unity at which they arrived later. Accordingly they were led to combat the foreign elements, foreign nationally and dogmatically, whether these elements came from without, as, *e. g.,* the Arabs or they existed within, as the Jews. At this point of history, the national struggle and the confessional struggle intermingle. With the persistent barbarism of the feudal system the struggle was naturally fierce, the more so that it was instinctive rather than rational, especially so on the part of the people, for the church or the popes and the synods at least proceeded upon reasoning. With these general principles given we shall see how they acted upon and in what manner they influenced the special and particular manifestations of anti-Judaism. To this end we must say a word about the commercial and financial role of the Jews, of their activity and their spirit.

Only towards the end of the eighth century the activity of the Western Jews developed. Protected in Spain by the Khalifs, given support by Charlemagne who let the Merovingian laws fall into disuse, they extended their commerce which until then centered chiefly in the sale of slaves. For this they were, indeed, particularly favored by circumstances. Their communities were in constant communication, they were united by the religious bond which tied them all to the theological centre of Babylonia whose dependencies they considered themselves up to the decline of the exilarchate. Thus they acquired very great facilities for exporting commerce, in which they amassed considerable fortunes, if we are to believe the diatribes of Dagobard, [63] and later those of Rigord, [64] which, with all their exaggeration of the property of the Jews must not, yet, be entirely rejected as unworthy of credence. [65] Indeed, with regard to this wealth of the Jews, especially in Prance and Spain,

[63] *De Insolentia Iudaeorum* (Patrologie Latine, v. CIV)

[64] *Gesta Philippi Augusti.*

[65] For the position of Southern Jews at the time of Philip the Fair, cf. Simeon Luce (*Catalogue des documents du Tresor des Chortes* (Revue dee Etudes Juives, v. I, 3.)

we possess the testimonies of chroniclers and the Jews themselves, several of whom reproached their coreligionists for devoting to the worldly welfare much more time than to the worship of Jehovah. "Instead of calculating the numerical value of the name of God," says the Kab-balist Abulafia, "the Jews prefer to count their riches."

Parallel with the general advance we really see this preoccupation with wealth grow among the Jews and their practical activity concentrating on a special business: I mean the gold business. Here we must emphasize a point. It has often been said, and it is re-peated still, that the Christian societies had forced the Jews into this position of creditor and usurer, which they have for a long time kept: this is the thesis of the philosemites. On the other hand the antisemites assert that the Jews, from time immemorial, had natural inclinations for commerce and finance, and that they but followed their normal disposition, and that nothing had ever been forced upon them. In these two assertions there is a portion of verity and a portion of error, or rather that there is room to comment on them, and especially to give them a hearing.

At the time of their national prosperity the Jews, like all other nations, for that matter, had a class of the rich, which proved itself as eager for gain and as hard to the lowly as the capitalists of all ages and all nations have proven. The antisemites, as well, who make use of the texts of Isaiah and Jeremiah, e. g., to prove the constant eternal rapacity of the Jews, act very naively, and, thanks to the words of the prophets, can but establish,—and puerile it is,—the existence, in Israel, of possessors and poor. If they examined impartially the Judaic codes and precepts only, they would acknowledge that legislation and morals prescribed never to charge interest on debts. [66] Taking all in all, the Jews were, in Palestine the least mercantile of the Semites, in this re-gard much inferior to the Phoenicians and Carthaginians. It was only under Solomon that they entered into intercourse with the other nations. Even at that time, it was a powerful corporation of Phoenicians that was engaged in the banking business at Jerusalem. However, the geographical position of Palestine prevented its inhabitants from devoting themselves to a very extensive and considerable traffic. Nevertheless, during the first captivity and through the contact with the Babylonians, a class of merchants had formed, and from it came the first Jewish emigrants, who established their colonies in Egypt, Cyrenaica and Asia Minor. In all cities that admitted them they formed active communities, powerful and opulent, and, with the final dispersion, important

[66] "Thou shalt not lend upon usury to thy brother; usury of money, usury of victuals, usury of anything that is lent upon usury: unto a stranger (nokhri) thou mayest lend upon usury." Deuter. XXIII. 19-20.

Nokhri means a transient stranger; a resident stranger is *get.*

"And if thy brother be waxen poor, and fallen in decay with thee; then thou shalt relieve him: *yea, though ho be a stranger,* or a sojourner; that he may live with thee. Take no usury of him or increase." Levit. XXV, 35-36.

"Lord, who shall abide in Thy tabernacle? . . . *He that* putteth not out his money to usury." (Psalm, XV, 1-5). "Even to a non-Jew," adds the Talmudic commentary, (*Mak-koth* XXIV). Consult also: Eyod. XXII 25; Philo, Do Charitate; Josephus, *Antiquitatcs Judaeorum,* B. IV, ch. VIII; Selden, B. VI., ch. IX).

groups of emigrants joined the original groups which facilitated their installation. To explain the attitude of the Jews it is accordingly not necessary to fall back upon a theory of the Arian genius and the Semitic genius. Indeed, we well know the traditional Roman cupidity and the commercial sense of the Greeks. The usury of the Roman *feneratores* had no limit any more than had their bad faith; they were encouraged by the very harsh laws against the debtors,—a worthy daughter of that law of the Twelve Tables which granted to the creditor the right of cutting pieces of flesh from the live body of an insolvent borrower. In Rome gold was absolute master, and Juvenal could speak of the *"sanctissima divit-iarum maiestas"* [67] As to the Greeks, they were the cleverest and boldest of speculators; rivalling the Phoenicians in the slave-trade, in piracy, they knew the use of letters of exchange and maritime insurance, and, Solon having authorized usury, they never did away with it.

As a nation the Jews differed in nothing from other nations, and if at first they were a nation of shepherds and agriculturists, they came, by a natural course of evolution, to constitute other classes among them. And devoting themselves to commerce, after their dispersion, they followed a general law which is applicable to all colonists. Indeed, with the exception of cases when he goes to break virgin soil, the emigrant can be only an artisan or merchant, as nothing but necessity or allure-

[67] The Hebrew Sibyl speaks of "the execrable thirst for gold, of the passion for sordid gain which goads the Latins on to the conquest of the world."

ment of gain can force him to leave his native soil. Therefore, the Jews coming into Western cities acted in no way differently from the Dutch or English when they established business offices. Nevertheless, they came soon enough to specialize in the money business, for which they have been so bitterly reproached ever since, and in the fourteenth century they constituted quite a coterie of changers and lenders: they had become the bankers of the world. They are accused of having created popular loan banks, and they become the figure-heads for the lords and rich bourgeois. This was a fatal proceeding, if we remember the particular notion entertained by the church concerning money, and also the economic conditions prevailing in Europe from the twelfth century on.

The Middle Ages considered gold and silver as tokens possessing imaginary value, varying at the will of the king, who could order its rate according to the dictations of his fancy. This notion was derived from Roman law, which refused to treat money as a merchandise. The church inherited these financial dogmas, combined them with the biblical prescriptions which forbade loan on interest, and was severe, from its very start, against the Christians and ecclesiastics even that followed the example of the *fenera tores,* who advanced money at 24, 48 and even 60 per cent., when the legal rate of interest was 12 per cent. The canons of councils are quite explicit on this point; they follow the teaching of the Fathers, Saint Augustin, Saint Chrysostom, Saint Jerome; they forbid loans and are harsh against those clerics and laymen who engage in the usurer's business. Their severity did not prevent usury entirely, but it lessened it by branding it with infamy. At the same time social conditions were such as to make usury inevitable, and in these conditions the synods could change nothing whatever. During several centuries feudalism had plundered communities of their possessions and increased its territories at the expense of communal lands. On the disappearance of serfdom, economic slavery took the place of personal slavery, a portion of the population was forced into vagabondage, which accounts for those bands of vagabonds, beggars and thieves, that overran the roads of France in the fourteenth century. The other portion was compelled to work for wages or they lived as farm-ers and tenants on the soil which had been their own.

At the same time, in the twelfth and thirteenth centuries, the wage system were established, the bourgeoisie developed, grew rich and acquired privileges and franchises: capitalistic power was now born. Commerce having taken on a new form, the value of gold increased and the passion for money grew with the importance which the currency had acquired.

Indeed, on one hand were the rich, on the other—the peasants, landless, subject to the tithe and prestations; workingmen dominated over by the capitalist laws. To cap it all, perpetual wars, revolts, diseases and famines. Whenever the year was bad, the money gave out, the crop failed, an epidemic came, the peasant, the proletarian, and the small bourgeois were forced to resort to borrowing. Hence, by necessity there were to be borrowers. But the church had forbidden loan at interest, and capital does not choose to remain unproductive, but during the Middle Ages capital could only be either merchant or lender, as money could be made pro-ductive in no other way. As far as the ecclesiastical decisions had any influence, a great part of the Christian capitalists did not want to begin an open revolt against their authority; there was also formed a class of reprobates for whom the bourgeoisie and nobility often acted as silent partners. It consisted of Lombards, Caeorsins, to whom the princes, the lords granted the privileges of loaning on interest, gathering a part of the profits which were considerable, as the Lombards lent money at 10 per cent. a month ;)or of unscrupulous foreigners, like Tuscan emigrants settled in Istria who went in usury to such extremes that the community of Triest sus-pended, in 1350, all executions for debts for three years. This did not take away the ground from under the usurers, but as I have said they found obstacles which the church placed in the way of their operations (the council of Lyons of 1215 wanted to declare the wills of usurers void).

As for Jews, these obstacles did not exist. The church had no moral power over them, it could not forbid them, in the name of the doctrine and dogma, to engage in money exchanging and banking. The Jews, who at this epoch were mostly merchants and capitalists, profited by this liberty and the economic condition of the peoples among whom they lived. In this path the ecclesiastic authorities encouraged, rather than restrained them, and the Christian bourgeois kept them busy in it by furnishing them with capitals and employing them as dummies. Thus a religious conception of the functions of capital and interest, and a social system which ran counter to this conception, led the Jews of the Middle Ages to adopt a profession cried down but made necessary ; and in reality they were not the cause of the abuses of usury, for which the social order itself was responsible. Thus we see that, in part, motives foreign to them, to their nature, to their temperament, brought them to this position of pawnbrokers, money changers and bankers, but it is but just to add that they had been prepared, for this by their very position, and this position they surely had sought. If they did not cultivate land, if they were not agriculturists, it is not because they possessed none, as has often been said; the restrictive laws relative to the property rights of the Jews came at a date posterior to their settlement. They own property, but had their domains cultivated by slaves, for their stubborn patriotism forbade them to break foreign soil. This patriotism, the notion which they attached to the sanctity of their Palestinian father land, the allusion which they kept alive in them of the restoration of that fatherland and this particular faith which made them consider themselves exiles who would one day again see the holy city,—all this drove them above all other foreigners and colonists to take up commerce.

As merchants they were destined to become usurers, given the 'conditions which the codes had imposed upon them and the conditions they had imposed upon themselves. To escape persecution and annoyance they had to make themselves useful, even necessary, to their rulers, the noblemen upon whom they depended, to the church whose vassals they were. Now the nobleman, the Church—despite its anathemas—needed gold, and this gold they demanded from the Jews. During the Middle Ages gold became the great motive power, the supreme deity; alchemists spent their lives in search of the magistery which was to produce it, the idea of possessing it inflamed the minds, in its name all kinds of cruelties were committed, the thirst of riches laid hold of all souls; later on, for Cortez and Pizarro, the successors of Columbus, the conquest of America meant the conquest of gold. The-Jews fell under the universal charm—the same under which the Tempters had fallen—and for them it was particularly fatal, because of their state of mind and the civil status imposed upon them. To acquire a few scanty privileges, or rather, in order to exist, they turned brokers in gold, but this the Christians sought as eagerly as they. More than that, under the constant menace of banishment, always acamp, forced to be nomads, the Jews had to guard against the terrible eventualities of exile. They had to transform their property so as to make it more convertible into money, that is, to give it a more movable form, and they were the most active in developing the money value, in considering it as a merchandise, hence the lending and—to recoup for periodic and unavoidable confiscations—the usury.

The creation of guilds,—merchant and craft— guilds and their organization, in the thirteenth century, finally forced the Jews into the condition to which they had been led by the social conditions—general and special—under which they lived. All these organizations were, so to speak, religious organizations, brother-hoods which none joined but those who prostrated themselves before the standard of the patron saint. The ceremonies attendant upon the initiation into these bodies being Christian ceremonies, the Jew could not but be shut out from them: and so they were. A series of prohibitions successively shut them out of all industry and all commerce, except that in odds and ends and in old clothes. Those who escaped this disqualification did so by virtue of special privileges for which they oftenest paid too dearly.

However, this is not all; other more intimate causes were added to those I have just enumerated, and all joined in throwing the Jew more and more out of society, in shutting him up in the ghetto, in immobilizing him behind the counter where he was weighing gold.

An energetic, vivacious nation, of infinite pride, thinking themselves superior to the other nations, the Jews wished to become a power. They instinctively had a taste for domination, as they believed themselves superior to all others by their origin, their religion, their title of a "chosen race," which they had always ascribed to themselves. To exercise this kind of power the Jews had no choice of means. Gold gave them a power which all political and religious laws denied them, and it was the only one they could hope for. As possessors of gold they became the masters of their masters, they dominated over them, and this was the only way to deploy their energy and their activity.

Would they not have been able to display it in some other fashion? Yes, and they tried it, but there they had to fight their own spirit. For many long years they had worked in the intellectual line, devoted themselves to sciences, letters, philosophy. They were mathema-ticians and astronomers; they practised medicine, and, if the school of Montpellier was not founded by them, they surely helped in developing it; they had translated the works of Averroes and of the Arabic commentators of Aristotle; they had revealed the Greek philosophy to the Christian world, and their metaphysicians Ibn Gabirol and Maimonides had been among the teachers of the schoolmen. [68] For years they had been the depositories of knowledge; like the initiated of old they held the torch which they handed over to the Westerners; with the Arabs, they had taken a most active part in the efflorescence and expansion of the admirable Semitic civilization which had arisen in Spain and Southern France and had ushered in and prepared the way for the Renaissance. Who stopped them in this advance? They themselves.

Their doctors endeavored to confine Israel to the ex- elusive study of the law in order to preserve Israel from outside influences, pernicious, it was said, to the integrity of the law. Efforts to this effect had been made since the time of the Maccabees, when the Helle-nizers constituted a great party in Palestine. Beaten at first, or, at least, hardly listened to, those who later acquired the name of obscurantists, kept at their task. When Jewish intolerance and bigotry grew in the twelfth century, when exclusiveness increased, the struggle between the partisans of profane science and their opponents became fiercer, it blazed up after the

[68] Cf. S. Munk, *Melanges de philosophic juive ct arabe.*

death of Maimonides and ended in the victory of the obscurantists.

In Ms works, particularly in the ***Moreh Nebukhim*** (Guide of the Perplexed) [69] Moses Maimonides attempted to reconcile faith and science. As a convinced Aristotelian, he wished to unite peripatetic philosophy with the Mosaic faith, and his speculations on the nature of the soul and its immortality found followers and ardent admirers, as well as fierce detractors. The latter reproached him for sacrificing dogma to metaphysics and scorning the fundamental beliefs of Judaism, e. g., the resurrection of the dead. As a matter of fact, especially in France and Spain, the Maimun-ists were led to neglect, the ritual practices and petty ceremonies of worship: bold rationalists, they had allegoric interpretations for the biblical miracles, as the disciples of Philo before them, and thus they escaped the tyranny of religious precepts. They claimed the right of taking part in the intellectual movement of the time and mingling in the society in which they lived, without giving up their beliefs. Their opponents clung to the purity of Israel, to the absolute integrity of its worship, its rites, and its beliefs; in philosophy and science they saw the most deadly enemies of Judaism and maintained that the Jews were destined to perish and scatter among the nations, if they did not recover their wits and did not reject everything that was not of the Holy Law. No doubt they were right from their narrow and fanatical point of view, but thanks to them the Jews continued everywhere as a foreign race, jealously guarding its laws

[69] Guide des Egares (Translated by S. Munk).

and customs, resigned to intellectual and moral death rather than to the physical and natural death of fallen nations.

In 1232, Rabbi Solomon of Montpellier issued an anathema against all those who would read the ***Moreh Nebukhim*** or would take up scientific and philosophic studies. This was the signal for the struggle. It was violent on both sides, and all weapons were resorted to. The fanatical rabbis appealed to the fanaticism of the Dominicans, they denounced the ***Guide of the Perplexed*** and had it burned by the inquisition: it was the work of Solomon of Montpellier, but it marked the overthrow of the obscurantists. Still this defeat did not end the struggle. It was renewed at the end of the century against Jacob Tibbon of Montpellier by Don Astruc of Lunel, supported by Solomon Ben Adret of Barcelona. At the instigation of a German doctor, Asher Ben Yechiel, a synod of thirty rabbis met at Barcelona, with Ben Adret in the chair, and excommunicated all those who read books other than the Bible and the Talmud, when under twenty-five years.

A counter-excommunication was proclaimed by Jacob Tibbon, who, at the head of all Provencal rabbis, boldly defended condemned science. All was in vain: those wretched Jews, whom everybody tormented for their faith, persecuted their coreligionists more cruelly and severely than they had ever been persecuted. Those whom they accused of indifference had to undergo the worst punishments; the blasphemers had their tongues cut; Jewish women who had any relations with Christians were condemned to disfigurement: their noses were subjected to ablation. Despite this, Tibbon's followers persisted. It was due to them, that Jewish thought did not completely die out in Spain, France and Italy during the fourteenth and fifteenth centuries. Even such men as Moses of Narbonne and Levy de Bagnols, as Elias of Crete and Alemani, the teacher of Pico di Mirandola, as well as later Spinoza, were all isolated men. As for the mass of Jews, it had completely fallen under the power of the obscurantists. Hereafter it was separated from the world, its whole horizon was shut out; to nourish its spirit it had nothing but futile talmudic commentaries, idle and mediocre discussions on . the Law. Like the mummies swaddled in their bandlets, it was shut up and choked in ceremonial practices: its rulers and guides had it shut up in the tightest and most abominable of dungeons. Hence a terrible deadening and awful decadence, a sinking of intellectualism, a compression of the brain which made them incapable of grasping any idea.

Henceforth the Jew thought no longer. And what need had he of thinking since he possessed a minute, precise code, the work of casuist legists, which could give answer to any question that it was legitimate to ask? For believers were forbidden to inquire into problems which were not mentioned in this code—the Talmud. The Jew found everything foreseen in the Talmud: the sentiments, the emotions, whatever they might be, were designated; prayers, formulas, all ready-made, supplied the means for expressing them. The book left room neither to reason nor to freedom, inasmuch as in instruction the legendary and gnomical portions were almost proscribed,—to lay stress upon the law and ritual. Through such an education the Jew not only lost all spontaneity, all intellectuality: he saw his morality decrease and weaken. Taking into account actions only, and that, too, external ones, accomplished mechanically and not with a moral purpose, the Talmudists equally restricted the Jewish soul; and between the worship and religion which they preached and the Chinese system of prayer-mills, there is but the difference between the complex and the simple. True, by the tyranny they had exercised over their flock they developed in each the ingenuity and spirit of craftiness necessary to escape from the net which closed without pity; but they also increased the natural positivism of the Jews by presenting to them as their only ideal the material and personal happiness, a happiness which one could attain on earth if one knew how to bind oneself to the thousand religious laws. To attain this selfish happiness, the Jew, whom the prescribed ceremonies rid of all care and trouble, was fatally led on to strive after gold, for under the existing social conditions which ruled him, as they ruled all the people of that epoch, gold alone could give him the gratification which his limited and narrow brain could conceive; Thus, by himself and by those around him; by his own laws and by those imposed upon him; by his artificial nature and circumstances, the Jew was directed to gold. He was prepared to be changer, lender, usurer, one who strives after the metal, at first for the pleasures it could afford and then afterwards for the sole happiness of possessing it; one who greedily seizes gold and avariciously immobilizes it. The Jew having become such, anti-Judaism became more complicated, social causes intermingled with religious causes; the combination of these causes explains the intensity and gravity of the persecutions which Israel had to undergo.

Indeed, the Lombards and Caorsins, for instance, were the object of popular animosity; they were hated and despised but they were not victims of systematic persecutions. It was deemed abominable that Jews 6hould have acquired wealth, especially because they were *Jews.* Against the Christian who cheated him, and was neither better nor worse than the Jew, the poor wretch when plundered felt less anger than against the Israelite reprobate, the enemy of God and man. When the deicide, even so the object of terror, had become the usurer, the collector of taxes, the merciless agent of the fisc,—the terror increased; it became intermingled with hatred on the part of the oppressed and downtrodden. The simple minds did not seek the real causes of their distress; they only saw the proximate causes. For the Jew was the proximate cause of usury; by the heavy interest he charged he caused destitution, severe and hard misery; accordingly, it was upon the Jews that enmities fell. The suffering populace did not trouble themselves about responsibilities; they were neither economists nor reasoners; they only ascertained that a heavy hand weighed upon them: that was the hand of the Jew, and the people rushed upon him. They did not rush upon him alone; when at the limit of their endurance, they often attacked all the rich, indiscriminately killing Jews and Christians alike, In Gascony and southern France the *Pastoureaux* destroyed 120 Jewish communities, but the Jews were not their only victims; they invaded castles, they exterminated the nobles and the propertied. In Brabant, the peasants who besieged Genappe, the residence of the Jews, did not spare their own coreligionists. Similarly , when King Armleder raised the tramps-in the Rhine lands, he had in his train not only *Juden-schlager* (Jew beaters), but also slayers of the rich. Only that among the Christians the propertied alone suffered violence at the hands of the rebels, the poor were spared; among the Jews the rich and the poor were exterminated indiscriminately, for, before any crime, they were guilty of being Jews. To the wrath for being plundered the mob added the aversion to being plundered by cursed ones, and no consideration restrained the plundered, as the accursed were of a strange race, forming a people apart.

At all events, the masses, restrained by authority and law, rarely attacked the capitalists in general; to goad them on to revolt a terrible accumulation of miseries was necessary. But with reference to the Jews their ill-feeling was not restrained at all; on the contrary, it was encouraged. This was a means to divert attention, and every now and then kings, nobles or burghers offered their slaves a holocaust of Jews. This unfortunate Jew was utilized for two purposes during the Middle Ages. They employed him as a leech, let him swell up, fill himself with gold, then they made him clear; or, whenever popular hatred was too bitter, he was subjected to corporal punishment which was profitable to the Christian capitalists, who thus paid a tribute of propitiary blood to those whom they oppressed.

To give satisfaction to their wretched subjects, the kings would from time to time proscribe Jewish usury, would cancel debts; but oftenest they tolerated the Jews, encouraged them, being sure to derive benefit from them through confiscation or by taking their place as creditors. Nevertheless these measures were always but temporary, and governmental anti-Judaism was purely political. They banished the Jews either to mend their finances, or to elicit the gratitude of the small fry by partly relieving them of the heavy burden of debt; but they would soon recall the Jews, as they could find no better tax collectors. However, anti-Jewish legislation was, as we have said, most frequently forced upon the royal power by the church, either by the monks or the popes and synods. Even the regular clergy and the secular clergy acted upon different principles.

The monks addressed themselves to the people, with whom they were in constant touch. In the first place they preached against the deicides, but they represented these deicides as domineering, while they should have been bent forever under the yoke of Christendom. All these preachers gave expression to popular grievances. "If the Jews fill their granaries with fruit, their cellar with victuals, their bags with money and their chests with gold' said Pierre de Cluny: [70] "it is neither by tilling the earth, nor by serving in war, nor by practicing

[70] Peter the Venerable, abbot of Cluny: *Tractatus adversua Judaeorum inveteratom duritiam* (Bibl. des Peres Latins, Lyons).

any other useful and honorable trade, but by cheating the Christians and buying, at low price, from thieves the things which they have stolen." They overheated the passions which needed only expression, and in their homilies and sermons they laid particular stress on the social side. They thundered against the "infamous" nation "which lives by pillage," and while their invec-tives were prompted by zeal in proselytism, they posed especially as avengers, who had come to punish "the insolence, avarice and hard-heartedness" of the Jews. And they found a hearing. In Italy, John of Capistrano, "the scourge of the Hebrews," was stirring up the poor against the usury and obduracy of the Jews. He continued his work in Germany and Poland, leading gangs of poor wretches and desperadoes who exacted expiation for their sufferings from the Jewish communities. Ber-nardinus of Feltre followed his example, but he was haunted by more practical notions, among others by that of establishing mont-de-pietes to counteract the rapacity of the lenders. He travelled all over Italy and Tyrol, demanding the expulsion of the Hebrews, inciting insurrections and riots, causing the massacre of the Jews in Trent.

The kings, nobles and bishops did not encourage this campaign of the regulars. They protected the Jews from the monk Radulphe, in Germany; in Italy, they set themselves against the preachings of Bernardinus of Feltre, who accused the princes of having sold themselves to Yechiel of Pisa, the wealthiest Jew of the peninsula; in Poland, Pope Gregory XI. stopped the crusade of Jan of Ryczywol. The rulers had every interest to suppress these partial uprisings; from experience they knew that when the bands of starvelings were through slaughtering the Jews, they would kill those who possessed too great wealth, those who enjoyed excessive privileges, or those lords, counts or barons, whose power weighed too heavily on the shoulders of tax-payers. The Pastoureaux, the Jacquerie, the faithful followers of the Armcleders, afterwards the peasants of Munzer, had demonstrated that the holders of power were not unreasonable in their fear: by protecting the Jews to a certain degree they protected themselves.

As for the Church, it kept to theological anti-Judaism, and, being essentially conservative, favoring the mighty and rich, it took care not to encourage the passions of the people. I speak of the official Church, abounding in prebendaries; striving for unity and centralization, cherishing dreams of universal domination; the Church of the Synods, the law-making Church, and not the church of petty priests and monks which was stirred by the same passions as agitated the lowly. But if the church sometimes interfered in behalf of the Jews when they were the object of the mob's fury, it nursed this fury and supplied it with fuel by combatting Judaism, even though combatting it from different motives.

Faithful to its principles, it vainly persecuted the spirit of Judaism in all its forms. It could not get rid of it, as this Jewish spirit had inspired it in its earliest stages. It was impregnated with it as the beach-sands are impregnated with the sea-salt which rises to their surface, and despite its efforts from the second century on to rebuff its origin, to thrust far away all memory of its original foundation, it still preserved the marks of it. In seeking to realize its conception of Christian states directed and ruled over by the Papacy, the church strove to reduce all anti-Christian elements. Thus it inspired Europe's violent reaction against the Arabs, and the struggle of the European nationalities against Mohammedanism was a struggle at once political and religious.

Still the Moslem danger was external, but the internal dangers threatening the dogma proved quite as grave for the church. As it had become all-powerful, as it had attained the maximum of Catholicity, it gave support to heresy less readily; beginning with the eighth century the legislation against heretics grew more severe. Formerly benign and confining itself to canonic penalties, hereafter it appealed to the secular powers, and the Vaudois, Albigenses, Beghards, Apostolic Brothers, Luciferians were treated with cruelty. The limit of this movement was reached in the inquisition which the Pope Innocent III. instituted in the thirteenth century. Henceforth, a special tribunal, backed by civil authority, obedient to its orders was to be the sole judge, and pitiless at that, of heresy.

The Jews could not be overlooked in this legislation. They were persecuted not as Jews—the church wished to preserve the Jews as a living testimony of its triumph —but because they instigated people to judaization, either directly or unconsciously, by the very fact of their existence. Had not their philosophers sent forth metaphysicians like Amaury de Bene and David de Dinan ? What is more, were not certain heretics judaizing? The Pasagians of Upper Italy observed the Mosaic law; the Orleans heresy was a Jewish heresy; an Albigens sect maintained that the doctrine of the Jews was preferable to that of the Christians; the Hussites were sup-ported by the Jews; accordingly, the Dominicans preached against the Hussites and the Jews, and the imperial army that advanced against Jan Ziska massacred the Jews on its way.

In Spain, where the mingling of Jews and Christians was considerable, the Inquisition was instituted by Gregory XI, who gave it its constitution, to surveil the judaizing heretics and the Jews and Moors, who, though not subjects of the Church, were subject to the will of the Holy Office whenever "by their words or their writings they urged the Catholics to embrace their faith." More than that, the popes recalled the canonic decisions to the minds of the Kings of Spain, because the *fueros,* i. e., Castillian customs which superseded the Visigothic laws, had granted equal rights to Jews, Christians and Moslemites.

All these ecclesiastic measures reinforced the anti-Jewish sentiments of kings and nations; they were the prime causes; they upheld a special state of mind, which political motives emphasized with the kings; social motives—with the nations. Owing to it, anti-Judaism became general, and no class of society was free from it, for all classes were more or less guided by the Church or inspired by its teachings, all of them were or thought themselves harmed by the Jews. The nobility took offense at their riches; the proletarians, the artisans and peasants, in a word the small people, were provoked by their usury; as for the bourgeoisie, the merchant class, the dealers in money, it was in permanent rivalry with the Jews, and their constant competition engendered hatred. The modern contest between Christian and Jewish capital assumes shape in the fourteenth and fifteenth centuries, the Catholic bourgeois looks with calm eyes on the murder of Jews, which rids him of an often successful rival.

Thus everything concurred to make of the Jew an universal foe, and the only support that he found during this terrible period of several centuries was with the popes, who, while abetting the passions of which they made capital, still wanted to guard earefully this witness of the excellence of the Christian faith. If the Church preserved the Jews, it often was not without schooling and punishing them. The Church forbade giving them public positions that might confer upon them authority over Christians; it instigated the kings to adopt restrictive measures against them; it imposed upon them distinctive badges, the *rouelle* and hat; it shut them in those ghettoes, which the Jews had often accepted and even sought in their eagerness to separate themselves from the world, to live apart, without mixing with the nations, to preserve intact their beliefs and their race; so that in many points the edicts bidding the Jews to remain confined in special quarters really but sanctioned an already existing state of affairs. But the chief task of the Church was to combat the Jewish religion dogmatically. However, controversies, numerous as they were, did not suffice for this; laws were issued against the Jewish books. The reading of the *Mishna* in synagogues had already been prohibited by Justinian;- after him no laws were passed against the Talmud, until the time of Saint Louis. After the controversy between Nicholas Donin and Yechiel of Paris (1240) Gregory IX ordered to burn the Talmud; this order was repeated by Innocent IV (1244), Honorius IV (1286), John XXII (1320) and the anti-pope Benedict XIII (1415). Moreover, the Jewish prayers were expurgated and the erection of new synagogues was forbidden.

The civil laws expounded the ecclesiastical decrees and were inspired by them, as, e. g., the laws of Alfonso X of Castile, in the code of *Siete Partidas,* [71] the dispositions of Saint Louis, those of Phillip IV, those of the German emperors and the Polish kings. [72] The Jews were forbidden to appear in public on certain days; a personal toll was imposed upon them as if on cattle; they were sometimes forbidden to marry without authorization.

To the laws one must add the customs—vexatious customs—like that of Toulouse, which made the syndic of the Jews subject to boxing on the ear. The mob insulted them during their holidays and sabbaths; it profaned their cemeteries; on leaving the Mysteries and Passion plays it would lay their houses waste.

Not content with vexing them, with expelling them, as did Edward I in England (1287), Phillip IV and Charles VI in Prance (1306 and 1394), Ferdinand the Catholic in Spain (1492), they killed the Jews everywhere.

[71] *Novellae,* 146. Title XXIV.

[72] *General Statute of Ladislas Jagellon*. Art. XIX.

When on their way to liberate the Holy Tomb, the Crusaders prepared themselves for the Holy War by the immolation of Jews; whenever the black plague or a famine raged, the Jews were sacrificed in holocaust to the angered divinity; whenever extortions, misery, hunger, destitution maddened the people, they would avenge themselves on the Jews, who were made victims of expiation. "What's the use of going to fight the Mohammedans," cried Pierre de Cluny, [73] "when we have among us the Jews, who are worse than the Saracens?"

What was to be done against an epidemic unless to kill the Jews who conspired with the lepers to poison the wells? And so they were exterminated in York and London; in Spain at the instigation of St. Vincent Ferrer; in Italy, where John of Capistrano preached; in Poland, Bohemia, France, Moravia, Austria. They were burned in Strassburg, Mayence, Troyes. In Spain the Marranos mounted the scaffold by the thousands; elsewhere they were ripped open with pitchforks and scythes; they were beaten to death like dogs.

Surely the prophets who had called upon Judah—in punishment for his crimes—the terrible wrath of God, had never dreamed of more frightful misfortunes than those that befell him. When reading the Jewish martyrology, such as the Avignonian, HaCohen, [74] lamented in the sixteenth century, the martyrology, which extends from Akiba, torn to pieces by iron curry-combs, on to the executed of Ancona praying in the flames, to the heroes

[73] Loc. cit.

[74] *Emek-ha-Bacha, La Vallee des Pleurs.* Translated by Julien See.

of Vitry who immolated themselves, one is overcome with pity. *The Valley of Tears* is the name of the book which sounded the call for mourning. "I have called it *The Valley of Tears*" says the ancient chronicler, "because it is the proper title for it. Whoever reads it will gasp for breath, his eyes will suffuse with tears, and with hands on his loins he will exclaim: 'How long, 0 my Lord? "

What crimes could have deserved such frightful punishments? How poignant must have been the afflictions of those beings! In those evil hours they cuddled one to the other and felt themselves brethren; the bond that joined them was fastened more tightly. To whom could they tell their plaints and their feeble joys, if not to themselves? From these general desolations, from these sobs was born an intense and suffering brotherhood. The ancient Jewish patriotism became still more exalted. These outcasts, maltreated all over Europe, and marching with bespattered faces, got it into their heads to feel Zion and its hills brought back to life, to conjure up —what a supreme and sweet consolation!—the beloved banks of the Jordan and the lake of Galilee; they arrived there through an intense solidarity. Amidst the groans and oppressions they were forced more than ever to live among themselves and to band more closely. For did they not know that on their journeys they would find a safe refuge with the Jew only, that if sickness befell them on the way, a Jew alone would help them like a brother, and that if they died far from theirs, Jews alone could bury them according to their rites and say the customary prayers over their bodies?

Still, to understand exactly the position of the Jews during these Dark Ages, one must compare it with that of the people surrounding them. The persecutions of the Jews would go on now that their exclusive character would render them more sorrowful. In the Middle Ages the proletarians and the peasants were not much better off; after being shaken up by terrible upheavals, the Jews would enjoy periods of comparative tranquillity, of which the serfs knew nothing. Steps were taken against them, but what steps were not taken against the Moris-coes, the Hussites, the Albigenses, the Pastoureaux, the Jacques, against the heretics and the outcasts? From the eleventh to the end of the sixteenth century, abominable years fell out, and the Jews suffered from it not a whit more than did those among whom they lived. They suffered for other reasons, and traces of it were left impressed in a different way. But as the manners had grown softer, hours of greater happiness for them were born. We shall see what changes the Reformation and the Renaissance were to bring about in their position.

CHAPTER VI.

ANTI-JUDAISM FROM THE TIME OF THE REFORMATION TILL THE FRENCH REVOLUTION.

Position of the Jews at the Beginning of the Sixteenth Century.—Defeat of the Moors.—Banishment from Spain.—Softening of the Manners.—The Last Persecutions.—The Inquisition in Portugal.—The Renaissance and the Reformation of the Church.—The Attacks upon the Supremacy of Rome.—The Humanists and the Talmud.—Reuchlin and Pfeffer-korn.—The Reformation and the Jewish Spirit.— The Bible.—Luther and the Jews.—Transformation of the Social and the Religious Question.—The Peasant Wars.—The Jews no Longer the Chief Enemies of the Church.—The Christian State.—Catholicism, the Reformed and the Jews.— The Popes and Judaism.—Measures Against the Talmud and Conversions.—Anti-Jewish Legislation.—Molestations and Outrages.—Dogmatic Anti-Judaism.—The Re-calling of the Jews.—The Jews of Europe in the Eighteenth Century.—The Jews in the Netherlands, England, Poland, Turkey.—The Portuguese Jews in France.— The Intellectual and Moral Condition of the Jews.—Kabbalism and Messianism.— Sabbatai Zevi and Franck.—The Mystic Sects: the Chassidim and New-Chassidim, the Donmeh and the Trinitarians.—Talmudism.—Joseph Caro and the ***Schulchan Aruch;*** the Pilpul.—Jewish Reaction Against the Talmud.—Mardochec-Kolkos, Uriel Acosta, Spinoza.—Mendelssohn, the Meassef and the Jewish Emancipation.— Humanitarian Philosophy and the Jews.—The Social State and the Jews. —The Economic and the Political Objections.— Maury and Clermont-Tonnerre; Rewbel and Gre-goire.—The Revolution.—The Appearance of the Jews in Society.

When the first brea in of freedom swept over the world at the dawn of the sixteenth century, the Jews were but a nation of captives and slaves. Cooped up in the ghettoes, whose walls their own foolish hands helped only to make thicker, they were retired from human society, and, for the most part, lived in a state of lamentable and heartrending abjection. Their intellect had become atrophied, as they had themselves barred all the doors and shut all the windows through which air and light might have come to them. Under the influence of the surrounding nations, special and disgraceful legislations, under the depressing and baneful influence of the Talmudists, they had acquired during the whole of the Middle Ages that specific physiognomy, which they have lost in our days only, and which many still preserve in Poland, Rumania, Russia, Hungary, Bohemia and several parts of Germany; a physiognomy which habitual humility had rendered base, and obsequious, which the circumstances of existence had made fearsome and sickly, which the exclusive instruction by rabbis had imprinted with cunning and hypocrisy, but which suffering had refined, at times illumed with passive sadness and sorrowful resignation. The number of those who had escaped this abasement was very limited, and the Jews who suc-ceeded in keeping a free brain and proud spirit were in the lowest minority. These were mostly physicians, as medicine is the only science permitted by the Talmud; at the same time there were philosophers occasionally, and we shall see the role they played in Italy during the Renaissance. As for the mass of the Jews they had no capabilities for anything outside of commerce and usury. However, they had no rights whatever, no capacities, no road was open to them, and the few paths which they could still take were closed for them by their own doctors, who thus acted as allies of the Christian legists.

These latter had been inspired in their work by the Church doctrines which Thomas Aquinas had expressed in such bold relief. *Judaei sunt servi,* the master said energetically; the law considered them in no other wise. Toward the end of the fifteenth century, the Jew had become the serf of the Imperial Chamber in Germany; in France he was the king's serf, the serf of the lord, less even than a serf, for a serf could still own something, while a Jew in reality had no property; he was a thing rather than a person. The king and the lord, the bishop or the abbot, could dispose of all his belongings, i. e., of all that seemed to belong to him, since for him the possibility of owning was purely fictitious. He was taxable at will; he was subjected to fixed imposts, without prejudice to confiscations, and while, on the one hand, the Church was making exery effort to attract to it the Jew, on the other hand, the baron and church dignitaries kept him in his condition. If he turned to Christianity ho lost his possessions in favor of the lord, who was anxious to make good the loss of the taxes which he could no longer levy on the convert, and thus it was to his interest to remain in the slaves' prison. He was looked upon as a beast, impure and useful at that, as lower than a dog or hog, to which the personal toll likened him, however; he was the one forever accursed, he upon whom it was lawful, even meritorious, to shower the blows which the Crucified had received in Pilate's pretorium.

The only country where the Jews could claim the dignity of human beings was closed to them at the opening of the sixteenth century. The capture of Granada and the conquest of the Moorish Kingdom had deprived the Jews of their last refuge. The whole of Spain became Christian on the day (January 2, 1492) when Ferdinand and Isabella entered the Mohammedan city. The holy war of the Spaniards against the infidels ended victoriously, and the Moors in existence were cruelly persecuted in spite of the security which had been granted them. The victory having aroused on the one hand fanaticism, and the national sentiment on the other, Spain, now free from the Moors, wished to get rid of the Jews, whom the Catholic king and queen expelled the very year of Boabdil's fall, while the Inquisition doubled the severities against the Marranos and the descendants of the Moriscoes.

Still, the time of great sorrows had passed for the Jews, notwithstanding that the circumstances to which they had been reduced were lamentable. They began to descend the hill which they had so laboriously climbed, and if they found as yet no complete security in their paths, they met with more humaneness, more pity. The manners soften at this epoch, the souls become less rude, people actually acquire the idea of a human being; this age when individualism increases, better understands the individuals; while personality develops, more tenderness is displayed towards the personality of the other.

The Jews felt the effects of this state of mind. They were despised all the same, but they were hated in a less violent way. It was still sought to attract them to Christianity, but that was by persuasion. They were banished from a good many cities and countries; they were driven from Cologne and Bohemia in the sixteenth century; the trade-bodies of Frankfort and Worms, led by Vincent Fettmilch, forced them to leave those cities; but as serfs of the Imperial Chamber, they were efficiently protected by their suzerain. If Leopold I sent them out of Vienna, if later on Maria Theresa expelled them from Moravia, these decrees of exile had but a temporary effect, their consequences were felt but for a short time; and when the Jews re-entered the cities by virtue of undoubted tolerance, they were not molested. The massacres of Franconia and Moravia, the funeral piles of Prague, were exceptions in the sixteenth century, and as for the extermination ordered in Poland by Chmielnicki, in the seventeenth century, they reached the Jews by ricochet only.

Hereafter there have been no systematic persecutions, except those kept up in Spain against the Jewish converts, and in Portugal when introduced by the Pope Clement VII, at the request of John III, and after the massacres of 1506. Even there the inquisition was intrusted to the Franciscans, who had showed themselves less cruel than the Spanish Dominicans.

Still-the Jew did not change. Such as we have seen them right in the Middle Ages, we find them also at the moment of the Reformation; morally and intellectually the mass of the Jews was perhaps even worse. But if they had not changed, those by their side had changed. People were less believing, and therefore less inclined to detest heretics. Averroism had prepared this decadence of faith, and the part played by the Jews in the spread of Averroism is well known; so that they thus had worked for their own benefit. The majority of Averro-ists were unbelievers, or more or less assailed the Christian religion. They were the direct ancestors of the men of the Renaissance. It is owing to them that the spirit of doubt, as well as the spirit of investigation, had worked itself out. The Florentine platonists, the Italian Aristotelians, the German humanists came from them; thanks to them Pomponazzo composed the treatises against the immortality of the soul; thanks to them, too, among the thinkers of the sixteenth century sprang up the theism which corresponded with the decadence of Catholocism.

Animated by such sentiments, the men of this period could not glow with religious indignation against the Jews. Other preoccupations engaged them, though, and they had to abate two powerful authorities—scholasticism and the supremacy of Home. The struggles of the pre-ceding century, the schism of the West, the license in the manners of the clergy, simony, the sale of benefices and indulgences, all these had weakened the Charch and im-paired the Papacy. There were protests rising against them on all sides. The authority of councils was being proclaimed above that of the pope. A distinction was made between the Universal Church, which was infallible, and the Roman Church, which was liable to error. The seculars and the regulars were in dispute, voices were heard demanding change. "The clergy must be made moral," said the Father of the Vienna Synod (1311). After them, it was declared that it was necessary to reform "the head and the limbs." The movement of the Hussites, that of the Frerots, the Fraticel-lians, the Beghards, had already been a protest against the wealth and corruption of the Church; but Papacy was incapable of reform, and the Reformation had to take place outside of and against it.

The Humanists were its promoters. Everything turned them away from Catholicism. The Greeks of Constantinople, fleeing from the Turks, had brought to them the treasures of the ancient literatures. By discovering a new world Columbus was to open for them unknown horizons. They were finding new reasons for combatting scholasticism,thatoldservant-maid of the Church. The humanists were becoming skeptics and pagans in Italy, but in Germany the emancipating movement which they helped to bring about was becoming more religious. To beat the scholastics the humanists of the empire became theologians, and went to the very sources in order to arm themselves better; they learned Hebrew, not as Pico di Mirandola and the Italians had done, in the way of a dilettant or out of love for knowledge, but in order to find therein arguments against their opponents.

During these years which ushered in the Reformation, the Jew turned educator, and taught the scholars Hebrew; he initiated them into the mysteries of the kabbala after having opened to them the doors of Arabic philosophy. Against Catholicism he equipped them with the formidable exegesis which the rabbis had cultivated and built up during centuries: the exegesis which protestantism, and later on rationalism, would make good use of. By a singular chance the Jews, who had consciously or unconsciously supplied humanism with weapons, had also given it the pretext for its first serious battle. The contest for or against the Talmud was the forerunner of the disputes over the Eucharist.

The struggle started at Cologne, the city of the inquisition and capital of the Dominicans. A converted Jew, Joseph Pfefferkorn, once more denounced the Talmud before the Christian world, and, with the aid of the great inquisitor, Hochstraten, obtained from the Emperor Maximilian an edict authorizing him to examine the contents of the Jewish books and destroy those which blasphemed the Bible and the Catholic faith. From this decision the Jews appealed to Maximilian, and succeeded in having the power originally conferred upon Pfefferkorn transferred to the archbishop elector of Mayence. As his advisors the archbishop took the doctors, the humanists, and among them Reuchlin, who felt no unbounded sympathy for the Jews, having even attacked them once upon a time. But though he scorned the Jews in general, he was a hebraizer for all that, and as such was doubtless more interested in the Talmud than in the inquisitorial tribunal with its arrests. He, therefore, violently fought the projects of Pfefferkorn and the Dominicans, and not only declared that the books of the Israelites ought to be preserved, but even maintained that chairs of Hebrew ought to be created in the universities. Reuchlin was accused of having sold himself for the gold of the Jews. He replied with a terrible pamphlet, *The Mirror of the Eyes,* which was condemned to be burned. Thenceforth the Jews, who were the original cause of the debate, were forgotten, the humanists and Dominicans alone occupied the stage, and the latter being given their final blow by the *Letters of Obscurantists,* were condemned by the archbishop of Speyer and deserted by the pope, who, a few years previous, had granted the Antwerp printers the privilege of printing the Talmud.

But new times were approaching; the storm foreseen by everybody broke over the Church. Luther issued at Wittenberg his ninety-five theses, and Catholicism not only had to defend the position of its priests, but was also forced to fight for its essential tenets. For a moment the theologians forgot the Jews, they even forgot that the spreading movement took its roots in Hebrew sources. Nevertheless, the Reformation in Germany and England as well was one of those movements when Christianity acquired new force in Jewish sources. The Jewish spirit triumphed with Protestantism. In certain respects the Reformation was a return to the ancient

Ebionism of the evangelic ages. A great portion of the protestant sects was semi-Jewish, the anti-trinitarian doctrines were later preached by the protestants, by Michel Servet and the two Socins of Sienna among others. Even in Transylvania anti-trinitarianism had flourished since the sixteenth century, and Seidelius had asserted the excellence of Judaism and of the Decalogue. The Gospels had been abandoned for the Old Testament and the Apocalypse. The influence exercised by these two books over the Lutherans, the Calvinists and especially the Reformers and the English revolutionists, is well known. This influence continued to the nineteenth century; it produced the Methodists, Pietists, and particularly the Millenaries, the men of the Fifth Monarchy, who in London dreamed with Venner of a republic and allied themselves with the Levellers of John Lilburne.

Moreover, Protestantism, at its inception in Germany, endeavored to win over the Jews, and in this respect, the analogy between Luther and Mohammed is striking. Both had drawn their teachings from Hebrew sources, both wished to have the remains of Israel stamp with approval the new dogmas which they were formulating. This, in fact, presents the by no means least curious side of this nation's history. While detested, despised, humiliated, spat upon and bespattered, outraged, martyred, locked up and beaten; the Jew is still the one from whom Catholicism expects the ultimate reign of Jesus; the Church hopes for and demands the return of the Jews, which, for the Church, would mean the supreme testimony of the truth of its beliefs, and it is to the Jews, too, that the Lutherans and Calvinists appeal for it. It seems even as if the latter would have been completely convinced of the justice of their cause had the sons of Jacob come to them. But the Jews had always been the stubborn people of the Scriptures, the people with the hard nape, rebellious against injunctions, tenacious, fearlessly faithful to its God and its Law.

Luther's preaching proved vain, and the irascible monk issued a terrible pamphlet against the Jews. [75] "The Jews are brutes," he said; "their synagogues are pig-sties, they ought to be burned, for Moses would do it, if he came back to this world. They drag in mire the divine words, they live by evil and plunders, they are wicked beasts that ought to be driven out like mad dogs".

In spite of these violent outbursts and excitement, in spite of the numerous controversies, which had taken place between the protestants and Jews, the latter were not ill-treated in Germany; people had no spare time to busy themselves with them. On the one hand, the Luth-erans and Calvinists had their hands full with controversies among themselves; the discussions over the Eucharist, the impana-tion and invination over the trinity and the nature of Christ, sufficiently engaged their minds, and the sects were so numerous—Crypto-calvinists and Antinomists, Adiaphorists and Majorists, Osiandrists and Synergists, Memnonites and Syner-chists, etc.—that the struggle of one with the other had to absorb all their activity. On the other hand, the social and religious conditions had quite changed, and this change was ad-vantageous to the Jews, who saw other preoccupations keep their enemies busy.

Overwhelmed with miseries, decimated by war, ruined,

[75] ***The Jews and their Lies.*** Wittenberg, 1558.

reduced to slavery, a prey to destitution and famine, the peasants of the six-teenth century no longer went for the Jewish money-lender or the Christian usu-rer, but they aimed higher; they attacked in the first place a whole class—of the rich—and then the social order as a whole. The revolt was general; at first it was the peasants of the Netherlands, then, and chiefly, those of Germany. All over the Empire they founded secret societies, the ***Bundschub,*** [76] the. Poor Conrad, the Evangelic Confederation. The peasants of Speyer and of the banks of the Rhine rose in 1503; the bands of Joss Fritz, in 1512; the peasants of Austria and Hungary, in 1515; those of Suabia, in 1524; those of Suabia, Alsace and the Palatinate, in 1525. All marched with the battle cry: "In Christ there is no longer master or slave." The tradesmen joined them; knights, like Goetz von Berlichingen, placed themselves at their head, and they massacred the nobles and set the castles and convents on fire.

Munzer went even further; he fought not only against the barons, bishops and the rich, those "Kings of Moab," but also against the very principle of authority. "No more authority," he cried, "but that which is accepted and freely chosen." In the code of twelve articles which he edited, he wanted the enfranchisement of the serfs, and when he mounted the scaffold on having lost the bat-tle of Frankenstein, he testified that it had been his desire to "establish equality in Christendom; that all things should be common and each and all have according to need." The twelve articles were translated into French, and were spread abroad in Lorraine, where the

[76] The confederate shoe.

peasants rose up, too, at the moment when Hutter and Gabriel Scherding were going to establish the communities of Moravia, when anabaptism was spreading in Switzerland, in Bohemia and in the Netherlands. In this formidable movement which convulsed a part of Europe until 1535, everywhere leaving deep traces, the Jews had been neglected, they had ceased to be the scapegoat, and the poor wretches, famished and miserable, no longer fell upon them.

Were they as happy in the Catholic countries? Yes, for there, too, they ceased to be the chief and sole enemies of the Church, and it was no longer they that were feared.

The Protestants made people forget the Jews; the Protestants' existence threatened the ancient conception of the Catholic State, and this secular conception brought upon the Protestants of France, Italy and Spain persecutions identical with those which the Jews had once undergone.

Still, after the council of Trent, the reformed papacy once more turned to the Jews. The relaxation of religious ideas brought in Italy a rapprochement between a certain class of Jews and the various classes of society. First, the humanists, the poets, visited the Jewish scholars, philosophers and physicians. This familiarity had begun in the fourteenth century, when Dante was seen to have for his friend the Jew Manoello, the cousin of the philosopher Giuda Romano; it continued in the fifteenth and the sixteenth centuries. Alemani was the teacher of Picondi Mirandola, Elias del Medigo publicly taught metaphysics in Padua and Florence, Leo the Hebrew published his platonic dialogues on love. The Jewish printers, like the scholar

Soncino, were in constant touch with the literature of the period; his library was the centre of Hebrew publications, and he even rivalled Aldo by publishing Greek authors. Hercules Gonzago, bishop of Mantua and disciple of the Jew Pomponazzo of Bologna, accepted the dedication of Jacob Mantino, who had translated the ***Compendium*** of Averroes, while other princes encouraged Abraham de Balmes in his work of translation. [77] And not only the skeptical, even unbelieving faction, of the Hellenists and Latinists, worshippers of Zeus and Aphrodite more than of Jesus, were on good terms with the Jews, but the lord and the bourgeois were likewise. "There are," says the bishop Maiol, "persons, and often persons of quality, both men and women, who are so foolish and senseless as to take counsel with Jews over their most intimate affairs, to their own detriment. They (the Jews) are seen visiting the houses and palaces of the great ones, the dwellings of officers, councillors, secretaries, gentlemen, both in the city and country." People did not content themselves with receiving Jews, they went to their houses, and, what is more, attended their religious ceremonies. "There are among us," says again Maiol, "some who visit and superstitiously revere the synagogues"; and, addressing them, he exclaims: "You hear the Jews blow their trumpets on the days of their festivities, and you run with your families to look at them." Thus it went on during the seventeenth century. In Ferrara they went to hear the sermons of Judah

> [77] Abraham de Balmes translated into Latin the greatest part of Averroes's writings, and his translations were in use in the Italian universities until the end of the seventeenth century.

Azael, and, in 1676, Innocent XI threatened with ex-communication and a fine of fifteen ducats those who frequented the synagogues. Did then the popes still fear the Jewish influence over their believers? After the terrible shock which had just disturbed the Church, they more than ever wished to guarantee security to the Catholic dogma. "The Talmud might be upheld," the Council of Trent decreed, "if the wrong it contains were removed; for portions of the Talmud can serve to defend the faith and to prove to the Jews their obstinacy." The popes were of a different opinion. Julius III had the Talmud burned in Rome and Venice upon denunciation by Solomon Romano, a converted Jew; Paul IV condemned it again at the request of another convert, Vit-torio Eliano; Pius V and Clement VIII did likewise.

During the dogmatic and theological reaction which followed the Reformation, the Roman Church, friendly to the Jews heretofore, came to be the only government, almost the only power, systematically to persecute Judaism. Paul IV revived the ancient canonic laws and had the Marranos burned; Pius V banished the Jews from his domains, except from Rome and An-cona, after having issued his Constitution against the Jews, while the Spaniards, as they penetrated further into Italy, were driving them from Naples, Genoa and Milan.

Another concern engaged the Church at all events. To persecute the Jews and burn their books was good; to convert them was better. This had been the constant preoccupation of the theologians, christian doctors and the fathers. In the fifteenth century, the councils were busying themselves with the conversion of the Jews. The Basel Council had ordered preaching to the Jews in Germany, and granted important privileges to the converts. The popes of the sixteenth century compelled the Jews to attend certain sermons and there had the good word preached to them by their own apostates. A third of the Jews of Borne had to be present in turn at the sermons. And while Sadolet was limiting at Avignon the pontifical privileges accorded the Jews, while a tax of ten ducats per year was levied on synagogues for the instruction of those who intended to abjure Judaism, Paul IV was building houses of refuge where catechumens were fed, dressed and cared for.

The other sovereigns had not the same motives as the popes to attend to the Jews. And so, from the sixteenth century on, legislation against the Jews ceased. We find only the edict of Ferdinand I against Jewish usury—in Germany; a few decrees in Poland, and much later, the prohibitions of Louis XV and Louis XVI. Again to find anti-Jewish legislation, it will be necessary to study modern Russia, Rumania and Servia, which we shall shortly do.

Anti-Judaism consisted chiefly in molestations and outrages. The populace delighted in jeering the Jews, and the grandees often gave them a chance to do it. Leo X, that ostentatious pontiff, who was fond of buffoonery— he had at his side two monks to divert him with their pleasantries—would order races between Jews, and, being very shortsighted, would watch them, glass in hand, from the heights of his balconies. During the carnival in Borne the people would parody the burial of rabbis, and a Jew would be marched through the city streets, mounted backward on a donkey and holding the animal's tail in his hand. [78] On the ghetto-gates a sow was carved, and they were often covered with obscene groups, in which rabbis were represented. [79] The sow symbolized the synagogue—exactly as with the Israelites the Roman Church was designated by the Hebrew name for hog— and the Jews were constantly reminded of it; a painter once even related at Wagenseil how he had painted a sow on the door-leaf of the arch of a synagogue which he was engaged to adorn.

With the scholars, the learned and the theologians, anti-Judaism was becoming dogmatic and theoretical. True they wanted to bring the Jews back, but by soft measures. It was no longer a question of burning their books, but of translating them. It was said that now that the Christian faith had struck deep enough roots, there was no danger to believers from publishing Hebrew books, as had been done in the case of those of the

[78] E. Rodocanachi: *Le Saint-Siege et let Juifs.* Paris, 1891.

[79] Luther: *Tractatue de Sohemhamphorasch.* Altenburg (*Opera,* V. VIII). These obscene groups were called Schemhamephor-asch. Its origin is as follows: these words Schemhamephor-asch mean "the name of God distinctly pronounced, the quadril-iteral name written and read with the four letters: yodt he, wau, he." (Munk, Translation of the *Guide of the Perplexed,* v. I, p. 267, note 3). This is the name of which Maimonides says: "Before the creation of the world there were but the Most Holy One and His Name only." (*Guide of the Perplexed,* v. I, ch. 61). This was the mysterious name; a magic power was ascribed to it, and the rabbis dressed up as magicians, who were represented on the groups I have just mentioned, were understood to reveal the Name to the sow. Hence the appellation Schemhamephorasch.

Arians and other heretics. Thus it would be possible to know the polemic practices of the Israelites, and it would thus be possible successfully to combat them.

This study brought about a result quite different from that expected. By scrutinizing the Jewish spirit one came nearer to the Jews, and thereby became more sympathizing with them. Men, like Richard Simon, e. g., who had prepared themselves for scientific exegesis, through talmudists and hebraizing researches, could not look with hatred upon those from whom they held their knowledge. Others were anxious to know when the Jews would be called to Christian communion. The seventeenth century was the most propitious time for the disputes over the recalling of the Jews. In France this question as to whether the Jews would be recalled at the end of the world or before it—divided Bossuet and the Figurists led by Duguet. [80] In England the Millenaries proclaimed the return of the Jews. [81] They flourished particularly in the eighteenth century, in which Worth-ington, Bellamy, Winchester and Towers described the approaching times of the millenium. In Germany also this opinion had its advocates, such as Bengel, e. g. In France, not only did the convulsionaries of Saint-Menard proclaim the approaching entry of the Jews into the Church, but some were seen entertaining these dreams

[80] On this point consult Duguet, ***Regies pour Vintelligence des Saint-es Ecri ures,*** 1723. Bossuet, ***Discours sur VHistoire univer-sette,*** part II. Rondet, ***Dissertation sur le rappel des Juifs,*** Paris, 1778. Anonymous, ***Lettre sur le provche retour des Juifs,*** Paris, 1789, etc.

[81] Gregoire, Histoire des seotes religiouses, v. II (Paris, 1825).

until our days, and in 1809 President Agier fixed upon 1849 as the year of the conversion of the Jews.

All over Europe the Jews enjoyed the greatest tranquillity during the eighteenth century. In Poland alone they fared badly for having once lived too well. They had been prosperous there up to the middle of the seventeenth century. Rich, powerful, they had lived on an equal footing with the Christians, treated as though of the people amid whom they lived; but they could not help giving themselves up to their usual commerce, their vices, their passion for gold. Dominated by the Talmudists they succeeded in producing nothing beyond commentators of the Talmud. They were tax collectors, spirit—distillers, usurers, seigneurial stewards. They were the noblemen's allies in their abominable work of oppression, and when the Cossacks of Ukraina and Little Russia had risen, under Chmielnicki, against Polish tyranny, the Jews, as accomplices of the lords, were the first to be massacred. It is said that over 100,000 of them were killed in ten years, but just as many Catholics and especially Jesuits, were killed as well.

Elsewhere they were very prosperous. Thus, in the Ottoman Empire, they were simply liable to the tax on foreigners and subject to no other restrictive regulations, but nowhere was their prosperity so great as in the Netherlands and England. Marranos fleeing the Spanish Inquisition had settled in the Netherlands in 1593, and thence settled a colony in Hamburg, then, later on, under Cromwell, one in England, whence they had been banished for centuries and whither Menasse-ben-Israel brought them back. The Dutch, as practical and circumspect a people as the English, utilized the commercial genius of the-Jews and turned it to their own enrichment. Besides, indisputable affinities existed between the spirit of these nations and the Jewish spirit, between the Israelite and the positive Dutchman or the Englishman, whose character, as Emerson says, can be brought to an irreducible dualism, which makes his nation one of greatest dreamers and most practical people, a thing which may be said of Jews as well.

In Prance Henry II. had authorized the Portuguese Jews to settle in Bordeaux, where, on the strength of the granted privileges, confirmed also by Henry III., Louis XIV., Louis XV. and Louis XVI., they acquired great wealth in maritime commerce.

In the other cities of Prance there were few of them, and, besides, those residing in Paris or elsewhere had settled there only because of the administrative tolerance. In Alsace alone there was a great agglomeration.

Their splendid condition provoked no violent demonstrations; now and then protests would be heard, they would say with Expilly: "With infinite grief one sees how such base people, who had been received in the capacity of slaves, possess costly furniture, lead a refined life, wear gold and silver on their garments, dress showily, perfume themselves, study instrumental and vocal music and ride horseback for mere diversion." At the same time, greater and greater toleration was shown them from day to day; the world was drawing nearer to them. Were they, in turn, drawing nearer to the world? No. They seemed more and more to attach themselves to their mystic patriotism; the further they went, the more the dreams of Kabbala haunted them, with ever re-newed confidence they awaited the messiah, and never had the pseudo-Messiahs been received with so much enthusiasm as they were in the seventeenth and eighteenth centuries. The Kabbalists exhausted arithmetical ' combinations to calculate the exact date of the coming of him, who was so longed for. Toward 1666, the date most commonly designated as the sacred date, all Jews of the Orient were raised by the preachings of Sabbatai Zevi. From Smyrna, where Sabbatai had proclaimed himself Messiah, the movement spread to the Nether-lands, and England even, and everybody expected the restoration of Jerusalem and of the holy kingdom from the King of Kings, as Sabattai was called. The same enthusiasm was displayed in 1755 when Frank appeared in Podolia as the new Messiah. Numerous mystic sects formed around all these enlightened ones: that of Don-meh, which leaned towards the Mohammedans; that of the Chassidim, of the New Chassidim, and that of the Trinitarians, who approached Christianity in professing the dogma of a God at once one and triple. [82]

These hopes which the illuminism of the Kabbalists entertained, helped to keep the Jews apart, but those who were not seduced by the speculations of dreamers, were weighed down by the yoke, of the Talmud, a yoke at all events even ruder and more humiliating. So far from decreasing, the* Talmudic tyranny had even increased since the sixteenth century. At this time Joseph Caro had edited the ***Shulchan Aruch,*** a Talmudic code,

[82] Peter Beer, ***Le Judaisme et ses Series.***

which—according to the traditions inculcated by the rabbinists—set up as laws the opinions of the doctors. Up to our time the European Jews had lived under the execrable oppression of these practices. [83] The Polish Jews improved even upon Joseph Caro and refined the already enormous subtleties of the ***Shulchan Aruch*** by making additions thereto, and they introduced the method of ***Pilpul*** (pepper-grains) into their instruction.

Accordingly, as the world grew kinder to them, the Jews—at least the masses—retired into themselves, straitened their prison, bound themselves with tighter bonds. Their decrepitude was unheard of, their intellectual sinking was equalled only by their moral debasement; this nation seemed dead.

However, the reaction against the Talmud had proceeded from the Jews themselves. Mordecai Kolkos, [84] 1721.

of Venice, had already published a book against the Mishna; in the seventeenth century, Uriel Acosta [85] violently fought the rabbis, and Spinoza [86] exhibited little affection for them. But anti-talmudism displayed itself particularly in the eighteenth century, at first among the mystics, such as, e. g., the Zoharites, disciples of Franck, who declared themselves enemies of the doctors of the law. At any rate these opponents of the rabbanites were unable to extricate the Jews from their abjection. To begin this task, it was necessary for Moses

[83] In Russia, Poland and Galicia they are extant even to-day.

[84] Consult Wolf, ***Bibliotheca Hebraco,*** v. II, p. 798. Hamburg.

[85] ***Exemplar vitae humanae.*** (Published by Limbroch, 1687).

[86] ***Tractatus Theoloffico.-Politicm.***

Mendelssohn, a Jew and philosopher at the same time, to array the Bible against the Talmud. His German version (1779)—was a great revolution. It was the first blow dealt to the rabbinical authority. The Talmudists, too, who had once wished to kill Kolkos and Spinoza, violently attacked Mendelssohn, and prohibited, under penalty of excommunication, to read the Bible which he had translated.

These outbursts of rage were of no avail. Mendelssohn had followers: young men, his disciples, founded the periodical *Meassef,* which advocated the new Judaism, endeavored to snatch the Jews from their ignorance and humiliation, and prepared their moral emancipation. As for political emancipation, the humanitarian philosophy of the eighteenth century was working hard to bring it about. Though Voltaire was an ardent Judoephobe, the ideas which he and the Encyclopaedists represented were not hostile to the Jews, as being ideas of liberty and universal equality. On the other hand, if the Jews really were isolated in the various states, they still had some points of contact with those surrounding them.

Capitalism had by this time developed among the nations; stock-jobbing and speculation were born; the Christian financiers applied themselves to them with a zeal, just as they had applied themselves to usury, just as they had, in the capacity of farmers-general, collected imposts and taxes. The Jews could, therefore, take their place among those whom "discounts were enriching at the public's expense, and who were masters of all possessions of the French of all classes," as already Saint Simon was saying.

The economic objections which were raised against their possible emancipation had no longer the same import as in the Middle Ages, when the church wanted to make the Jews the only representatives of the class of money-brokers. As for the political objections, that they formed a State within the State, that their presence as citizens could not be tolerated in a Christian society and was even injurious to it, they remained valid until the day when the French Revolution dealt its direct blow to the conception of a Christian State. And so Dohm, Mirabeau, Clermont-Tonnerre, the Abbot Grégoire were right with regard to Rewbel, Maury and the Prince de Broglie, and the Constituent Assembly obeyed the spirit which had guided it since its inception when it declared on September 27, 1791, that the Jews would enjoy in France the rights of actual citizens. The Jews were on the threshold to society.

CHAPTER VII.

ANTI-JUDAIC LITERATURE
AND THE PREJUDICES.

Anti-Judaism of the Pen and its Forms.—Theological Anti-Judaism.—The Transformation of Christian Apologetics.—Judaization and its Enemies.—An-selm of Canterbury, Isidore of Seville.—Pierre de Blois.—Alain de Lille.—The Study of Jewish Books.—Raymond de Penaforte and the Domini-cans.—Raymund Martin and the *Pugio Fidei.*— Nicholas de Lyra and His Influence.—Anti-Jewish Theological Literature and the Conversions.— Nicholas de Cusa.—The Converted Jews and Their Role.—Paul de Santa Maria, Alfonso of Valladolid. —Anti-Talmudism and the Converts: Pfefferkorn. —The Controversies Over the Talmud and the Jewish Religion.—Controversies of Paris, Barcelona and Tortosa.—Nicholas Donin, Pablo Christiani and Geronimo de Santa Fé.—The Extractions *Tal-mut.* —Social Anti-Judaism.—Agobard, Amolon, Peter the Venerable, Simon Maiol.—Polemic Anti-Judaism.—Alonzo da Spina.— *Le Livre de l'Albo-raique* .—Pierre de Lancre.—Francisco de Torre-joncillo and the *Centinela Contra Judios.* —Polemic Anti-Judaism and the Prejudices.—The Jews and the Accursed Races.—Jews, Templars and Sorcerers.—Ritual Murder.—The Defense of the Jews.— Jacob ben Ruben, Moses Cohen of Tordesillas, Shem-Tob ben Isaac Shaprut—Jewish Polemic Literature in Spain in the Fifteenth Century.— Anti-Christianity.—Chasdai Crescas and Joseph Ibn Shem Tob.—The Attacks Against the New Testament.— The Nizzachon and The Book of Jo-seph the Zealot—The Toldoth Jesho .—Attacks Against the Apostates.—Isaac Pulgar, Don Vidal Ibn Labi.—Transformation of Scriptural Anti-Judaism in the Seventeenth Century.—The Converters.—The Hebraizers and the Exegetists: Bux-torf and Richard Simon.—Wagenseil, Voetius, Bartolocci.—Eisenmenger.—John Dury.—The Re-lationship and Similarity of Anti-Jewish Works. The Imitators.— The Ancient Literary Anti-Judaism and the Modern Antisemitism.—Their Affinities.

We have studied only the legal and the popular anti-Judaism from the eighth century to the French Revolution. We have seen how anti-Jewish legislation, at first canonic and later civil, was little by little instituted. We have shown how the populace had been partly prepared by the decrees of the popes, kings and republics, to hate and abuse the Jews, and how far this exasperation of the people, the massacres it committed, the insults and outrages it showered, had given the counter-blow to this legislation. We have shown that up to the fifteenth century, the accusations weighing over the Jews, had grown each year, so that they had reached their maximum at this period, and from then on went decreasing, that the codes had ceased to be applied rigorously, that customs had gradually fallen into disuse, that few, if at all, new laws were made, and that the Jew thus marched towards liberation.

However, there is a kind of anti-Judaism to which we have paid no special attention, and which we must hereafter examine. While the Church and the monarchies issued laws against the Jews, the theologians, philosophers, poets, and historians were writing about them. It is the role, the working and the importance of this anti-Judaism of the pen that we still have to examine.

It was not born under the same influences; diverse causes engendered it, and according to these causes it was theological or social, dogmatic or even polemic. Not that all these anti-Jewish writings can be classified under one category to the exclusion of any other; on the contrary, there are few of them that can be referred exclusively to one of these types, and yet, according to their principal tendency, they can be registered under one of the rubrics that I have just indicated. Theological anti-Judaism alone has produced clearly cut works, written without social cares, and these works, however little characteristic they may be, may be dogmatic and polemic at the same time.

Theological anti-Judaism, chronologically the first, naturally had apologetic ways at its inception; it could not be otherwise as Judaism was fought only to glorify the Christian faith and prove its excellence. As we have said, they ceased producing apologetic writings towards the end of the fourth century; the young church, in the intoxication of its triumph, did no longer think it necessary to prove its superiority, and as representatives of the apologetic manner, we find in the fifth century only the *Altercation of Simon and Theopilus* of Evagrivs, [87] in which the *Altercation of Jason and Papiscus* of Aris-to of Pella was imitated and even plagiarized; after that one has to come to the seventh century to find the three books of Isidore of Seville directed against the Jews. [88]

When scholasticism was born, apologetics reappeared. Scholasticism from its very 6tart was a servant-maid of the dogma, but a reasoning servant that attempted to explain the Trinity metaphysically, and the discussions on nominalism and realism were of such importance during the Middle Ages, only because these two theories were applied to the interpretation of the Trinity. The whole of metaphysics of this time turned around the nature and divinity of Christ. Hence the importance for the scholastic theologians of defending this divinity against those even who denied it; and were not the Jews just those whose denial was most stubborn? It was necessary, therefore, to convince these obstinates, and thus the apologies sprang up again, and all or nearly all of them were addressed to the Jews.

They had two ends in view: they defended the Catholic dogmas and symbols, and they combatted Judaism. They set themselves against that judaizing which the church, its doctors, philosophers and apologists had always feared, imagining the Jew as a sort of wolf that prowled around the sheep-fold in order to carry the sheep away from a happy life. These were the senti-

[87] Consult the *Spicilegium* of Achery, vols. X and XV.

[88] Isidore of Seville, *De Fide Catholica ex vetere et novo Testamento contra Judaeos* (Opera, vol. VII). Migne, P. L., lxxxiii.

ments that guided, e. g., Cedrenus [89] and Theophanes [90] when they wrote their *ontra Judaeos,* and Gilbert Crépin, abbot of Westminster, in his *Disputatio Judei cum Christiano de fide Christiana.* [91]

The form of these writings was little varied; they reproduced almost servilely the classic arguments of the Fathers of the Church, and their wording followed similar patterns. To analyze one of them means analyzing all Thus, e. g., Pierre de Blois's *Against the Perfidy of the Jews,* [92] enumerated through thirty chapters the testimonies which the Old Testament, and especially the prophets, contain in favor of the divine Trinity and Unity, of the Father and the Son, of the Holy Spirit, of the Messianism of Jesus Christ, of the Davidic descent of the Son of Man, and of his incarnation. He ended, by proving, on the basis of the same authorities, that the Law had been transmitted to the Gentiles, that the Jews had been doomed to reprobation, but that the remnants of Israel would nevertheless one day be converted and saved. Guibert de Nogent, in his *De Incarnatione adversus Judaeos,* [93] Rupert in his *Annulus sivedialogus inter Christianum et Judeum de fidei sacramentis;* [94] Alain de Lille in his De Fide Catholica; [95] many others to enumerate whom would be tiresome, proceeded in the

> [89] *Duputatio contra Judaeos.* Opera, Editio Basileensis, p. 180.
>
> [90] *Contra Judaeos.* Lib. VI.
>
> [91] Migne, P. L., Ch. IX.
>
> [92] *Liber contra perfidia Tudaeorum.* Opera, Paris, 1519.
>
> [93] *Opera,* Paris, 1651.
>
> [94] Migne, P. L., CLXX.
>
> [95] "Migne, P. L., CCX.

same way, developing the same arguments, dwelling upon the same texts, resorting to the same interpretations. As a whole, all this literature was one of extreme mediocrity; I know little that is more inane, and Anselm of Canterbury himself failed to make it more interesting when he composed his *De Fide seu de Incarnatione verbis contra Judaeos.*

Yet these writings, discussions, fictitious dialogues hardly, if at all, attained their object. They were consulted by clergymen only, and were thus directed at converts; rabbis read them in very rare cases; their own biblical exegesis and science being much superior to those of the good monks, these latter rarely were at an advantage. At all events they never convinced those whom they were to convince, and they could not effectively fight the Jews, as they did not know the taldumic and exegetic commentaries, from which the Jews drew their weapons and forces. Things changed in the thirteenth century. The works of Jewish philosophers had spread and exercised considerable influence on the scholasticism of the time; men like Alexandre de Hales had read Maimonides (Rabbi Moses) and Ibn Gebirol (Avi cebron), and they bore the impress of the teachings exposed by the ***Guide of the Perplexed and the Fountain of Life.*** Curiosity was awakened, people wanted to know Jewish thought and dialectics, at first for philosophical motives, then to fight against the Jews with better success.

The dominican Raymond de Penaforte, confessor of James I. of Aragon, and a great converter of the Jews, bade the Dominicans to learn Hebrew and Arabic to be able better to persuade and battle with the Jews. He established schools for the instruction of monks in these two languages and was the pioneer of Hebrew and Arabic studies in Spain. He thus started a line of apologists who were no longer contented with collecting the passages of the Old Testament that foreshadowed the Trinity or prophesied the Messiah, but who endeavored to refute the rabbinical books and Talmudic assertions.

All these ***shields, ramparts, strongholds of faith,*** a host of treatises and demonstrations, came from this movement. In these pamphlets the Jews were "slain with their own glaive," "pierced with their own sword," i. e., ***they were being convinced of their ignominy and convicted of falsehoods*** by means of their own argumentation, such as the monks found it, or at least thought they found it, in the Talmud.

The best known among all these theological lampoons are those published by the dominican Raymund Martin, "a man as remarkable for his knowledge of Hebrew and Arabic writings as for that of Latin works." [96] These squibs bear characteristic enough titles: Capistrum Judaeorum (Muzzle of the Jews) **and** Pugio Fidei (Dagger of the Faith) [97] The second had the greatest circulation. "It is well," Raymund Martin said therein, "that the Christians take in hand the sword of their enemies, the Jews, to strike them with it?" Starting

[96] Augustin Giustiniani, *Linguae Hebreae* (1656).

[97] *Pugio Fidei* (Paris, 1661). (Cf. Quetif, *Bibl. Scriptorum domini-canorum,* v. I, p. 396, and the edition of Carpson, Leipzig, 1687).

thence and with this very wide-spread notion that God had given Moses an oral law as commentary to the written law and containing the revelation of the Trinity and the divinity of Jesus, Martin tried to prove, by means of Biblical, Talmudic and Kabbalistic texts, that the Messiah had come and that the tenets of Catholicism were irrefutable. In two chapters, [98] he simultaneously fell upon Judaism, which he represented as reprobate and abominable.

During the thirteenth and fourteenth centuries the *Pugio Fidei* was quite in vogue among the monks, especially the Dominicans, ardent defenders of the faith. It was studied, consulted, plagiarized. The number of writings which were inspired by Raymund Martin and for which the Pugio Fidei served as the prototype and even mould, was considerable. Among others those of Porchet Salvaticus, [99] Pierre de Barcelona, [100] and Pietro Galatini [101] may be named.

Still even Martin's knowledge was not perfect, and as we shall presently see, the rabbis very often worsted their opponents in their controversies. The anti-Jews needed better weapons: the Franciscan, Nicholas de Lyra, supplied them. He had made a careful study of rabbinical literature, and his hebraic attainments, their extent, variety and solidity led to the belief that he was

[98] Chh. XXI-XXII, *de Reprobatione et Faetore doctrinae Inu-dae-orum,*

[99] ***Victoria adversus itnpios Hebreos et sacris litteris*** (Paris, 1629). Wolf, Bibl. Hebr. v. I, p. 1124.

[100] Consult Fabricius, Bibliotheca Latina, on Peter of Barcelona (Petrus Barcinonensis).

[101] ***De Arcanis catholicae veritatis libris*** (Sorcino, 1518).

of Jewish origin, which is of little probability. At all events, he was the precursor of modern exegesis, which is the daughter of Jewish thought and whose rationalism is purely Jewish; he was the ancestor of Richard Simon. Nicholas de Lyra declared that the literal explanation of the text of the Scriptures should form the foundation of ecclesiastic science, and that the text and its meaning once established four meanings should be derived therefrom: the literal, allegoric, moral and anagogic. [102] Nicholas de Lyra expounded his researches in the ***Postilla*** and the ***Moralitates,*** collected and recast later into a larger work. Hereafter this was the arsenal to draw upon in the polemics against the Jews, as well as for the defense of the Gospels against the Jewish attacks, for Nicholas de Lyra had refuted, in his ***De Messia,*** [103] the criticisms passed on the Old Testament by the Jews. Numerous editions of Nicholas de Lyra's works appeared, commentaries, notes and addi-tious thereto were made, and in the matter of exegesis even Luther was his pupil.

But praiseworthy as it was to combat the Jews, it was still more meritorious to convince them, and most of the polemist monks did not forget that the conversion of

[102] Throughout the Middle Ages they believed in this fourfold meaning of the Scriptures, and the following distict expressed its import:

Littera gesta docet, quid credas, allegoria;

Moralis, quid agass quo tendas anagogia.

[103] De Messia, eiusque adventu practerito tractatus una cum

responsione ad Judaei argumenta XIV contra veritatem evangeliorum (Venice. 1481).

Judah was one of the aims of the church. While the councils took steps to convert the Jews, the writers, on their part, endeavored to be convincing, several of them, the more practical, went so far as to seek ground for reconciliation. So, e. g., by making certain concessions he was even ready to accept circumcision—Nicholas de Cusa wanted to unite all religions into one, with the Trinity as its principal dogma. The ancient *"obstinatio Judaeorum"* which maintained divine unity resisted these attempts, and the overtures of the Christians were generally received with disfavor. However, conversions were not infrequent, and I mean not only those brought about by violence, but also those obtained by persuasion. These converted Jews played a very great role in the anti-Jewish literature as well as in the history of the persecutions. Toward their coreligionists they proved themselves the most cruel, unjust and treacherous of adversaries. This is generally characteristic of converts, and the Arabs converted to Christianity or Christians turned to Islam witness that this rule allows of very few exceptions.

A host of sentiments united in maintaining this bilious disposition among the apostates. Above all they wished to give proof of their sincerity: they felt that a sort of suspicion surrounded them at entering into the Christian world, and the affectation of piety which they proclaimed did not seem sufficient to them to dispel the suspicions.

Nothing did they fear so much as the accusation of lukewarmness or sympathy with their former brethren, and the way in which the Inquisition treated those it deemed relapsers, was not calculated to diminish the fears entertained by the proselytes. Accordingly, they simulated an excess of zeal which in many, if not all, upheld a genuine faith. Some of them, convinced of having found salvation in their conversion, made even efforts to win over their coreligionists to the Christian faith; among these the church found several of its most fearless and eagerly listened to converters. [104] They did not stop at publishing apologies; in the churches they preached to the Jews whom the canonic decrees obliged to attend sermons as obedient auditors. Such were Samuel Nachmias [105] baptized under the name of

Morosini; Joseph Tzarphati, who assumed the name Monte at his baptism; [106] the rabbi Weidnerus, who con-vinced a great number of the Jews of Prague of the excellence of the Trinity. Some even informed against the Jews that they had abandoned the rigors of the ecclesiastical and civil laws. About 1475, for instance, Peter Schwartz and Hans Bayol, both converted Jews, instigated the inhabitants of Ratisbon to sack the Ghetto; in Spain, Paul de Santa-Maria instigated Henry III. of Castile to take measures against the Jews. This Paul de Santa-Maria, previously known under the name of Solomon Levi of Burgos, was not an ordinary personality. A very pious, very learned rabbi, he abjured at the age of forty, after the massacres of 1391, and was

[104] For the antisemitic literature of the Jewish apostates consult Wolf, *Bibl. Hebr.,* v. I.

[105] *Via della Fede* (Wolf, Bill. Hebr., p. 1010).

[106] *Treatise on the Confusion of the Jews.* (Wolf, *Bibl. Hebr.,* p. 1010).

baptized along with his brother and four of his sons. He studied theology at Paris, was ordained priest, became bishop of Cartagena and afterwards chancellor of Castile. He published an *Examination of the Holy Writ,* —a dialogue between the infidel Saul and the convert Paul,—and issued an edition of Nicholas de Lyra's *Postilla,* supplemented by his *Additiones* and glosses. He did not stop at that in his activity. He is generally found the instigator in all the persecutions which befell the Jews of his time, and he hunted the synagogue with a ferocious hatred; and yet in his works he confined himself to theologic polemics. [107]

But not all converts were like Paul de Santa-Maria. To believe Poggio who had learned Hebrew from a bap-tized Jew, they were, generally speaking, little educated, and of mediocre intelligence: "Stupid,' say he, "crazy and ignorant as are, as a rule, the Jews who baptize." This class of catechumens proved itself the most spiteful. Those, however, who constituted it, were provoked by their coreligionists, who bitterly hated their apostates and missed no opportunity to abuse them, so that numerous laws had to be promulgated forbidding the Jews to throw stones at the renegades and soil their clothes with oil and fetid liquids. When unable to maltreat them the Jews would insult and rail at the converts. The new Christians replied to these insults by publishing satires on the rabbis, as did Don Pedro Ferrus and Diego of Valencia, or by abusing their opponents in bulky dogmatic treatises, in the manner of Victor de

[107] Cf. Wolf, *Bibl. Hebr.,* I, p. 1004; and Joseph Rodriguez de Castro, *Bibliotheca Espanola* (Madrid, 1781;, vol. I, p. 235.

Carben. [108] They did not forget to resort to theologic demonstration, but often preferred invention and even calumny. At times they would unite both methods, as in the case of Alfonso of Valladolid (Abner of Burgos), who published simultaneously concordances of the law and treatises of violent polemics: the *Book of God's Battles* and the *Mirror of Justice* [109].)

But the Talmud was the great antagonist of the converts, and one that had to withstand most of their wrath. They constantly denounced it before the inquisitors, the king, the emperor, the pope. The Talmud was the execrable book, the receptacle of the most hideous abuses of Jesus, the Trinity and the Christians; against it Pedro de la Caballeria wrote his *Wrath of Christ Against the Jews,* [110] Pfefferkorn, his *Enemy of the Jews,* [111] in which he congratulated himself upon "having withdrawn from the dirty and pestilential mire of the Jews," and Jerome of Santa Fé, his *Hebreomastyx* [112] The Catholic theologians followed the example of the converts, most frequently they had about the Talmud no other notions beyond those given them by the converts.

Usually auto-da-fés followed these denunciations of the Talmud, but they were, as a rule, preceded by a dis-

[108] Three treatises against the Jews 1. *Propugnaculum fidei ehristia-*

nae (1510) ; 2. ***Judaeorum erroris et moris*** (Cologne, 1509) ; 3. ***De vita et moribus Judaeorum*** (Paris, 1511). Cf. Wolf, Bill. Hebr., v. IV, p. 578.

[109] Bibliotheque Nationale, manuscript of Spanish origin, No. 43; cf. Isidore Loeb, Revue des Etudes Juives, v. XVIII).

[110] ***Tractatus Zelus christi contra Judaeos, Saracenos et infi-deles*** (Venice, 1542).

[111] ***Hostis Judaeorum*** (Cologne, 1509).

[112] Hebreomartyx (Frankfort, 1601).

putation. This custom of disputations goes back to deep antiquity. We know that already the Hebrew doctors held disputations with the apostles. On several occasions rabbis and monks were seen contending in eloquence in the presence of the Emperors of Borne and Byzantium in order to convince their audience of the excellence of their cause, and the Chazar King made up his mind to embrace Judaism only after a discussion, in which a Jew, a Christian and a Mohammedan took part, so, at least, the legend relates. [113] These discussions were, however, rarely public, the church feared their consequences; it feared Jewish subtlety, clever at finding objections which embarrassed the defenders of the Catholic faith and troubled the believer. There remained in use only private discussions between ecclesiastical dignitaries and Talmudists, and few auditors were admitted to these meetings, except under rare and important circumstances, in which cases a legal sanction followed the dispute. In these queer disputes, in which one side acted as judge at the same time, the Jews were, in general, the stronger. Their more concise dialectics, their more genuine knowledge, their more serious and subtle exegesis, gave them an easy advantage. In spite of this, or rather, because of this, the Jews were very prudent in their assertions, they appeared in the most courteous light, and heeded those melancholy words of Moses Cohen of Tordesillas, addressed to his brethren:

[113] Juda Hallevy, ***Liber Cosri.*** Translated by John Buxtorf, Jr., 1660—a German translation with an introduction was published by H. Jolowics and D. Cassel, ***Das Buck Kuzari,*** 1841, 1858.

"Never let your zeal carry you away to the point of uttering stinging words, for the Christians hold the power and may silence the truth with fist-blows." These coun- sels were followed, but in spite of the precautions taken, at the end of the argument the Jew, who was always wrong in the end, was beaten to death.

However, the informers were usually commanded to sustain their charges. In 1239, a converted Jew, Nicholas Donin of La Rochelle, brought before the pope, Gregory IX., a charge against the Talmud. Gregory ordered the copies of the book to be seized and an inquest made. Bulls were sent out to the bishops of Prance, England, Castile and Aragon. Eudes de Chateauroux, chancellor of the University of Paris, directed the investigation in France, the only country where the bulls had produced an effect. The disputation was ordered, and took place in 1240, between the informer, Nicholas Donin, and four rabbis: Yechiel of Paris, Jehuda ben David Melun, Samuel ben Solomon, and Moses of Coucy. The discussion was long, but Donin's skill finally divided the rabbis; the Talmud was condemned and burned a few years later.

In 1263, Raimond de Penaforte arranged at the Ara-gonian court a dispute between the rabbis, Nachmani of Girone (Bonastruc de Porta), and the Dominion, Pablo Christiani, a converted Jew and a zealous converter. This time Nachmani was victorious after a four-day disputation on the coming of Messiah, on the divinity of Jesus, and the Talmud. The king himself accorded him an audience, received him very cordially and loaded him with presents. But such victories were exceptional, as the Jewish books were most frequently condemned by the judges beforehand, whatever the skill of their defenders. Thus, a baptized Jew, Joshua Lorqui d'Al-canis, known under the name of Geronimo de Santa Fé, physician to the anti-pope Benedict XIII., called, with a view to making converts, a debate which opened in 1417 at Tortosa. Geronimo exerted himself to prove by Talmudic texts that Messiah had come and that it was certainly Jesus. As adversaries he had the most famous doctors of Spain, Don Vidal Benveniste ibn Albi, Joseph Albo, Zerachya Halevi Saladin, Astruc Levi of Daroque and Bonastruc of Girone. The controversy took place before the anti-pope, surrounded by his cardinals; it lasted sixty days, but no conversions resulting from it Geronimo de Santa Fé issued an address to the court against the Talmud, and the reading of it was forbidden.

These controversies increased in number in Spain during the fourteenth and fifteenth centuries. Thus the convert Alfonso of Valladolid had a dispute with his former coreligionists at Valladolid; John of Valladolid, another convert, had a dispute with Moses Cohen de Tordesillas on the proofs of the Christian faith contained in the Old Testament, but was defeated in the contest; Shem-Tob ben Isaac Shaprut had at Pampeluna a controversy on the original sin and redemption, with the cardinal Pedro de Luna, later anti-pope Benedict XIII. Many more might be mentioned, all of them proving what amount of trouble the Jews were giving the church and how eagerly conversion was desired and solicited. Still all these disputes were courteous up to the moment the Inquisition was introduced. The theologians made every effort to prepare priests and monks so as to pre-vent the Catholic faith from suffering a blow, and for this purpose, they composed extracts that were intended to enlighten the defenders of Christ on the faults found with the Talmud. A few of these guides have been preserved, as, e. g., the ***Extractions Talmut,*** edited by Eudes de Chateauroux, after the auto-da-fé of 1242, and the ***Censura et Confutatio libri Talmut,*** [114] a work composed by Antonio d'Avila, and a prior of the convent of the Holy Cross of Segovia, and addressed to Thomas de Torquemada. All these manuals were placed in the hands of the Spanish inquisitors and served for reference in the trials of the Marranos and Jews.

But alongside of the Jew, considered the enemy of Jesus and the foe of Christianity, there was the Jew, the usurer, the money-dealer, he upon whom fell a part of the hatred of the oppressed and the poor, he whom the rising bourgeoisie was beginning to envy and hate. I have pictured that Jew at work, how he had come to the exclusive pursuit of gold, and how he became the object of popular passions as a sort of victim of expiation, the scape-goat for all the sins of a society that was no better than he. If the populace oftenest killed the deicide, it also fell upon the clipper of ducats; its anti-Judaism was not religious only, but social as well. The case was similar with anti-Judaism of the pen. If certain bishops and ecclesiastical writers confined themselves to defending the symbols of their faith against Jewish

[114] Ms. 351 of the Spanish collection of the Bibliotheque Na-tionale (Cf. Loeb, Revue des Etudes Juives v. XVIII).

exegesis, if they fought against this Jewish spirit,—the terror of the church that was, nevertheless, deeply impregnated with this spirit,—others followed the example of the Fathers who had thundered against Jewish rapaity and the rapacity of the rich in general. To the theological treatises issued by them they added addresses to the court intended to combat the lenders on pawned articles, those who lived by usury. Agobard, [115] Amolon, [116] Rigord, [117] Pierre de Cluny, [118] Simon Maiol [119] were these anti-Jews. They were among those whom the wealth of the Jews revolted more than their ungodliness, who were more scandalized by their luxury than by their blasphemies. No doubt, for them the Jews were the most hateful adversaries of the truth, the worst of the unbelievers; [120] they are the enemies of God and Jesus Christ; they call the apostles apostates; they scoff at the Bible of the Septuagint; [121] in their daily prayers they curse the Saviour under the name of the Nazarene; they build new synagogues as if to insult the Christian religion ; they Judaize the believers, they preach the Sab-bath to them and they persuade them to take a rest on Sabbath. But, besides, the Jews oppress the people; they hoard up wealth that is the fruit of usury and plun

[115] *De Insolcntia Judaeorum* (Patrologie latine v. CIV).

[116] *Existola scu liber contra Judaeos* (Patrologie latine, v. OXVI).

[117] *Gesta Philippi Augusti,* 12-16.

[118] *Tractatus adversus Judaeorum inveteratam duritiam* (Bibll-otheque des Peres latins. Lyons).

[119] Lea J ours caniculaircs (Dierum canioularium) translated by P. de Rosset (Paris, 1612).

[120] Agobard, *loc. cit.*

[121] Amolon, *loc. cit.*

der; [122] they hold the Christians in servitude; they possess enormous treasures in the cities which had received them, e. g., in Paris and Lyons; they commit larceny, they acquire money by evil methods; "everything passes through their hands, they insinuate themselves into houses and gain confidence; by their usury they draw the sap, the blood and the natural vigor of the Christians." [123] They sell counterfeit jewels, they receive stolen goods, they coin base money, cannot be trusted, collect their debts twice over. In brief, "there is no wickedness in the world which the Jews are not guilty of, so that they seem to aim at nothing but the Christians' ruin." [124]

To this picture of the *perfidia Judaeorum,* the anti-Jews, like Maiol or Luther, [125] added abundant abuse, and soon anti-Judaism became purely polemic. The theological and social considerations now occupy but a limited place in the books of Alonzo da Spina, [126] especially Pierre de Lancre [127] and Francisco de Torrejoncillo. [128] The *Sentinel Against the Jews,* a pamphlet by the last named, is particularly curious. Written in Spain at the beginning of the seventeenth century, it was aimed at the Marranos, who, it was said, invaded all the civil and

[122] Pierre de Cluny, *loc. cit.*

[123] Agobard, *loc. cit.* —Rigard, *loc. cit.*

[124] S. Maiol, *loc. cit.*

[125] *The Jews and their falsehoods* (Wittenberg, 1568).

[126] *Fortalitium Fidei* (Nurenberg, 1494). Wolf, Bibl. Hebr., v. I, p. 1116.

[127] *L'lncredulite et mecreance du sortilege pleinement convaincue* (1622).

[128] *Centinela contra Judioas* (Cf. Loeb, Revue des Etudes Juives, v.

V.)

religious offices. It consisted of fourteen books and showed that the Jews were presumptuous and liars, that they were traitors, that they were despised and dejected, that those favoring them came to an evil end, that neither they nor their work could be trusted, that they were turbulent, self-conceited, seditious, that the church preserved them only that in their midst might be born their Messiah the anti-Christ, who will be vanquished to allow Israel to recognize his error. At any rate Francisco de Torrejoncillo may be considered amiable if one compare his pamphlet with a singular little work of the same epoch bearing the title, ***Book of the Alboraique.*** [129] The Alboraique was Mohamet's mount, a queer animal, neither horse, nor mule, nor ox, nor donkey; to this singular animal the author of the squib likens the new Christians, the Marranos, who are Alboraiques as being neither Jews nor Christians. Thereupon the pamphleteer declares that the Jews or Marranos possess all the characteristics of the Alboraique, and he lays down one of the most extraordinary parallels. Mohamet's mount had the ears of a harrier, but the Alboraiques are dogs; it had the body of an ox, but the Alboraiques think only of the material welfare and of filling their stomach; it had a serpent's tail, but the Alboraiques spread the poison of heresy.

Had all the polemists limited themselves to allegorical comparisons, not much harm would have come to the Jews. But some did not hesitate to relate the most extraordinary things about these accursed ones, and the

[129] Bibliotheque Nationale, Spanish section, Ms. No. 356 (Loeb, Revue de* Etudes Juivcs v. XVIII).

anti Jewish polemic literature enregistered all the popular prejudices, even made them worse; it originated new ones and perpetuated them in all instances. The wildest stories about the Jews were circulated; they were represented with monstrous features; the most abominable deformities, the blackest vices, the most heinous crimes, the most despicable habits were attri-buted to them. They have, so it was declared, the figure of a he-goat, they have horns and a caudal appendage, [130] they are subject to quinsy, to scrofula, to blood-flux, stinking infirmities which make them lower their heads, [131] they have hemorrhoids, bloody sores on their hands, they cannot spit; at night their tongue is overrun with worms. The belief in these diseases peculiar to the Jews had come from Spain, in the fourteenth century; later on they were arranged in lists, the oldest of which belongs to 1634. In these lists, to each of the twelve tribes its special disease is assigned. Those of Reuben's tribe, is was said, had laid their hands on Jesus, accordingly their hands dry up whatever they touch; those of Simeon's tribe had nailed Jesus,—and they have bloody stains on their feet four times a year; "let his blood fall upon us!" they all had cried, and, therefore, their children are born with a bloody arm and on Holy Friday they throw blood from their anus. Purely mystical, then, was the origin of this belief in the maladies of the Jews; it may even be said that it was the rhetorical figures and allegorical similes, only objectified and made concrete, that gave rise to these fables. Legends grew up which had for

[130] *Centinela con ra Judios.*

[131] Pierre de Lancre, *loc. cit.*

their starting point a metaphor, like the legend of the smell of the Jews. Fortunatus is the first to speak of it —for it seems probable that the passage from Ammianus Marcellinus often referred to was misquoted, [132] and he speaks of it in a figurative sense: [133] "The baptismal water removes the Jewish odor; the purified flock will exhale a new fragrancy." Besides, the notion of fragrancy was associated with that of purity; to say of a blest man that he died in the fragrancy of sanctity really meant that this saint had the gift of emitting divine balms. When we read the lives of Saint Dom-inicus, of Anthony of Padua, of Francois de Paule, we see that they had enjoyed that privilege. On the contrary, the vicious, the impious, all those whose soul was impure, would exhale an infected odor. Saint Phillip de Néri, so his biographer asserts, would distinguish the incontinent vices of men by the odor, and thus he would divine the presence of the devil; Dominique de Paradis and Gentille de Ravennes also possessed this faculty. As for the devil, everybody concurred in saying, during the Middle Ages, that he revealed his presence by a poisoned goat-smell. The Jew, who was the worst of the impious, and the true son of Satan, could not, accordingly, help exhaling atrocious emanations. Strange to say, the Jews had similar notions of the relations between sin and ill smell, and according to Maimonides,

> [132] Ammianus Marcellinus, B. XXII. It is certain that the ***Judaeorum foetentium*** of which Marcus Aurelius complained, cornea from a blunder or the spite of the copyist, and that ***foe-tentium*** —ill-smelling—was substituted for poetentium-turbulent, which the Ms. of Ammianus contained.
>
> [133] Fortunatus, ***Carmine,*** 1. V.

the Serpent had thrown its stench on the race of Eve, but the faithful Jews had been preserved.

Thus can be explained some other anti-Jewish prejudices; but though it is evident that the likening of the Israelites to the evil spirit caused the he-goat figure and horns on their foreheads to be attributed them, still many of these beliefs remain inexplicable. They all arise, in part, from the fact that the retired life of the Jews, their venerable habit of keeping aloof, not to mingle with those surrounding them—ever served to excite excessively the popular imagination. Whenever individuals or groups of individuals willingly fenced themselves in or were fenced in, the same phenomenon occurred; people would forget the causes which had brought on this seclusion and the isolated would be endowed with passions, vices, and infirmities, deemed the more horrible, as these recluses were detested. The same thing happened with certain conventual associations, with secret societies, with militant religious or-ders, with all groups, which in any way lived away from the masses, whether for mystical, national or political reasons,—it mattered little. The populace is naturally curious, more than that, it is strongly imaginative, inclined to make up legends, to originate fables, and very naively at that, in a childish fashion. A word, a sentence, an association of ideas suffice; at the slightest indication it rears up dreams, invents stories, of which it is impossible to extricate the origin. Whatever is hidden disquiets, troubles, preoccupies it. It seeks for the motives that make a class of people shelter themselves in a collective solitude, and finding none, invents them; at all events, though it may discover some real motives, it cannot help inventing imaginary ones. All those who belonged to what is known as the accursed races were made the subject of these fables and legends.

With reference to the Cagots of the Pyrenees, the Gahets of Guienne, the Agotacs of the Lower Pyrenees, the Couax of Bretagne, the Oiseliers of the duchy of Bouillon, the Burrins of l'Ain, the Capots, the Trangots, the Gesitans, the Coliberts,—the same assertions were made as of the Jew.' [134] They exhale, it was said, a stinking and infectious odor, they wither fruits by holding them in their hands, they are subject to the flux of blood, they have a caudal appendage, they emit blood from the navel on Holy Friday, they have dim eyes, they droop their heads, they cannot expectorate. With slight variations, these stories were repeated about the Arians, Manicheans, Cathari, Albigenses, Patarians, in general, of all heretics.

As to the Templars, concerning whom so many similar abominations had been spread, they, above all others, can be likened unto the Jews. Like the latter, they were hated for their pride, their ostentation, their wealth in the midst of general misery, their eagerness for gain, their shameless use of means of acquisition, their making usurious contracts. They were hated because they advanced money on chattels and fiefs on condition that these fiefs and chattels remained theirs in case of the borrower's death; because the Templars' Order possessed a greater part of the French territory in the thirteenth century and formed a commonwealth within the state,

[134] Michel, Les Races *maudites,* Paris, 1847.

the Templars having and recognizing no master but God. [135] We see then that the same causes produce the same results, create the same animosities, give rise to the same beliefs.

Were not the Templars said to "burn and roast the children they begat by young girls, and to sacrifice to and anoint their idols with the fat taken off"; [136] were not

the Cagots said to make use of Christian blood? Does not the charge of ritual murder weigh over the Jews as it had weighed over those wretches, the lepers, whom
the Middle Ages treated as the Jew's brethren, thus taking up again the assertions
of Manetho, repeated by Chaere-mon, Lysimachus, Posidonius, Apollonius Molon
and Apion, just as it had weighed over the sorcerers, who were also likened to the
Jews? But we shall come back to this question when we speak of the modern antisemites.

What was the attitude of the Jews in the face of all these attacks and abuses
which the theologians and po-lemists directed at them? They vigorously defended
themselves. They opposed exegesis to exegesis; they opposed their logic to their opponents' arguments; they an-swered insults and calumnies with calumnies and insults; which is but normal, natural, inevitable, but all the same these insults fatally
rebounded against them. If the anti-Jewish literature is enormous, the defensive
literature of the Jews, as well as their anti-Christian literature—

[135] Lavocat, **Proces des Freres de l'ordre du Temple,** Paris, 1888.

[136] Lavocat, **loc. cit.**

for the Jews oftentimes took up the offensive—is quite considerable. [137]

The first controversial work belonging to the Israelite literature of the Middle
Ages, was the **Book of the Lord's Wars,** written in 1170, by Jacob ben Ruben.[138]
It was made up of twelve chapters, or gateways, proving that Messiah had not yet
come, which, however, for the exe-getic rhetoricians, was just as easy as, if not
easier than to prove the opposite. But it was not enough to prove that Jesus was not
the awaited Messiah; it was equally necessary to prove the superiority of the Jewish
religion to those who were establishing, irrefutably, the superiority of the Christian
religion, and this was easy for both sides, as each drew from the Bible what suited
it. The Talmudists made use of the New Testament even to confirm their Judaic
dogmas. This was done by Moses Tohen de Tordesillas, in his **Support of the Faith,**
while Shem-Tob ben Isaac Shaprut resumed, in the form of a dialogue between a

Unitarian and a Trinitarian, the ideas propounded by Jacob ben Ruben. [139]

The polemic literature was greatly developed in Spain

[137] It would be necessary to devote a whole chapter to the anti-Christian literature, which I cannot possibly do here, where anti-Judaism is the main question, and I shall simply indicate the Jewish reaction. The Jewish endeavor against "Christian idolatry" was great indeed. To get some idea of it, it will sufice to glance over the Bibliotheca Judaica antichristiana of J.B. Rossi (Parma, 1800). Besides, the catalogue compiled by Rossi is not perfectly exact; still it enables one to gauge the polemic activity of the Jews, which finds its equal only in that of the Christians (Cf. also Wolf and Wagenseil, *loc. cit.*)

[138] Loeb, *Revue des Etudes Juives,* v. XVIII

[139] Shem-Tob ben Isaac Shaprut, *The Touchstone* (Loeb, *loc. cit.*).

in the fifteenth century. The time was a hard one for the Jews of the Peninsula. The Church doubled its efforts to convert them; disputes, pamphlets, treatises increased in numbers. The Jews fought against prose-lytism resorting to it under the last extremity, and later on, at the moment of the final banishement, the greatest part of them chose exile without the hope of return, rather than conversion. While the monks sought in the Pentateuch and the Prophets arguments in support of the Christian symbols, the Jews endeavored to lay plain the differences which divide the two creeds, and were fighting Catholicism in order to confirm the faith in the soul of those who vacillated. Like Chasdai Crescas they studied their opponents' theology. Thus armed, Jacob ibn Shem Tob wrote the *Objections to the Christian Religion,* [140] Simon ben Zemach Duran published a *Philosophical Examination of Judaism,* a special chapter of which, entitled "Bow and Shield," contained a critique of Christianity.

In imitation of the ecclesiastical writers and inquisitors, the rabbis wrote books for the use of those who were challenged in disputes. A kind of vade these books pointed out the vulnerable sides of the Christian dogmas; and if, on the one hand, there were publications like "Judaism Defeated with Its Own Weapons," on the other hand were composed works like "Christianity Defeated with Its Own Arms," i. e., with those found in the New Testament. In anti-Christian literature the Gospels played the part of the Talmud in anti-Jewish

[140] Cf. Graets, v. IV.

literature. Beginning with the eleventh or twelfth century they were often assailed, and numerous discussions took place between rabbanites and theologians. These discussions were sometimes gathered in collections, where they were presented in a light favorable to Jewish dialectics. Presently these collections came to be used as manuals; among them were the ancient Nizzachon (Victory) of Rabbi Mattathiah; the Nizzachon of Lipman de Mülhausen; the one by Joseph Kimhi; the *Strength" ening of the Faith,* by Isaac Troki, [141] and the *Booh of Joseph the Zealot.* [142] Still this was not sufficient for the fervor of the Jews. Having prepared the minds for future debates, having assailed the Catholic doctrines, not in oratorical tournaments only, but in apologies as well, they wrote abusive pamphlets, like that famous *Toldot Jesho,* the life of the Galilean which goes back to the second or third century, and which Celsius possibly was acquainted with. [143] This Toldot Jesho was published by Raymund Martin, Luther translated it into German; Wagenseil and the Dutchman Huldrich also published it. It contained the story of Pantherus the soldier and the legends representing Jesus as a magician. After defending the Bible and Monotheism the Jews turned upon those who were their most dangerous enemies—the converted. If they had refuted Raymund

[141] Wagenseil in his *Tela ignea Satanae* (Altdorf, 1681), reproduces all these treatises in print

[142] Zadoc Kahn, *The Book of Joseph the Zealot* (Revue des Etudes Juives,, vols. I and III).

[143] *For the Toldot Jesho,* cf. *Tela ignea Satanae,* Wagenseil, v. II,

5, 189, and B. de Rossi, Biblotheoa Judaica antichristiana (Parma, 1800), p. 117.

Martin [144] and Nicholas de Lyra [145], they refuted with still greater energy Jerome de Santa Fé, the Santa Fé whom his former coreligionists called Megaddef, i. e., blasphemer. At Jerome they were incensed. Don Vidal ibn Labi, Isaac ben Nathan Kalonymos, [146] Solomon Duran, several others, wrote to give the lie to the "calumniator." The same was done by Isaac Pulgar against Alfonso of Valladolid, [147] by Joshua ben Joseph Lorqui and Proflat Duran. [148] The apostates of the Middle Ages were not treated perceptibly better than of yore, in the first century of the Christian era, when a curse that was to smite them was added to the daily prayers; from the tenth till the sixteenth or seventeenth century, they repeated against them what the Talmud said of the Min-cans, the ancient Judeo-Christians and the Ebionites. Of course, all these Jewish books were not accepted without protests; they also called forth numerous refutations, which in turn gave rise to replies.

In the seventeenth century anti-Judaism took on another form. The theologians were succeeded by erudites, scholars, exegetes. Anti-Judaism became milder and more scientific; it was represented by hebraizers, often of great attainments, like Wagenseil, [149] Bartolocci, [150] Voe-

[144] Wagenseil, *loc. cit.*

[145] ***Magna Biblothica Rabbinioa*** (Rome, 1693-95).

[146] Solomon ben Adret, of Barcelona, refuted the ***Pugio Fidei.***

[147] Chayimibn Musa refuted Nicholas de Lyra in his ***Shield and Sword*** (Graetz, loo. cit.)

[148] Letter of Combat (Graetz, *loc. cit.,* and Rossi, Bibloth. antichrist, (p. 100).

[149] ***Dialogue against the Apostates*** (Loeb, *loc. cit.*)

[150] ***Alteca Boteca*** (Loeb, *loc. cit.*)—De Rossi, Dizionario degli ***autori***

Ebrei (Parma, 1802), p. 89.

tius, [151] Joseph de Voisin,[152] etc. These men studied Jewish literature and manners in a more serious way. Thus Wagenseil denied ritual murder; [153] though saying that the Talmud contained "blasphemies, impostures and absurdities," Buxtorf declared that it also contained things of value for the historian and philosopher. [154] Yet the same ideas persisted which had inspired the authors of the preceding centuries. The object was always to prove the truth of the Christian faith and dogmas on the basis of the Old Testament; the anxiety to convert the Jews ever haunted the souls, the recall of Israel was spoken of, means of bringing them back were proposed; [155] the apostates invoked the Zohar and Mishna in favor of Jesus, [156] and the polemic literature was still in bloom under Eisenmenger, whose *Judaism Unveiled?* [157] has inspired many contemporary antisemites; under Schudt, [158] later under Voltaire. It is true that literary anti-Judaism, particularly that of combative tendencies and pam-

[151] *Disputations Sclectae* (Utrecht, 1063).

[152] *Theologia Judaeorum* (1647).

[153] *Benachrichtung wegen einiger die Judenschaft angekenden Sochen* (Altdorf, 1709).

[154] *Dictionn. chaldeo-talmudico-rabbinique* (Basiliae, 1639) and *Synagoga Judaica* (Hanau, 1604).

[155] Pean de la Croullardiere, *Methode facile pour convaincre Us heretiques* (Paris, 1667), which contains a "method of assailing ad converting the Jews"; Thomas Bell' Hader, *Dottrina facile e breve per reduire VHebreo al oonosoimento del veto Messia e Salvator del Mondo* (Venetia 1608).

[156] Conrad Otton, *Gali Razia* (Secrets unveiled), (Nurenberg, 1005).

[157] *Judaism Unveiled* "(Frankfort, 1700).

[158] *Compendium Historiae Judaicae* (Frankfort, 1700) and *Judaeus Christicida gravissime peceans et vapulans* (1760).

phleteers, is varied but little. Most of the anti-Jewish writers imitate one another, without scruple; they plagiarize without even taking the trouble to verify the assertions of their predecessors. One book of the kind is responsible for similar others: Alonzo da Spina draws his inspiration from Batallas de Dios, by Alfonso of Valladolid; Porchet Salvaticus, Pietro Galatini, Pierre de Barcelona republish, under different names, Raymund Martin's *Sword of the Faith;* Paul Fagius and Sebastian Münster [159] help themselves to the *Book of the Faith.*

In spite of this, and independently of the dissimilarities I have noted, anti-Judaism, from the seventeenth century on, is in all respects quite different from the anti-Judaism of the preceding centuries. The social side gets gradually the upperhand of the religious side, though this latter continues to exist. The question is asked, not whether the Jews are wrong in being usurers, or merchants, or deicides, but whether, as Schudt [160] says, the Jews ought to be tolerated in a State or not, whether it is lawful to admit Jews into a Christian commonwealth, as John Dury [161] inquires, about 1655, in a pamphlet directed against Cromwell's protégé, Menasseh ben Israel. This is the social standpoint which we shall see developing henceforth in literary anti-Judaism; a part of modern antisemitism will rest on the theory of a Christian State and its integrity, and in this wise it will be connected with the ancient anti-Judaism. In the course of this book we shall have to examine more closely

[159] *Revue des Etudes juives,* v. V, p 57.

[160] *Loc. tit.*

[161] *A Case of Conscience* (London, 1655).

the affinities and differences which unite and separate these two kinds of anti-Judaism.

CHAPTER VIII.

MODERN LEGAL ANTI-JUDAISM.

Emancipated Judaism.—The Position of the Jews in Society.—Usury and the Affairs in Alsace.—Napo-leon and the Administrative Organization of the Jew-ish Religion.—The Great Sanhedrin.—The Re-strictive Laws and the Progressive Liberation in France.—The Emancipation in the Netherlands.— Emancipation in Italy and Germany.—The Anti-Napoleonic Reaction and the Jews.—The Revival of Anti-Jewish Legislation.—Popular Movements.— Emancipation in England.—In Austria.—The Revolution of 1848 and the Jews.—The End of Legal Anti-Judaism in the West.—Eastern Anti-Judaism. —The Jews in Roumania.—The Russian Jews.— The Persecutions.—The Social Question and the Religious Question.

After preliminary discussions, as a result of which any decision on the eman-cipation of the Jews was adjourned, the Constituent Assembly voted, on September 27,1791, on a motion by Duport, and thanks to Regnault de Saint-Jean-d'Angély's intervention, the admission of the Jews to the rank of citizens. This decree had been ready for a long time, prepared as it was through the work of the commission assembled by Louis XVI, with Malesherbes in the chair; prepared by the writings of Leasing and Dohm, of Mirabeau and Grégoire. It was the logical outcome of the efforts made for some time by the Jews and the philosophers; in Germany Men-delssohn had been its promoter and most active advocate, and in Berlin Mirabeau drew his inspiration at the side of Dohm in the salons of Henriette de Lemos.

A certain class of Jews had, however, already been emancipated. In Germany the court Jews (Hofjuden) had obtained commercial privileges; even titles of nobil-ity were being conferred upon them for money. In France the Portuguese Marranos returned to Judaism, enjoyed great liberties and prospered under the supervision of their syndics at Bordeaux, very indifferent nevertheless to the fate of their un-fortunate brethren, though very influential: one of them, Gradis, failed to secure a nomination as deputy to the States-General. In Alsace even, several Jews obtained important favors, as, e. g., Cerf Berr, purveyor to the armies of Louis XV, who granted him naturalization and the title of Marquis de Tombelaine.

Thanks to all these privileges, there sprang into existence a class of rich Jews which came into contact with the christian society; open-minded, subtle, intelligent, refined, of extreme intellectualism, it had given up, like so many Christians, the letter of religion or of the faith even, and retained nothing but a mystic idealism which, for good or ill, went hand in hand with a liberal rationalism. The fusion between this group of Jews and the elite led by Lessing, was brought about above all in Berlin, a young city and centre of a kingdom which was rising to fame, an easygoing city, with little tradition. Young Germany gathered at the houses of Henrietta de Lemos and Rachel von Varnhagen; with the Jews, German Romanticism ended in impregnating itself with Spinozaism; Schleiermacher and Humboldt were seen visiting there, and it may be said that if the Constituent Assembly decreed the emancipation of the Jews, it was in Germany that it had been prepared.

At any rate, the number of these Jews qualified to mingle with the nations, was extremely limited, the more so because the majority of them—like Mendelsson's daughters, like Boerne and Heine later on—ended by converting, and thus no longer existed as Israelites. As for the mass of Jews, it was in quite different circumstances.

The decree of 1791 freed these pariahs from a secular servitude; it broke the fetters with which the laws had bound them; it wrested them from all kinds of ghettos where they had been imprisoned; from, as it were, cattle it made them human beings. But if it was within its power to restore them to liberty, if it was possible for it to undo within one day the legislative work of centuries, it could not annul their moral effect, and it was especially impotent to break the chains which the Jews had forged themselves. The Jews were emancipated legally, but not so morally; they kept their manners, customs and prejudices—prejudices which their fellow citizens of other confessions kept, too. They were happy at having escaped their humiliation, but they looked around with diffidence and suspected even their liberators.

For centuries they had looked with disgust and terror at this world which was rejecting them; they had suffered from it, but they still more feared to lose their personality and faith from contact with it. More than one old Jew must have looked with anxiety at the new existence which opened before him; I should not even be surprised if there were some in whose eyes the liberation appeared a misfortune or abomination. Many of these miserable beings cherished their humiliation, their seclusion which kept them far from sin and contamination, and the efforts of the majority were bent on remaining what they were, among *strangers* in whose midst they were cast. . The enlightened, intelligent part of the Jews, the reformers, who suffered from their inferior position and from the degradation of their coreligionists —these worked for emancipation, but even they could not at once transform those for whom they had reclaimed the right of being human creatures.

As the decree of emancipation did not. change the Judaic self, the way in which this self manifested itself was not changed either. Economically the Jews remained what they were—be it understood that I speak of the majority—unproductive, i. e., brokers, money-lenders, usurers, and they could not be otherwise, given their habits and conditions under which they had lived. With the exception of an insignificant minority among them, they had no other aptitudes, and even nowadays a great many Jews are in the same plight. They did not fail to apply these aptitudes, and during this period of unrest and disorder they found occasion to apply them more than ever. In France they availed themselves of events, and the events were favorable for them. In Alsace, for instance, they acted as auxiliaries to the peasants, whom they lent the funds necessary for the purchase of national property. Already before the revolution they were the home-bred usurers in this province, and the objects of hatred and contempt; [162] after the Revolution, the very peasants who had erstwhile forged quittances [163] to escape from the clutches of their creditors, now appealed to them. Thanks to the Alsatian Jews, the new ownership continued, but they meant to draw profit from it with a plentiful, usurious hand. The debtors raised a protest; they pretended they would be ruined if no aid were forthcoming, and in this they exaggerated, as they, who previous to 1795 had nothing, had eighteen years later acquired 60,000,000 francs' worth of estates on which they owed the Jews 9,500,000 francs. Nevertheless, Napoleon lent ear to them, and suspended, during one year, judicial decisions in behalf of the Jewish usurers of the Upper Rhine, the Lower Rhine, and the Rhine provinces. His work did not stop at that. In the preambles of the decree of suspension of May 30, 1806, he showed that he did not consider the repressive

[162] Mention must be made that, as in the Middle ages, the Alsatian Jews were the "dummies" and intermediaries of the Christian usurers, (Cf. Halphen, ***Recueil des lois et decreta concer-nant les Israelites,*** (Paris, 1851), and the ***Petition des Juifs etablis en France addressee a l'Assemblee nationale le*** 28 janvier 1790).

[163] On the Alsatian Jews before and after the Revolution, consult: Gregoire, ***Essai sur la Regeneration des Juifs;*** Dohm, ***De la Reforme politique des Juifs;*** Paul Fauchille, ***La Question Juive en France Sous le premier Empire*** (Paris, 1884).

measures sufficient, but wanted the source of the evil done away with.

"These circumstances," said he, "caused us at the same time to consider how urgent it was to revive among those subjects of our country who profess the Jewish religion, the sentiments of civic morals, which have unfortunately been deadened with a great number of them through the state of humiliation in which they have languished too long, and which is not our intention to maintain and renew."

To revive or rather to give birth to these sentiments, he wanted to bend the Jewish religion to suit his discipline, to hierarchize it as he had hierarchized the rest of the nation, to make it conform to the general plan. When first consul he had neglected to take up the question of the Jewish religion, and so he wanted to make amends for this failure by convoking an Assembly of Notable Jews for the purpose of "considering the means of improving the condition of the Jewish nation and spreading the taste for the useful arts and professions among its members," and of organizing Judaism administratively. A list of questions was sent out among prominent Jews and when the answers had come in, the Emperor called together a Great Sanhedrin vested with the power of bestowing a religious authority upon the responses of the first assembly. The Sanhedrin declared that the Mosaic law contained obligatory religious pro-visions, and political provisions; the latter concerned the people of Israel when an autonomous nation, and had, therefore, lost their meaning since the Jews had scattered among the nations; it also forbade to make, in the future, any distinctions between Jews and Christians in the matter of loans, and entirely prohibited usury.

These declarations showed that the prominent Jews belonging for the most part to the minority I have mentioned, knew to adapt themselves to the new state of affairs, but could in no way make any presumption upon the dispositions of the mass. Therein Napoleon deceived himself; his fondness for order, regulation and law, his faith in their efficiency played him false. He doubtless imagined that a Sanhedrin was a council, but it was nothing of the kind. The Sanhedrin decisions had absolutely no import except as personal opinions, they were in no way binding upon the Jews, they carried no authority, and there were no sanctions to enforce them. The only piece of work of this assembly was administrative—that of organizing consistories; as for the moral work it was naught, and the men assembled were incapable of changing manners. They knew it too well themselves, however, and they simply recorded what was common property; thus they abolished polygamy which had been out of use for centuries. It required the candor of Napoleon the legist to believe that a synod could enjoin love for the neighbor, or forbid usury which the social conditions facilitated. The imperial prohibition for Jews against providing substitutes for military service—this for the purpose of making them better realize the grandeur of their civic duties—was bound to have the same effect as the prescriptions of the synod. [164] The case was the same with the decree of

[164] Halphen, *Recueil des lois et deorets.*

March 17, 1808, forbidding the Jews to engage in commerce without a personal license issued by the prefect, or to take mortgages without authorization; besides, Jews were forbidden to settle in Alsace and the Rhine provinces, and the Alsacian

Jews were forbidden to enter other *departments* unless to engage in agriculture, [165] These decrees issued for ten years, did not turn one Jew into an agriculturer, and if any of them became chauvinists, the obligation of serving in the army had something to do with it. These were the last restrictive laws in France; the legal assimilation was consummated in 1830, when Lafltte had the Jewish creed incorporated in the budget. This meant the final downfall of the "Christian State," though the lay state was not, as yet, completely established. The last trace of the ancient distinctions between Jews and Christians disappeared with the abolition of the oath *More Judaico,* in 1839. Nor was the moral assimilation complete.

So far we have been speaking of the emancipation of the French Jews, it remains to examine the influence it had on the Jews of Europe. [166] From the moment of the

[165] Halphen, *loc. cit.*

[166] In this book I shall not speak of the modern Jews of the Mohammedan countries, Turkey, Asia Minor, Tripoli, Persia. It is quite evident that the enmity there rests on quite different causes from those in Christian lands, and quite different principles, or at least notions and instincts, guide the Mohammedans. In the contemporary meaning of the word, antisemitism does not exist in any of these countries, nevertheless the hostility to Jews, especially popular hostility, is very great there. To determine the causes thereof it would require a special study, which I shall undertake later on; in this study I shall take up the Tunisian and Algerian Jews, with the understanding that I shall not deal with the grievances of the French antisemites against them, grievances similar to those which we are about to treat here, although some of them, as, for instance, the national grievance, are hardly tenable. I shall simply deal with the more interesting aspects and the causes of hatred between Arabs and Jews.

foundation of the Batavian Republic, in 1796, the National Assembly gave the Jews in the Netherlands the rights of citizenship, and their position regulated later by Louis Bonaparte was settled in a decisive way by William I, in 1815. As a matter of fact, the Dutch Jews enjoyed important privileges and quite a deal of liberty since the sixteenth century: the Revolution was but the decisive cause of their total liberation. In Italy and Germany emancipation was brought to the Jews by the armies of the Republic and the Empire. Napoleon became the hero and god of Israel, the awaited liberator, he whose mighty hand was breaking the barriers of the Ghetto. He entered all cities greeted by the acclamations of the Jews—witness the way in which Heinrich Heine extolled him—who felt that their cause was linked with the triumph of the eagles. And for this reason the Jews were the first to feel the effects of the Napoleonic reaction. A return to anti-Judaism went hand in hand with the exaltation of patriotism. The emancipation was a French act; it was, therefore, necessary to prove it bad, besides, it was a revolutionary act, and there was a reaction against the Revolution and the ideas of equality. While the Christian State was being re-established, the Jews were being banished. In Germany in particular this antique religious conception of the State again came to life with a new splendor, and in Germany, especially, anti-Judaism manifested itself more acutely, but the revival of anti-Jewish legislation was general. In Italy legislation had been resumed in 1770; in Germany the Vienna Congress abolished all imperial provisions for Jews, leaving them only the rights granted by the lawful German governments. As a result of the decisions of the Congress, the cities and communities showed themselves harsh toward the Jews. Lubeck and Bremen expelled them; like Rome, Frankfort shut them up anew in their ancient quarters. [167] Naturally, popular movements followed suit of the legal measures. At this moment of overheated patriotism, any restriction of the rights of strangers met with approval; for the Jews were as ever the strangers par excellence, who best represented noxious strangers, and so, about 1820, i. e., the moment when this state of minds reached its paroxysm, the mob fell, in many places, upon the Jews and badly maltreated them, even if it did not massacre them.

The thirty years following the disappearance of Napoleon did not witness any great progress for the Jews. In England where they were, as a matter of fact, treated liberally enough, they were, nevertheless, always considered dissidents, and, like the Catholics, were subject to certain obligations. Little by little only did they see their condition modified, and the history of their emancipation is an episode in the struggle between the House of Commons and the House of the Lords.

[167] At this moment the Jews entered suit against the city of Frankfort to contest the legality of the city's decisions. This sult was the occasion of violent anti-Jewish polemics.

Not before 1860 were they completely assimilated with the other English citizens.

In Austria they had been partly emancipated by the Toleration edict of Joseph II. (1785), but had to undergo the same reaction; the Revolution was too fatal for the Austrian House, that the latter should even put up with this well-nigh equality of the Jews which a democratic and philosophic sovereign had granted. Only in 1848 the Austrian Jews became citizens. [168] At the same time their emancipation was achieved in Germany, [169] Greece, Sweden, and Denmark. Once more they owed their independence to the revolutionary spirit which once again came from France. However, we shall see that they were not strangers to the great movement

> [168] The constitution of March 4, 1849, proclaimed the equality before the law. But as this constitution was abolished in 1851, an ordinance of July 29, 1853, restored the old legislation against the Jews. Successive Amendments were added to it, and the Constitution of 1867 finally restored equality before the law and liberated the Jews.

In Hungary the law emancipating the Jews was also voted in 1867 by the Chamber of Deputies, on motion by the Government. (Cf. Wolf, ***Oeschichte der Juden in Wien,*** Vienna, 1876; Kaim, ***Ein Jahrhundert der Judenemancipation.*** Leipzig, 1869.)

> [169] The German Constituent Assembly voted the equality of all citizens before the law, on May 20, 1848. The Parliament of Frankfort did likewise, and the principle of this equality was incorporated in the German constitution of 1849. At any rate many States retained the restrictions against the Jews till the time of the Law of the Northern Federation of July 8,

1869, which abolished all the "restrictions of civil and political rights that still existed and were based on difference in religion." (Cf. Kaim, *loc. Cit.* and *Allegemeine Zeitung dcs Judenthums* for the years 1837, 1849, 1856, 1867, 1869). After the Franco-German which had not adopted it before the organization of the Empire. war. this law was forced upon those States like Bavaria, e. g.

which agitated all Europe; in some countries, notably in Germany, they aided in preparing it, and they were the advocates of liberty. They also were among the first to benefit thereby, as legal anti-Judaism may be said to have come to an end in. the Occident after 1848. Little by little the last obstacles fell, and the last restrictions were abolished. The fall of the temporal power of the Popes, in 1870, did away with the last occidental Ghetto, and the Jews now could become citizens even in St. Peter's city.

Since then anti-Judaism has transformed, it has become purely literary, it has come to be but an opinion, and this opinion has no longer had its effect on laws. But before examining this antisemitism of the pen which in certain countries existed until 1870, side by side with restrictive regulations, we must speak of the Christian States of Eastern Europe, where the anti-Judaism is even now legal and persecutionary, i. e., of Roumania and Russia.

The Jews have lived in Roumania, [170] i. e., the Moldau-Valachian lands, since the fourteenth century, but they came there in numbers at the beginning of this century only, and are about 300,000 in all, as a result of Hungarian and Russian emigration. For many long years they lived undisturbed. They naturally depended upon the boyars who hold the power in this country, and they leased the sale of spirits from these noblemen, who held the monopoly therefor. As they were indispensable to

[170] Desjardins, *Les Juifs de Moldavies* (Paris, 1867).—Isidore Loeb, *La Situation des Israelites en Turquie, en Serbie et en Roumanie* (Paris, 1877).

the noblemen as tax-collectors, fiscal agents and all sorts of middlemen, the nobles were rather inclined to grant them privileges, and they only had the excess of popular superstitions or passions. The official persecutions of the Jews began only in 1856, when Roumania adopted the representative system and the power thus fell into the hands of the bourgeois class. The Paris treaty of 1858, which preceded the union of Moldavia and Val-achia, bestowed the enjoyment of civil rights upon the Moldau-Valachians ***without distinction of creed.*** Despite the formal text of the treaty, the Jews were denied the benefits of naturalization, and replying to repres-en-tation made to it the Roumanian government asserted that the Jews were aliens. Thenceforth restrictive measures grew more serious. The Jews could not obtain any rank, they were deprived of the right of permanent domicile in country places, they were forbidden to hold real estate—except in cities—or lands, or vineyards. They were prohibited to take estates on lease, to keep hotels and taverns outside of cities, to retail spirits, to have Christian domestics, to build new synagogues. Some of these decisions were passed arbitrarily by certain municipalities; in other villages, on the contrary, the Jews were tolerated. This state of affairs lasted till 1867. At this time the minister Jean Bratiano published a circular in which he recalled to mind the fact that the Jews had no right to live in rural communities, or to take there property on lease. As a result of this circular the Jews were expelled from the villages they inhabited, they were condemned like vagabonds, and the expulsions continued till 1877; they were generally called forth by the uprisings in Bucharest, Yassy, Galatz, Tecucin, as well as in other places, and during these uprisings cemeteries were profaned and synagogues burned.

What were, what are still the causes of this special legislation, and of this animosity of the Roumanians towards the Jews? They are not exclusively religious, and despite the persistence of ancestral prejudices, it is not a case of a confessional war. The Roumanian Jews constituted, especially at the moment of the formation of Roumania, agglomerations completely isolated from the bulk of the population in the Moldau-Val-achian lands. [171]They wore a special garb, lived in quarters set apart in order to escape contaminations, and spoke a Judaeo-German jargon, which rounded off their marks of distinction. They lived under the domination of their rabbis, narrow-minded, limited, ignorant Tal-mudists, from whom they received in Jewish schools— heder—and education which was conducive to their intellectual abasement and their degradation.

They were the victims of this isolation which was due to their guides, the rab-binists. The patriotic passions were particularly aroused in this land, which was being born, was acquiring a nationality and striving for unity. There has been a pan-Roumanism, just like pan-Ger-manism or pan-Slavism. There were discussions on the

> [171] This condition has not changed since, and only a small number of Jews, by entering universities and obtaining there intellectual development, succeeded in tearing themselves away from the exclusionist prejudices of the mass which is still sunk in the stupor, from which antitalmudic instruction alone can recover it

Roumanian race, on its integrity, its purity, the danger threatening it from adulteration. Associations were formed to counteract foreign encroachment, and Jewish encroachment in particular. Schoolmasters, university professors were the soul of these societies; just as in Germany, they were the most active antisemites. They looked upon the Jews as agents and apostles of Germanism, and they became the instigators of restrictive legislation in order to repel and restrain them. They reproached the Jews with forming a state within a state, which was true, but—and that is the everlasting inconsistency of anti-Judaism—they passed laws to retain them in the condition they considered dangerous. They asserted that the Jewish education crippled the brains of those receiving it, that it rendered them unfit for social life, which was but too correct, and yet they were going to shut the Jews out completely from obtaining the education given to Christians, exactly the one that would lift them from their degradation.

But the college-bred were not the sole antisemites in Roumania, and there were economic causes beside patriotic causes. As I have said, antisemitism was born with the advent of the bourgeoisie, because this bourgeois class, composed of merchants and manufacturers, came into competition with the Jews who displayed their activity exclusively in commerce and in-dustry, when not in usury. The bourgeoisie had every interest in the passage of protective laws, which, though nominally directed at strangers and not at the Jews, principally aimed at placing obstacles to the expansion of their formidable rivals. It achieved its point by skilfully fomenting disturbances which gave their representatives in Parliament a chance to propose new regulations. Thus these diverse causes of antisemitism may be reduced to a single one—national protection-Ism—and very clever it is, as simultaneously with denying the Jews all civic rights on the ground that they are strangers, it forces them into military service, which again is a contradiction, as none but a citizen can form a part of a *national army.* [172]

Harder still, more miserable than in Roumania, is the condition of the Jews in Russia. Their history in that country, where they arrived in the third century B. C. and founded colonies in Crimea, has been that of the Jews of all Europe. They were banished in the twelfth century never to be recalled. Nevertheless, at present Russia counts 4,500,000 Jews (see footnote), and to say, as the antisemites maintain, that the Jews have invaded it is nonsense, for Russia has acquired them by seizing White Russia in 1769 and late on the Polish provinces and Crimea, which contained a great number of Jews. At the moment of this conquest it was out of the question to apply the ukase of 1742 which banished the Jews once more. On the one hand, it was not an easy thing to drive out several million individuals into the neighboring states; on the other, commerce, industry, and particularly the treasury, would have fared ill from such wholesale expulsion. Catherine II. then granted the Jews equal rights with her Russian subjects, but the

[172] I believe the truth of this will be admitted by the most irra-tional chauvinist, be he a Turk, Bulgarian, Russian, German, Englishman or even a Frenchman.

Senate ukases of 1786, 1791 and 1794 curtailed these privileges and confined the Israelites within White Rus-sia and Crimea—thenceforth constituting the *Jewish territory*—and Poland. Only in certain cases and under special conditions were they allowed to leave the limits of this territorial Ghetto.

In Russia all modern antisemitism, which is official antisemitism *par excellence,* consists in keeping the Jews from escaping the Senate ukases just spoken of. Russia has resigned herself to her Jews, but she wants to leave them where she found them. Still there were favorable or rather less unfavorable times for the Jews. Alexander I. permitted them in 1808 to settle in the crown lands on condition of engaging there in agriculture; Nicholas I. gave them permission to travel when their business required it, they were allowed to attend the universities; and under Alexander II. their position improved still further. [173]

After the death of Alexander II. the autocratic reaction became monstrous in Russia: an abominable reawakening of absolutism was the answer to the bomb of

[173] N. de Gradovski, *La Situation legale des Israelites en Russie* (Paris, 1891).—Tikhomirov, *La Russie politique et sociale* (Paris, 1888).—*Les Juifs de Russie* (Paris, 1891).—Prince Demidoff-San-Donato, *La question juive en Russie* (Bruxelles, 1884).—Anatole Leroy-Beau lieu, *L'Empire des Tzars et les Russes* (Paris, 1881-82-89). [English translation, London and New York, 1894].—Weber et Kempster, *La Situation des Juifs en Russie* (Resume of a report to the United States Government by its delegates).—Leo Errera, *Les juifs Russes* (Bruxelles, 1893).—Harold Frederic, *The New Exodus* (1892).

the nihilists. The national orthodox spirit was overexcited, the liberal and revolutionary movement was charged to foreign influences, and the Jews were made the scapegoats, in order to divert the people from the nihilistic propaganda; hence the massacres of 1881 and 1882, during which the mob burned Jewish houses, robbed and killed the Jews, saying: "Our daddy, the Tsar, wants it."

After these disturbances General Ignatyeff promulgated the "May Laws" of 1882. They read as follows:

1. As a temporary measure and until the general revision of the laws regulating their status, Jews are forbidden to settle hereafter outside of cities and towns. Exception is made with regard to Jewish villages already in existence where the Jews are engaged in agriculture.

2. Until further order all contracts for the mortgaging or renting of real estate situated outside of cities and towns to a Jew, shall be of no effect. Equally void is any power of attorney granted to a Jew for the administration or disposition of property of the above-indicated nature.

3. Jews are forbidden to do business on Sundays and Christian holidays; the laws compelling Christians to close their places of business on those days will be applied to Jewish places of business.

4. The above measures are applicable only in the governments situated within the Jewish pale of settlement.

These laws were enacted *as a temporary measure.* Accordingly, a commission presided over by Count Pahlen met in 1883 to settle finally the Jewish question, The conclusions of this commission were quite liberal in spirit; it recommended that certain civil rights be given to the Jews. Owing to the influence of Pobyedonost-seff, the Procurator of the Holy Synod, the report of the Pahlen Commission was buried, and the *May Laws* have remained in force. Since that time, and especially from 1890 on, the persecutions redoubled. The "pale" was narrowed by forbidding the Jews to enter certain fortified places, and by creating a frontier belt where the Jews could not reside. The ukase of 1865 of Alexander II., allowing "skilled" artisans to choose a domicile throughout the empire was abrogated. Thus nearly 3,000,000 Jews were crowded into the cities of the pale of settlement, while a million was spread over Poland, and 500,000 privileged—merchants of the first rank, financiers and students—all over Russia.

In the cities of the pale of settlement the Jews constitute a majority, and the conditions of their existence are frightful. Crowded in unhealthy habitations, where they live in the worst of poverty, ravaged by misery beside which the misery found in Paris, Berlin and London is prosperity; with "slack-time" during a part of the year, with work during the other part on con-dition of accepting wages so ridiculously low that their scale often falls to 8 or 10 cents a day; multiplying incessantly because of their very destitution, these wretches are in the slow agonies of death and are the foreordained victims of cholera, typhoid fever and all pests. From day to day their condition grows more serious, their distress increases, they are crowded together in the cities like cattle, without hope of deliverance in sight; they have only the choice of three things; conversion, emigration or death. It is just what the Procurator of the Holy Synod, Pobyedonostseff foresaw, when he demanded the application of the Ignatyeff Laws.

Other measures, besides this systematic crowding, were taken against the Jews. They were shut out of certain occupations and certain professions; those sheltered in hospitals as invalids were sent away; employees of railroads and steamship companies were dismissed; the number of those who could enter universities, colleges and high schools was limited; they were barred from becoming attorneys, physicians, engineers, or at least their opportunties for entering these professions were restricted; even their own schools were closed to them, they are not admittd even to hospitals, they are burdened with special taxes on their rents, inheritances, the animals they kill for meat, the candles they light on Friday evenings, the skull-caps they wear during religious ceremonies, even when these are of a private nature.

Besides these official taxes imposed by the government, the Jews are under the exploitation of the Russian administration and police, the basest, the most corrupt and venal in all Europe. Half the income of the middle class Jews, says Weber and Kempster, and Harold Frederic, goes to the police. Every Jew in easy circumstances is the victim of constant extortion. As for those (and they are the majority), who are too poor to be able to pay, they are subjected to the most loathsome, most inhuman treatment, forced to bow to all the whims of brutal policemen who domineer and martyrize them, as they martyrize also the nihilists and the suspects of liberalism whom the horrible autocracy of the Tsar places in their power. [174]

Why this treatment, this abominable persecution? Because, say the antisemites, these four and a half million Jews exploit the ninety million Kussians. How do they exploit them ? By usuary. Still nine-tenths of the Russian Jews own nothing, there are hardly ten to fifteen thousand Jews in Russia who possess capital. Of these ten to fifteen thousand some are merchants, others are money lenders and probably usurers; finally, an insignificant minority who have from time immemorial lived in villages, lend money to the peasants. True, these few were driven from the villages, but the merchants, financiers, and all those in general, who are rich and can pay for the privileges, were left quite undisturbed., If, therefore, the exploiters were aimed at, a mistake was made, because the artisans and poor wretches were chiefly hit by it. Has at least the condition of the peasants improved ? No. The Russian peasant, burdened with taxes since the time of his emancipation, exploited by the fisc and the officers of the gov-ernment agents, is the fated prey of usurers. The Jew's place was everywhere taken by the ***kulak*** [175] (a peasant

[174] The condition of the Jews in Russia, compared with that of the native people, is absolutely the same as in the Middle ***Ages.*** The Russian peasant and the workingman are pretty nearly as wretched as the Jew. They, too, are subjected to annoyances and arbitrary rule, but they are not persecuted, and have, to a certain degree the right of migrating.

[175] Russ. kulak, literally fist.

usurer), who, even previously had been playing havoc in all Russian villages where there were no Jews—i. e.j in the majority of the country districts. But no measures were taken against the ***kulak.*** Thus, the expulsion of the Jews has not for its object the protection of the peasants. They also turn people to drunkenness, we are asssured. But Katkoff, who could not be suspected of bias in favor of the Jews, said more than once that alcoholism is much more widespread in central and northern Russia, where there are no Jews, than in the Southwest, where they are engaged in inn-keeping. It is quite natural: alcohol, which becomes a necessity to the wretches whose nourishment is insufficient, is still more necessary in the cold countries. Though the Jews may not be saloon-keepers and others may replace them, yet the expulsion of the Jews is not a fight against alcoholism, as no measure has been taken against the Christian retailers who outnumber the Jewish retailers.

We shall not deal with the frauds with which Jewish business men are charged, as exactly these business men occupy a privileged position; as for the lawlessness of a part of the miserable mass, those of whom it is made up "would not have food if they did not rob," [176] and so they are in the same position with a great number of orthodox Russians whom the social and economic condition of Russia forces to resort to unscrupulous methods, in order to make a living. [177]

> [176] A great part of these grievances is better founded with reference to the Jews of Poland, and yet the Jews there are not driven back into cities as are those of the "pale of settlement."
>
> [177] Tikhomirov, loc. cit.

What are then the real causes of antisemitism ? They are political and religious. Antisemitism is by no means a popular movement in Russia; it is purely official. The Russian people, laden with misery, crushed under taxes, groaning under the most atrocious of tyrannies, embit-tered by administrative violence and governmental abuse of power, burdened with suffering and humiliation is in an unberable condi-tion. Generally resigned, they are liable to yield to passions; their uprisings and re-volts are formidable; antisemitic riots are the proper thing to divert popular anger, and that is why the government encouraged them and often provoked them. As to the peasants and workingmen, they fell upon the Jews because, they said, "the Jew and the nobleman are of a pair, only it is easy to thrash the Jew. [178] Thus is ex-plained the plundering of rich Jewish merchants, of wealthy money-lenders, often of poor Jewish workmen, and it is heart-rending to see these disinherited fall upon one another instead of uniting against the op-pressive tsarism.

The possibility of a union between these two camps of misery is, perhaps, fore-seen by those whose interest it is to engender and keep their antagonism and who actually saw the rioters burn many Christian houses during the riots of 1881 and 1882. After Alexander II.'s death it became urgent to blot out of the moujiks' and proletarians' memories the nihilists' attempts at liberation. The revolution was more than ever the frightful hydra and dragon, against which Holy Russ

[178] Tikhomirov, *loc, cit.*

was to be protected. To accomplish it a return to orthodox ideas was thought necessary. All evil, it was said, comes from the foreign, the heretical, that which pollutes the sacred soil. It was the theory of Ignatyeff, of Pobyed-onostseff, and of the Holy Synod, and doubtless of the unhappy Alexander III., whom fear drove insane, and whom Polyedonostseff guided like a weak-minded child. A rush was made against the Jews, just as measures were taken against Germans, Catholics, Lutherans, against all those who were not of the Slavic race and did not belong to the Greek orthodox church. [179] At all events, the persecution of the Jews was more active, for with regard to them no attention had to be paid to diplomatic discretion with which they came into a clash in the case of the Catholics, Lutherans or Germans. Had the Russian Catholics been massacred, all Europe would have arisen; the Jews could be killed with impunity. However, just like the Roumanian Jews, the Jews of Russia are distinguished from the rest of the population by their manners, customs and education—excepting an enlightened very intelligent minority of young Jews, who rushed into the universities before their doors were closed on them. They have an internal organization—the Kahal, which gives them a sort of self-government, and to denounce them as dangerous is easier, as well as of great benefit to established institutions and

[179] One of the queerest things is the approval given by certain religions antisemites of France and Germany—through chauvinism or passion—lo the actions of the Tsar's government In approving the Tsar's persecution against the Jews, they implicitly approve those against the Catholics and Lutherans, who are so dear to them.

the orthodox capitalists who thus escape the popular passions whose explosion is ever to be feared.

The religious origin of the official antisemitism has often been denied; yet it cannot be denied, and the Russians will yet probably give up even Panslavism in order to arrive at religious unity, a unity which to some of them, at least, seems indispensable for the unity of the State. The national and the religious question are but one in Russia, the Tsar being simultaneously the temporal and spiritual head, Caesar and Pope; but to faith more importance is attached than to race, and the proof is that a Jew who is willing to be converted is not perse-cuted. On the contrary, the Jew is encouraged to embrace orthodoxy. Prom fourteen years of age on, any Jewish child may be baptized against the will of his parents; a convert when married is free from the ties which unite him with his wife or children, a woman convert cancels her matrimonial ties by the very process of her conversion, but the non-converted consorts are always treated as married. Finally, when baptizing, adult converts receive from fifteen to thirty rubles, and children from seven to fifteen rubles. To induce the Jews still further to embrace the Greek faith, the rabbinical schools were suppressed; the number of synagogues was limited— the Moscow synagogue was closed up in 1892 as "an in-decent thing;"—JewB are even forbidden to gather for prayer. What then becomes of the antisemites' complaints against the Jews if they admit into their midst converted Jews, knowing as they do perfectly well that baptism would not make those who are not artisans, but middlemen and capitalists [180] change their positive function in the community.

Thus we may say that in eastern **Europe** where the actual condition of the Jews fairly well represents what had been their condition in the Middle Ages, the causes of antisemitism are twofold: social causes, and-religious causes combined with patriotic ones. It now remains for us to see what are the causes that maintain antisemitism in the countries where it has become antisemitism of the pen instead of legal antisemitism, and, first of all, to examine this transformation and the phenomena to which it has given rise.

> [180] I could but sketch the general outlines of Roumanian and Russian antisemitism. To make a complete story of them would require more than these few pages, within which it was impossible to give a social picture of Roumania and Russia, and to expound the moral, psychological, ethnologi-

cal and economic position of the Jews in these countries.

CHAPTER IX.

MODERN ANTISEMITISM AND ITS LITERATURE.

The Emancipated Jew and the Nations.—The Jews and the Economic Revolution.—The Bourgeoisie and the Jews.—The Transformation of Anti-Judaism., —Anti-Judaism and Antisemitism.—Instinctive Anti-Judaism and Antisemitism of the Reason.— Legal Anti-Judaism and Antisemitism or the Pen. —Classification of the Antisemitic Literature.— Christian Antisemitism and the Anti-Judaism of the Middle Ages.—Anti-Talmudism.—Gougenot de Mousseaux,, Chiarini, Rohling.—Christian-Socialist Antisemitism.—Barruel, Eckert, Don Deschamps.— Chabeauty.—Edouard Drumont and the Pastor Stoecker.--Economic Antisemitism.—Fourier and Proudhon; Toussenel, Capefigue, Otto Glaguu.— Ethnological and National Antisemitism.—Hegel-ianism and the Race Idea.—W. Marr, Treitschke, Schoenerer.—Metaphysical Antisemitism.—Schopenhauer.—Hegel and the Hegelian Extreme Left. —Max Stirner.—Dühring, Nietzsche and Anti-Christian Antisemitism.—Revolutionary Antisemitism.—Gustave Tridon.—The Complaints of the Antisemites, and the Causes of Antisemitism.

The emancipated Jews scattered among the nations just like strangers, and, as we have seen, it could not be otherwise, since for centuries they formed a nation among the nations, a special people preserving its characteristics thanks to the strict and precise ritual, as well as owing to the legislation which kept it apart and tended to perpetuate it. As conquerors, not as guests did they come into modern societies. They were like a penned-in flock; suddenly the barriers fell and they rushed upon the field opened to them. They were not warriors, what is more, the moment was not favorable to an expedition of a small band, but they made the only conquest for which they were armed, the economic conquest for which they had been preparing for so many long years. They were a race of merchants and money-dealers, perhaps degraded by mercantile practice, but, thanks to this very practice, equipped with qualities which were becoming preponderant in the new economic system. And so it was easy for them to take to commerce and finances, and, it must be repeated, they could not act otherwise. Crowded together, oppressed for centuries, ever curbed in their soarings, they had acquired a formidable power of expansion, and this power could find application in certain channels only; their efforts were limited, but their nature was not changed, and it was not changed on the day of their liberation either, and they marched ahead on the road which was familiar to them. However, the state of affairs was particularly favorable to them. At this period of great overthrows and reconstructions, when nations were being modified, new principles established, new social, moral and metaphysical conceptions wrought out, they were the only ones to be free. They were without any attachments to those surrounding them; they had no ancient patrimony to defend, the heritage which the former society was leaving to nascent society was not theirs; the thousand ancestral ties which linked the citizens of the modern state with the past, could not influence their conduct, their intellectuality, their morality; their spirit had no shackles.

I have shown that their liberation could not change them, that a number of them regretted their past of isolation, and even if they did endeavor to remain themselves, if they did not assimilate, they marvelously adapted themselves, by the very force of their special tendencies, to the economic conditions which had affected the nations since the beginning of the nineteenth century.

The French Revolution was above all an economic revolution. If it is considered as the termination of a struggle between classes, it must be viewed as the consummation of a struggle between two forms of capital, viz.: real property and personal property, or landed cap-ital, and industrial and speculative capital. With the supremacy of the nobility the supremacy of landed capital disappeared, too, and the supremacy of the bourgeoisie brought on the supremacy of industrial and speculative capital. The emancipation of the Jew is linked with the growth of the prevalence of industrial capital. So long as landed capital retained the political power, the Jew was deprived of any right; the Jew was liberated on the day when political power passed to industrial capital, and that proved fatal. The bourgeoisie needed help in the struggle it undertook; the Jew was for it a valuable ally, whom it was its interest to emancipate. Since the days of the Revolution, Jew and bourgeois marched hand in hand, together they sustained Napoleon at the moment when dictatorship be-came nec-essary to defend the privileges gained by the Third Estate, and when the imperial tyranny became too heavy and oppressive for capitalism the bourgeois and the Jew, united and preluded the fall of the Empire by forestalling provisions at the time of the Russian campaign and helped to bring about the final disaster by calling forth slumps at the exchange and buying the disloyalty of marshals.

At the beginning of the great industrial development, after 1815, when canal, mine, and insurance companies were formed, the Jews were among the most active in promoting combination of capital. Moreover, they were the most skilful, because the spirit of combination had for centuries been their only support. But they were not content to aid in bringing about in this practical way the triumph of industri-alism, they gave their aid in a theoretical way, also. They gathered around Saint-Simon, the philosopher of the bourgeoisie; they worked at diffusing and developing his teaching. Saint-Simon had said: [181] "The manufacturers must be entrusted with the administration of the temporal power," and "the last step that remains for industry to make is to obtain the direction of the State and the chief problem of our time is to secure to industry a majority

[181] Saint-Simon, ***Du Systeme industriel*** (Paris, 1821).

in our parliaments." He had added: [182] "The industrial class must occupy the first rank, because it is the most important of all; because it can do without all the others, while none other can do without it; because it exists by its own forces, by its personal labors. The other classes must work for it, because they are its creatures and because it sustains their existence; in a word, as everything is made by indus-try, everything must be made for it." The Jews helped to realize the Saint-Simonian dream; they proved themselves the most trustworthy allies of the bourgeoisie, inas-much as in working for it they worked for themselves and, in all Europe, they were in the front rank of the liberal movement, which from 1815 till 1848 succeeded in establishing the domination of bourgeois capitalism.

This role of the Jews did not escape the class of landed capitalists, and we shall see that therein lay one of the causes of the anti-Judaism of the conservatives, but to the Jews it was not worth so much as the recognition of the bourgeoisie. When the latter had firmly established its power, when it became restful and secure, it discovered that its ally, the Jew, was its formidable competitor, and it reacted against it. Thus the conservative parties, made up, as a rule, of capitalist agricultures, became anti-Jewish in their fight against industrial and speculative capitalism, represented chiefly by the Jew, and industrial and speculative capitalism became anti-Jewish in its turn, on account of Jewish competition. Anti-Judaism, which had been religious

[182] Saint-Simon, *Catechisme des Industriels, ler Cahier* (Paris, 1823).

at first, became economic, or, rather, the religions causes, which had once been dominant in anti-Judaism, were subordinated to economic and social causes.

This transformation, which corresponded with the change in the role played by the Jews, was not the only one. Once a matter of sentiment, the hostility towards the Jews became one of reason. The Christians of yesterday hated the deicides instinctively, and they never attempted to justify their animosity: they showed it. The antisemites of to-day conceived a desire to explain their hatred, i. e., they wanted to dignify it: anti-Judaism moulted into antisemitism. How was this anti-semitism manifested? It had no other way of expression but through the printing press. Official anti-semitism was dead in the West, or it was dying; as a result anti-Jewish legislation, too, was disappearing; there remained theoretical antisemitism, it was an opinion, a theory, but the antimesites had a very distinct object in view. Up to the time of the Revolu-tion literary anti-Judaism sustained legal anti-Judaism, since the Revolution and the emancipation of the Jews, literary antisemitism has striven to restore legal anti-Judaism in the countries where it no longer . exists. It has not, as yet, achieved that, and we have to study only the manifestations of the antisemitism of the pen, manifestations, some of which represent the opinion of the many, for, if literary antisemites have supplied reasons to the unconscious antisemites, they were produced by them; they attempted to explain what the flock felt, manifested, and if they have at times ascribed strange and improbable motives, they often but echoed the sentiments of their inspirers. What were these sentiments? We shall see if we examine the anti-semitic literature, and at the same time we shall disentangle the manifold causes of contemporary antisemit-ism.

Except in the case of some of them, it is impossible to classify the antisemitic works under too narrow categories, as each of them often presented manifold tendencies. Still they each have a dominant idea, in accordance with which their classification may be settled, always remembering that a work approaching a definite type does not belong solely and exclusively to it. We shall, then, subdivide antisemitism into Christian, Socialist, economic, ethnological and national, metaphysical, revolutionary and anti-Christian antisemitism.

Christian Socialist antisemitism was generated by the permanency of religious prejudices. If the Jews had not changed on entering into society, the sentiments felt toward them for so many long years would not have disappeared either. The Jews owed their emancipation to a philosophical movement coinciding with an economic movement and not to the abolition of secular prejudices against them. Those who thought the Chris-tion State the only State possible looked with disfavor upon the intrusion of the Jews, and anti-Talmudism was the first manifestation of this hostility. The Talmud which was justly considered the religious strong-hold of the Jews was assailed and a host of polemists devoted themselves to proving how much the teachings of the Talmud were opposed to the teachings of the Gospel. Against the book they resumed all the complaints of the controversialists of yore, those enumerated by the Jewish apostates in debates, and repeated in the thirteenth century by Raymund Martin, those raised by Pfefferkorn and later on by Eisenmenger. Not even the method or the make-up was changed; the same moulds were made use of; in writing pamphlets the same traditions were followed as those of the dominican inquisitors, and not a whit more of critical acumen was put to use in the study of the Talmudic "deep." Nevertheless, concerning the Jew, his dogmas, his race, the Christian antisemites of our time have the same notions as the Jews of the Middle Ages had. The Jew preoccupies and haunts them, they see him everywhere, they trace everything back to him, they have the same conception of history as had Bossuet. For the bishop, Juduea was the centre of the world; all events, disasters and joys, conquests and the downfalls, as well as the foundings of empires had for its primary, mysterious and ineffable cause the whims of a God faithful to the Bene-Israel, and this people, wanderer, founder of kingdoms and captive, in turn, had continually directed mankind toward its only goal: the coming of Christ. Ben Hadad and Sennacherib, Cyrus and Alexander, seem to exist only because Judah exists, and because Judah must now be exalted and then humiliated, until the hour when he will enjoin upon the world the law which must come from him. But what Bossuet had conceived for the purpose of unheard of glorification, the Christian antisemites renew that with quite opposite ends in view. For them the Jewish race, the scourge of the nations, scat-tered over the earth, accounts for the misfortunes and blessings of the alien nations in whose midst it had settled, and the history of the Hebrews once more becomes the history of monarchies and republics. Scourged or tolerated, banished or admitted, they, by the very fact of these political vicissitudes, account for the glory of the states or even their decadence. To tell the story of Israel, is to tell the story of Prance, or Germany, or Spain. This is what the Christian anti-semites see, and their antisemitism is thus purely theological, it is the antisemitism of the Fathers, that of Chrysostom, Saint Augustin, Saint Jerome. Before the birth of Jesus, the Jewish people was the chosen people, the beloved son of God; since the time it had disowned the Saviour, since it had become a deicide, it had become the fallen people par excellence, and having before brought the world's salvation, it now causes its ruin.

In certain works, as, e. g., in the little known book by Gougenot des Mousseaux, ***The Jew, Judaism and the Judaization of the Christian. Nations,*** [183] this conception is very clearly set forth. To Gougenot the Jews are "for ever the elect nation, the noblest and most august of nations, the nation issued from the blood of Abraham, to which we owe the mother of God." At the same time the Jews are the most perverse and unsociable of beings. How does he reconcile these contradictions? By opposing the Mosaic Jew to the Talmudist, the Bible to the Talmud. This is the way in which most of the Christian antisemites proceed. "Judaism and not Mosaism stands in the way of a radical reformation of the Jews,"

[183] Gougenot des Mousseaux, *Le Juif, le Judaisme et la Judai-action des peuples Chretiens* (Paris, 1869).

says the abbot Chiarini in a memoir composed as "a guide to reformers of the Jews." [184]

Whatever their affinities and kinship with the anti-Jews of the Middle Ages, the anti-Talmudists, at all events, take a little different point of view. Formerly, the blasphemies against the Christian religion were chiefly sought in the Talmud, or arguments in support of the divinity of Jesus Christ were sought there; hereafter this book's enemies hunt it especially as an anti-social, pernicious and destructive work. The Talmud, according to them, makes the Jew an enemy of all nations, but if some of them, like des Mousseaux and Chiarini are guided, like the theologians of yore, above all by the desire to bring Israel back to the bosom of the church, [185] others, like Doctor Rohling, [186] are rather inclined to suppress him and they declare him forever in-capable to be of any good. Quite the contrary; since, they say, not only are his teachings incompatible with the principles of Christian governments, but because he even seeks to ruin these governments in order to draw profit therefrom.

It is easy to understand that after the upsettings caused by the French Revolution, the conservatives felt

[184] Chiarini, *Theorie du Judaisme* (Paris, 1830).

[185] The anxiety for the future role of the Jews is expressed in a striking book by Leon Bloy, *Le Salut par lea Juifs* (Paris, 1892). In the volume of documents and notes written as a sequel to Dom Deschamps' work on *Secret socteties,* Claudio Jan net expresses the opinion that the Jews are undoubtedly destined to lead the world back to God. This is exactly the ancient theo-logical belief.

[186]Eng. translation. A. Rohling, *Le Juif selon le Talmud* (Paris, 1888). Translated from the German.

called upon to hold the Jews responsible for the destruction of the ancient regime. When they cast a glance around them after the storm had passed away, one of the things that must have given them the greatest surprise was surely the position of the Jew. But yesterday the Jew was nothing, he had no right, no power, and now he was shining in the front rank; not only was he rich, but he could even be doctor and govern the land, as he paid his tax. Him particularly did the social change favor. In the eyes of a representative of the past, of tradition, it looked as if a throne had been overthrown and European wars let loose solely in order that the Jew might acquire the citizen's rank, and the declaration of the Bights of Man seemed to have been but a declaration of the rights of the Jew. Accordingly, the Christian antisemites did not stop at being incensed at the Jews' speculations over national property or the military supply, [187] but applied to them the old juridical saying: fecisti qui prodes ("thou hast done it who profittest thereby.") If the Jew indeed had profited by the Revolution in this respect, if he had derived from it so great a benefit, it means that he had prepared them, or rather, to say, he had helped along with all his forces.

Nevertheless it was necessary to explain how this despised and hated Jew, considered a thing, had obtained the power of accomplishing such deeds, how he had prepared so formidable a might. Here comes in a theory, or rather a philosophy of history familiar to the Cath-

> [187] I do not mean to say that the Jews were the only ones to speculate in this way; on the contrary, they were in the insignificant minority among those who did the speculation.

olic polemists. According to these historians, the French Revolution whose counter blow has been universal, and which has transformed the institutions of Western Europe, was but the capping of a secular con-spiracy. Those who attribute it to the philosophical movement of the eighteenth century, to the excesses of monarchical governments, to a fatal economic change, to the decrepitude of a class, the enfeeblement of a form of capital, to the inevitable evolution of the ideas of authority and State, to the enlargement of the idea of an individual—all those are grievously in error, according to the historians I am speaking about. They are blind people who do not see the truth: the Revolution was the work of one or several sects, whose establishment goes back to great antiquity, sects brought out by the same desire and the same principle: the desire for domination and the principle of destruction. These sects proceeded according to a clearly defined, inexorably followed up plan—toward the destruction of monarchy and church; through their countless ramifications they covered Europe with a string of close meshes, and, with the help of the most underhand, abominable means, they succeeded in undermining the throne—the only upholder of social and religious order.

The Genesis of this conception of history is easy to find. It took its origin under the Terror itself. The part taken by the Masonic lodges, by the Illumines, the Red-Crosses, the Martinists, etc., in the Revolution, had vividly struck certain minds which were carried away to exaggerate the influence and role of these societies. A thing which particularly astonished these superficial observers, was the international character of the Revolution of 1789 and the simultaneousness of the movements it called forth. They contrasted its general effect with the local effect of the previous Revolutions, which had agitated, as, e. g., in England, only the countries where they took place, and, in order to account for this difference they attributed the work of centuries to a European association with representatives in the midst of all nations, rather than to admit that the same stage of civilization and similar intellectual, social, moral and economic causes, could have simultaneously produced the same effects. The very members of these lodges, of these societies, helped in spreading this belief. [188] They, too, exaggerated their importance, they not only asserted to have worked, during the eighteenth century, for the changes then in the process of preparation —which was true—but they even claimed to have been their distant initiators. This, however, is not the place to debate this question; suffice it to have stated the existence of these theories: we are going to show how they came to the assistance of the Christian antisemites.

The first writers to set forth these ideas confined themselves to stating the existence of "a peculiar nation which was born and had grown in darkness, amidst all civilized nations, for the purpose of subjecting all of them to its rule," [189] as, e. g., the cavalier de Malet, brother

[188] Louis Blanc, *Histoire de la Revolution Francaise,* vol. II, p. 74.

[189] *Recherches historiques et politiques qui prouvent Vexistence d'une secte revolutionnaire, son antique origine, son organisation, ses moyens ainsi que son but; et devoilent entierement tunique cause de la Revolution Francaise, par le Chevalier de Malet Paris, Gide fils, libraire, 1817.*

of the conspiring general, wanted to prove in a book, little-known and very poor at that. Men like P. Barruel, in his *Memoirs on Jacobinism,* [190] like Eckert in his works on Free Masonry, [191] like Dom Deschamps, [192] like Claudio Jannet, like Crétineau Joly, [193] have developed and systematized this theory, they have even endeavored to prove its reality and though they did not attain their aim, they have at least gathered all the elements necessary to undertake so curious a history as that of secret societies. In all their works, they were led to examine what had been the position of the Jews in these groups and sects, and, struck by the analogies presented by the mystagogic rites of Masonry as compared with certain Judaic and Kabbalistic traditions, [194] misled by the Hc-

[190] Barruel, *Memoires sur le Jacobinisme* (1797-1813). Father Barruel was the first to expound these ideas, and those who followed him have, properly speaking, only imitated or continued his work.

[191] Eckert, *La Frane-Maconnerie dans sa veritable signification* (Liege, 1854).— *La Franc-Maconnerie en ellememe* (Liege, 1859).

[192] Dom Deschamps, *Lee Societes Secretes et la Societe,* with an introduction, notes and documents by Claudio Jannet Paris, 1883.

[193] Cretineau Joly, *L'Englise romaine avant la Revolution.* Paris

1863.

[194] On the Hebrew traditions in Free-Masonry, and on the points of similarity between the Free-Masons and the ancient Essenians, of. Clavel, *Histoire pittoresque de la Franc-Maconnerie* (Paris, 1843); Kauffmann
et Cherpin, *Histoire philosophique de la Franc-Maconnerie* (Lyons,
1856) and an article by Moise Schwab on the Jews and the Free-Masons,
published in the *An-nuaire des Archives israelites pour l'an 5620*
(1889-1890). Consult also the various works of J. M. Ragou on Free-Masonry (Paris, Dentu).

brew pomp which characterizes the initiation in these lodges, they arrived at
the conclusion that the Jews had always been the inspirers, guides and masters of
Free-Masonry, nay, more than that, they had been its founders, and that they, with
its aid, persistently aimed at the destruction of the church, from the very time of its
foundation.

They went further in this path, they wanted to prove that the Jews had preserved
their national constitution, that they were still ruled by princes, the Nam, who led
them to the conquest of the world, and that these enemies of mankind possessed a
formidable organization and tactics. Gougenot des Mousseaux, [195] Rupert, [196]
de Saint-André, [197] the abbot Chabeauty,[198] have supported these assertions.
As for Edouard Drumont, the whole pseudo-historic portion of his books, when not
borrowed from father Loriquet, is nothing but a clumsy and uncritical plagiarism of
Barruel, Gougenot, of Dom Deschamps and Crétineau Joly. [199]

Whatever the case may be, with Drumont, as with pastor Stoecker, Christian
antisemitism transforms or

[195] Gougenot des Mousseaux, *loc. cit.*

[196] Rupert, *L'Eglise et la Synagogue* (Paris, 1859).

[197] De Saint-Andre, *Francs Macons et Juifs* (Paris, 1880).

[198] A Chabeauty, *Las Juifs nos Maitres* (Paris, 1883).

[199] It must be noted that in his France *Juive* (I mean in its first chapters) Drumont does not quote Gougenot des Mousseau or Barruel even once; he quotes, in passing, Dom Deschamps three times and Cretineau de Joly's *Vendee Militaire* once, and yet he laid these writers under heavy contribution. Unless his "historical documents" had been furnished him by the disciples of those I have just mentioned—that is quite possible. Let it be understood here, that this refers to Drumont as historian and not as polemist.

rather it borrows new weapons from several sociologists. TThough Drumont fights the Jew's anti-clericalism, though Stoecker, in his anxiety to win the name of a second Luther, rises against the Jewish religion as destructive of the Christian State, other preoccupations engage them; they attack Jewish wealth and attribute to Jews the economic transformation which is the work of the 19th century. They still persecute in the Jew, the enemy of Jesus, the murderer of a God, but they aim particularly at the financier, and therein they join hands with those who preach economic antisemitism.

This antisemitism has manifested itself since the be-ginning of Jewish financiering and industrialism. If we find only traces of it in Fourier [200] and Proudhon, who confined themselves to stating only the role of the Jew as middle-man, stock-jobber and non-producer, [201] it gave life to men like Toussenel [202] and Capefigue; [203] it inspired such books as *The Jews Kings of the Epoch* and the History of Great Financial Operations; and later on, in Germany, the pamphlets of Otto Glagau

[200] Fourier, *Le Nouveau Monde industriel et societaire* (Paris, librairie societaire, 1848).

[201] In Earl Marx (Annates franco-allemandes, 1844, p. 211) and in Lassalle, the same estimates of the parasite Jew may be found as in Fourier and Proudhon.

[202] Toussenel, ***Les Juifs rois de l'Epoque*** (Paris, 1847). Tous-senel followed up this book with a violent campaign in the newspaper, ***La Democratic pacifique.*** However, the antisemitic movement vas quite violent, under the July monarchy, and numerous pamphlets were published against the Jewish financiers.

[203] Capefigue, ***Histoire des grandes operations financiers*** (Paris, 1856).

against the Jewish bankers and brokers. [204] However, I have already pointed out the origin of this antisemitism, how, on the one hand, the landed capitalists held the Jew accountable for the predominance of industrial and financial capitalism, so hateful to them, how, on the other hand, the bourgeoisie, stocked with privileges, turned against the Jew, its erstwhile ally, henceforth its competitor and a foreign competitor at that; for to his position as a non-assimilated stranger the Jew owes the excessive animosity shown him, and thus economic antisemitism is bound up with ethnologic and national antisemitism.

This last form of antisemitism is modern, it was born in Germany, and from the Germans the French antisem-ites have derived their theory.

This doctrine of races, which Renan advocated in France [205] was wrought out in Germany under the influence of the Hegelian doctrines. It gained the ascendancy in 1840 and particularly in 1848, not only because German policy pressed it into service, but because it was in accord with the nationalist and patriotic movement that produced nations, and with that striving for unity which characterized all European nations.

The state, so they said, must be national; the nation

[204] Otto Glagau, ***Der Boersen und Grundergeschwindel in Berlin,*** (Leipzig, 1876). ***Let bcsoins de l'Empire ei le nouveau Kulturkampf*** (Osnabruck, 1879).

[205] During the last years of his life Renan had given up his theory of races, their inequality and their mutual superiority or inferiority. These theories will be found set forth quite clearly and lucidly in Gobineau's in many ways remarkable book, *L'in-egalite des races* (Paris, Firmin Didot 1884).

must be one, and must include all the individuals speaking the national language and belonging to the same race. More than that, it is of importance that this national State reduce all the heterogeneous elements, i. e., the foreigners. For the Jew, not being an Aryan, has not the same moral, social and intellectual conceptions as the Aryan; he is irreducible, and therefore he must -be eliminated, or else he will ruin the nations that have received him, and some among the nationalist and ethnologic antisemites assert that the work has already been accomplished.

These notions, resumed since then by von Treitschke [206] and Adolph Wagner in Germay, by Schoenerer in Austria, Pattai in Hungary and, at a much later date, by Drumont in France [207], were reduced, for the first time, to a system by W. Marr, in a pamphlet which had a certain echo in France: *The Victory of Judaism over Germanism.*[208] In it Marr declared Germany the prey of a conquering race, the Jews, a race possessing everything

[206] H. von Treitschke, *Ein Wort ueber unser Judenthum* (A Word about Our J ews). Berlin, 1888.

[207] Drumont is the type of the assimiiator antisemite who has flourished in France these last years, and who has overrun Germany. A talented polemist, vigorous journalist and sprightly satirist, Drumont is a historian of poor documentary evidence, a mediocre sociologist and especially philosopher, and can under no circumstances be compared with men of H. von Treitschke's, Adolph Wagner's and Eugen Duhring's standing. Yet, in the development of antisemitism in France and Germany even he has played a considerable role, and he has exercised a great influence as a propagandist.

[208] W. Marr, *Der Sieg des Judenthums ueber das Germvanthum* (Berne, 1879). In the *Journal des Debats* of Nov. 5, 1870, Bourdeau de-

voted an essay to this pamphlet.

and wanting to judaize Germany, like France, however, and he concluded by saying that Germany was lost. To his ethnologic antisemitism he even admixed the metaphysical antisemitism which, if I may say so, Schopenhauer had professed, [209] the antisemitism consisting in combatting the optimism of the Jewish religion, an optimism which Schopenhauer found low and degrading, and with which he contrasted Greek and Hindoo religious conceptions.

But Schopenhauer and Marr are not the only representatives of philosophical antisemitism. The whole of German metaphysics combatted the Jewish spirit, which it considered essentially different from the *Germanic spirit,* and which for it stood for the past as contrasted with the present. While the Spirit is realized in the world's history, while it advances, the Jews remain at a lower stage. Such is the Hegelian thought, that of Hegel and also of his disciples of the extreme left— Feuerbach, Arnold Huge and Bruno Bauer. [210] Max Stir-

[209] "A God like that Jehovah," says Schopenhauer, "who, as *animi causa,* for its own pleasure and from the *joy of heart* produces this world of misery and lamentations, and who even glories in it and applauds himself with his —this is too much. Let us then, at this point, consider the religion of the Jews as the last among the religious doctrines of the civilized nations, and this will be in perfect accord with the fact that it is the only one that has absolutely not a trace of immortality." (*Parerga und Paralipomeno,* v. II, ch. XII, p. 312, Leipzig 1874).

[210] We shall return to this question in our *Economic History of the Jews,* when speaking of the role of the Jews in Germany in the nineteenth century.—Cf. Hegel, *Philosophie des Rechts;* Arnold Huge, *Zwei Jahre in Paris;* Bruno Bauer, *Dic Juden-frage;* L. Feuerbach, *Das Wesen des Christenthums.*

Ner [211] developed these ideas with much precision. To his mind, universal history has until now passed through two ages: the first, represented by antiquity, during which we had to work out and eliminate "the negro stage of the soul;" the second, that of Mongolism, represented by the Christian period. During the first age man depended upon things, during the second he is swayed by ideas, waiting until he can dominate them and free himself. But the Jews, these precociously wise children of antiquity, have not passed out of this *negro stage of the soul.* In spite of all their sagacity and their intelligence, which, with little effort, masters things and makes them subserve man, they cannot discover the spirit which consists in holding things as not having happened. In Dühring we find another more ethical than metaphysical form of philosophical antisemtism. In several treatises, pamphlets and books, [212] Dühring assails the Semitic spirit and the Semitic conception of the divine and of ethics, which he contrasts with the conception of the Northern peoples. Pushing the deductions from his premises to their logical end and still following up Bruno Bauer's doctrine, he assails Christianity which is the last mani-festation of the Semitic spirit: "Christianity," says he, "has above all no practical morality such as is not capable of ambiguous interpretation and thus might be available and sane. The nations will, therefore, not be done

[211] Max Stirner, *Der Einzige und sein Eigenthum.* Leipzig, 1882, pp. 22, 25, 31, 69.

[212] Particularly in *The Parties and the Jewish Question. Die Juden-frage als Frage der Racenschaedlichkeit.*

with the Semitic spirit until they have expelled from their spirit this present second aspect of Hebraism."

After Dühring, Nietzsche, [213] in his turn, combatted Jewish and Christian ethics, which, according to him, are the *ethics of slaves* as contrasted with *the ethics of masters.* Through the prophets and Jesus, the Jews and the Christians have set up low and noxious conceptions which consist in the deification of the weak, the humble, the wretched, and sacrificing to it the strong, the proud, the mighty.

Several revolutionary atheists, Gustave Tridon [214] and Regnard [215] among them, have espoused, in France, this Christian antisemitism which, in its final analysis, is reduced to the ethnologic antisemitism, just like as is the strictly metaphysical antisemitism.

The different varieties of antisemitism may, then, be reduced to three: Christian antisemitism, economic antisemitism, and ethnologic antisemitism. In our examination just made we have pointed out that the grievances of the antisemites were religious grievances, social grievances, ethnologic grievances, national grievances, intellectual and moral grievances. To the antisemite the Jew is an individual of a foreign race, incapable of adapting himself, hostile to Christian civilization and religion; immoral, antisocial, of an intellectuality different from the Aryan intellectuality, and, to cap it all, a depredator and wrongdoer.

[213] Frierich Nietzche, Human, all too Human (1879), Beyond Good and Evil; The Genealogy of Morality (1887).

[214] Gustave Tridon, *Du Molochitme juif.* (Bruxelles, 1884).

[215] A. Regnard, *Aryens et Semites.* (Paris, 1890).

We shall now examine these grievances in regular order. We shall see whether they are well-founded i. e., whether the real causes of contemporary antisemi-tism correspond to them, or they are but prejudices. Let us first turn to the study of the ethnologic grievance.

CHAPTER X.

THE RACE.

The Ethnologic Grievance.—The Inequality of Races.— Semites and Aryans.— Aryan Superiority.—The Struggle of Semites and Aryans.—The Semitic Share in the so-called Aryan Civilizations.—The Semitic Colonization.—The First Years of the Christian Era and the Judeo-Christians.—The Jewish Elements in the European Nations.—The Idea of Race Among the Jews.—Jewish Superiority.—The Origins of the Jewish Race.—Foreign Elements in the Jewish Race.—Jewish Prosely-tism.—In Pagan Antiquity.—After the Christian Era.—The Uralo-Altaic Infiltrations in the Jewish Race.—The Khazars and the Peoples of the Cau-casus.—Different Varieties of Jews.—Dolichoceph-als and Brachycephals.—Ashkenazim and Sephar-dim.— The Jews of China, India and Abyssinia.— Modification Through Surroundings and Language. Jewish Unity. — Nationality.

The Jew is a Semite, he belongs to a strange, noxious, disturbing and inferior race—such is the ethnologic grievance of the antisemites. What does it rest upon? It rests upon an anthropological theory which had given rise or at least justification to an historical theory: the doctrine of the inequality of races, of which we must speak first of all.

Since the eighteenth century attempts have been made to classify men and distribute them under well-defined, distinct and separate categories. As a basis for it quite different indices were taken: the section of the hair— oval section for negroes with woolly hair, or round sec-tion; [216] the shape of the skull—broad or elongat-ed; [217] the color of the skin. This last classification has prevailed: nowadays three races of mankind—the negro, the yellow, and the white race—are distinguished. Different aptitudes are ascribed to these races, and they are arranged in the order of their superiority in a ladder of which the negro race occupies the lowest and the white race the highest round. Similarly, in order to account still better for this hi-erarchy of the human races, the religious doctrine of monogenism, which declares that mankind has descended from a single couple,—is rejected, and against it is set up polygenism which admits of the simultaneous appearance of numerous different couples,—a more logical and rational conception and more in keeping with real-ity.

Has this classification any serious and actual bases? Does the belief in mono-genism or in polygenism allow of

[216] Ulotrichi and Leiotrichi.

[217] Brachyciphals and Dolichocephals.

asserting that there are elect and reprobate races? Not by any means. If monogenism is accepted, it is evident that men, as descendants of one common pair, possess the same qualities, the same blood, the same physical and psychic constitution. If, on the contrary, polygenism, i. e., the initial existence of an indefinite and considerable number of heterogeneous bands inhabiting the earth, is accepted, it becomes impossible to maintain the existence of originally superior or inferior races, for the first social groupings were effected through the amalgamation of these heterogeneous bands whose respective qualities and virtues we should not be able to determine, and, still less, to classify. "All nations," says Gumplowicz, [218] "the most primitive that we meet with at the first dawn of historic times, will be for us the products of a process of amalgamation (already ended during the prehistoric times) among the heterogeneous ethnic elements." Thus, if the point of view of the identity of origin is taken, the ethnologic hierarchy is inadmissible, and, with Alexander von Humboldt, it may be asserted that" there are no ethnic stems that are nobler than others."

Race is, however, a fiction. No human group exists that can boast of having had two original ancestors and having descended from them without any adulteration of the primitive stock through mixture; human races are not pure, i. e., strictly speaking, there is no such thing as a race. "There is no unity," says Topinard : 1 the races have divided, scattered, blended, intercrossed in all degrees and directions since thousands of centuries; most of them gave up their language in favor of that of their

[218] L. Gumplowicz, LA Lutte des races (Paris, 1893).

conquerors, then gave the same up for a third, if not a fourth language; the principal masses have disappeared and now we find ourselves face to face with peoples and not races." The anthropologic classification of mankind has consequently no value whatever.

It is true that, in default of anthropologic characteristics, the partisans of the ethnologic hierarchy, fall back upon linguistic characteristics. As languages are classified according to their evolution into monosyllabic, agglutinative, inflectional and analytical—the "election" or "reprobation" of those who speak them has been established on the basis of these various forms of language. This claim is at all events untenable, for the Chinese, with their monosyllabic language, are inferior neither to the Yakuts nor the Kamchatkans, whose speech is ag-glutinative, nor to the Zulus who speak an inflectional language; and it would be easy to prove that the Japanese and Magyars, whose language is agglutinative are in no way inferior to certain so-called Aryan nations speaking an inflectional language. Still, we know that the fact of speaking the same language does not imply the identity of origin; conquering races have from times immemorial forced their language upon other strange races, though these latter had no inborn tastes for it; the classification of languages can, consequently, in no way determine the ethnic classification of mankind.

Nevertheless, and however untenable this doctrine of the inequality of races, whether from the linguistic or from the anthropologic point of view, it has been quite dominant in our times, and nations have chased and still chase this chimera of ethnologic unity, which is but the heritage of an ill-informed past and, truth to tell, a form of regress. Antiquity had the greatest claims to purity of blood, and at present the race idea is most widespread and most deeply rooted among the African negroes and certain savages. This is simple. The first collective ties were blood ties; the first social unit, the family, was founded on blood; the city was considered as the family enlarged, and at the historical dawn of every city, legend placed an ancestral couple, just as an initial couple was placed in certain religions, at the early stage of mankind. [219] When new human elements came upon these agglomerations, it was necessary to perpetuate this belief in the original identity, and this was attained by the fiction of adoption, and in these remote civilizations only the child of the tribe or city, or the adopted one, had a place. In all primitive legislations, the foreigner was an enemy against whom precaution was necessary, a disturber who perplexed beliefs and ideas. At the same time collective bodies became less uniform as they grew. If an interrupted filiation is considered the exclusive mark of unity,—we have seen that even in the prehistoric times vast hordes had been formed through the agglomeration of heterogeneous bands and that the first historic states had, in their turn been made up through the ag-

> [219] The tenth chapter of Genesis presents one of the most perfect types of this belief, in the genealogy of the descendants of Noah's sons; an ancestor is placed at the head of each human group of each nation.

glomeration of these hordes, who could no longer claim the same ancestor for each of its members. In spite of all, this idea of the community of origin has survived till our days. That is because it takes its origin in an essential need: the need of homogeneity, unity, the need which impels all societies to reduce their dissimilar elements, and this belief in the purity of blood is but an external manifestation of the need of unity, it is a way of expressing this necessity, a neat, simple and satisfactory way for the unconscious and the savage, but at all events insufficient and particularly undemonstrable for him who is not satisfied with the appearance of things.

All the same the theory of the inequality of races rests on a real fact; its formula ought to be: the inequality of nations, for there is every evidence that the destiny of different nations has not been similar, but this does not mean that the inequality of these nations was original. It simply means that certain nations were placed in more favorable geographical, climatic and historical conditions than those enjoyed by other nations, and that, consequently, they could develop more happily, more harmoniously; but not that they had better dispositions or better-formed brains. The proof thereof is in the fact that certain nations of the would-be superior white race have founded civilizations by far inferior to those of the yellow or even the negro races. There are not, therefore, any *originally* superior peoples or races, but there are nations which "*under certain conditions* have founded more powerful monarchies *and more lasting civiliza-tions.*" [220]

[220] Leon Metchnikoff, *La Civilisation et les Grands Fleuves.*

Whatever they be, true or false, these ethnologic principles which concern us, have, by the very fact of their existence,—been one of the causes of antisemitism; they have supplied a scientific appearance to a phenomenon which we shall later recognize as national and economic and, through them, the grievances of the anti-semites were fortified with pseudo-historical and pseudo-anthropological arguments. Indeed, not only was the existence admitted of three races,—negro, yellow and white, —ranged in hierarchic order, but even in these races subdivisions, categories, were established. At first it was asserted that the white race alone and some families of the yellow race were capable of founding superior civilizations; presently this white race was divided into two branches: the Aryan race and the Semitic race; finally it was maintained that the Aryan must be considered the most perfect race. Even in our days the Aryan race has been subdivided into groups, and this enabled anthropologists and chauvinistic ethnologists to declare either that the Celtic or the Germanic group must be considered as the pure wheat of this Aryan race, already superior as it was. Modern historians place at the basis of Oriental antiquity this problem which, though insoluble, they deem paramount. To which stock do the ancient nations belong? Are they Aryans, Turanians or Semites ? This is the question put at the outset of all researches on the nations of the Orient. Thus, consciously or unconsciously, history is modeled after the ethnic tables of Genesis—tables also met with among the Babylonians and the primitive Greeks—which accounted in a rudimentary way for the diversity of human groups, by the existence of sprouts issued from single parents, each sprout then producing a nation. Thus it is the Bible again that lends assistance to the antisemites, for in ethnography and history we are still clinging to the explanations of the Genesis—Shem, Ham and Japhet, only replaced by the Semite, the Turanian and the Aryan, however impossible it may be to justify these divisions linguistically, anthropologically or historically. [221]

Without stopping to discuss whether the negro races are capable of civilization or not [222] we must see what is understood under the names Aryans and Semites.

Aryans is the name of all peoples whose language is derived from Sanskrit, a language spoken by a human group called arya. Now, this group "presents no scientifically demonstrable unity except from the exclusively linguistic point of view." [223] All anthropologic unity is undemonstrable: the cranial measurements, indices, numbers, furnish no proof. In this Aryan chaos are found Semitic types, Mongolian types, all types and all varieties of types, from the one which is capable of de-

[221] The classification is pretty nearly of a piece, with the claim of the feudal classes, who justified, in the Middle Ages, their tyranny by pretending to be Japhetites, while the peasant and the serf were Hamites, a fact which made legitimate the relations of superior and inferior.

[222] We know that that wonderful civilization of Ancient Egypt was in great part the work of negroes, who were helped by the reds, the Semites, Turanians and some of those white tribes, in our days still represented by the African Tuaregs, who have never founded any society or anything lasting. There still exist in Africa imposing ruins which testify to the existence of a negro civilization, strongly developed at one historical epoch.

[223] Leon Metchnikoff, *loc. cit.*

veloping morally, intellectually and socially, np to the one that remains in everlasting mediocrity. There may be observed dolichocephals and brachycephals, men with brown skin, others with yellowish and yet others with white skin. Still, despite the fact that some tribes of Aryan language had no development perceptibly superior to that of some agglomerations of negroes, it is not a whit less energetically asserted that the Aryan is the most beautiful and noblest of the races, that it is the productive and creative race *par excellence,* that to it we are indebted for the most wonderful metaphysics, the most magnificent lyric, religious and ethical productions and that no other race ever was or is susceptible of a like expansion. To arrive at such a result, an abstraction is naturally made from the indisputable fact that all his-torical organisms had been formed of the most dissimilar elements, whose respective share in the common work it is impossible to determine.

The Aryan race, then, is superior, and it has proven its superiority by resisting the rule of a fraternal and rival race—the Semitic. This latter is a ferocious, brutal race, incapable of creative power, devoid of any ideal, and Universal History is represented as the history of the conflict between the Aryan and the Semitic race, a conflict which we witness even at present. Each anti-semite affords proof of this secular conflict. Even the Trojan War becomes, with some, the struggle between the Aryan and the Semite, and through the exigencies of the case, Paris becomes a Semitic brigand who ravishes Aryan beauties. Later on the Median Wars form a phase of this great contest, and the great king is pictured as the leader of the Semitic Orient falling upon the Aryan Occident; then it is Carthage disputing with Rome over the Empire of the World; then Islam advances against Christendom, and all through it is pointed with pleasure that the Greek has defeated the Trojan and Artaxerxes, that Rome triumphed over Carthage, and Charles Martel checked Abder-Rahman. Just as they recognize Semites in the Trojans, the apologists of the Aryans (on the other hand) do not want to see anything but Aryans in those heterogeneous and barbarous hordes that besieged the wealthy Ilium and in the Medes who subjugated Assyria and of whom only one tribe—the Arya-Zantha—was Aryan, while the majority was Turanian, no doubt. They want to prove that Summer and Accad, the educators of the Semites—were Aryans, and some have ascribed this noble origin even to ancient Egypt. They have done even something better than that with Semitic civilizations, they have computed the good and the evil, and nowadays it is an article of antisemitic faith, that whatever is acceptable or perfect in Semitism had been borrowed of the Aryans.

The Christian antisemites have thus reconciled their faith with their animosity, and not stopping short even before heresy, they have admitted that the prophets and Jesus were Aryans, [224] while the anti-Christian antisemites

> [224] This theory, which has the immense advantage of not resting on any foundation, sprang up in Germany and passed from there into France and Belgium. De Biez and Edmond Picard have in turn upheld it, but they did not bring any even illusory proof in support of their assertions. (Cf. Antisemiten—Spiegel, pp. 132, s22., Danzig, 1892).

consider the Galilean and the nobis (prophets) as deserving condemnation and inferior Semites.

Does what we know of the history of ancient and modern nations give us the right to accept as genuine this rivalry, this struggle, this instinctive opposition between the Aryan and the Semitic race? By no means, since Semites and Aryans have intermingled in a continuous way, and since the Semitic share in all so-called Aryan civilizations is considerable. Ten centuries before the Christian era the Phoenician cities of the Mediterranean had sent out emigrants to the islands, and, after founding cities which covered the Northern coast of Africa, from Hadrumete and Carthage to the Canary Islands, successively colonized Greece, which the Aryan invaders found so peopled by yellow natives and Semitic colonists that Athens was an entirely Semitic city. The case was the same in Italy, Spain, France, where the Phoenician navigators, e. g., founded Nimes just as they had founded Thebes in Boeotia and came to Marseilles just as they had made land in Africa. These diverse elements amalgamated later on and were brought into harmony through the effect of the climate, mental, intellectual and moral surroundings, but they did not remain inactive. The Semites transformed the Hellenic genius, i. e., by introducing into it strange elements, they gave it an opportunity of modifying itself. From this point of view, the history of Hellenic myths is curious and instructive, and this Semitic contribution may be grasped by comparing Hercules to Melkart, or Ashtoreth to Aphrodite. Likewise, the Phoenician cups and vases, exported in great numbers by the merchants of Tyre and Sidon, served as models for the Greek artists, and thus enabled the subtle mind of the Ionians and Dorians to interpret the myths represented on them, and the Phoenician image-trade helped out much the Greek iconologic mythology. [225] Again, the Phoenicians brought to the Hellenes the alphabet borrowed from the hieroglyphics of ancient Egypt; they taught them the mining industry and the working of metals, just as Assyria's pupil, Asia Minor, made them familiar with sculpture, and we still possess monuments testifying to this influence.—*e. g.,* the lions of the Mycenaean Acropolis and those Hellenic goddesses which have preserved the types we meet with on the Babylonian baked-clay tablets. With their marvelous sense of harmony and beauty, with their science of order, of orchestration, as it were, they wrought up these oriental ideas, transformed and purified them, but, for all that, the Greek people was an amalgam of quite different Aryan, Turanian and Semitic, even perhaps Hamitic, races, and it owed its genius to causes other than the nobility and purity of its origin.

Still the modern antisemites would rigorously admit the importance of the Semites in the history of civilization, but would make a classification even there. There are, they say, superior and inferior Semites. The Jew is the latter type, of the Semites, essentially unproductive, from whom men have received nothing and who can give nothing. It is impossible to accept this assertion. It is true that the Jewish nation has never displayed any

[225] Cf. Clermont-Ganneau, *L'Imagerie phenicienne et la Mythologic iconologique chest let Grecs.* Paris, 1880; and Let *An-tiquites orientates,* Paris, 1890.

great aptitudes for the plastic arts, but, through the voice of its prophets, it has accomplished a moral work by which every nation has been benefited; it has worked out some of those ethical and social ideas which are the leaven of humanity; if it has not had any divine sculptors and painters, it has had wonderful poets, it has, above all, had moralists who had worked for universal brotherhood, prophetic pamphleteers who made living and immortal the idea of justice, and Isaiah, Jeremiah, Ezekiel, despite their violence, fierceness even, have made heard the voice of suffering which wants not only to be protected against execrable force, but to be freed from it.

However, if the Phoenician element had incorporated itself with the Pelasgian, Hellenic, Latin, Celtic and Iberian elements, the Jewish element, by intermingling with others, has also contributed to the formation of those agglomerations which later on united to form the modern nations. The Jew, too, came to sink and disappear in that enormous crucible which Asia Minor presented, and where the most diverse nations were cast. Slowly hellenized, the Jews in Alexandria turned the city into one of the most active centres of Christian propa-ganda. They were among the first to convert; they formed the nucleus of the primitive Church in Alexandria, Antioch, Rome, and after the disappearance of the Ebionites they were absorbed in the total mass of Greek and Soman converts.

Throughout the Middle Ages Jewish blood was inter- mingling with Christian blood. Cases of wholesale conversion were exceedingly numerous, and it would make interesting reading to recount those of the Jews of Braine, [226] of Tortosa, [227] those of Clermont converted by Avi-tus, the 25,000 converted, as tradition goes, by Vincent Ferrer,—all of whom disappeared in the midst of the nations among whom they lived. If the Inquisition hindered, or at least tried to hinder, judaization, it favored the absorption of the Jews, and were the Christian anti-semites logical they would curse Torquemada and his successors, who helped to pollute Aryan purity by the adjunction of the Jew. The number of Marranos in Spain was enormous. In nearly all Spanish families, a Jew or a Moor is found at some point of their genealogy; "the noblest houses are full of Jews," they said, [228] and the cardinal Mendoza y Bovadilla wrote in the sixteenth century a pamphlet on the flaws in Spanish lineages. [229] It was the same everywhere, and from the number of apostates antagonizing their former coreligionists we have ascertained that the Jews were accessible to Christian seduction.

We have thus made answer to those who maintain the purity of the Aryan race; we have pointed out that this race, like all the others, was a product of countless mixtures. Not to speak of the prehistoric times we have made it clear that the Persian, Macedonian and Roman conquests made worse the ethnologic confusion which in-

[226] Saint-Prioux, ***Histoire de Braine.***

[227] The Jews of Tortosa converted in thousands after the conference opened at the instigation of Jerome de Santa Fe.

[228] ***Centinela contra Judios.***

[229] Francisco Mendoza y Bovadilla, ***El Tizon de la Nobleza Es-pano-***

la, o maculas y sambenitos de sus Linajes (Barcelona, 1880; Bibliotheca de obras raras).—Cf. also Llorente, ***Histoire de l'Inquisition*** (Paris,
1817).

creased in Europe still further during the invasions. The so-called Indo-German-
ic races, stock-full of alluvions even before, intermingled with Chudians, Ugrians,
Uralo-Altaians. Those among the Europeans who believe themselves descended in
line direct from Aryan ancestors do not keep in mind those so diverse lands which
these ancestors had traversed in their long journeys, nor all the tribes which they
had swept along with them, nor all those which they found settled wherever they
tarried,— tribes of unknown races and of uncertain origin, obscure and unknown
tribes whose blood is still running in the veins of those who boast themselves heirs
of the legendary and noble Aryans, as the blood of the yellow Dasyus and black
Dravidians flows under the skin of the white Arya-Hindoos.

But the idea of Semitic superiority is in no way more justifiable than the idea
of Aryan superiority, and yet it was upheld with as much verisimilitude. Theorists
were found who asserted and even tried to prove that the Semites were the flower
of mankind, and that from them came whatever good there was in the Aryans.
Surely one day there will appear, if it has not yet happened, an ethnologist who will
be led by his patriotism to prove with equal obviousness that the Turanian ought to
occupy the highest place in history and anthropology.

At present, the Jews—who consider themselves the highest incarnation of
Semitism—help in perpetuating this belief in the inequality and hierarchy of races.
The ethnologic prejudice is universal, and those even who suffer from it are its
most tenacious upholders. Antisem-ites and philosemites join hands to defend the
same doctrines, they part company only when it comes to award the supremacy.
If the antisemite reproaches the Jew for being a part of a strange and base race, the
Jew vaunts of belonging to an elect and superior race; to his nobility and antiquity
he attaches the highest importance and even now he is the prey of patriotic pride.
Though no longer a nation, though protesting against those who see in him the representative of a nation encamped among strange nations, he nevertheless harbors in

the depth of his heart this absurdly vain conviction, and thus he is like the chauvinists of all lands. Like them he claims to be of pure origin, while his assertion is no more well-founded, and we have to examine closely the assertion of Israel's enemy and of Israel himself: to wit, that the Jews are the most united. stable, inpenetrable, irre-ducible nation.

We possess no documents to determine the ethnology of the nomadic Bene-Israel, but probable it is that the twelve tribes constituting this people, according to the tradition, did not belong to a single stock. They were doubtless heterogeneous tribes, for, in spite of its legends, the Jewish nation cannot, any more than the other nations, boast of having originated from a single couple, and the current conception which represents the Hebrew tribe as subdividing into sub-tribes [230] is but a legendary and traditional conception,—that of the Genesis,—and one which a portion of historians of the Hebrews have wrongly accepted. Already composed of various unities among which doubtless were Turanian and Kushite

[230] Ernest Renan, *Histoire du peuple d'Israel,* v. I.

groups, i.e., yellows and blacks, [231] the Jews added still other strange elements while living in Egypt and in the land of Canaan which they conquered. Later on Gog and Magog, the Scythians, coming in Josiah's reign to Jerusalem's gates, probably left their impress on Israel. But starting with the first captivity the mixtures grow in number. "During the Babylonian captivity," says Mai-monides, [232] "the Israelites mingled with all sorts of foreign races and had children, who formed, owing to these unions, a kind of a new confusion of tongues," and yet this Babylonia, where there were cities like Mahuza, almost entirely peopled by Persians converted to Judaism, was deemed to contain Jews of a purer race than the Jews of Palestine. Said an old proverb: "For the purity of the race, the difference between the Jews of the Ro-man provinces is just as perceptible as the difference between dough of mediocre quality and dough made of the flour of meal; but, compared to Babylonia, Judea itself is like mediocre dough."

This means that Judea had undergone many vicissitudes. It had. always been the transit ground for the Mizraim and Assur; afterwards, on returning from captivity, the Jews united with the Samaritans, Edomites and Moabites. After the conquest of Idumea by Hyrcan,

> [231]Three elements are found at the basis of every civilization: the white, the yellow and the black. We see it in Egypt, where they adjoined a red element, in Mesopotamia, in India, every-where where great empires arose, and it may almost be asserted that the co-operation of these three types of mankind is necessary to establish durable civilizations.

> [232] Maimonides, *Yad Hazaka* (the powerful hand), Part I, chap. 1, J4.

there were Jewish and Idumean unions, and it was said that, during the war with Rome, the Latin conquerors had begotten sons. "Are we perfectly sure," said Rabbi Ulla, melancholically, to Judah-ben Ezekiel, "that we are not descended from pagans who dishonored the young daughters of Zion after the capture of Jerusalem?"

But what was most conducive to the introduction of foreign blood into the Jewish nation was proselytism. The Jews were a propagandist nation *par excellence,* and from the construction of the Second Temple and particularly after the dispersion, their zeal was considerable. They were exactly those of whom the Gospel says, that they ran over "earth and sea to make a proselyte," [233] and with perfect right could Rabbi Eliezer exclaim: "Where-fore has God scattered the Jews among the nations? To recruit for Him proselytes everywhere." [234] There are abundant proofs of the proselyting ardor of the Jews, [235] and during the first centuries before the Christian era Judaism spread with the same vigor as characterized Christianity and Mohammedanism later on. Rome, Alexandria, Antioch—where nearly all the Jews were converted gentiles—Damask, Cyprus were the centres of fusion, as I have already pointed out. [236] Nay, more, the Hasmonide conquerors compelled the vanquished Syrians to circumcise; kings, carrying their subjects along, converted, as, e. g., the family of Adiabenus, and the pop-

[233] Matth. xxiii.

[234] Talmud Babli, *Pesaohim,* f. 87.

[235] Horace, Sat. IV, 143.—Josephus Bell. *Jud.,* vii, III., 3.— Dio Camilla, xxxvii, xvii, etc., etc.

[236] Cf. Ch. II; ch. III and ch. IV.

illation was very mixed in certain cantons of Palestine itself, as was the case with Galilea, in that "circle of gen-tiles" where Jesus was to be born.

The Jewish propaganda did not cease after the Christian era, it was practiced even by force, and when, tinder Heraclius, Benjamin of Tiberias conquered Judaea, the Palestinian Christians converted by the wholesale. The persistence—the continuity of this propaganda as I have said, was one of the causes of theologic antisemitism. For centuries long, the councils legislated, and measures were taken to prevent the Jews from attracting the believers to them, to forbid them to circumcise their slaves, to prohibit them to marry Christians. But up to the moment of general persecutions, i. e., until it became dangerous to be a Jew, the canonic prescripts were powerless to check these proselytisms and, at times, when a great event took place or a scandal broke out, we can see Jewish propaganda at work. A bishop, converted in 514, afterwards the deacon Bodon, [237] demands circumcision and assumes the name of Eliezer. Often the popes intervene with their bulls—as e. g., Clement IV, in 1255.and Honorius IV, in 1288. The kings even take a hand in the matter, as did Phillip the Fair, who, in 1298, in-structed the justiciars of the realm "to punish the Jews who convert to their own faith Christians, by means of gifts."

All over Europe the Jews attracted proselytes, thus rejuvenating their blood by the admixture of new blood. They made converts in Spain where successive councils at Toledo forbade mixed marriages; in Switzerland,

[237] Amolon, *Liber contra Judaeos.*—Migne, Patr. Lat. CXVI.

where a decree of the fourteenth century sentenced young girls to wearing Jewish hats for having begotten children by Israelite fathers; in Poland, in the sixteenth century, in spite of Sigismund I's edicts, if we are to believe the historian Bielski. [238] And they not only made these unions with the so-called Aryan nations in Europe, but also with the Uralo-Altaians and Turanians; there the infiltration was more considerable.

On the shores of the Black and the Caspian Sea, the Jews had established themselves in great antiquity. The story goes that during the war he waged against King Tachus (361 B. C.) in Egypt, Artaxerxes Ochus wrested the Jews from their land and transferred them to Hyr-cania on the Caspian shore. Even if their establishment in this region is not so old as claimed by this tradition, they still were settled there long before the Christian era, witness the Greek inscriptions of Anape, Olbia and Panticapea. They emigrated in the seventh and eighth centuries from Babylonia and came to the Tatar cities, Kertsh, Tarku, Derbend, etc. About 620 they converted there a whole tribe, the Khazars, [239] whose territory was in the neighborhood of Astrakhan. Legend seized upon this fact, which greatly stirred up the Jews of the West, but, despite of this, there can be no doubt about it. Isidore of Seville, a contemporary of the event, mentions it, and afterwards Chasdai Ibn-Shaprut, minister of the Khalif Abd-er-Rahman, corresponded with Joseph, the last

[238] Bielski, ***Chronicon rerum Polonicarum.***

[239] Vivien de Saint-Martin, ***Lea Khazars*** (Paris, 1851).—C. C. d'Ohlson, ***Lea Peuplea du Caucase,*** Paris, 1828.— ***Revue dea Etudes juives,*** v. XX, p. 144.

Khagan of the Khazars, whose kingdom was destroyed by Svyatoslav, prince of Kieff.. The Khazars exercised a great influence over the neighboring Slav tribes, the Polyane, Syeveryane and Vyatichi, and made numerous proselytes among them.

The Tatar peoples of the Caucasus also embraced Judaism in the twelfth century, according to the report of the traveler Petachya of Ratisbon. [240] In the fourteenth century, there were numerous Jews in the hordes, which, with Mamay at their head, invaded the lands surrounding the Caucasus. It was in this nook of Eastern Europe that actively went on the fusion of Jews and Uralo-Al-taians; here the ***Semite*** mixed with the ***Turanian,*** and even now, in studying the nations of the Caucasus, one meets with traces of this mixture among the 30,000 Jews of that country and the tribes surrounding them. [241]

Thus this Jewish race represented by Jews and anti-semites as the most unassailable, most homogeneous of races, is strongly multifarious. Antropologists would in the first place divide it into two well-defined parts: the dolichocephals and the brachycephals. To the first type belong the Sephardic Jews—the Spanish and Portuguese Jews as well as the greater part of the Jews of Italy and Southern France; to the second may be assigned the

[240] Basnage, ***Histoire des Juifs,*** v. IX, p. 246; and Wagenseil, ***Exercitationes.***

[241] Among the Chechens inhabiting the East and Northwest of the Caucasus, as well as among the Andis of Daghestan, the Jewish type is very widespread. The Tats of the Caspian Sea are considered to be Jews, and there are many Jews among the Tatar tribes, as the Kumiks, for instance. (Cf. Eckert, Der Kaukasus und $eine Volker, Leipzig, 1887).

Ashkenazim, i. e., the Polish, Russian and German Jews. [242] But the Sephardim and the Ashkenazim are not the only two known varieties of Jews; these varieties are numerous.

In Africa are found agricultural and nomadic Jews, allied with the Kabyls and Berberians, near Setif, Guel-ma and Biskra, at the frontier of Morocco; in caravan they go as far as Timbuctoo, and some of their tribes, on the borders of Sahara, like the Daggatouns, are black tribes, [243] as also are the Fellah Jews of Abyssinia. [244] In India, one finds white Jews in Bombay, and black Jews in Cochin China, but the white Jews have in them mela-nian blood. They settled in India in the fifth century, after the persecutions of the Persian King Pheroces, who banished them from Bagdad. Their settling is at all events assigned to a more remote date: the coming of the Jews into China, i. e., before Christ. As to the Jews of China, they are not only related to the Chinese surrounding them, but they have also adopted the practices of the Confucian religion. [245]

The Jew, consequently, has incessantly been transformed by the environments in which he stayed. He has changed because the different languages which he has

[242] For the dollchocephalous Jews of Africa and Italy, cf. the works of Pruner-Bey (*Memoire de la Societe d'anthropologies* II, p. 432 and III, p. 82) and Lombroso.—For the brachycephalous Jews cf. Copernlcki and Mayer, *Physical Characteristics of the Population of Galicia,* Cracow, 1876 (In Polish).

[243] Mardochee Aby Serour, *Les Daggatouns,* Paris, 1880.

[244] On the Fellahs cf. Abbadie, *Nouvelles annates des Voyages,* 1840, III, p. 84, and Ph. Luzzato, Archives Israelites, 1851-1854.

[245] Elle Schwartz, *God's Nation in China.* Strassburg, 1880.— Abbe Sionnet, *Essai sur les Juifs de la Chine,* Paris, 1887.

spoken, have introduced into his mind different and opposite notions; he has not remained such as a united and homogeneous people ought to be, but, on the contrary, he is, at present, the most heterogeneous of all nations, one that presents the greatest varieties. And this pretended race whose stability and power of resistance friend and foe agree in extolling, affords us the most multifarious and most opposite types, since they range from the white to the black Jew, passing by way of the yellow Jew, not to speak of the secondary divisions,—Jews with blonde and red hair, and brown Jews with black hair.

Consequently, the ethnologic grievance of the anti-semites does not rest upon any serious and real foundation. The opposition of the Aryans and the Semites is artificial; it is not correct to say that the Aryan race and the Semitic race are pure races, and that the Jew is a single and unvarying people. Semitic blood has mingled with Aryan blood and Aryan blood has mixed with Semitic blood. Aryans and Semites have both, furthermore, received an admixture of Turanian blood and Hamite, Negro or Negroid blood, and in the Babel of nationalities and races which the world is at present, the preoccupation of those who seek to discover who among his neighbors is an Aryan, a Turanian, a Semite, is a vain pursuit.

In spite of this there is a portion of truth in the grievance which we have examined, or, rather, the theories of the antisemites about the inequality of races and Aryan superiority, in one word, the anthropologic prejudices are but the veil which covers some real causes of anti-semitism.

We have said that there are no races, but there are peoples and nations. What is improperly called a race is not an ethnologic unit, but is an historic, intellectual and moral unit. The Jews are not an ethnos, but they are a nationality, they are diversified types, it is true, but what nation is not diversified? What makes a people is not unity of origin, but unity of sentiments, ideas, ethics. Let us see whether the Jews do not present this unity, and whether we cannot find therein, in part, the secret of the animosity shown them.

CHAPTER XI.

NATIONALISM AND ANTISEMITISM.

The Jews in the World.—Race and Nation.—Are the Jews a Nation?—The Midst, the Laws, the Cus-toms.—The Religion and the Rites.—The Language and Literature.—The Jewish Spirit.—Does the Jew Believe in His Nationality?—The Restoration of the Jewish Empire.—Jewish Chauvinism.—The Jew and the Strangers to His Law.—Is the Talmud Anti-Social ?—Once and Now.—The Permanence of Prejudices.—Jewish Exclusiveness and Persistence of the Type.—The Principle of Nationalities in the Nineteenth Century.—In Germany and Italy.—In Austria, in Russia and Eastern Europe.—Panger-manism and Panslavism.—The Idea of Nationality, the Jew and Antisemitism.—The Heterogeneous Elements in the Nations.—Elimination or Absorption.—National Egoism.—Preservation or Transformation.—The Two Tendencies.—Patriotism and Humanitarianism.—Nationalism, Internationalism and Anti-Semitism.—Jewish Cosmopolitanism and the Idea of Fatherland.—The Jews and the Revolution.

There are about eight million Jews scattered over the face of the earth, [246] nearly seven-eighths of which inhabit Europe. [247] Among these Jews figure the Bedoween Jews living on the confines of Sahara, the Daggaouns of the

[246] It is very difficult to estimate exactly the Jewish population of the world. On the one hand the antisemites overdraw the probable figures, desirous as they are of proving the Jewish invasion; on the other hand, the Jews or the philosemites, led on by contrary interests, in their turn diminish these figures. Thus the antisemites readily give the number as nine millions, if not all ten, the philosemites or the Jews (Cf. Loeb, article "Jew" in Vivien de Saint-Martin's ***Dictionaire de Geographie.***—Th. Reinach, ***Histoire des Israelites***) give the number at 6,300,000; but in their estimate they set down the number of Russian Jews at 2,552,000, which is much below the actual figures of 4,500,000 at the least (Leo Efrera, ***Let Juifes Russes***). I have therefore adopted 8,000,000 as the total population, which seemed to ma the figure nearest approaching the truth. [The figure is an underestimate; the number of Russian Jews, according to the Russian census of 1897, was 5,700,00.—Translator.]

[247] It is possible that the increasing emigration of Polish and Russian Jews to the United States should cause a difference in in these figures. At present there are about 250 or 300 thou-sand Jews in the United States, [about 1,135,00 in 1902.— Translator] and if their number does not enormously increase from year to year, it means that the Jews of the United States have a very marked tendency to blend in the surrounding population. This refers to the fact that the majority of the Jewish immigrants belong to the working class.

desert, the Fellahs of Abyssinia, the black Jews of India, the Mongoloid Jews of China, the Kalmuk and Tatar Jews of the Caucasus, the blonde Jews of Bohemia and Germany, the brown Jews of Portugal, Southern France, Italy and the Orient, the dolichocephalous Jews, the bra-chycephalous and sub-brachycephalous Jews, all Jews, who, according to the section of their hair, the shape of their skull, the color of their skin, could be classified, on the strength of the best principles of ethnology, into four or five different races, as we have just shown.

By comparing, *e. g.,* the inhabitants of the different departments of France, we might, in exactly the same way, prove that the differences observable between a Provencal and a Breton, a Niceois and a Picardian, a Nor-mandian and Aquitanian, a Lorrain and a Basque, an Auvergnat and a Savoyard do not permit the belief in the existence of the French race.

Still, proceeding in this way, we shall really have proven that the race is not an ethnologic unity, i. e., that no people is a descendant of common parents, and that no nation has been formed from the aggregation of cells of this kind. But we shall by no means have proven that there exists no French people, a German people, an English people, etc., and we should not be able to do it, since there exists an English literature, a German literature, a French literature, different literatures all of them, expressing in a different way common sentiments, it is true, but whose objective and subjective play upon the various individuals affected by them is not the same, sentiments common to human nature, but ones which each man and each collection of men feels and expresses in a different way. We have had to reject the anthropologic notion of race, a notion which is erroneous and which we shall see to have given origin to the worst opinions, the most detestable and least justifiable vanities, that anthropologic notion which tends to make of each people an association of proud and egoistic recluses, but we are forced to admit the existence of historical units i. e., separate nations. For the idea of race we substi-tute the idea of nation, and again we have to make an explanation, for the nineteenth century based its belief in nationalities on its belief in race, and an innate race at that.

What is commonly understood by race? According to Littré, a nation is a "union of human beings inhabiting the same territory subjected or not subjected to the same government, and having had common interests long enough to allow of ***considering them as belonging to the same race.***" To this definition of a nation Littr6 opposes that of a people: "A multitude of human beings who even though not inhabiting the same country, have the same religion and are of the same origin." According to Mancini, [248] a nation is a "natural community of human beings united by their country, origin, manners, language, and being conscious of this community." To follow Bluntschli, [249] a people may be defined as follows: "The community of spirit, sentiment, race, which has become hereditary in a mass of human beings of different pro-

[248] Mancini, ***Delia Nazionalita come fondamento del diritto delle genti.*** Naples, 1873.

[249] Bluntschli, ***Theorie generate de VEtat.*** (Traduction A. de Piedmatten) Paris, 1891.

fessions and classes; a mass which—leaving the political bond out of consideration—feels united by culture and origin, especially by language and manners, and which is strange to others." As for nation, again to follow Bluntschli, it is a "community of men united and or-ganized into a state." Thus it is plain that in order to succeed in discriminating a people from a nation one must introduce either a territorial unity, as does Littré, or a state unity as does Bluntschli; in other words, an outside matter, one above those constituting the people and the nation which can actually be identified.

To sum up. Customarily a nation is called an agglomeration of individuals having in common their territory, language, religion, law, customs, manners, spirit, historic mission. Now, we have seen that a common race, innate race, a race implying the same origin and purity of blood is but a fiction; the idea of race is not necessarily linked with the conception of a nation—proof that the Basques, Bretons, Provencals, belong all to the French nation, though very different anthropologically. As for territorial community, it is not a whit more necessary; the Poles, e. g., possess no common territory, and yet there is a Polish nation. Language, too, does not seem indispensable, and indeed one may refer to Switzerland, Austria, Belgium, in which countries two or several languages are spoken, but these countries, organized,—with the exception of Switzerland,—federatively, permit us on the contrary, to assert that language is clearly the sign of nationality, since in all of them those speaking the same language strive to group together, in other words, that one language tends to become preponderant and destroy the others. Religion was formerly one of the most important forces that contributed to the formation of peoples. We cannot possibly realize what Home, Athens or Sparta had been, if we disregard the Gods of Olympus and the Capitolium; the same is true of Memphis, Nineveh, Babylon and Jerusalem, and what becomes of the Middle Ages if we leave out Christianity? The influence of religion was preponderant for centuries long, but since a few years it has had a very limited power, and in certain countries only, as in Russia, for instance, the unity of faith is sought for and is made one of the constitutive and indispensable elements of nationality. Elsewhere multiplicity of religious confessions is no obstacle to unity; still it is well to add, that in all European lands religion was the first unity known, and that, leaving the Ottoman Empire out of account, all the European States and peoples were first of all Christian States and peoples. The Reformation was the last religious effort aiming at unity, and after the religious war the toleration edicts marked the end of the domination of dogmas over nationalities. Still, Christianity has left its impress on manners, customs, morality. However its principles, metaphysics, ethics be judged, it has been one of the most important factors in the life of the European nations and the individuals composing them; it is the common ground on which the various edifices have been built; it is one of the fundamental notions to which a good many others were added, which have been worked in various ways but are found in the strata of modern societies. Christianity was one of the steady elements of the spirit of various peoples of the old and the new continent, but what has differentiated the peoples and created their personality—was the manners, customs, art, language with the thousand peculiar ideas which it generates by means of its literature, and philosophy. The dissimilarity of individuals is caused by the different way in which they interpret general and common ideas, as also by the different way in which they are impressed by phenomena and the manner in which they construe them. It is the same with collective bodies. They consist of various beings, each of whom, it is true, is a substance apart, but all follow certain directions in common. What gives these directions? Language, next, also, the traditions, interests and historic destinies belonging to all these beings in common. But to this must be added—as was done by Mancini,—the consciousness of this community. This consciousness was slowly worked out in the course of ages, through thousands of blows from outside, thousands of struggles within, but the nations began to exist only on the day when they came to this self-consciousness, and once born this consciousness became one more factor for nationality. Without it there is no nationality; but once it exists it reacts, in its turn, on the brains of each individual and this national self-consciousness, the last to be formed, is also the last to disappear, after the territory, manners, practices, customs, and religion have disappeared and literature no longer lives.

Nations, consequently, do exist. These nations may sometimes not be organized under the same government; they may have lost their fatherland, their language, but the nation continues as longer as have not disappeared this self-consciousness and the consciousness of that com-munity of thought and interests which they represent by the fictitious background of race, filiation, origin and purity of blood.

Now let us turn to the Jew. We have seen that he does not exist, as far as race is concerned, and those are in error who say: "There is no longer a Jewish people, there is a Jewish fellowship closely united with a race." [250] It remains to inquire whether the Jew is not a part of a nation composed, like all nations, of various elements, and nevertheless possessing unity. Now, if we leave aside the Abyssinian Fellaheen, some little known nomadic Jewish tribes of Africa, the black Jews of India, and the Chinese Jews, we arrive at the conclusion that by the side of the pointed out differences which distinguish these Jews they possess also common peculiarities, a common individuality and a common type. Still, the Jews have lived in quite contrasting countries, they were subjected to very diverse climatic influences, they were surrounded by very dissimilar peoples. What is it that succeeded in keeping them such as they have remained until to-day? Why do they continue to exist otherwisc than as a religious confession? This is due to three causes: one depending on the Jews—religion; another for which they are partly responsible—their social con-dition; the third, which is external—the conditions which have been forced upon them.

No religion has ever moulded soul and spirit as has the Jewish religion. Nearly all religions have had a

[250] A. Franck, lecture on "Religion and Science in Judaism," in ***Annuaire de la Societe des Etudes Juives,*** 2nd year.

philosophy, ethics, a literature alongside of their religious dogmas; with Israel religion was simultaneously ethics and metaphysics, nay, more, it was law. The Jews had no symbolic independence from their legislation; no, after the return from the second captivity, they had Yahweh and his Law, each inseparable from the other. To become" part of the nation one had to accept not its God only, but also all legal prescriptions emanating from Him and bearing the stamp of sanctity. Had the Jew had only Yahweh, he would probably have vanished in the midst of the different peoples that had received him, just as had vanished the Phoenicians who carried only Melkart with them. But the Jew had something more than his God—he had his Torah, his law, and by it he has been preserved. He not only did not lose this law when losing his ancestral territory, but, on the contrary, he has strengthened its authority; he has developed it; he has increased its power as well as its property. After the destruction of Jerusalem the law became the bond of Israel; he lived for and by his law. But this law was minute and meddlesome, it was the most perfect manifestation of the ritual religion—into which the Jewish religion turned under the influence of its doctors, an influence which may be contrasted with the spiritualism of the prophets whose tradition Jesus carried on. These rites which foresaw every act in life, and which the Talmudists made infinitely complicated, have given shape to the Jewish brain, and everywhere, in all lands, they have shaped it in the same manner. Though scattered, the Jews thought the same way in Seville, York, Ancona, Ratisbon, Troyes and Prague; they had the same feelings and ideas about human beings and things; their viewed things through the same eye-glasses; they judged according to similar principles, of which they could not get rid, since there were no small and grave obligations in the law, all of them had the same import, as they all emanated from God. All those attracted by the Jews were caught in the terrible gear which kneaded the minds and cast them into a uniform mould. Thus the law created peculiarities; these peculiarities the Jews transmitted to one another, as they constituted everywhere a close association keeping strictly aloof, in order to be able to perform the legal prescriptions, and thus having still more power of preservation as it was opposed to penetration. The law created not only particularities but it created types as well: a moral type as well as a physical type. The influence which the exercise of mental faculties and the direction of these faculties have on the physiological individual is well known. It is known that certain human beings engaged in the same intellectual pursuits acquire special and similar traits. Under our very eyes professional types are in the process of formation, and Gal-ton's experiments with this creation of common characteristics by means of common thought are well known. The Jewish type has been formed in a way analogous to that in which were formed and are still forming the type of a physician, the type of a lawyer, etc., types produced by the identity of the social and psychic function. The Jew is a confessional type; such as he is he has been made by the law and the Talmud; more powerful than blood or climatic varieties, they have developed in him the characteristics which imitation and heredity have perpetuated.

Social characteristics were added to these confessional characteristics. We have spoken [251] of the role played by the Jew during the Middle Ages, how internal and external causes, proceeding from economic and psychological laws, led them to become almost exclusively traders, and above all dealers in gold at a time when capital was forced to be creditor in order to be productive. This role was general; the Jews filled it in all countries, not in any particular one only. To their common religious preoccupations were consequently added common social preoccupations. As a religious being the Jew was already thinking in a certain way wherever he was; as a social being he again thought identically; thus other peculiarities were created, which, too, spread peculiarities, the formation of which was general and simultaneous with all Jews. But however he isolated himself, the Jew was not alone; the peoples he lived among reacted on him and could be causes of changes. The natural midst is not everything for a man living in society. True, its influence is great, and sometimes it may, in a high degree contribute to the formation of nations, [252] but there is a social midst whose influence is not less considerable, and this social midst is created by the laws, manners and customs. Had the Jews lived in different social surroundings, they would, no doubt,

[251] Chapt. VII.

[252] For instance the transformations of the Anglo-Saxons in the United States of America, and the transformations of the Dutch in the Transvaal.

have been different mentally as well as physically. [253] This was not the case, and their social and political midst was the same everywhere. In Spain, France, Italy, Germany, Poland, the legislation against the Jews was identical, a fact quite easy of explanation as in all these lands the legislation was inspired by the church. The Jew was placed under the same restrictions, the same barriers were built around him, he was ruled by the same laws. He had kept apart, and so they kept him apart; he had endeavored to distinguish himself from the others, and they distinguished him; he had retired into his abode to be able to perform freely his rites,—he was shut up in his Ghettoes. The Jew obtained a territory on the day he was imprisoned in these Jewries, and the Israelites lived since then exactly like a people that had a fatherland of its own; in these special quarters they preserved their customs, manners and secular habits, scrup-ulously transmitted by an education which was everywhere guided by the same invariable principles.

This education did not preserve the traditions only, it was preserving the language. The Jew spoke the language of the country he inhabited, but he spoke it only because it was indispensable in his business transactions; once at home he made use of a corrupt Hebrew or of a jargon of which Hebrew formed the basis. For writing purposes he employed Hebrew, and the Bible and the Talmud do not constitute the whole of Hebrew litera-

[253] If I seem to say that all Jews are alike physically, I want to speak of their general physiognomy only, which is their common property, without prejudicing the truth about the differences which I have stated.

ture. The Jewish literary productivity from the eighth to the fifteenth century
was very great. There has been a neo-hebraic poetry of the synagogue, which was
par-ticularly copious and brilliant in Spain; [254] there has been a Jewish religious
philosophy which was born with Saadiah in Egypt and which Ibn Gebirol and Mai-
mon-ides developed afterwards; there has been a Jewish theology since the time
of Joseph Albo and Jehuda Halevi, and Jewish metaphysics—that is the Kabbala.
This literature, this philosophy, this theology, these metaphysics were the common
property of the Israelites of all countries. Up to the moment when the obscurantist
efforts of the rabbis had closed their ears and their eyes,—their spirit drew upon the
same source, they were roused by the same thoughts, they dreamt the same dreams,
they made merry to the same rhythms, the same poetry, the same preoccupations
went with them and thus they underwent the same impressions, which similarly
shaped their spirit, that Jewish spirit composed of a thousand diverse elements and
still not perceptibly different from the ancient Jewish spirit, at least in its general
tendencies, for those who aided in creating it were brought up on the ancient law.

Thus, consequently, the Jews had the same religion, manners, habits and customs, they were subjected to the same civil, religious, moral and restrictive laws;
they lived in similar conditions; in each city they had their own territory, they
spoke the same language,

[254] Cf. Munk, *De la Poesie hebraique apres la Bible,* in Temps of
Jan. 19, 1835, and the works of Zunz, Rappoport and Abraham Geiger. Cf.
also Amador de los Rios, *Histoire des Juifs d'Es-pagne* (1875).

they enjoyed a literature, they speculated over the same persisting and very
old ideas. This alone was sufficient to constitute a nation. They had even more than
that: they have had the consciousness of being a nation, that they had never ceased
to be one. After they had left Palestine, in the first centuries before the Christian
era, a bond always tied them to Jerusalem; after Jerusalem had been plunged in
flames, they had their exilarchs, their Nassis and Gaons, their schools of doctors,
schools of Babylon, Palestine, then Egypt, finally of Spain and France. The chain of

tradition has never been broken. They have ever-considered themselves exiles and have deluded themselves with the dream of the restoration of Israel's kingdom on earth. Every year, on the eve of the Passover they have chanted from the depth of their whole beings, three times the sentence: *"Leshana haba b'Yerushdlaim"* (the next year in Jerusalem!). They have preserved their ancient patriotism, even their chauvinism; in spite of disasters, misfortunes, outrages, slavery, they have considered themselves the elect people, one superior to all other peoples, which is characteristic of all chauvinist nations, the Germans as well as the French and English of to-day. At one time in the beginning of the Middle Ages, the Jew was really superior, because, he, the inheritor of an already ancient civilization, the possessor of a literature, philosophy and above all experience, which should have given him the advantage, came into the midst of barbarian children. He lost that supremacy, and in the fourteenth century even, his was already a culture lower than the general culture of those in the same class with him. But he has religiously kept this idea of supremacy, has kept on looking with disdain and scorn upon all those who were strangers to his law. However, he was taught to be such by his book, the Talmud pervaded by a narrow and ferocious patriotism. The book has been charged with being anti-social, and there is some truth in this accusation; it has been claimed that it is the most abominable code of law and ethics, and therein lay the error, since it is neither more nor less execrable than all particularist and national codes. If it is anti-social, it is so only in that it represented and still represents a spirit differing from that of the laws in force in the country where the Jews lived and that the Jews wanted to follow their code before following the one to which every member of society was amenable, and again it is unsocial only in a relative sense, as the law was not always uniform and custom invariable in all parts of the States. At one moment of history it appeared fatally anti-human, because it remained immutable while everything was changing. Its brutality has been exposed by the Christian antisemites, because this brutality shocked them directly, but in saying, "Kill even the best of Goyim," Rabbi Simon ben Jochai was no more cruel than was Saint Louis, who thought that the best way of arguing with a Jew was to plunge a dirk in his belly, or than the Pope Urban III. when he wrote in his bull: "Everybody is allowed to kill an excommunicate if it is done from zeal for the church."

One thing, besides, has to be taken into account. Some modern Jews and philosemites have rejected with horror those aphorisms and axioms that had been national aphorisms and axioms. They say that the invectives against the *goyim,* the Mineans, were directed at the Romans, the Hellenes, the Jewish apostates, but they were never aimed at the Christians. There is a great deal of truth in these assertions, but there is also a great deal of error. Indeed, a portion of the prescriptions against strangers, prescriptions that were the work of the Jews defending their national spirit, must be referred to the time when the Jewish nationality was menaced, when the Jewish spirit was broken in by the Greek spirit, and when Hellenic influence threatened to become preponderant. Maledictions became more violent afterwards, beginning with the Roman Wars; everything was deemed permissible against the oppressor, every kind of violence, of hatred was extolled, and the Talmud but echoed these sentiments, it catalogued the precepts and words, and it perpetuated them. When Judaism was fought by the rising Christianity, all the hatred and wrath of hired assassins, patriots, pious people turned upon the Jews who were converting themselves—the Mineans. When deserting the national faith they deserted the battle against Rome and the enemy; they were traitors to their country, to the Jewish religion; they lost interest in a struggle that was vital for Israel; gathered around their new temples they looked with an eye of indifference upon the fall of the national glory, the disappearance of their autonomy, and not only did they not fight against the she-wolf, but they even unnerved the courage of those listening to them. Against them, against these anti-patriots, formulas of malediction were drawn up; the Jews placed them under the ban of their society, it was lawful to kill them, just as it was lawful to kill "the best of *goyim.*" Similar exhortations would be found at all periods of patriotic struggles, among all nations; the proclamations of the generals, the calls to arms of the tribunes of all ages contain just as odious formulas. When the French, for instance, invaded the Palatinate, it must have been a rule, nay, even a duty, for all Germans to say: "Death even to the best of Frenchmen!" Similarly, when the Germans, in their turn, entered France, it was doubtless the Frenchman's turn to say: "Death even to the best of Germans!" It is cruel, execrable war that generates these sentiments, and anti-human ferocity manifests itself whenever this warrior spirit is awakened by the circumstances. It is further said that with the Jews these precepts have represented only personal opinions, and by their side may be found moral formulas as humane, brotherly and as full of compassion as the Christian formulas. This is true, and in the spirit of the Fathers who had written these maxims, gathered in the ***Pirke Aboth,*** [255] these humanitarian maxims had a general meaning, but the Jew of the Middle Ages who found them in his book attributed to them a restricted meaning; he applied them to those of his nation. Why? Because this book, the Talmud, contained also egotistic, cruel and nationalist precepts directed against strangers. Preserved in this book of enormous authority, in this Talmud which to the Jew has been a code, an expression of their nationality, which has been their soul,—these cruel or narrow-minded as-

[255] ***Pirke Aboth*** (Traite des Principes), with a French translation and notes by A. Crehange (Paris, Durlacher).

sertions have acquired at least a moral if not a legal force. The Talmudist Jew who found them attributed to them a permanent import, he applied them to all his enemies, he made of it a general rule toward strangers to his faith, his law, his beliefs. There came a day when the Jew had but one enemy in Europe the Christian who persecuted, hunted, massacred, burned, martyrized him. As a consequence he could not experience any very tender feeling toward the Christian, the more so that all the efforts of the Christian were bent on destroying Judaism, on annihilating the religion which from that time on constituted the Jewish fatherland. The goy of the Maccabees, the Minean of the doctors, turned into the Christian, and to the Christian all the words of furious hatred, wrath and despair found in the book, were applied. To the Christian, the Jew was a despicable being, but to the Jew the Christian became the ***goy,*** the execrable stranger, who fears no pollution, who maltreats the elect nation, one through whom Judah suf-fers. This word ***goy*** comprehended all the passions, scorns, hatreds of persecuted Israel—against the stranger, and this cruelty of the Jews toward the non-Jew is one of the things that best prove how long-lived the idea of nationality was among the children of Jacob. They have always believed themselves a people. Do they still belive it at present ?

Among the Jews who receive a Talmudic education, and this means the majority of the Jews in Russia, Poland, Galicia, Hungary, Bohemia and the Orient, the idea of nationality is still as alive at present as it had been during the Middle Ages. They still form a people apart, fixed, rigid, congealed by the scrupulously observed rites, by the unvarying customs and the manners; hostile to every innovation, to every change, rebelling against all attempted efforts to detalmudize him. In 1854 the rabbis anathematized the Oriental schools founded by French Jews, where profane sciences were taught; at Jerusalem, an anathema was hurled, in 1856, against the school established by Doctor Franckel. In Russia and Galicia, sects like those of the New Chas-sidim are still opposing all attempts made to civilize the Jews. In all these countries only a minority escapes the Talmudic spirit, but the mass persists in its isolation, and however great its abjection and its humiliation, it ever holds itself the chosen people, the nation of God.

This intolerant aversion toward the stranger has disappeared among the Western Jews, the Jews of France, England, Italy and a great portion of the German Jews. [256] The Talmud is no longer read by these Jews, and the Talmudic ethics, at least the nationalist ethics of the Talmud, have no longer any hold on them. They no longer observe the 613 laws, have lost their fear of impurity, a horror which the Eastern Jews have preserved; the majority no longer know Hebrew; they have forgotten the meaning of the antique ceremonies; they have transformed the rabbinic Judaism into a religious rationalism; they have given up the familiar observances, and the religious exercise has been reduced by them to passing several hours in the year in a synagogue listening to hymns they no longer understand. They can't attach themselves to a dogma, a symbol; they have none of it;

[256] I leave apart the. Polish Jews of Germany.

in giving up the Talmudic practices they have given up what made their unity, that which contributed to forming their spirit. The Talmud had formed the Jewish nation after its dispersion; thanks to it, individuals of diverse origin had constituted a people; it had been the mould of the Jewish soul, the creator of the race; it and the restrictive laws of the various societies have modeled it. It appears that with the legislators abolished, the Talmud left in disdain, the Jewish nation should inevitably have died, and yet the Western Jews are Jews still. They are Jews, because they have kept perennial and liv-ing their national consciousness; they still believe they are a nation, and, believing that, they preserve themselves. When the Jew ceases to have the national consciousness he disappears; so long as he has this consciousness, he continues to be. He has, he practices his religious faith no longer, he is irreligious, often even an atheist, but he continues to be, because he has a belief in his race. He has kept his national pride, he always fancies himself a superior individuality, a different being from those surrounding him, and this conviction prevents him from assimilating himself, for, being always exclusive, he generally refuses to mix through marriage with the peoples surrounding him. Modern Judaism claims to be but a religious confession; but in reality it is an ***ethnos*** besides, for it believes it is that, for it has preserved its prejudices, egoism, and its vanity as a people—a belief, prejudices, egoism and vanity which make it appear a stranger to the peoples in whose midst it exists, and here we touch upon one of the most profound causes of anti8emitism. Antisemitism is one of the ways in which the principle of nationali-ties is manifested.

What is this question of nationalities? By it is un-derstood "the movement which carries certain popula-tions, of the same origin and language, but constitut-ing a part of different States,—to unite in such a way as to make a single political body, a single nation." [257]

Simultaneously with proclaiming the rights of the the land, formerly the prop-erty and domain of the peoples the Revolution overthrew the old conception of rule and dynasty on which the nations were founded; the land, formerly the property and domain of the kings, now became the domain of the people that occupied them. The royal government in itself constituted the national unity,—the representative, constitutional government placed that unity somewhere else: in the community of origin and language. The artificial bond being broken, a natural bond was sought for; there have been efforts on the part of nations to acquire an individuality; they all strove for the unity they lacked. It was about 1840 that nationalist ideas espe-cially mani-fested themselves, they began the work, and contemporary Europe was founded through them. The theory of a National State was wrought out by the savants, historians, philosophers, poets of a whole generation. "Every people has been called to form a State, has a right to organize into a State. Mankind is made up of peoples, the world must be divided into corresponding nations. *Each people is a State, each State a national body"* [258] This theory, these ideas became mighty and irresistible

[257] Laveleye, *Le Gouvenment dans la Democratic,* v. I, p. 53 (Paris, 1801).

[258] Bluntschli, *Theorie generate de l'Etat,* p. 84.

forces. They are what made the unity of Germany, of Italy, and they have been the causes of *irredentism;* they, too, are what creates separatism in Ireland and Austria, what calls forth the struggles between the Magyars and Slavs, the Chekhs and Germans. On these ideas of nationalities Russia and Germany have been and are resting to make up their empire, Pangermanic or Pan-slavic; and is not this Panslavism, and this Pangerman-ism what agitates the East of Europe, do not the destinies of that part of Europe depend on this remote or near clash of theirs?

It would be out of place to discuss here the legitimacy or illegitimacy of this movement. It will suffice for our purpose merely to state its existence. How do the peoples construe this tendency into unity? In two ways: either by uniting under the same government all individuals who speak the national language, or by reducing all heterogeneous elements coexisting in the nations, for the benefit of one of these elements which becomes preponderant and whose characteristics henceforth become the national characteristics. Thus the Germans have endeavored to assimilate the Alsatians and Poles; the Russians compel the Poles to maintain the Russian universities which denationalize them; in Austria the Germans try to absorb the Chekhs; in Hungary, "Slovak orphans are taken from the places where their native tongue is spoken and removed to Magyar comitats." [259] If these heterogeneous elements do not let themselves be absorbed, there comes a struggle, a violent struggle often, which is manifested in many

[259] J. Novicow, *Les luttes entre societes humaines,* Paris, 1893.

various ways—from persecution down to expulsion in some cases.

Now, in the midst of the European nations the Jews live as a confessional community, believing in the lat-ter's nationality, having preserved a peculiar type, special aptitudes and a spirit of their own. In their struggle against the heterogeneous elements which they contained, the nations were led to struggle against the Jews, and antisemitism was one of the manifestations of the effort made by the peoples in order to reduce these strange individualities.

To be reduced, these individualities must be absorbed or eliminated, and the process of social reduction does not differ perceptibly from the process of physiological reduction. In the beginning, when heterogeneous human bands covered the earth, they began to struggle for existence and did not think it possible to develop unless by suppressing the stranger who existed by their side. Cannibalism is the first degree of elmination. When the nations were formed by the fusion and homogeneization of heterogeneous hordes, they tended rather to absorb the stranger, although the tendency toward elimination still existed. Having reached a certain stage of development, the primitive societies came to aim at isolation, exclusivism, mutual hatred; while in the process of formation these national characteristics thus escaped all shocks, all changes, and exclu-siveness was, perhaps, indispensable for a certain time, in order that types might be formed. When these types were solidly formed, it became useful to add new cells to the original aggregate owing to the danger that this aggregate might crystallize and immobilize, as happened in certain cases. Accordingly, the stranger was allowed to enter the nation, but this was allowed with great precautions by surrounding the naturalization and adoption with a thousand regulations, and whoever wished to remain a stranger in society was placed under very annoying restrictions. The laws were very hard on those who were not nationalists. The Jewish law is charged with being merciless toward the non-Jew, but the Roman law was not tender with the non Roman, who was without rights as the non-Greek was in Athens and Sparta. Even to-day national exclusivism or egoism is manifested in the same way, it is still as alive as was the family egoism of which it is but an extension. It may even be said that by a kind of regression it is actually asserting itself with more force. Every nation seemingly wants to rear around itself a Chinese wall, there is talk of preserving the national patrimony, the national soul, the national spirit, and the word guest regains in contemporary civilizations the same meaning as it had acquired in Roman law: the meaning of *hostis,* enemy. The economic and political rights of the immigrant are being restricted in every possible way. There is opposition to immigration, strangers are even expelled when their number grows too great, they are considered a menace to the national culture which they modify; no account is taken of the fact that therein lies a life condition of this very culture. It means that we live at a period of changes and that the future does not open quite clearly before the peoples. Many people are troubled about the future; they are attached to the old customs, in every transformation they see the death of the society of which they are a part, and as conservatives opposed to this transformation they deeply hate whatever is likely to bring a modification, everything that is different from them, i. e., the strange.

To these nationalist egoists, to these exclusivists, the Jews appeared a danger, because they felt that the Jews were still a people, a people whose mentality did not agree with the national mentality, whose concepts were opposed to that ensemble of social, moral, psychological, and intellectual conceptions, which constitutes nationality. For this reason the exclusivists became antisem-ites, because they could reproach the Jews with an ex-clusivism exactly as uncompromising as theirs, and every antisemitic effort tends, as we have seen already, [260] to restore those ancient laws restricting the rights of the Jews who are considered strangers. Thus is realized this fundamental and everlasting contradiction of nationalist antisemitism: antisemitism was born in modern societies, because the Jew did not assimilate himself, did not cease to be a people, but when antisemitism had ascertained that the Jew was not assimilated, it violently reproached him for it, and at the same whenever possible it took all necessary measures to prevent his assimilation in the future.

At all events, there exist contrary, opposing tendencies by the side of these nationalist tendencies. Above nationalities there is mankind; now, this mankind, so fragmental at the start, composed of thousands of inimical tribes that were devouring one another, is be-

[260] Ch. ix.

coming a very homogeneous mankind. The different peoples possess a common ground, despite their differences; a general conscience is formed above all the national consciences; formerly there had been civilizations, now we advance towards *one civilization;* once upon a time Athens resisted its neighbor Sparta; from now on, even if dissimilarities between one nation and another persist, the similarities are accentuated. As by the side of his special qualities constituting his essence and personality, each individual in a nation possesses qualities in common with those who speak the same tongue and have the same interests as he, just so civilized mankind acquires similar characteristics, though each nation preserves its physiognomy. More frequent from day to day, the relations among the peoples bring on a more intimate communion. Science, art, literature, become more and more cosmopolitan. Hu-manitarianism takes its place by the side of patriotism, internationalism by the side of nationalism, and presently the idea of mankind will acquire more force than the idea of fatherland, which is being modified and is losing some of that exclusivism which the national egoists wish to perpetuate. Hence the antagonism between the two tendencies. To internationalism, which is already so powerful, patriotism is opposed with unheard of violence. The old conservative spirit is elated; it is in training against cosmopolitanism which will some day defeat it; it fiercely fights those who are in favor of cosmopolitanism, and this is again a cause of antisemitism.

Though often exceedingly chauvinist, the Jews are essentially cosmopolitan in character; they are the cosmopolitan element of mankind, says Schaeffle. This is quite true, since they have always possessed in a high degree that mark of cosmopolitanism—the extreme facility of adaptation. On their arrival into the Promised Land they adopted the language of Canaan; after a seventy year sojourn in Babylonia, they forgot Hebrew and re entered Jerusalem, speaking an Aramaic or Chaldee jargon; during the first century before and after the Christian era, the Hellenic tongue pervaded the Jewries. Once dispersed the Jews fatally became cosmopolites. Indeed they did not again attach themselves to any territorial unit, and have had only a religious unity. True, they have had a fatherland, but this fatherland, the most beautiful of all, as, however, every fatherland is, was placed in the future, it was Zion renewed, with which no land is compared or camparable; a spiritual fatherland which they loved so ardently that they became indifferent to every land, and that every land seemed to them equally good or equally bad. Finally they lived under such and so terrible circumstances that they could not be expected to have a fatherland of their choice, and, with the aid of their instinct of solidarity, they have remained internationalists.

The nationalists have been led to consider them as the most active propagators of the ideas of internationalism; they even found that the example alone of these country-less laymen was bad, and that by their presence they undermined the idea of fatherland, that is any special idea of fatherland. For this reason they became antisemites or rather for this reason their antisemitism took on added force. They not only accused the Jews of being strangers, but even destructive strangers. The conservatism of the exclusivists connected cosmopolitanism with revolution; it upbraided the Jews first for their cosmopolitanism, and then for their revolutionary spirit and activity. Has the Jew, indeed, any leaning toward revolution? We shall examine that.

CHAPTER XII.

THE REVOLUTIONARY SPIRIT IN JUDAISM.

Communism and Revolution.—The Jewish Agitation.— The Optimism and Eudaemonism of Israel.—The Theories of Life and Death.—Immortality of the Soul and Resignation.—Materialism and Hatred of Injustice.—The Contract Idea in Jewish Theology. —The Idea of Justice.—The Prophets and Justice. —The Return from Babylon, the Ebionim and the Anavim.—The Conception of Divinity.—Divine Authority and Government on Earth.—The Zealots and Anarchism.—Human Equality.—The Rich Man and Evil.—The Poor Man and Good.—Yah-wehism and Liberty.—Free Will, Human Reason and Divine Power.—Jewish Individualism.— Jew-ish Subjectivity and the Feeling of Self.—Hebraic Idealism.—The Idea of Justice, the Idea of Equality, the Idea of Liberty, and Their Possible Re-alization.—Messianic Times.—The Messiah and Revolution.—The Revolutionary Instinct and Tal-mudism.—The Modern Jews and Revolution.

To inquire into the revolutionary tendencies of Judaism does not mean to examine Jewish Communism. Moreover, from the fact that the so-called Mosaic institutions had been inspired by socialistic principles it should not necessarily be inferred that the revolutionary spirit has always guided Israel.

Communism and revolution are not inseparable terms, and if nowadays we cannot utter the first word without fatally evoking the other,—this is due to the economic conditions governing us and to the fact that the transformation of the present-day societies, based as they are on individual property, is considered impossible without a violent tearing up. In a capitalistic State the communist is looked upon as a revolutionist, but it is not taken into account that a partisan of private capital would be treated in similar fashion in a communistic State. In the one and the other case this conception would be correct, for communist or individualist would in turn display both discontent and desire for. change, and that is the characteristic of the revolution-ary spirit.

If it can be said, with Renan, of the Jews that they have been an element of progress or at least of transformation, if they could be regarded as the ferments of revolution, and that, too, at all times, we shall see, it is not because of these laws on gleaning, on the workmen's wages, on the sabbatic and jubilee years, which are found in the Exodus, Numbers, Leviticus, ets., [261] but because they have always been malcontents.

I do not mean to claim thereby that they were mere

[261] Leviticus, xix, xxv; Exodus, xxii; Numbers, xxv.

mudslingers and systematic opponents of all government, for they were not wrought up against an Ahab or Ahaziah only,—but the state of things did not satisfy them; they were forever restless, in the expectation of a better state which they never found realized. Their ideal not being one of those which are satisfied with hope—they had not placed it high enough for that— they never could lull their ambitions with dreams and phantoms. They thought they had a right to demand immediate satisfactions and not remote promises. Hence this constant agitation of the Jews, which had manifested itself not only in prophetism, Messianism and Christianity that was its supreme consummation, but as well since the time of the dispersion, and then in an individual manner.

The causes that gave birth to this agitation, which kept it up and perpetuated it in the souls of some modern Jews, are not external causes such as the tyranny of a ruler, of a people or ferocious code; they are internal causes, i. e., such as pertain to the very essence of the Hebrew spirit. The reasons of the sentiments of revolt with which the Jews were animated must be sought in the idea they had of God, in their conception of life and death.

To Israel, life is a boon, the existence granted to man by God is good; to live is in itself good luck. When, in a strait moment, the Ecclesiastes [262] declared that the day of death was preferable to that of birth, he was troubled by Hellenic thought, and his aphorism had but an individual value. According to the Hebrew, life must

[262] Eccles. vii. 1.

give a being all the joys and only from it they must be expected.

By contrast, death is the only evil that can afflict man, it is the greatest of calamities; it is so horrible, so frightful that to be struck by it is the most terrible of punishments. "May death serve me as expiation," the dying would say, for he could not conceive of a more serious punishment than that consisting in death. The only recompense that the pious earnestly desired was that Yahweh might make them die sated with days, after years passed in abundance and jubilation.

Besides, what recompense other than this could they have expected? They did not believe in the future life, and it was late, perhaps only under the influence of Parsism, that they began to admire the immortality of the soul. For a Jew, his existence ended with life, he was sleeping till the day of resurrection, he had nothing to hope for except from existence, and the punishments that threatened vice, just as the satisfactions that accompanied virtue, were all of this world.

The philosophy of the Jew, or more properly speaking, his eudaemonism, was simple; he says with the Ecclesias-tes. "I have found out that there is happiness in rejoicing only and in giving one's self comforts during life." [263] A realist, therefore, he sought to develop himself to the best of his desires; having but a limited number of years allotted to him, he wanted to enjoy it, and he demanded not moral pleasures, but material pleasures, suitable to embellish, to make comfortable the existence. As there was no paradise, he could expect only tangible favors

[263] Eccles, iii. 12.

from God, in return for his fidelity, his piety; not vague promises, good for those seeking beyond, but formal realizations, resulting in an increase of fortune, an augmentation of well-being. If the Jew saw himself defrauded of the advantages he thought were due his attachment, his soul was profoundly disturbed; with Job he preferred to believe he had sinned unknowingly, and that having made him expiate his errors by poverty Yahweh would treat him like that very Job to whom was granted "the double of whatever he had possessed. [264]

Having no hope of future reward the Jew could not resign to the misfortunes of life; it was only at a very late date that he could console himself in his misfortunes by dreaming of celestial happiness. To the scourges befalling him he replied neither with the Mohammedan's fatalism, nor with the Christian's resignation, but with revolt. As he possessed a concrete ideal, he wanted to realize it, and whatever retarded its advent aroused his wrath.

The peoples that believed in a world beyond, those who deluded themselves with sweet and consoling chimaeras and let themselves be lulled to sleep with the dream of eternity; those that possessed the dogma of rewards and punishments, of paradise and hell, all these peoples accepted poverty and sickness with bowed heads. The dream of future rejoicing kept them up, and without anger they put up with their sores and their privation. They consoled themselves of the injustices of this world by thinking of the mirth that would be their

[264] Job, xiii.10.

dise pleasures, they consented to bend, without complaint, before the strong who tyrannized them.

"The hatred of injustice is strikingly diminished through the assurance of rewards beyond the grave," says Ernest Kenan. Indeed, to him who believes in the life eternal during which immutable and sovereign justice shall reign, of what import are these short earthly iniquities from which death gives release? The faith in the immortality of the soul is a counselor of resig-lot in the other world; in the expectation of the para-nation ; this is so true, that the uncompromising attitude of the Jew subsides as the belief in eternity grows stronger in Israel.

But this idea of the continuity and persistence of the personality contributed nothing to the formation of the moral being with the Jews. In earliest times they did not share the hopes of the later Pharisees; after Yahweh had closed their eyelids, they expected only the horror of Sheol. Accordingly, life was for them the important thing; they sought to beautify it with all blessings, and these mad idealists, who had conceived the pure idea of one God, were, by a startling yet explicable contrast, the most untractable of sensualists. Yahweh had assigned to them a certain number of years on earth; in this existence, always too short to suit the Hebrew, He demanded of them a faithful and scrupulous worship; in return, the Hebrew claimed positive advantages from his Lord.

The idea of contract dominated the whole of Jewish theology. When the Israelite fulfilled his duties toward Yahweh, he demanded reciprocity. If he thought himself wronged, if he considered his rights had not been respected, he had no good reason to temporize, for the minute of happiness he lost was a minute stolen from him, one which could never be returned to him. Accordingly, he looked to a punctual fulfilment of mutual obligations; he wanted a correct balance to exist between his God and himself; he kept a strict account of his duties and his rights, this account was part of the religion, and Spinoza could justly say: [265] "With the Jews the religious dogmas did not consist in instructions, but in rights and prescriptions; piety meant justice, impiety meant injustice and crime."

The man whom the Jew lauds is not a saint, not a resignee: it is the just man. The charitable man does not exist for those of Judah's people; in Israel there can be no question of charity, but only of justice: alms is but a restitution. Besides, what did Yahweh say? He has said: "Just balances, just weights, a just ***ephah,*** and a just ***hin*** shall ye have ;" [266] he has also said: "Thou shalt not respect the person of the poor, nor honor the person of the mighty; but in righteousness shalt thou judge thy neighbor." [267]

Prom this conception of the primitive times of Israel came the law of retaliation. Simple spirits, imbued with the idea of justice, were obviously bound to come to: "An eye for an eye, a tooth for a tooth." The rigor of the code softened only then when a more exact idea of equity was obtained.

[265] ***Tract. Theolog. Polit., chap.*** xvii.

[266] Levit, xix, 15.

[267] Levit., xiz. 86.

The Yahwehism of the prophets reflects these sentiments. What the God they praise wants is: "Let judgment run down as waters and righteousness as a mighty stream;" [268] he says: "I am the Lord which exercise lov-ingkindness, judgment and righteousness in the earth; for in these things I delight." [269] To know justice is to know God, [270] and justice becomes an emanation from divinity; it takes on the character of a revelation. With Isaiah, Jeremiah, Ezekiel it formed part of the dogma, it had been proclaimed during the Sinaitic theophanies, and little by little is born this idea: Israel must realize justice.

This desire guides all great prophets before and during the captivity. Should the elect people not practice justice it will be punished for it as for its idolatry. If it is led into captivity it is not simply because it had worshipped Ashera and Kamosh, had sacrificed on high places, had disgraced the sanctuary, but as well because it is rotten with iniquity.

All prophetic schools were imbued with these thoughts. The prophets believed themselves sent to work for the advent of justice. Obviously, what struck them most was the inequality in conditions. As long as there would be poor and rich, there would be no hope for the reign of equity. According to the inspired nobis (prophets) the rich were a hindrance to justice and this latter was to be brought about only by the poor. Accordingly the anavim and ebionim (the afflicted and the poor)

[268] Amos, v, 24.

[269] Jeremiah, ix. 24.

[270] Jeremiah, xxii, 15-16.

gathered around their protectors, the prophets. With them they protested against the extortions; in return, the prophets presented them as models, and from them drew the portrait of the just man: "The just is he that walketh righteously and speaketh uprightly; he that despiseth the gain of oppressions, that shaketh his hand from holding of bribes, that stoppeth his ears from hearing of blood, and shutteth his eyes from seeing evil." [271] They pointed out their duties to the rich and said in the name of Yahweh: "Is not this the fast I have chosen? to loose the bands of wickedness, to undo the heavy burdens, and to let the oppressed go free, and that ye break every yoke? Is it not to deal thy bread to the hungry, and that thou bring the poor that are cast out to thy house?" [272]

On returning from Babylon, the Jewish population formed a considerable nucleus of ***poor, just, pious, humble, and saints.*** A great portion of the Psalms came from this midst. These Psalms are for the most part violent diatribes against the rich; they symbolize the struggle of the ***ebionim*** against the mighty. When addressing the possessors, the sated, the Psalmists readily say with Amos: "Hear this, O ye that swallow up the needy, even to make the poor of the land to fail,"[273] and in all these poems written between the Babylonian exile and the Maccabees (589-167) the poor is glorified. He is God's friend, His prophet, His anointed; he is good,

[271] Isaiah, xxxiii, 15.

[272] Isaiah, lviii, 6-7.

[273] Amoa, viii, 4.

his hands are pure; he is upright and just; he is part of the flock of which God is the shepherd.

The rich is the wicked, he is the man of violence and blood; he is knavish, perfidious, haughty; he does evil without motive; he is contemptible, for he exploits, oppresses, persecutes and devours the poor. But his great crime is that he does not do justice; that he has bribed judges who condemn the poor beforehand. [274]

Incited by the words of their poets, the ***ebionim*** did not slumber in their misery, they did not delight in their misfortunes, they did not resign to poverty. On the contrary, they dreamed of the day that would avenge the iniquities and oprobriums heaped upon them, the day when the wicked would be hurled down and the just exalted: the day of the Messiah. For all these humble ones the Messianic era was to be an era of justice. Did not Isaiah speak of this time when he said: "I will also make thy officers peace, and thine exactors righteousness. Violence shall no more be heard in thy land. And they shall build houses, and inhabit them; and they shall plant vineyards, and eat the fruit of them. They shall not build, and another inhabit; they shall not plant and another eat."

When Jesus comes he will repeat what the ***ebionim*** Psalmists had said, he will say: "Blessed are they which do hunger and thirst after righteousness, for they shall be filled;" [275] he will anathematize the rich, and will exclaim: "It is easier for a camel to go through the eye

[274] Psalms, xxvi, 10; lxxxii, 2-3; xxii; xlviii; xlix; cii, 1, 2; cvii, etc.

[275] Matth., v, 6.

of a needle than for a rich man to enter the Kingdom of God." [276] On this point the Christian doctrine will turn out to be purely Jewish, not at all Hellenic, and Jesus will find his first adherents among the *ebionim.*

Thus the conception the Jews formed of life and death furnished the first element of their revolutionary spirit. Starting with the idea that good, that is justice, was to be realized not beyond the grave—for beyond the grave there is sleep, until the day of the resurrection of the dead,—but during life, they sought justice, and never finding it, ever dissatisfied, they were restless to get it.

The second element was given them by their conception of divinity. It led them to conceive the equality of men, it led them even to anarchy; a theoretic and sentimental anarchy, since they always had a government, but a real anarchy, for they never accepted with cheerful heart this government, whatever it were.

Whether worshipping Yahweh as their national God, or when they rose with their prophets to the belief in one and universal God, the Jews never speculated over the essence of Divinity. Judaism never set for itself any essential metaphysical questions, whether about the "beyond" or the nature of God. "Sublime speculations have no connection with the Scripture," says Spinoza, "and, as far as I am concerned, I have not and could not learn, from the Holy Writ, any of the eternal attributes of God"; [277] and Mendelssohn adds: "Judaism has not revealed unto us any of the eternal truths." [278]

[276] Mark, x. 25.

[277] Spinoza, *Letters,* xxxiv.

[278] Mendelssohn, *Jerusalem.*

The Jews looked upon Yahweh as a ceiestial monarch, who would give a charter to his people and enter into engagements with it, demanding, in return, obedience to his laws and prescriptions. In the eyes of the ancient Hebrews and, later on, the Talmudists, the Bene-Israel alone could enjoy the prerogatives granted by Yahweh ; in the eyes of the prophets, all nations could lawfully claim these privileges, because Yahweh was the God Universal, and not the equal of Dagon or Beelzebub.

But Yahweh was "the supreme head of the Hebrew people"; [279] He was the all-powerful and formidable lord, the only king, jealous of His authority, cruelly punishing those who showed themselves rebellious against His omnipotence. In good luck, as in ill-luck, a pious Jew had ever to have recourse to Him. To turn to men and not to God Yahweh was a crime, and having made an alliance with Home and Mithridates I., Judas Macca-baeus incurred this anathema of Rabbi José, son of Jo-hanan: "Accursed be he who places his reliance in creatures of flesh and who removes his heart from Yahweh!" Yahweh is thy fort, thy shield, thy citadel, thy hope, say the Psalms.

All Jews are Yahweh's subjects; He has said it Himself: "For unto me the children of Israel are servants." [280] What authority can, then, prevail by the side of the divine authority? All government, whatever it be, is evil, since it tends to take the place of the government of God; it must be fought against, because Yahweh is the

[279] Munk, *Palestine.*

[280] Leyit.. xxv. 56.

only head of the Jewish commonwealth, the only one to whom the Israelite owes obedience.

When insulting the Kings, the prophets represented the sentiment of Israel.

They were giving expression to the thoughts of the poor, the humble, all those who, being directly ill-used by the power of the Kings or of the rich, were more inclined, for that very reason, to criticize or deny the good coming from this tyranny.

Holding Yahweh alone as their lord, these **anavim** and **ebionim,** were ever driven to revolt against human magistracy; they could not accept it, and during the periods of uprising Zadok and Judah the Galilean were seen carrying with them the zealots by their cry: "Call none your master!" Zadok and Judah were logical: if we place our tyrant in heavens we cannot endure one down here.

No authority being compatible with Yahweh's, it fatally followed that no man could rise above the others; the merciless lord of heavens brought equality on earth, and already primitive Mosaism had in it this social equality. Before God all men are equal; they are equal before the law, since the law is a divine emanation, and the unfortunate have the right, in speaking of the rich, to say to Nehemiah: "Our flesh is as the flesh of our brethren; our children as their children." [281]

God himself commands this equality, and again the mighty are the obstacle to its realization. The humble, who live in common, practice it; they follow the communistic precepts of Leviticus, Exodus, Numbers, precepts inspired by preoccupations with equality. As for the rich, they forget that God had made all men from the same clay, they disown the equality proclaimed by God. Thus they oppress the people, they fill their houses with the spoils of the poor, they browse his vineyard, they make of widows their prey, of orphans their booty, [282] and owing to them inequality exists.

At them, at these possessors and these grandees the prophets hurl the anathema; the psalmists thunder: "0 Lord God, to whom vengeance belongeth; 0 God, to whom vengeance belongeth, show thyself!" [283] they cry. They rebuke the rich for the abundance of his treasures, his luxury, his love of pleasures; whatever contributes to raise him materially above his brethren; whatever can give him the impious arrogance of deeming himself made of other dust than that of which is made the mountain-shepherd who pastures his sheep and fears God; whatever makes him forget this divine truth; men are equal to one another, since they are the children of Yahweh who pretended giving each of his subjects an equal share of the earth they tread on, an equal share of joys and blessings.

The Israelite's hatred toward the rich abettor of injustice was tangled up with the hatred toward the rich denier of the prescriptions of equality. As he could not attribute divine origin to riches, as he could not believe that Yahweh distributed it, thus breaking the pact which bound him with his nation, the Hebrew decreed that all wealth came from evil, from sin; he said that all property was ill acquired. To make his ideas of justice and

[281] Nehemiah, v, 5.

[282] Isaiah, iii, 14; x. 2.

[283] "Psalms, xciv, 1.

equity agree with reality, which showed him David taking Uri's wife and Ahab despoiling Naboth, he was de-claring that the prosperity of the wicked was a pure phantom, that it lasted little; that, sooner or later, the formidable Sabaoth stretched his right hand upon those who violated his law, and made them return to naught.

Yet the poor, the *anavim,* did not see their wishes being accomplished; before them, ever defying their misery, the rich were making a display of themselves. They would then attribute to their own sins the distress with which they were afflicted; they would carry their hopes forward to the time of Messiah, when all men would be judged with equity, when all would be equal, all free, for they possessed the love of liberty.

This passion contributed also to the formation of the revolutionary spirit of the Jews, and speaking of liberty I do not mean political liberty. The idea of political liberty was born in Israel particularly at the time of the Antiochi and during the Soman sway, when Epiphanes, or Sidetes, Aulus Gabinius, or the other proconsuls, fomented religious persecutions, thus provoking the great nationalist movements of the Zealots and Assassins.

But if the conception of political liberty was tardy, that of individual liberty ever existed among the Jews, for it was an inevitable corollary of their dogma of divinity, it proceeded from their theory of man's creation.

According to this theory, all power belonged to God, and the Jew could be ruled by Yahweh only. He gave account of his deeds to **Adonai** alone, who rules the heavens and earth; none of his fellow-creatures had a right to restrain his activity or to impose his will upon him; with regard to creatures of flesh he was free and was to be free. This conviction incapacited the Hebrew for discipline and subordination, it led him to reject all shackles with which the kings or patricians would have wished to bind him, and the princes of Judaea ever held sway over a people of rebels, incapable of submitting to any yoke or coercion.

One might believe that so thinking the Jews abdicated liberty into the hands of the Lord whom they recognized; nothing of the kind, and they have never been fatalists like the Mohammedans. Over against Yahweh they claimed their free will, and without caring for the contradiction they stood up erect in the face of Him to assert the reality, the inviolability of their self, while they bowed to the whims of their Lord.

Were they not created after the image of God, and was not their nature partaking of this God? Just because they were fashioned after their Creator, their human brethren must not commit the sacrilege of oppressing them; but Yahweh, who had given men the gift of intelligence, was not at liberty to prevent them from directing this intelligence according to their will. The story of the dispute between Rabbi Eliezer and the rabbis, his colleagues, gives us a sufficiently typical sample, and is worth quoting.

In the course of a doctrinal discussion, the divine voice was heard and, breaking in upon the debate, gave right to Rabbi Eliezer. The colleagues of the favored man did not accept the decision of heaven; Rabbi Joshua, one from among them, arose and declared: "Not mysterious voices, but the majority of sages must hereafter decide questions of doctrine. Reason is no longer hidden in heaven, the Law is no longer in the heavens; it has been granted on earth, and it is the task of human reason to comprehend and explain it." [284]

If the divine words met with such a reception when they allowed themselves to force individuals and to wish to impose upon man's reason a will foreign to his own will, how were man's words received ? Renan was right when saying of the Semites: 'There is nothing, there-fore, in these souls to resist the uncontrollable feeling of self," [285] and this was more particularly true of the Jews.

After Yahweh they believed in self only. To the unity of God there corresponded the unity of being; to God absolute—absolute being. Accordingly, subjectivity has ever been the fundamental trait of the Semitic character; it has often led the Jews to egoism, and having once exaggerated this egoism, certain Talmudists ended with recognizing, in the matter of duties, nothing but duties to one's self. This subjectivity, as much as monotheism, accounts for the incapacity shown by the Jews in all plastic arts. As for their literature it was purely subjective; the Jewish prophets, like the psalmists, like the poets of Job and the Song of Songs, like the moralists of the Ecclesiastes and the Book of Wisdom, knew only themselves and generalized their feelings or their personal sensations. This subjectivity also allows to understand why the Jews have at all times, even in our days, shown so much aptness for music—that most subjective of all arts.

[284] Talmud, *Baba Mezia,* 50a.

[285] Ernest Renan, *Histoire generate des langues semitiques.*

Thus they were undeniably individualists, and these men, BO eager to pursue earthly interests, appear to us,— thanks to their uncompromising conception of existence, —as untractable idealists. Now, an individualist imbued with idealism is and will always be in revolt. He will never want to allow anybody to violate his sacred self, and no will will be able to prevail over his.

We have separated all the elements of which was formed the revolutionary spirit in Judaism; they are: the idea of justice, of equality and of liberty. Still, if among the nations Israel was the first to preach these ideas, other nations upheld them at various moments of history, and for all that they were not revolted peoples like the Jewish people. Why? Because, though convinced of the excellence of justice, equality and liberty, these people did not hold their complete realization as possible, in this world at least, and therefore they did not work solely for their advent.

The Jews, on the contrary, not only believed that justice, liberty and equality could be the sovereigns of the world, but they thought themselves specially intrusted with the mission of working for this reign. All the de-sires, all the hopes these three ideas gave birth to ended by crystallizing around one central idea: that of the Messianic times, of the coming of Messiah, who was to be sent by Yahweh to establish the power of these queens of the earth.

The prophets kept up Israel in this dream of an era of happiness and prosperity, and the Psalms of the period after the exile further contributed toward increasing the belief in a blessed epoch when the wicked shall be no more, when "the meek shall inherit the earth; and shall delight themselves in the abundance of peace." [286] From the return from Babylon up to the very agony of the Jewish nation, this Messianic dream lulled the Jews. The tyranny of Antiochus, the Roman oppression, rendered these hopes but more indispensable to the Jews. They consoled themselves of their trials by dreaming of the day of their deliverance; the liberator's image formed little by little before them, and it was all alive in the 60ul of those who heard the voice of John the Baptist exclaim: "The Kingdom of Heavens is to come!" in the heart of those who went after Jesus.

Quite a literature was born of these hopes which so many men played false with during the first century be-fore and after the Christian era; but here I can mention but *The Book of Daniel, The Psalms of Solomon, The Assumption of Moses, The Book of Enoch, The Fourth Book of Ezra, the Sibylline Oracles;* it is impossible for me to analyze these revelations and oracles. Nearly all of them foretell the hour which will witness the Messianic times open; they describe the signs that will announce the Messiah. They also agree in saying that this moment will bring the death of evil, and the Sibyl sums them all up when soothsaying: "From the starry heavens Messiah will descend to men,and with him holy concord, faith, love, hospitality. He will drive iniquity, reprehension, envy, anger, folly, from this world. No more poverty, murders, evil wranglings, dark quarrels, nocturnal thieveries. No more of that which is perverse. . . . The pious men will live happily in cities and

[286] Psalms, xxxvii, 11.

rich estates." [287] The earth will be delivered of injustice, inequality will be known no longer and all men will be free.

Israel did not want to trust any one of those who represented themselves as the Messiah. He rejected all those who said they had been sent from God; he has re-fused to hear Jesus, Bar-Cochba, Theudas, David Alroy, Serene, Moses of Crete, Sabbatai-Zevi. It means that Israel never saw his ideal become real. None of the prophets that came to him has brought the divine justice, triumphant equality or indestructible liberty in the folds of his robe; at the voice of these anointed the Jews did not see chains fall, prison-walls crumble, the rod of authority rot, the ill-gotten treasures of the rich and de-spoilers scatter like empty smoke.

Notwithstanding their long bondage, despite the years of martyrdom which have been their lot, in spite of the centuries of humiliation, which have debased their character, depressed their brains, cramped their intelligence, changed their tastes, their customs, their aptitudes, the debris of Judah have not abjured their so vivid dream, which had been their support and inspiration during the wars for independence.

The funeral-piles, massacres, spoliations, insults, everything contributed to make dearer to them the justice, the equality and the liberty which during many long years were for them the emptiest words. The great voice of the prophets proclaiming that the wicked will be punished one day has always found an echo in these tenacous souls that did not like to bend, and despised

[287] *Sibyllino Oracles,* iii, 573. 685.

this so miserable reality in order to delude themselves with the idea of the future time; that future time, of which Amos and Isaiah, Jeremiah and Ezekiel, and all those have spoken who sang Mizmorim (psalms), to their own accompaniment on stringed instruments. However gloomy the present, Israel never ceased to believe in the future.

The Jews were told: "Why do you await Messiah; obdurate, know ye not that he has come?" They answered with sarcasm, they shrugged their shoulders and replied: "The Messiah has not come, for we are suffer-ing, for famine desolates the land, for the black pest and the nobleman burden the sorrowful wretches!" But when they would be told that their Meshiach would never come, they would lift up their bowed down heads and, stubborn that they were, would say: "Meshiach will come one day and on that day will be understood the word of the Psalmist: '1 have seen the wicked in great power and spreading himself like a green bay tree. Yet he passed away and lo! he was not; yea, I sought him, but he could not be found' [288] and the poor, the just are those who will possess the earth."

The narrow practices into which their doctors had pressed the Jews, have put to slumber their instincts of revolt Under the bonds of the Talmudic laws, they felt tottering in them the ideas that had ever sustained them, and it could be said that Israel could be vanquished only by himself. Still the Talmud did not debase all Jews; among those who rejected it there were some who persisted in the belief that justice, liberty and

[288] Pialms, xxxvii, 35-36]

equality were to come to this world; there were many of them who believed that the people of Yahweh was charged with working for this coming. This makes it plain why the Jews were implicated in all revolutionary movements, for they took an active part in all revolutions, as we shall see when we study their role during all periods of trouble and change. [289]

It remains now to know how the Jew has manifested these revolutionary tendencies, whether he was actually (as he is accused) an element of disturbance in modern societies; and thus we are led to examine the religious, political and economic causes of antisemitism.

[289] It would require a long study to show the role of the Jews In the revolutions. We hope to undertake this study, and we shall bring together, at present, only its elements; it will form part of a book in which we intend to take up again this whole chapter as well as a part of the following chapter; there we shall make a more detailed criticism of the ideas which we have expressed, and we shall examine whether the Jews at all times or at least some among the Jews at all times had not attempted to realise these ideas.

CHAPTER XIII.

THE JEW A8 A FACTOR IN THE TRANSFORMATION OF SOCIETY.—POLITICAL AND RELIGIOUS CAUSES OF ANTISEMITISM.

The Jew as a Revolutionist—The Jews of the Middle Ages and the Spirit of Skepticism.—Jewish Rationalism and Christianity.—The Jews and Secret Societies.—The Role Played by the Jews in the French Revolution and in the Upheavals of the Nineteenth Century.—The Jews and Socialism.—Political, Social and Religious Changes at Work in Present-day Society.—The Grievances of the Conservative Elements and Antisemitism.—The Jew as a Menace to Public Order and a Solvent of Society.—The Judaization of Christian Nations and the Decay of Faith.—Is the Jew Still anti-Christian?—The Persistence of anti-Jewish Prejudices.—Ritual Murder.

—The Jews and the Talmud.—The Synagogue and the Spirit of Religious Indifferentism Among the Jews.—The Emancipated Jew.—Liberalism, Anti-clericalism and the Jews.—Judaism and the Christian State.—The Modern Struggle.—The Spirit of Conservatism versus the Spirit of Revolution.— Tradition and Change.—Antisemitism in an Age of Transition.—The Jew in Society.

Thus it would seem as if the grievance of the anti-Semite were well founded; the Jewish spirit is essentially a revolutionary spirit, and consciously or otherwise, the Jew is a revolutionist. Not content, however, with this, antisemitism would have it that the Jews are the very cause of revolution. Let us see what truth there is in the charge.

Taking him as he was, the tendencies of his nature and the direction of his sympathies made it inevitable that the Jew should play an important part in the revolutions of history; and such a part he has not failed to play. Nevertheless it would be too much to say, with the great mass of Israel's enemies, that every public commotion, every uprising, every political overturning has originated with the Jews, or has been provoked or occasioned by the Jews, and that governments change and take on new forms because the Jew in his secret counsels has plotted such changes and transformations. In maintaining such a proposition we violate the simplest of historical laws, by assigning to a minute cause a totally disproportionate effect, and concentrating our attention upon one phase of historical development to the exclusion of a thousand others of its manifold aspects. Had the Jews perished to a man behind the walls of Zion, the destiny of nations would not have been changed, and though the Jewish element were wanting to this wondrous totality which we call progress, society would have developed notwithstanding. Other forces would have taken the place of the Jews and accomplished what the Jews have accomplished in the general scheme. Given the Bible and Christianity, the intellectual and moral mission of the Jew would have been carried out without him. The Jew, therefore, is not the animating force of the world, nor our sole guide to a newer life. At the same time, those who, in an excess of caution, would represent the Jew as exercising no influence at all in historical evolution, or, going further still, assert that the Jew is essentially inimical to progress, fall into as grave an error as do the antisemites.

The Jew, it is said, is non-progressive; it is necessary to see in what sense and after what fashion this is true. The Jew is non-progressive in so far as regards himself, in clinging tenaciously to his traditions, his modes of worship and his customs. So loath is he to abandon the old that stagnation has resulted, and we may study the life of the Middle Ages in the Jewries of Galicia, Poland and Russia. But in reality it is not so much Judaism which is non-progressive as Talmudism. We have just seen that it is the Talmud alone that can subdue the Jew and tame his rebellious instincts, and it is the study of the Talmud, obligatory and exclusive, that has prevented the Jew from drinking at the real fountain-head, the Bible; the doctors have stifled the prophets. Still, we must not forget that the Talmudists were at one time philosophers also, and philosophers of the rationalist school. [290] In the tenth century the Rabbinites, following in the footsteps of the Karaites, attempted to ground religion upon philosophy. Saadiah, *gaon* of Sora, main-

[290] The Talmud is, as a matter of fact, permeated with the spirit of rationalism; witness the famous controversy between Rabbi Eliezer and his colleagues, in which it was maintained that miracles can not afford sufficient evidence of truth (Talmud, *Baba Mezia,* 69).

tained that side by side with the authority of Scripture and tradition ran the authority of reason, and he preached "not only the right, but the duty, of applying the test of reason to religious belief." [291] In the eleventh century, Ibn Gebirol, known to the scholastics as Avice-bron, gave life to the Arabian philosophy by the publication of his *Fons Vitae.* Of Maimonides and of his work I have already spoken.

It was these rationalist thinkers and philosophers who from the tenth to the fifteenth century, that is, to the Renaissance, took an active part in what might be termed the universal revolution of humanity. To a certain extent they helped Man to free himself from the bonds of religion; and, even if at the beginning of this period they were not fully conscious, perhaps, of the nature of the work they were performing, they accomplished their work nevertheless. At a time when orthodoxy and the Christian faith constituted the foundation of States, he who ventured to attack the established dogmas of faith or gave aid to those who assailed them, was naturally a revolutionist.

Theologians who resort to reason for the defence of dogma, will inevitably end by asserting the superiority of reason to dogma, with fatal results to the latter. Exegesis and freedom of investigation are powerful destroyers, and it is the Jews who originated biblical exegesis, just as they were the first to criticize the forms and doctrines of Christianity. Already had the Jews of Palestine assailed the doctrine of the Incarnation as implying

[291] S. Munk, ***Melanges de philosophic juive et arabe*** (Paris, 1859), p. 478.

a degradation of the divine essence, and therefore impossible, an idea which Spinoza was to take up later in his ***Tractatus theologico-politicus.*** The polemic carried on by the Jews against the Christians was based upon this idea and upon what might be called positivist reasoning. We have an example of the latter in Origen's ***Contra Cel-sum,*** for we know that Celsus had borrowed his rationalist arguments from the Jews of his time. The importance of the controversial literature of the Middle Ages has already been shown. [292] If we study closely we find in it all the arguments advanced by the scholars of our own day. It might, indeed, be maintained in denial of the revolutionary role said to have been played by the Jews, that the greater part of their exegesis was addressed to Jews only, and that it consequently could not have been a means of inciting to change, inasmuch as the Jew knew well how to reconcile the results of textual criticism with the minutiae of his practices and the integrity of his faith. This, however, is not altogether true, for Jewish doctrines did find their way out of the synagogue, and this in two different ways. In the first place, the Jews could always find an opportunity for proclaiming their ideals, thanks to the prevalence of public disputation. In the second place, they were the means of disseminating the Arabian philosophy, and were its expounders at a time, twelfth century, to be precise, when Al Farabi and Ibn Sina were being anathematized in the mosques, and orthodox Mussulmans were feeding the fires with the writings of the Arabian Aristotelians. The Jews of this period translated the writings of Aris-

[292] Chapter vii.

totle and of the Arabian philosophers into Hebrew, and these, retranslated into Latin, afforded the scholastics an opportunity for becoming acquainted with Greek thought. The most famous of the scholastics, "men like Albertus Magnus and St. Thomas Aquinas, studied the works of Aristotle in Latin versions made from the Hebrew." [293]

The Jews did not stop there. They preached the materialism of the Arabian philosophers which was to prove so destructive to the Christian faith, and carried abroad the spirit of skepticism. Their activity was such as to give rise to a general belief in the existence of a secret society sworn to the destruction of Christianity. [294] During the thirteenth century, a century which witnessed the rapid development of that complex of humanism, skepticism and paganism which we call the Renaissance, at a time when the Hohenstaufen defended the cause of science against dogma, and showed themselves the pro-tectors of Epicureanism, the Jews occupied the first place among scholars and rationalist philosophers. At the Court of the Emperor Frederick II, "that hotbed of irreligion," they were received with favor and respect. It was they, as Renan has shown, [295] that created Averro-ism; it was they who established the fame of that Ibn-Roshd, that Averroes whose influence was destined to become so great. Without doubt they had their share, too, in the dissemination of the "blasphemies" of the im-

[293] S. Munk, *loc. cit.*

[294] Cf. the poetic account of the ***Descent of St. Paul into Hell,*** cited by Ernest Renan in his ***Averroes et l'Averroisme,*** p. 284.

[295] E. Renan, *loc. cit.*

pious Arabians; blasphemies which an Emperor, fond of science and of philosophy, encouraged. These find their type in the so-called "Blasphemy of the Three Impostors," Moses, Jesus and Mahomet, invented by the theologians, and their spirit is tersely summed up in the saying of the Arabian soufis, "What care I for the Kaaba of the Mohammedan, the synagogue of the Jew, or the convent of the Christian!" Truly has Darmesteter written : "The Jew was the apostle of unbelief, and every revolt of the mind originated with him, whether secretly or in the open. In that immense foundry of blasphemy maintained by the Emperor Frederick and the princes of Suabia and Aragon, he acted a busy part." [296]

Another thing also is worthy of notice. If the Jews as followers of Averroes, or as unbelievers, skeptics and blasphemers, sapped the foundations of Christianity in spreading the doctrines of materialism and rationalism, they were also the creators of that other enemy of Catholic dogma, pantheism. In fact the *Fons Vitae* of Avice-bron was the well at which numerous heretics drank. It is even quite possible that David de Dinant and Amaury de Chartres, were influenced by the *Fons Vitae* which they knew in a Latin translation made in the twelfth century by the archdeacon Dominique Gundissa-linus. It is certain that Giordano Bruno borrowed from the *Fons Vitae,* whence his pantheism came in part. [297]

If, therefore, the Jews were not solely responsible for the destruction of religious doctrine and the decay of

[296] James Darmesteter: *Coup d'oeil sur L'histoire du peuple juif,* Paris, 1881.

[297] P. 582.

faith, they may at least be counted among those who helped to bring about such a state of desuetude and the changes which followed. If they had never existed, the Arabians and the heterodox theologians would have filled their place; but they did exist, and existing they were not idle. Moreover the Hebrew genius worked not only through them, for their Bible became a powerful aid to all advocates of freedom of thought. The Bible was the soul of the Reformation, just as it was the soul of the religious and political revolution in England. Bible in hand, Luther and the English recusants blazed the path to liberty, and it was through the Bible that Luther, Melanchthon and others broke the yoke of Roman theocracy and overthrew the tyranny of dogma. But they made use, too, of that Jewish scholarship which Nicholas de Lyra had transmitted to the Christian world. ***Si Lyra non lyrasset, Lutherus non sal-tasset,*** it used to be said, and Lyra had studied with the Jews; in fact, he was so steeped in the science of Hebrew exegesis that he was taken for a Jew himself. Here, too, however, it must be remembered, that the Jews were not the cause of the Reformation the absurdity of such a contention is patent), though they certainly were its promoters. This is the line which should separate the impartial historian from the antisemite. The antisem-ite says the Jew is the "designer, the constructor and the chief engineer of revolutions." [298]

The historian confines himself to the task of investigating the role which the Jew, given his genius, his char-

[298] Gougenot des Mousseaux, *Le Juif, le judaisme et le judaise-tion dee peuples chretiens* (p. 25).

acter and the nature of his philosophy and his religion, could possibly have played in the revolutionary process and in the work of revolution itself. By the revolutionary process, I mean the intellectual progress of revolution, or rather what the conservatives call revolution, but which may be described as comprising, on the one hand, the slow but steady subversion of the Christian state and the undermining of religious authority, and on the other hand a parallel development on economic lines. I have just shown, very briefly, it is true, the part played by the Jews in the spread of new ideas during the Middle Ages, as well as at the beginning of the Reformation, and during the Italian Renaissance when Jewish Averroists, like Elias del Medigo, taught at the university of Padua, the last refuge of Arabian philosophy. [299] We might pursue the subject still further in showing what Montaigne, for instance, that half-Jew, owed to his ancestry, and whether it was not from that source that he drew his unbelief and his skepticism. It would be necessary to go still further, to study the critical method of the rationalist Spinoza, and to discover its relation to the Christian exegesis of the Scriptures. It would be necessary to show what were the Jewish elements in the metaphysical system of him whom his contemporaries picttured as the prince of atheists, [300] and who,

> [299] J. Burekhart, ***La civilisation en Italic au temps de la Renaissance*** (Paris, 1885).

> [300] On Spinoza, as an atheist, consult the ***Life of Spinoza,*** by Colerus, an opponent of his; of the numerous works published against Spinoza and the atheistic movement of the seventeenth century, see Kortholt, ***De Tribus Impostoribus,*** which revives the legend of Averroism; also the treatise of the learned Mu-saeus, professor of theology at Jena, "a man of great genius," says oar friend Colerus, "who ***Spinozam pestilentium foctum acutissimis, queis solet, telis confodit.*** " The monstrous cartoons of Spinoza bearing the legend "Signum reprobations in vulta gerens," are well known.

according to Schleiermacher, was drunk with God. It would be necessary, finally, to trace the influence of Spinoza's teachings on philosophic thought, especially at the end of the eighteenth and the beginning of the nineteenth centuries, when the weazened little Jewish lens-maker became the master and the "daily refuge" of Goethe, [301] the saint adored by Novalis and Schleiermacher, the inspiration of the earliest romanticists and metaphysicians of Germany.

In like manner we would have to inquire what was the importance, I will not say of the Jew, but of the Jewish spirit throughout the period of fierce revolt against Christianity which characterized the eighteenth century. We must not forget that in the seventeenth century, scholars like Wagenseil, Bartolocci, Buxtorf and Wolf, had brought forth from oblivion old volumes of Hebrew polemic, written in refutation of the Trinity and the Incarnation and attacking all dogmas and forms of Christianity with a bitterness entirely Judaic, and with all the subtlety of those peerless casuists who created the Talmud. They gave to the world not only treatises on questions of doctrine and exegesis, like the *Nizzachon* or the *Chizuk Emunah,* [302] but published blasphemous tractates and pseudo-lives of Jesus, of the character of the *Toldoth Jesho.* The eighteenth century repeated, concerning Jesus and the Virgin, the outra-

[301] Goethe, Memoires, liv; xvi; *Annates,* 1811.

[302] See Chap. vii.—Wolf, Bibl. Hebr., vol. iv, p. 639.

geous fables invented by the Pharisees of the second century; we find them in Voltaire and in Parny, and their rationalist satire, pellucid and mordant, lives again in Heine, in Boerne and in Disraeli; just as the powerful logic of the ancient rabbis lives again in Earl Marx, and the passionate thirst for liberty of the ancient Hebrew rebels breathes forth again in the glowing soul of Ferdinand Lassalle.

I have sketched here, and that in the broadest strokes, the function performed by the Jews in the development of certain ideas which helped to bring on the general revolution; but I have not yet shown how the activity of the Jew revealed itself in the very work of revolution. I believe I have established the fact, on more than one occasion, that the Jews acted as a leaven upon the economic development of the age, [303] even though their influence may have proved to be, as the partisans of the old régime assert, a source of disorder; order and stability being represented by the Christian monarchical state. If we are to believe Barruel, Crétineau-Joly, Gougenot des Mousseaux, Dom Deschamps, Claudio Jannet, all those who see in history the mere work of secret societies, the role played by the Jews in the political and social upheavals of history has been one of capital importance. True it is that, during the last years of the eighteenth century, secret associations exercised a great influence on the course of events, and though they may not have been formulators of the humanitarian, rationalistic and

[303] I hope to establish the point still more completely in my *Eco nomio History of the Jews,* of which *The Role of Jew in the Frennh. Revolution.* forms but a part

revolutionary theories of the time, such societies certainly were the cause of the enormously widespread dissemination of revolutionary ideas. They were, in fact, great centres of agitation. It cannot be denied that Free Masonry and Martinism were powerful agents in bringing about the revolution, but it must be remembered that their importance increased only as the theories for which they stood became predominant in society, and that, far from being the creators of that spirit of the times which was the fundamental cause of the Revolution, they were in themselves but one of its effects, though an effect to be sure which reacted in its turn upon the course of events.

What then was the connection between these secret societies and the Jews? The problem is a difficult one to solve, for respectable documentary evidence on the subject there is none. It is clear, however, that the Jews were not the dominant factors in these associations, as the writer whom I have just now quoted would have it; they were not "necessarily the soul, the heads, the grand-masters of Free Masonry," as Gougenot des Mous-seaux mantains. [304] It is true, of course, that there were Jews connected with Free Masonry from its birth, students of the Kabbala, as is shown by certain rites which survive. It is very probable, too, that in the years preceding the outbreak of the French Revolution, they entered in greater numbers than ever, into the councils of the secret societies, becoming, indeed, themselves the founders of secret associations. There were Jews in the circle around Weishaupt, and a Jew of Portuguese ori-

[304] Gougenot des Mousseaux, *loc. cit.*

gin, Martinez de Pasquales, established numerous groups of illuminati in France and gathered a large number of disciples, whom he instructed in the doctrines of reintegration.[305] The lodges which Martinez founded were mystic in character, whereas the other orders of Free Masonry were, on the whole, rationalistic in their teachings. This might almost lead one to say that the secret societies gave expression in a way to the twofold nature of the Jew, on the one hand a rigid rationalism, on the other that pantheism which, beginning as the metaphysical reflection of the belief in one God, often ended in a sort of Kabbalistic theurgy. There would be little difficulty in showing how these two tendencies worked in harmony; how Cazotte, Cagliostro, [306] Martinez, Saint-Martin, the Comte de Saint Gervais, and Eckartshausen were practically in alliance with the Encyclopaedists and Jacobins, and both, in spite of their seeming hos-tility, succeeded in arriving at the same end, the under-mining, namely, of Christianity.

This, too, then, would tend to show that though the Jews might very well have been active participants in the agitation carried on by the secret societies, it was not because they were the founders of such associations, but merely because the doctrines of the secret societies agreed so well with their own. The case of Marti-nez de Pasquales is an exceptionable one, and even with regard to him, it should be remembered that before he became the founder of lodges, Martinez had already been initi-

[305] M. Matter, ***Saint Martin et la philotophie inconnue.***

[306] The statement is often made that Cagliostro was a Jew, but the asser-tion is based on no real evidence.

ated into the mysteries of the illuminati and the Rosi-crucians.

During the Revolution the Jews did not remain inactive, considering how few their numbers were in Paris; the position they occupied as district electors, officers of legion, and associate judges, was important. There were eighteen of them in the capital, and one must wade through provincial archives to determine what part they played in affairs. Of these eighteen some even deserve official mention. There was the surgeon Joseph Ravel, member of the General Council of the Commune, who was executed on the ninth Thermidor; Isaac Calmer, President of the Commit-tee of Safety at Clichy, executed on the 29th Messidor, Year II; and Jacob Pe-reira, who had held the post of commissioner of the Belgian government with the army of Dumouriez, and who as a follower of Hébert, was brought to trial and condemned at the same time as his chief, and was executed on the 4th Germinal, Year II. [307]

We have seen how, as followers of Saint Simon, they brought about the economic revolution in which the year 1789 was but a step. [308] the important position occupied by d'Eichthal and Isaac Pereira in the school of Olinde Rodriguez. During the second revolutionary period, which begins in 1830, they displayed even greater ardor than during the first. They were actuated by motives of personal inter-

[307] See Emile Campardon, *he Tribunal revolutionnaire de Paris,* Paris, 1866.— *Proces instruit et juge au tribunal revolutionnaire contre Hebert et ses consorts* (1-4 Germinal), Paris, An. II.— Leon Kahn, *Les Juifs a Paris* (Paris, 1889).

[308] Capefigue, *Histoire des grandes operations financieres.* — Toussenel, *Les juifs rois de l'epoque.*

est, for in the great number of European countries they were not as yet completely emancipated. Those, there-fore, who were not revolutionists by temperament or principle, became such through self-interest. In laboring for the triumph of liberalism, they were looking for their own good. It is beyond a doubt that the Jews, through their wealth, their energy and their talents, supported and furthered the progress of the European revolution. During this period Jewish bankers, Jewish manufacturers, Jewish poets, journalists, and orators, stirred perhaps by quite different motives, were, nevertheless, all striving towards the same goal. "With stooping form, unkempt beard, and flashing eye," writes Cré-tineau-Joly, [309] "they might have been seen breathlessly rushing up and down everywhere in those countries which were unhappy enough to be afflicted with them. Contrary to their usual motives, it was not the desire for wealth that spurred them on to such activity, but rather the thought that Christianity could no longer withstand the repeated shocks which were convulsing society, and they were preparing to wreak on the cross of Calvary revenge for eighteen hundred and forty years of well-deserved suffering."

Nevertheless, it was not such feelings that animated Moses Hess, Gabriel Riesser, Heine, and Boerne in Germany, Manin in Italy, Jellinek in Austria, Lublincr in Poland, and many others besides who fought for liberty in those days. To discover in that all-embracing crusade which agitated Europe until the aftermath of 1848

[309] Crettneau-Joly, ***Histoire de Sonderbund,*** p. 195 (Paris, 1860).

the work of a few Jews intent on revenging themselves on the Nazarene, argues a remarkable mental attitude. Still, whatever may have been the end pursued, self-interest or idealism, the Jews were the most active, the most zealous of missionaries. We find them taking part in the agitation of Young Germany; large numbers of them were members of the secret societies which constituted the fighting force of the Revolution; they made their way into the Masonic lodges, into the societies of the Carbonari, they were found everywhere in France, in Germany, in England, in Austria, in Italy.

Their contribution to present-day socialism was, as is well known, and still is very great. The Jews, it may be said, are situated at the poles of contemporary society. They are found among the representatives of industrial and financial capitalism, and among those who have vehemently protested against capital. Rothschild is the antithesis of Marx and Lassalle; the struggle for money finds its counterpart in the struggle against money, and the worldwide outlook of the stock-speculator finds its answer in the international proletarian and revolution-ary movement. It was Marx who gave the first impulse to the founding of the International through the manifesto of 1847, drawn up by himself and Engels. Not that it can be said that he "founded" the International, as is maintained by those who persist in regarding the International as a secret society controlled by the Jews. Many causes led to the organization of the International, but from Marx proceeded the idea of a Labor Congress, which was held at London in 1864, and resulted in the founding of that society. The Jews constituted a very large proportion of its members, and in the General Council of the society, we find Karl Marx, Secretary for Germany and Russia, and James Cohen, secretary for Denmark. [310] Many of the Jewish members of the International took part subsequently in the Commune, [311] where they found others of their faith. In the organization of the socialistic party, the Jews participated to the greatest extent. Marx and Lassalle in Germany, [312] Aaron Libermann and Adler in Austria, Dobrojan Gherea in Roumania, are or were at one time its creators and its leaders. The Jews of Russia deserve special notice in this brief réumé. Young Jewish students, scarcely escaped from the Ghetto, have played an important part in the Nihilistic propaganda; some, among them women, have given up their lives for the cause of liberation, and to

[310] Besides Marx and Cohen, mention might be made of Neu-mayer, secretary of the bureau of correspondence in Austria; Fribourg, who was one of the directors of the Parisian Federation of the International to which belonged Loeb, Haltmayer, Lazarre and Armand Levi; Leon Frankel, director of the German section at Paris; Cohen who acted as delegate from the Cigar Makers' Union of London to the Congress of the International held at Brussels in 1868; Ph. Coenen who, at the same Congress, represented the Antwerp section of the International, etc. See O. Testat: *L'Internationale,* Paris, 1871; and *L'Internationale au ban de l'Europe* (Paris, 1871-72); Fribourg, *L'Association intenationale des travailleurs* (Paris, 1891).

[311] Among the others Fribourg and Leon Frankel.

[312] There are at present four Jewish social-democrats in the German Reichstag, and among the younger element in the ranks of the socialists, collectivists and communistic anarchists, the number of the Jews is very large. Of the reform party In Germany we may mention Doctor Hertzka, the founder of the Frel-land colony, an attempt at realising the ideal social organisation. (See *Eine Reise nach Freiland,* von Theodor Hertska.

these young Jewish physicians and lawyers, we must add the large number of exiled workingmen who have founded in London and in New York important labor societies, which serve as centres of socialistic and even of anarchistic propaganda. [313]

Thus have I briefly depicted the Jew in his character as a revolutionist, or at least have attempted to show how we might approach the subject. I have described his achievements both as an agent in the dissemination of revolutionary ideas, and as an actual participant in the struggle,, and have shown how he belongs to both those who prepare the way for revolution through the activity of the mind, and

those who translate thought into action. The objection may be raised that, in joining the ranks of revolution, the Jew as a rule, turns atheist, and ceases practically
to be a Jew. This, however, is true only in the sense that the children of the Jewish
radical lose themselves more easily in the surrounding population, and that as a
result the Jewish revolutionist is more easily assimilated. But as a general thing, the
Jew, even the extreme Jewish radical, can not help retaining his Jewish characteristics, and

> [313] In April the members of the Jewish revolutionary party in London,
> celebrated the anniversary of the founding of their club in Berner street. In
> reviewing the history of the social movement among the Jews, the orator
> of the occasion declared that "during the last seven years, the Jew has made
> his entrance as a revolutionary; and now wherever there are Jews, —in
> London, in America, in Austria, in Poland, and in Russia— there are Jew-
> ish revolutionists and anarchists." By seven years, the speaker was referring
> to the date when the proletarian class among the Jews first declared their
> adhesion to the revolutionary propaganda.

though he may have abandoned all religion and all faith, he has none the less
received the impress of the national genius acting through heredity and early training. This is especially true of those Jews who lived during the earlier half of the
nineteenth century, and of whom Heinrich Heine and Karl Marx may serve as fit-
ting examples.

Heine, who in France was regarded as a German, and was reproached in Germany with being French, was before all things a Jew. As a Jew he sang the praises
of Napoleon, for whom he entertained a fervent admira-tion common to all the
German Jews, who had been freed from their disabilities by the Emperor's will.
Heine's disenchantment, his irony, are the disenchantment and the irony of the
Ecclesiastes ;like Koheleth he bore within him the love for life and for the pleasures
of the earth; and before sorrow and disease ground him down death to him was
the worst of evils. Heine's mysticism came to him from the ancient Job. The only
philosophy that ever really attracted him was pantheism, a doctrine which seems to
come naturally to the Jewish philosopher who in speculating upon the unity of God

by instinct transforms it into a unity of substance. His sensuous-ness, that sad and voluptuous sensuousness of the ***Intermezzo,*** is purely oriental, and has its source in the Song of Songs. The same is true of Marx. The descendant of a long line of rabbis and teachers he inherited the splendid powers of his ancestors. He had that clear Talmudic mind which does not falter at the petty difficulties of fact. He was a Talmudist devoted to sociology and applying his native power of exegesis to the criticism of economic theory. He was inspired by that ancient Hebraic materialism, which, rejecting as too distant and doubtful the hope of an Eden after death, never ceased to dream of Paradise realized on earth. But Marx was not merely a logician, he was also a rebel, an agitator, an acrid controversalist, and he derived his gift for sarcasm and invective, as Heine did, from his Jewish ancestry.

Continuing the argument we might show what Boerne, what Lassalle, what Moses Hess and Robert Blum owed to their Hebrew origin, and the same with Disraeli; and thus we would prove the never-failing persistence, among thinkers, of the Jewish spirit, that Jewish spirit which we have already found in Montaigne and Spinoza. But if the writers, scholars, poets, philosophers, and sociologists of the Jewish race have preserved this spirit, is it also true of the mass of the people who actually constitute the main strength of socialism or anarchism? Here a distinction must be made. The Jews of whom I speak, the Jews of London, the United States, Holland, Germany and Australia have accepted revolutionary doctrines in so far as they belong to the proletariat, in so far, that is, as they are a part of that class which, for the future, is destined to be engaged in continuous warfare against capital; and if they embrace the cause of revolution they do so by virtue of certain social laws which drive them to such a course. Therefore they do not initiate revolution, but rather adhere to it, follow its progress, and put no obstacles in its way. And yet these groups of workingmen cut off from their ancient faith, and free from all religion, from all belief, in fact, are Jews in the national sense, even though they are no longer Jews in the religious sense. The Jews of London and of the United States, who, to escape the persecutions to which they are subjected in Poland and Russia, abandoned their native country, have formed associations among themselves in their new homes; they have organized societies calling themselves "Jewish-speaking groups," and as such have gained representation at the labor congresses. They speak a jargon which is a mixture of German and Hebrew, and not only employ it in their daily inter-course, but even publish their party organs in that vernacular and print them in Hebrew characters. The objection might of course be raised that, driven from their native country, and coming to a land the language of which was strange to them, they have been obliged to cling together, and that naturally they continue to make use of the vernacular which is familiar to them. This objection is true enough, but it may be pointed out that in other countries, as in the Netherlands and Galicia, the workingmen of Jewish nationality are likewise organized in separate associations.

The Jew, therefore, does take an active part in revolutions ; and he participates in them in so far as he is a Jew, or more correctly in so far as he remains Jewish. Is it for this reason, then, that the conservative elements among Christians are an-tisemites, and is this predisposition of the Jews for revolutionary ideas a cause of antisemitism? We may say at once that the great majority of conservatives overlook entirely the historic and educative role of the Jews. It is appreciated only, and that very imperfectly, by the theorists and the literary men among the antisemites. The hatred against Israel does not come from the fact that the Jews were instru-mental in bringing about the Terror, or that Manin lib-crated Venice, or that Marx orga-nized the International. Antisemitism, the antisemitism of the Christian conserva-tives, says: "If modern society is so different from the old regime; if religious faith has diminished; if the political system has been entirely changed; if stock-gambling, if speculation, if capital in its industrial and financial forms, knowing no spirit of nationality dominates now and is to dominate in the future, the fault rests with the Jew." Let us clearly examine this point. The Jew has been living for centuries in the midst of those nations which, so it is said, are now perishing on account of his presence. Why, it may be asked, has the poison taken such a long time to work? The usual answer is, because formerly the Jew was outside of society; because he was carefully kept apart. Now that the Jew has entered into society, he has become a source of dis-order, and, like the mole, he is busily engaged in undermining the ancient foundations upon which rests the Christian state. And this accounts for the decline of nations, and their intellectual and moral decadence: they are like a hu-man body which suffers from the intrusion of some foreign element which it can-not assimilate and the presence of which brings on convulsions and lasting disease.

By his very presence the Jew acts as solvent; he produces disorders, he destroys, he brings on the most fearful catastrophes. The admission of the Jew into the body of the nations has proved fatal to them; they are doomed for having received him. Such is the very simple explanation which the antisemites advance to account for the changes which society is undergoing. For them there are no such things as economic revolutions, no transformations in the nature of capital, no such changes in the human conscience. There are only two things which they take into consideration: formerly there was a flourishing and prosperous order of society based upon solid moral, political and religious principles; now men have overturned all the ancient moral standards, and have abandoned all the judicious and salutary ideas concerning the necessity of absolute authority and a priestly hierarchy to preserve the bonds of society. But, in former days, the Jew was not acknowledged a member of society; at present, on the contrary, he constitutes a very important element in it. Here, therefore, is a clear case of cause and effect, and the Jew has been made accountable for the work of ages, for the work of a thousand different forces which combine to produce national progress.

The accusation has not been limited to this alone. The Jew, it is said, is not only a destroyer, but also an up-builder; arrogant, ambitious and domineering, he seeks to subject everything to himself. He is not content merely to destroy Christianity, but he preaches the gospel of Judaism; he not only assails the Catholic or the Protestant faith, but he incites to unbelief, and then im-poses on those whose faith he has undermined his own conception of the world, of morality and of life. He is engaged in his historic mission, the annihilation of the religion of Christ Are the Christian antisemites right or wrong in this respect? Has the Jew retained his ancient notions; is he still in his actions anti-Christian? I say in his actions, because he is necessarily anti-Christian, by definition, in being a Jew, just as he is anti-Mohammedan, just as he is opposed to every principle which is not his own. The answer is that the Jew has retained his ancient animosities precisely where he has been kept outside of society; wherever he herds apart; in the Ghettoes, where he lives under the guidance of his rabbis, who unite with the powers in authority to pre-vent him from attaining light; everywhere, in fact, where the Talmud still dominates, and especially in eastern Europe where official antisemitism still prevails. In western Europe where the Talmud nowadays has lost its influence and the Jewish *cheder* has given place to the public school, the hereditary hatred of the Jew for the Christian has disappeared in the same proportion as the hatred of the Christian for the Jew. For we must not forget that though we speak frequently of the animosity of the Jew against the Christian, we speak very rarely of the animosity of the Christian against the Jew, a feeling which always thrives. Prejudice against the Jew, or, better still, the numerous prejudices against the Jew are not dead. People still believe in an odor peculiar to the Jews; a German antisemite goes so far as to declare that Pope Pius IX was a Jew, and that he became aware of the fact from the odor of the slipper which the Pope had extended for him to kiss. Others have retained a dim belief in certain diseases peculiar to the Jews, and by the side of antisemitic physicians, devoted to the discovery of Jewish maladies, there are writers who descant gravely upon the physical type of the Jewish tribes. We find in the publications of the antisemites all the ancient charges, which were brought forward in the Middle Ages, and which the seventeenth century revived, accusations which find support in popular belief. The most persistent of all accusations, however, and the one which typifies best the historic struggle of Judaism against Christianity, is the charge of ritual-murder. The Jew, it is maintained to the present day, has need of Christian blood in order to celebrate his Passover. What is the origin of this accusation which goes back to the twelfth century?

The first instance of such an accusation being brought against the Jews occurred at Blois, in 1171, when they were accused of having crucified a child during their celebration of Passover. Count Theobald of Chartres, after having caused the accuser of the Jews to undergo the ordeal by water, which proved favorable to him, condemned thirty-four Jewish men and seventeen Jewish women to be burnt.

We can see clearly enough why the Romans should have brought the identical charge against the early Christians. It arose from a materialistic conception of the Lord's Supper, from a literal interpretation of the words employed in consecrating the flesh and blood of Jesus. But how could the Jews, whose sacred books breathe forth a horror of blood, have given occasion, and still give occasion, for such a belief? This question must be discussed to the very bottom. We must examine the theories advanced by those who would have it that human sacrifice is a Semitic institution, whereas, as a matter of fact, it is found among all peoples at a certain stage of civilization. In this manner we would prove, as has in fact been proven, that the Jewish relig-ion does not demand blood. Can we, however, prove, in addition, that no Jew ever shed blood? Of course not, and throughout the Middle Ages there must have been Jewish murderers, Jews whom oppression and persecution drove to avenge themselves by assassinating their persecutors or even perhaps their children. Nevertheless, this does not afford a sufficient explanation for the popular belief which has its real origin in the widespread conviction that the Jew was irresistibly impelled every year and at the same time to reproduce exactly the murder of Christ. It is for this reason that in the legendary acts of the Infant martyrs the victims are always shown as crucified and undergoing the agony of Jesus: sometimes even they are represented as wearing a crown of thorns and with their sides pierced. To this general belief there were added the accusations, often justified, which were brought against the Jews as being addicted to the practice of magic. Throughout the Middle Ages the Jew was considered by the common people as the magician par *excellence.* As a matter of fact, a number of Jews did devote themselves to magic. We find many formulas of exorcism in the Talmud, and the demonology both of the Talmud and the Kabbala is very complicated Now it is well known the blood played always a very important part in the arts of sorcery. In Chaldean magic, it was of the utmost consequence; in Persia it was considered as a means of redemption, and it delivered all those who submitted themselves to the practices of Taurobolus and Kriobolus. The Middle Ages were haunted by the idea of blood as they were haunted by the idea of gold; for the alchemist, for the enchanter blood was the medium through which the astral light could work. The elemental spirits, according to the magicians, utilized outpoured blood in fashioning a body for themselves, and it is in this sense that Paracelsus speaks when he says that "the blood lost by them brought into being phantoms and larvae." To blood, and especially to the blood of a virgin, unheard of powers were assigned. Blood was the curer, the redeemer, the preserver; it was useful in the search for the Philosopher's Stone, in the composition of potions, and in the practice of enchantments. Now it is quite probable, certain, in fact, that Jewish magicians may have sacrificed children, and thence the genesis of ritual murder. The isolated acts of certain magicians were attributed to them in their character as Jews. It was maintained that the Jewish religion which approved of the Crucifixion of Christ, prescribed in addition the shedding of Christian blood; and the Talmud and the Kabbala were zealously searched for text that might be made to justify such a thesis. Such investigations have succeeded only through deliberate misinterpretation, as in the Middle Ages, or through actual falsifications like those recently committed by Dr. Rohling, and proven spurious by Delitzch. The result, therefore, is this, that whatever the facts brought forward, they cannot prove that the murder of children constituted, or still constitutes, a part of the Jewish ritual any more than the acts of the maréchal de Retz and of the sacrilegious priests who practised the "black mass" would prove that the Church recommends in its books assassination and human sacrifice.

Are there still in existence in the East sects maintaining such practices ? It is possible. [314] Do Jews constitute a part of such societies? There is nothing to support 6uch a contention. The general accusation of ritual murder, therefore, is shown to be utterly baseless. The murder of children, I speak of cases where murder was actually proved, and these are very rare, [315] can be attributed only to vengeance or to the practices of magicians, practices which were no more peculiar to Jews than to Christians.

The persistence of these accusations against the Jews is significant, in that it shows what old leaven of hatred still lies in the souls of the people against the murderers of Christ. For it stands to reason that a Christian anti-semite does not believe that the Jew of the present time who has abandoned his ancient customs, the Jew whom

[314] In 1814 a Christian sect arose in Bavaria, known as the Brothers and Sisters of Prayer, the members of which brought human sacrifices to God. The founder of this sect was called Poeschl. In Switzerland, in 1815, a certain Joseph Ganz, founded a similar association, to which he gave the same name, and which practised the same rites.

[315] Consult the report of Ganganelli, afterwards Pope Clement XIV, which, after an investigation into the charges of ritual murder brought

against the Jews, arrives at the conclusion of their absolute falsity. (*Revue des Etudes Juives,* April-June, 1880). It may be observed here that the bodies of children murdered for the purpose of magical practices were never found, the magicians having prudently burnt them.

he rubs up against in the street every day, really makes use of the blood of little children at certain periods and for his own welfare. The real feeling is that he belongs to a race which, through hatred of the name of Jesus, has prescribed ritual murder, and the antisemite is ready to declare that if the enlightened Jew has abandoned these abominable and obsolete customs, he has nevertheless preserved the feeling which made them possible. He no longer transpierces the Host, to make it shed blood, but he attacks Christ in attacking His Church; he is perpetually plotting the destruction of the Christian faith, he is busily planting the seeds of disorder, and he brings doubt upon the spirits of men. How much truth is there in these statements? It cannot be denied that the Orthodox Jew has certain prejudices against the Christian, but have not the Christians the very same prejudices against him? Nay, more, do not these feelings prevail between Protestants and Catholics? It is precisely the Orthodox Jew who is an element of conservatism. M. Anatole Leroy-Beaulieu was right in saying: "Is it the Jew of Poland, of Russia, or of Roumania that appears to you as a fabricator of revolution? Look at him. Is it he or the like of him that has succeeded in impelling the modern world into untrodden ways? Is it him we suspect of imperilling Christian civilization? Poor wretch; for that, he is too degraded, too poor, too ignorant, too indifferent to our religious and political quarrels. Question him; he will not understand you: but that is not all. He is in addition too much of a Jew, too religious, too devout, too faithful to tradition; in a word, too conservative." Among the nations of the West, the orthodox Jew likewise affords evidences of his conservatism. He holds to the law and to the regulations of society. He knows how to reconcile his Judaism with a spirit of patriotism, which in its excess amounts at times almost to Jingoism. As we have seen, it was only a minority of emancipated Jews who took part in the French Revolution. These emancipated Jews, even though they might abandon their faith, could not for all that cease to be Jews. And, indeed, how could they have done otherwise? By embracing Christianity, it is said, a course of action fol-lowed by some, but from which the majority have recoiled, as merely hypocrisy on their part, inasmuch as the emancipated Jew speedily arrives at a state of irre-ligion. They have therefore remained Jews by apathy. All those revolutionaries of the first half of the nineteenth century, of whom I have spoken, were brought up in Judaism, and if they abandoned Judaism in the sense that they no longer practised it, they remained its adherents in retaining the spirit of their nation.

The emancipated Jew, being no longer bound by the faith of his ancestors, and owning no ties with the old forms of a society in the midst of which he had lived an outcast, has become in modern nations a veritable breeder of revolutions. Now it has happened that the emancipated Jew has drawn perceptibly nearer to the Christian unbeliever; but instead of observing that the Christian has allied himself with the Jew, because he, too, like the Jew, has lost his religion, the antisemites would have us believe that the Jew, by his very contact, has undermined the faith of the Christians who have joined him. The Jews, therefore, are made responsible for the disappearance of religious belief, and the general decay of faith; and in doing so, moreover, the antisemite does not distinguish between the Jew who is still faithful to his religion and the emancipated Jew. To the impartial observer, however, it is not the Jew that is destroying Christianity. The Christian religion is disappearing like the Jewish religion, like all religions, which we may now observe in their slow agony. It is passing away under the blows of reason and of science. It is dying a natural death, because it essentially was in harmony with only one period of civilization, and because the further we advance, the less in harmony it is with changing conditions. From day to day our yearning for the irrational and our need of the supernatural is disappearing, and with them our need for religion, especially for the rites of religion: for those even who believe in God, do not believe in the necessity nor in the efficacy of worship.

Has the Jew taken part in this unfolding of the modern spirit? Certainly he has, but he is by no means the creator of it, nor even responsible for it, for he has merely brought an insignificant stone to the edifice which the ages have built up. Wipe the Jew out of existence, the decadence of Catholicism or Protestantism will not be retarded in the least. If the Jew gives us an impression to the contrary, it is because he has played a very great role in Germany, in Austria, in Prance, and in Italy, in the history of modern liberalism, and liberalism has advanced hand in hand with anti-clericalism. The Jew has indeed been an anti-clerical. He prepared the way for the Kulturkampf in Germany, he supported the Ferry laws in France. The general belief is that the Jew was a liberal because he was an anti-Christian, whereas the contrary is true. From this point of view it is only just to admit that the Jewish Liberals have been hurtful to Christianity, or, at least, that they have been the allies of those whose activity was inimical to Christianity. For the antisemite and conservative, to de-Christianize is to denationalize, which argues a con-fuson of thought on their part, in that they make nation and state synonymous. Anti-clerical liberalism does not denationalize. It does destroy the old Christian state. But the nineteenth century witnessed the last effort on the part of the Christian state to retain its dominance. The conception of a feudal state, based upon unity of belief, and in the advantages of which heretics and unbelievers could not participate, is opposed to the notion of a neutral and secular state, upon which the greater number of political entities are at present based. Thus anti-semitism represents one phase of the struggle going on between the two types of state of which we have just spoken. The Jew is the living testimony of the disappearance of that state which had its foundation in theological principles and the restoration of which is the dream of the Christian antisemite. The day when the Jew was first admitted to civil rights the Christian state was in danger. This is true, and the antisemites who say that the Jews have destroyed the idea of State could more justly say that the entrance of the Jew into society marked the destruction of the State, meaning by State the Christian State. In the eyes of the conservative, nothing indeed is BO significant as the presence of the Jew in modern society; and by a very common mode of reasoning they have made a cause out of that which is only an effect, because this effect in its turn acts, it is true, as a cause.

These, then, in brief, are the political and religious mainsprings of antisemitism. First and fundamental are hereditary dislike and prejudice; then, as a result of these prejudices, an exaggerated conception of the role which the Jews have played in the development and or-ganization of modern society; a conception in which the Jews appear as the representatives of the revolutionary spirit, against the spirit of established order; of change against tradition; a conception which makes them responsible in this age of transition for the fall of antiquated institutions and the disappearance of ancient beliefs.

CHAPTER XIV.

THE ECONOMIC CAUSES OF ANTISEMITISM.

Economic Antisemitism.—The Case Against the Jew. —The Moral Charge.— The Dishonest Jew.—Jewish Astuteness and Bad Faith.—The Corrupting Influence of the Talmud.—Restrictive Legislation and Jewish Fraud.—Mercantilism and Usury as Causes of Degradation.—Money and the Decline of Morality.—The Economic Charge.—The Jew and Present Social Conditions.—The Importance of the Jews in Capitalistic Society.—The Jew in Finance and in Industry.—The Jew as the Possessor of Capital.—Disadvantages under Which the Jew Labors under Present Conditions.—The Jewish Proletarians in Europe and America.—The Jews of the Middle Class.—The Relative Supremacy of the Jew. —Causes of Such Supremacy.— Jewish Solidarity versus Middle Class Individualism.—The Jewish Brotherhood.— Its Origin and Antiquity.—The Synagogues.—The Middle Ages.—The Ghettoes.— Modern Times.—The Kahal in the Countries of the East.—Minorities in Western Europe and the Solidarity of Classes.—Opposition Between Different Forms of Capital as a Cause of Antisemitism.— Agricultural Capital versus Industrial Capital.— The Jewish Stockbroker and the Small Trader.— Competition and Antisemitism.— Competition in the Banks of Capital and in the Labor Market.—Grievances Against the Jews and Economic Antisemi-tism.—Antisemitism and the Intestine Struggles of Capital.

After being assailed as a Semite, as a stranger, as a revolutionist, as an enemy to Christianity, the Jew is attacked as a factor in economic affairs. This has been the case ever since the dispersion. Already before our era the Romans and the Greeks were jealous of the privileges which permitted the Jews to carry on trade under more favorable conditions than the rest of the people, [316] and during the Middle Ages the usurer was hated as much as, if not more than, the murderer of Christ. [317] The condition of the Jews was changed at the end of the eighteenth century; and so favorable was the change to them that it tended to confirm, if not to increase, the feeling of antipathy with which they were regarded. Economic antisemitism to-day is stronger than it ever was, for the reason that to-day, more than ever, the Jew appears powerful and rich. Formerly he was not seen: he remained hidden in his Ghetto, far from Christian eyes. He had but one care, to conceal his wealth, that wealth of which tradition regarded him as the gatherer, and not the proprietor. The day he was freed from his disabilities, the day the restrictions put to his activities fell away, the Jew showed himself in public. Indeed, he showed himself with ostentation. He wished, after centuries of imprisonment, after years of oppression, to ap-

[316] Chap. ii.

[317] Chap. v.

pear a man; and he had the naive vanity of the savage. That was his way of reacting upon centuries of humiliation. On the eve of the French Revolution, they saw him humble, timid, an object of general contempt, exposed to insult and injury. They found him after the tempest, free, liberated from every constraint, and from a slave, become a master. Such a rapid exaltation was offensive. People were affronted by the wealth which the Jews had now attained the right to pile up, and recourse was had at once to the old accusation of the fathers, the charge that the Jew was an enemy to society. The wealth of the Jew, it was said, is gained at the expense of the Christian. It is acquired through deception, through fraud, through oppression, by all means and principally by detestable means. This is what I shall call the moral charge of the Antisemites, and it may be summed up thus: the Jew is more dishonest than the Christian; he is entirely unscrupulous, a stranger to loyalty and candor.

Is this charge well founded ? It was true and still is true in all those countries

where the Jew is kept outside of society; where he receives only the traditional Talmudic education; where he is exposed to persecution, to insult, and to oppression;
where people refuse to recognize in him the dignity and the independence of the
human being. The moral condition of the Jew is due partly to himself, and partly to
exterior circumstances. His soul has been moulded by the law which "he imposed
on himself, and the law which has been forced upon him. Throughout the centuries
he lived twice a slave: he was the bondman of the law, and the bondman of everyone. He was a pariah, but a pariah whom teachers and guides united to keep in a
state of servitude more complete than the ancient bondage of Egypt. From without
a thousand restrictions impeded his way, arrested his development, restrained his
activity; within he was confronted by an elaborate system of prohibitions. Outside the Ghetto he experienced the constraint of the law; within the Ghetto he
suffered the oppression of the Talmud. If he attempted to escape from the one, a
thousand punishments awaited him; if he ventured to depart from the other, he
exposed himself to the **Cherem,** that awful excommunication which left him alone
to the world. It would have been vain to attack these two hostile powers boldly; and
therefore the Jew attempted to triumph over them by guile. Both forms of oppression developed in him the instinct of cunning. He attained to an une-qualed talent
for diplomacy, to a subtlety rarely found. His natural finesse increased, but it was
employed for base purposes—to deceive a tyrannical God and despotic rulers. The
Talmud and anti-Judaic legislation united to corrupt the Jew to his very depths. Impelled by his teachers, on the one hand, by hostile legislation on the other, by many
social causes besides, [318] to the exclusive occupation of commerce and of usury,
the Jew became degraded. The pursuit of wealth ceaselessly prosecuted, debauched
him, weakened the voice of conscience within him, taught him habits of fraud. In
this war of self-preservation which he was forced to carry on against the world and
against the secular and religious law, he could conquer only by intrigue, and the
unhappy wretch, given

[318] Chap. v.

oyer to humiliations, to insults, forced to bow his head under blows and curses
and persecution, could avenge himself on his enemies, his tormentors, his execu-

tioners only by guile. Bobbery and bad faith became his weapons ; they were the only weapons of which he could possibly make use, and therefore he exerted himself to elaborate them, to sharpen them, and to conceal them.

When the walls of the Ghetto were overthrown, the Jew, such as he had been made by the Talmud and the legislative and social restrictions imposed upon him, did not change all at once. Upon the morrow of the Revolu-tion he lived just as he had lived upon its eve, nor did he alter his customs, his manners, and, above all, his spirit, as quickly as his condition in life had been altered. Liberated, he retained the soul of a slave, that soul which he is losing day by day as one by one the memories of his degradation are disappearing. To-day, in order to find the Jew as the antisemites represent him, we must go to Russia, to Roumania, to Poland, where discriminating laws still rage in full force, or to Hungary, Galicia and Bohemia, where the Jewish schools retain their exclusive domination. And if in Western Europe there are Jews of a certain category among those engaged in trade and speculation who are, by force of inherited instinct, still given to cunning, to intrigue and even to deception, they are no worse in this respect than the traders and speculators of the Christian faith, whom long experience in business has rendered unscrupulous. To such an assertion, however, the antisemites always have this answer ready: "The Jews have perverted the Christians, and even though it be confessed that the class of capitalists, entrepreneurs and traders shows itself harsh, cruel, grasping, faithless towards the exploited class, the fault rests with the Jews, who are responsible for present social conditions, nay, more, who are the very cause of such conditions." This is really the great economic charge against the Jews.

But here, too, the antisemites are the victims of an error. The Jew is not the cause of the present state of things which is, in reality, the result of a long evolution. It is true that he has played his part in the economic revolution which has resulted in establishing the supremacy of the bourgeoisie; but far from being the cause, he has been only one of the factors that have brought about such a transformation, by no means the sole factor, nor even the principal one. [319]

I have already shown [320] how in the course of time the bourgeoisie found in the Jew a powerful and marvel-ously endowed ally. During long centuries, while society was still plunged in the barbarism of the Middle Ages, the Jew, the trader of old, well armed, well provided with a fine mental equipment, and rich in the possession of ages of experience, was either the representative of capital as employed in commerce and in usury, or else aided in its creation. Nevertheless, these forms of capital did not attain their greatest influence until the labor of centuries had prepared the way for their domination and had transformed them into industrial and bonded capital. To accomplish this Capital needed those two great movements, the Crusades and the

[319] Chap. v.

[320] Chap. ix.

discovery of America, followed by the manifold colonial enterprises of Spain, of Portugal, of the Netherlands, of England, and of Prance, all the activity, in fact, of the age of commercial development. It needed the establishment of public credit and the rise of great banking institutions. It needed the rise of manufactures and the scientific discoveries which brought about the invention and the perfection of machinery. It needed all the elaborate legislation looking towards the restriction of the laborer's rights and wages, until the moment came when the proletariat was deprived even of the right of association; it needed all that and many other causes besides, causes historic, religious and moral, in order to make present-day society what it is. Those who maintain that the Jews are the sole cause of the present state of things succeed only in establishing their own absurdly marvelous ignorance.

Of course, as I have just said, the part played by the Jews in the development of modern society, was important, but its true character is very little known, or, at least, very imperfectly known, and that especially to the antisemites. It is not to this very elementary knowledge of the economic history of the Jews that antisemitism must be atributed. Our knowledge of the Jews since their emancipation is more complete; in France, under the Restoration and the July Monarchy, they stood at the head of the financial and industrial enterprise, and were among the founders of the great canal, railway and insurance companies. In Germany their activity was exceedingly great. They were at the bottom of all the legislation favorable to the carrying on of banking and exchange, the practice of usury and speculation. It was they who profited by the abolition, in 1867, of the ancient laws limiting the rate of interest. They were active in bringing about the enactment of the law of June 1870, which exempted stock companies from government supervision. After the Franco-German War, they were among the boldest speculators, and at a time when German capitalists were carried away by a passion for the creation of industrial combinations, they acted a no less. important part than had the Jews of Prance, from 1830 to 1848. [321] Their activity persisted until the financial panic of 1873, when the country squires and the small traders who had been ruined by the excesses of this Gründer Periode (the era of promoters) in which the Jew had played the most important part, gave themselves up to the most violent antisemitism, such, indeed, as proceeds only from injured interests.

Once the important part played by the Jews of this period had been proven, and, indeed, their importance was undeniable, people proceeded to the conclusion that the Jew was the possessor of capital *par excellence.* This became an added cause of hatred against him. The Jews, it was asserted, held everything, and the word Jew, after having been a synonym for knave, malefactor and usurer, came to be used as equivalent to rich. Every Jew is a capitalist; such is the common belief. The error of course is deep. The vast majority of Jews, nearly seven-eighths of the total number, in fact, live in extreme poverty. In Russia, in Galicia, in Roumania,

[321] Otto Glagau, *loc. cit.*

Servia and Turkey, their destitution is appalling. For the most part they are artisans, and as such they suffer equally with Christian wage-earners from present social conditions. They are, indeed, among the most disinherited of the proletariat. In the East End of London, in that congested Jewish population composed almost entirely of refugees from Poland, Jewish tailors, working twelve hours a day in the sweatshops, earn on an average twelve cents an hour. The majority, moreover, find employment only during three days in the week, a large number work only from two to three days a week, and at all times there is an unemployed population of from ten to fifteen thousand Jews living in a state of utter misery, verging on starvation. In New York, they are counted by the hundred thousand, and before the organization of the tailors' unions, many were forced to work twenty hours a day for five or six dollars a week. Since the foundation of the unions, however, though their earnings may not have increased, the hours of labor have been reduced to eighteen hours per day, and in some factories to sixteen. [322] In Russia their condition is still worse. In Vilna, Jewish women employed in the knitting mills receive forty kopecks (the kopeck is equal to one-half of a cent) for a day of fourteen hours. Fifty kopecks is the average wage for men in all of the trades, for a day varying from fourteen to twenty hours. The immense majority of working men crowded together within the cities of the Pale can find no market at all for their labor. [323] In Gali-

[322] Miss I. Van Etten, "The Russian Jews as Immigrants," *The Forum,* April, 1893.

[323] Leo En-era, *The Russian Jew.*

cia the condition of the working population is no better, and the same is true of Roumania.

There remain, then, about two million Jews in Western Europe and in the United States, who may be said to belong to the middle class. Of these two millions, however, it must be admitted that if they were of very little importance a hundred years ago, they are of very great importance to-day. Through their wealth, through their education, through their relations to one another, they occupy a place far out of proportion to their numbers. Compared with the general body of the population they are but a handful, and yet their position in life is such that they are to be seen everywhere, and in number seem to be legion. It is true that we must avoid the comon error of comparing them with the total population of any country, inasmuch as they do not generally live outside of towns, but confine themselves to the cities where they play a correspondingly important part. If we would arrive at some exact statistical basis we must compare them to the Christian population of their own class, that is, to the bourgeoisie of commerce, industry and finance. And yet even when we reduce the comparison to these two factors, the Jew versus the bourgeoisie, it is still in favor of the Jew.[324]. Wherefore, then, this pre-

> [324] It is customary to compare the two million Jews, who may be called the possessors of capital in various degrees, to the total mass of Christian inhabitants, overlooking the fact that the vast majority of Jews is composed of laborers and artisans. If we wish to consider the Jews as a nation, a nation with no determined geographical boundaries, we must endeavor to ascertain whether there are not among them both a class of wage-earners and class of capitalists, as indeed I have already proven, and then to compare the class of Jewish capitalists with the class of Christian capitalists. In this manner only can we attain a correct formula for the purpose of statistical comparison and a true version of things.

ponderance? Some Jews are in the habit of ascribing their economic supremacy to their intellectual superiority. This boast of Jewish superiority is not altogether true, or, at least, requires explanation. In the present bourgeois society, which is founded upon the exploitation of capital and upon exploitation by capital, where the power of wealth is supreme, where stock-jobbing and speculation are all-powerful, the Jew is certainly better equipped for success than any other body. Though he may have been degraded by his exclusive devotion to commerce through the ages, his experience has nevertheless endowed him with certain qualities which have become of surpassing value in the new organization of society. He is cold and calculating, supple and energetic, persevering and patient, clear and exact, qualities which he has inherited all from his ancestors, the money changers and traders of mediaeval times. When he devotes himself to commerce or to finance, he naturally profits by the educaton which his ancestors have undergone through centuries, an education which has rendered him, perhaps, not more suited for certain pursuits as his vanity suggests, but certainly more adaptable to them. In the present industrial struggle, he is better endowed, man for man,—I am speaking in general terms— than his competitors, and all things being equal, he must succeed because of his superior equipment. He has no need to make use of fraud, or, at least, to make more use of it than his neighbors, since his personal and inherited qualities are sufficient to assure him the victory.

Still the possession of such personal gifts is not sufficient to explain the preponderance of the Jews. Among the Christians, too, there are ancient merchant families; a section of the bourgeoisie has inherited qualities very similar to those of the Jews, and therefore it would seem, should be able to challenge the Jews successfully. The answer is that there are other, farther reaching causes, arising both from the nature of the Jew and from the charcater of modern society. Bourgeois society is based entirely upon competition between man and man in the field of the daily necessities of life. It affords us the spectacle of individuals fighting bitterly one against the other, of isolated units stubbornly disputing the victory and making use of their own individual resources. In this state of society Darwin's principle of the struggle for life dominates. This spirit governs the actions of every man, and tacitly it is recognized that victory ought to belong to the strongest, to him, that is, who is best equipped, whose body and whose spirit are most perfectly adjusted to the social conditions of existence. That form of activity which is based on solidarity, on common action, and on a common understanding, is to be found only outside of this class. Historians, philosophers and economists unite in recognizing only the principle of individual effort. It is only against its common enemies, against the proletariat and against those who attack capital that our capitalistic Bourgeoisie resorts to the principle of solidarity. If we conceive, then, in the midst of such a community, based upon egoistic action, associations of citizens strongly organized and gifted, animated for many centuries by the spirit of common action, and knowing by instinct and experience, the advantages which they may derive from union, it is certain that such organizations by - directing their activity towards the same end as that pursued by the scattered individuals around them will possess such an advantage in the struggle as to assure them an easy victory. This is just the role which is being played by the Jews of the middle class in modern society. They are desirous of winning the same prizes of life as the Christian; they enter the same field of battle; they have the same ambitions; they are just as keen, just as greedy, just as hungry for wealth, just as foreign to any form of justice that is not the justice of their caste, or that does not defend them against the classes they hold in subjection; they are, to sum up, just as immoral at bottom as the Christian in the sense that they consider only the advantages which they may obtain for themselves, and that the sole ambition of their lives is the acquisition of material goods, of which each hopes and strives to obtain the maximum. But in this daily struggle, the Jew, who, personally, as we have already seen, is better endowed than his competitors, increases his advantage by uniting with his co-religionists possessed of similar virtues, and thus augments his powers by acting in common with his brethren; the inevitable result being that they out-distance their rivals in the pursuit of any common end. In the midst of a disunited middle class, whose members are engaged in a perpetual struggle against one another, the Jews stand united as one. This is the secret of their success. Their solidarity is all the stronger in that it goes so far back. Its very existence is denied, and yet it is undeniable. The links in the chain have been forged in the course of ages until the flight of centuries has made man unconscious of their existence. It is worth our while to see how this bond of union was formed and how it was perpetuated.

Jewish solidarity dates from the Dispersion. Jewish emigrants and colonists took up their residence in foreign countries, and wherever they made their home they constituted a distinct society. Their communities centered around their houses of prayer, which they built in every town where they formed a nucleus. Everywhere they possessed numerous important privileges (see Chapters II and III.). The Diasporoi were invaluable allies of the Greeks in carrying on the work of eastern colonization, and strangely enough the Jews who adopted Hellenism, assisted in turn in Hellenizing the East. As a recompense they were allowed to retain their national homogeneity, together with full powers of self-government. This was the case in Alexandria, in Antioch, in Asia Minor, and in the Greek cities of Ionia. In almost every city they constituted corporations at the head of which was an ethnarch or patriarch, who, with the assistance of a council of leaders and a special tribunal, exercised all the powers of civil authority and of justice. The synagogues were "veritable small republics." [325] They were, in addition, the centres of religious and public life. The Jews came together in their synagogues, not only to listen to the reading of the Law, but also for

[325] E. Renan, *Vie de Jesus,* p. 142.

the discussion of their private affairs and for the purpose of exchanging views upon the general course of events. All the synagogues were closely connected in a vast federation which included within its scope the entire ancient world, progressing parallel with the expansion of the Macedonian power and Hellenistic civilization. They communicated with one another by messengers and kept one another in constant touch with events, the knowledge of which was likely to prove useful. They sought one another's counsel and rendered one another aid. At the same time, of course, the synagogues were bound together by a powerful religious tie. They preserved their independence, but they felt themselves sisters. The eyes of all Jews turned towards Jerusalem and towards the Temple, to which they sent their annual tribute, and the love which they felt for the Holy City, the passion with which they clung to their faith, served to bring to their mind their common origin and to cement their union. The small synagogues of the Grecian cities no less than the powerful Jewish colonies in Antioch and Alexandria were the creators of Jewish solidarity, both in its local and its world-wide aspects. In every city the Jewish traveller could count upon the aid of the community; when he arrived as an immigrant or as a settler, he was received as a brother, succored in his need and assisted in his designs, he was permitted to take up his home wherever he desired and he enjoyed the protection of the community which put all its resources at his disposal. He did not come as a stranger bound upon a difficult conquest, but as one well equipped and with protectors, friends, and brothers by his side. Throughout Asia Minor, the Archipelago, Cyrenaica and Egypt, a Jew might travel in perfect security; everywhere he was treated as a guest, everywhere he proceeded straight to the house of prayer, where he was sure to find a welcome. The Essenes carried on their propaganda in the same manner. They, too, created their little social centres, little associations in the very heart of the Jewish communities, and in this fashion they traveled from city to city, at their own free will taking no thought of the morrow.

At Home, where they lived in considerable numbers, [326] the Jews were as firmly united as in the cities of the Orient. "They are bound together by indissoluble bonds by the ties of loving sympathy," says Tacitus. [327] Thanks to their solidarity, they had acquired at Rome, as in Alexandria, such power that political parties feared them and sought their support. "You know," says Cicero, [328] "how great is the multitude of the Jews, how firm their union and their sympathy, how striking their political skill and their sway over the crowd in the assemblies."

When the Roman Empire fell, when the barbarian hosts invaded the ancient world, and triumphant Catholicism entered upon its career of expansion, the Jewish communities did not change. They were still powerful. organisms and the activity of their common life was such as to lend them great powers of resistance. In the midst

[326] E. Renan estimates the number of Jews in Rome at the time of Nero at from twenty to thirty thousand (*L'Antechrist,* p. 7, note 2).

[327] Hist. v. 5.

[328] Pro Flacco. xxviii.

of the universal upheaval they preserved their religious and social unity, two inseparable bonds to which they owe their prosperity. The members of the Jewish synagogues drew still more closely together. It was owing to this mutual support that they suffered nothing from the great changes that were going on about them. For some time, even after the Gothic and German kingdoms had been established Jewish communities preserved a certain degree of self-government. They were placed under a special jurisdiction and in the midst of those new societies they constituted veritable trading corporations in which none of the ancient solidarity was wanting. In proportion as the nations became more hostile to the Jews, in proportion as persecution and oppressive legislation increased, their solidarity increased. The external and internal forces which tended to imprison the Jews within the narrow circumference of their Ghettoes, only served to foster the spirit of union among them. Isolated from the world, they only tightened the bonds which held them together. Their common life nourished the desire for, and the need of, fraternal action. In other words, the Ghettoes developed the spirit of Jewish solidarity. In addition, the synagogues had succeeded in preserving their authority, so that while the Jews were subject to the harsh laws of king and of emperor, they had also a government of their own, councils of elders, and tribunals, to whose decisions they submitted.

Their general synods forbade, in fact, any Jew under the pain of anathema, from citing a fellow Jew before a Christian tribunal. [329] Everything drove them to

[329] These synods frequently met after the twelfth century, and constituted the first general assemblies of the Rabbis since the closing of the Talmud. Jacob Tarn (Rabbenu Tarn), the founder of the school of Tossafists, was the first to bring about the reunion of such assemblies, for the purpose, undoubtedly, of considering means of common resistance to persecution.

unity in those long years of horror and cruelty known as the Middle Ages. Had they been disunited they would have suffered still more. By common action they could defend themselves the more easily and escape some of the calamities that threatened them without end. Though their life was made miserable by the imposition of numerous regulations, the fraternal aid which they rendered one another enabled them frequently to evade the numberless burdens which were piled upon them. At the same time the ancient relations between synagogue and synagogue were maintained, and in this manner the cosmopolitan spirit of the Jews was preserved with their solidarity. The communities frequently came to one another's aid and instances of this bond of sympathy are plentiful, such as that very characteristic act of the Levantine Jews, who, after the martyrdom of the Jews of Ancona, made a common agreement to suspend all commercial relations with that town and to transfer their trade to Pesaro, where Guido Ubaldo had received the fugitives from Ancona. The Doctors and the Rabbis encouraged this feeling of solidarity which was further increased by the spirit of Talmudic exclusiveness. In the eleventh century a Rabbinical synod at Worms, forbade a Jewish landlord to rent out his house, occupied by a Jew, to a Gentile without the consent of the tenant. [330] and a council of the twelfth century forbade a Jew,

[330] Jost, ***Geschichte der Juden,*** Berln, 1820, Vol 2.

under the pain of anathema, to bring a fellow Jew be-fore a Christian tribunal. The Jewish community, or Kahal, made use of a powerful weapon against those who proved themselves lacking in the spirit of solidarity; it struck them with anathema and pronounced against them the **Cherem Hakahal** (the ban of the community). This excommunication fell upon all those who failed in their duty to the community; those, for instance, who refused to acknowledge the full value of their possessions in order to evade the taxes imposed for the maintenance of the synagogue; those who, in drawing up a legal in-strument with a fellow Jew, omitted to have such document attested by the notary of the community; those who would not submit to any decision arrived at by the Kahal for the common welfare; [331] finally, all those who by word or writing attacked the Law and the Talmud, and worked for the destruction of Israel. Mordechai Kolkos, Uriel Acosta and Spinoza were among the last.

In this manner, the action of time, the influence of hostile legislation and of religious persecution, and the need for mutual defense, have intensified the feeling of fellowship among the Jews. In our own day the powerful institution of the Kahal exerts its influence wherever the Jew is subjected to a rigorous regime, and even the reformed Jew, who has broken away from the narrow restrictions of the synagogue, and yields no obedience to the will of the community, has not forgotten the spirit of solidarity. [332] Once having acquired the sentiment

[331] Maurice Aron, **Histoire de Vexcommunication juive,** Nimes, A. Catelan, 1882.

[332] The **Alliance Israelite Universelle,** founded in 1860 by idolphe Cremieux, and numbering at present more than thirty thousand members, has served only to foster the fraternal spirit among the Jews. The aims of the Alliance are to ameliorate the intellectual and moral conditions of the Jews in the Orient @@@ the establishment of schools, to take measures for their relief from oppression, and to bring about their complete emancipation.

of union and fostered it by the habit of ages, they could not get rid of it in getting rid of their faith. It had become a social instinct, and social instincts, slowly formed, are slow to disappear. This also should be kept in mind: the Jew had taken his place as a member of society on a basis of equality with the rest of the people, but he nevertheless constituted a minority, and the law which impels minorities to unite may be said almost to be a corollary of the law of self-preservation. A number of individuals in the presence of an overpowering aggregation will perceive that to preserve their existence by the side of the majority, they must unite their forces in order to offer a successful resistance to an outside power which threatens to destroy them, that they must form a compact unit, become, in other words, an organized minority; not that it has leaders, or theoretic rulers, or a government and laws, but because it consists of small groups firmly united and acting in constant co-operation. A Jew will always obtain assistance from his co-religionists, provided he be found faithful to the ties of Jewish brotherhood; but, if on the contrary, he prove hostile to the sentiment of Jewish unity, he will meet with nothing but hostility. The Jew, even though he may have departed from the synagogue, is still a member of the Jewish free-masonry, [333] of the Jewish clique, if you will.

United, then, by the strongest feelings of solidarity, the Jews can easily hold their own in this disjointed and anarchic society of ours. If the millions of Christians by whom they are surrounded were to substitute this same principle of co-operation for that of individual competition, the importance of the Jew would immediately be destroyed. The Christian, however, will not adopt such a course, and the Jew must inevitably, I will not say dominate, the favorite expression of the antisemites, but certainly possess the advantage over others, and exercise that supremacy against which the Antisemites inveigh, without being able to destroy it, seeing that its reason lies not only in the middle class among the Jews, but in the Christian bourgeoisie as well. The accusations enumerated above are therefore the expression of hatred on the part of the Christian capitalist who sees himself outdistanced and supplanted by his Jewish rival; but such accusations do not constitute the basis of economic antisemitism, the real cause of which I have just demonstrated.

If we keep in mind, then, this conception of Jewish fellowship and the fact that the Jews at present, constitute an organized minority, we are not unjust in concluding that antisemitism is, in part, a mere struggle among the rich, a contest among the possessors of capital. In truth, it is the capitalist, the merchant, the manufacturer, the financier, among the Christians, who

[333] I am not speaking, of course, of Masonic lodges, but use the word Fret Masonry in the broad meaning of the term.

feels himself injured by the Jews, and not the Christian proletariat, who suffer no more from the class of Jewish employers than from their Christian masters; less, indeed, if we consider that in a case like this, where numbers count, the entrepreneur class among the Jews by comparison with the Christians amounts to little. This will explain why antisemitism is essentially the senti-ment of the middle classes, and why it is so rarely met with, except in the form of a vague prejudice among the mass of the peasants and the working classes.

This war within the ranks of capital does not reveal itself after the same fashion; it presents rather two aspects, according as it arises from the hostility between the landowning class and the capitalist class in the narrower sense, or from competition within the industrial class itself.

The agrarian capitalist, in his contest against the captain of industry, has embraced antisemitism, because to the territorial lord, the Jew is the representative of commercial and industrial capitalism. For this reason, in Germany, the Agrarian Protectionists, are bitter enemies of the Jews, who are among the most conspicuous champions of free trade. By instinct and self-interest the Jews are opposed to the physiocratic theory which would vest political power only in the owners of land; they maintain rather the theory of modern industrialism, which makes political power go hand in hand with industrial development. Jews and Agrarians both are probably unconscious, as individuals, of the part they are playing in the economic struggle, but their mutual hatred comes from this source, nevertheless. The man of the lower middle class, the small tradesman whom speculation has probably ruined has much clearer ideas of why he is an Antisemite. He knows that reckless speculation, with its attendant panics, has been his bane, and for him, the most formidable jugglers of capital, the most dangerous speculators are the Jews; which, indeed, is very true. Those even whose downfall has not been caused by speculation, ascribe their misfortunes indirectly to this cause which has destroyed a great part of the industrial and commercial capital of the world. But here, as everywhere, they make the Jew responsible for a state of things, of which he is far from being the sole cause.

The other form of economic antisemitism is more simple. It arises from the direct competition between Jewish and Christian brokers, manufacturers, and merchants. The Christian capitalist, acting for the most part, independently of his fellows, when confronted by the harmonious, if not united, opposition of the Jewish capitalists, finds himself necessarily at a disadvantage, and in the daily struggle for life frequently succumbs to his adversaries. He, therefore, suffers directly, from the rise of Jewish manufacturers and merchants. Hence his extreme animosity against the Jews, and the desire to break the power of his fortunate rivals. This is the most violent, the most bitter of all the manifestations of antisemitism, because it is the expression of the sentiments of those who feel themselves injured in their personal interests.

One might be tempted to find an indication of antisemitism proceeding from direct competition, in the display of hostility by the working classes against the Jews of London and New York. This, however, would not be exactly true. Russian and Polish immigration into England and the United States has brought about a considerable increase in the working population of the great industrial centres, and as a result has occasioned a great decrease in wages and brought about the rise of the hideous sweating system in the East End of London and on the East Side of New York. There has consequently been some agitation against the Jewish proletarians, especially against the members of the tailors' trades, who constitute a majority of the immigrants. This movement, however, has nothing inherently anti-semitic in it, but is similar to the opposition aroused among workingmen in other countries by the importation of foreign labor; such is the case with the Italian and Belgian laborers in Prance, whom the employers eagerly seize on at very great advantage to themselves. [334] The same is true of competition in the middle class. If there this movement is consciously antisemitic, it is not solely because the Jews form a freemasonry or a

[334] A clearer idea of economic antisemitism may be obtained from a study of the Chinese Question in America. Constituting a minority in race and religion and differently endowed from the Americans, the Chinese, through their firm organization, have aroused the fear of the capitalists, who accuse them of draining the country of its wealth, and of reducing wages by their entrance into the labor market The feeling of hostility against the Chinese has given rise, besides the anti-immigration law, to legislative measures greatly curtailing their rights, checking their influence, and limiting their opportunities. Similar measures have been proposed against German and Russian Immigration.

minority too well-organized. As a matter of fact the Protestants are organized after a similar fashion, and yet, save in rare instances, Anti-Protestantism does not rage any more in France than Anti-Catholicism in England, where in their turn the Catholics form a powerful minority. There must be another cause, and that; one of capital importance. It is this. The Jews, it is true, are a minority like the French Protestants or the German Catholics, but the Protestants in France and Catholics in Germany form a national minority, whereas the Jews are regarded as strangers. We find ourselves in the presence therefore of a struggle, which is not merely a contest betwen two forms of capital, or between a number of capitalists, but rather a conflict between national capital and capital which is looked upon as foreign. It is the continuation of the old historic contest, commenced in antiquity, when the Ionian cities "attempted to force the Jews resident within their walls to abjure their faith or to bear the weight of public disabilities." [335] It persisted throughout the Middle Ages, when the Jews were thought of by the young nations the people which had crucified God, when it was discovered, too, that this race of strangers had concentrated in their hands all wealth. When Christian commerce arose, it, too, attempted to crush a rival who seemed all the more dangerous because he was not sprung from the soil, and it succeeded in part by the establishment of fraternities, corporations, and orders, by the organization, that is, of Christian wealth.

This prejudice against the Jews has prevailed to the

[335] Theodore Mommsen, *History of Rome.*

present day, secret, instinctive rather than deliberate, and acquired by heredity. People still feel an intense bitterness against the deicides, and glance with no favorable eye at their riches, for they still find it difficult to understand how this tribe of miscreants and murderers, doomed to perdition, can legitimately be the owners of wealth. The belief is still held that the Jew cannot acquire wealth without plundering the sons of the soil— every owner of land looking upon himself as its child. If economic antisemitism therefore must be regarded as the manifestation of a struggle within the ranks of capital, we must not forget, too, that it is an outcome of the opposition between national and foreign wealth.

CHAPTER XV.

THE FATE OF ANTISEMITISM.

The Causes of Antisemitism.—Antisemitism of the Present Day and Anti-Judaism in Former Times.—The Permanent Cause.—The Jew as a Stranger and the Manifestations of Antisemitism.—The Jew and Assimilation.—The Jew and His Surroundings.— Modification of the Jewish Type.—The Disappearance of External Characteristics.—The Disappearance of Internal Characteristics.—The Religion of the Synagogue at the Present Day.—The Decline and Fall of Talmudism.—The Jew an Assimilated Element.—The Disappearance of Religious Prejudices Against the Jew.—The Decay of the Spirit of Particularism and National Exclusiveness.—The Progress of Cosmopolitanism.—Antisemitism and Economic Change.—The Struggle Against Capital. —The Capitalist Alliance.—Capital and Revolution. —The Antisemites as Adversaries of Revolution.— The End of Antisemitism.

We have seen then that the causes of antisemitism are, in their nature, ethnic, religious, political and economic. They are all causes of far reaching importance, and they exist not because of the Jew alone, nor because of his neighbors alone, but principally because of pre-vailing social conditions. Ignorant of the real cause of their sentiments, those who profess antisemitism, justify their opinion by accusations against the Jew which, as we have seen, do not at all agree with facts. Charges racial, charges religions, charges political and economic, none of these grievances of antisemitism are well ' founded. Some, like the ethnic grievance arise from a false conception of race; others like the religious and political charges, are due to a narrow and incomplete interpretation of historical evolution; and la9t of all, the economic count, has its justification in the necessity of concealing the strife going on within the capitalist class. None of these accusations is justified. It is no more correct to say that the Jew is a pure Semite than it would be to say that the European peoples are pure Aryans. There is, in fact, no legitimate basis for the very notion of Aryan and Semite, one superior to the other. We have seen that there is no such thing as race in the sense in which the word is generally employed, that is, to denote a human aggregate, descended from the same pair of primitive ancestors, and suffering no admixture of foreign elements throughout the entire course of its development. The belief which made purity of blood the basis of communal life, even though it must have been justified at a time when humanity consisted of a number of minute and heterogeneous groups, was no longer tenable when these groups united to form cities. The idea, nevertheless, persisted and became an ethnological fiction, which ancient cities embellished with legends in recounting the lives of their heroic founders. The fiction changed when cities in turn began to unite, and nations arose; but it survived just the same and gave rise to the construction of interminable genealogies for the purpose of establishing a common descent for all the members of the same State.

If it is true that the Jews are not a race, it is unjust to look upon them as the cause of undesirable change in modern society. This is really assigning them too important a role, a role of such importance indeed as to make the antisemites seem philosemites in fact. To make Israel the central figure of the world's history, the leaven of peoples, the awakener of nations, is absurd; nevertheless this is what both the friends and the enemies of the Jew are guilty of. Whether it be Bossuet or Drumont, they have ascribed to the Jew an exaggerated importance, which the latter, with characteristic untutored vanity, has not been loathe to accept. But of this vanity we must be rid. If the all-powerful Church has seen its influence decrease in spite of the desperate efforts of the bourgeoisie to revive it and if religious indifference advances with the growth of revolutionary ideas, the fault does not rest with the sons of Jacob. The Jews are not in themselves the creators of present conditions, but merely by the force of inherited habits have been more able to adapt themselves to prevailing circumstances. They are not the founders of this capitalistic, financiering, stock-jobbing, trading, manufacturing, society of ours, though they have profited by it more than any others. They enjoy at present many great advantages, not because they resort to methods of procedure which are unfair or dishonest, as their adversaries declare, but because in the course of centuries, hostile legislation, religions persecutions and the political and social restrictions under which they lived, have served to prepare them for the present form of society, by equipping them with superior weapons for the daily struggle of life.

Still though the Jews are not a race, they were, until our own days, a nation. They did not fail to perpetuate their national characteristics, their religion and their theological code, which was at the same time a social code. Though they were never guilty of working for the destruction of Christianity, and were never organized in a secret conspiracy against Jesus, they did lend aid to those who assailed the Christian religion, and in all attacks on the Church, they were ever in the front rank. In the same way, even if they did not constitute a vast secret society, implacably pursuing through the centuries as its object, the undermining of monarchy, they did render important aid to the cause of Revolution. In the nineteenth century they were among the most ardent adherents of the liberal, social, and revolutionary parties, to which they contributed men like Lasker and Disraeli, Crémieux, Marx and Lasalle, [336] not counting the obscure herd of agitators. To the revolutionary cause, too, they contributed their wealth. Finally, as I have just said, if they did not, by themselves, erect the throne of triumphant capitalism on the ruins of the old regime the were instrumental in its erection. Thus are the Jews found at the opposite poles of modern society. On

> [336] This is not the place to discuss the respective importance of these men, who differed among themselves in so many ways; it is sufficient here to recall the part they severally played.

the one hand they labor assiduously at that enormous concentration of wealth, which, no doubt, is bound to result in its expropriation by the State; on the other hand, they are among the most bitter foes of capital. Opposed to the Jewish money baron, the product of exile, of Talmudism, of hostile legislation and persecution, stands the Jewish revolutionist, the child of biblical and prophetic tradition, that same tradition which animated the fanatic Anabaptists of Germany in the sixteenth century, and the Puritan warriors of Cromwell. In the midst of the many transformations which our age has witnessed, they have not remained inactive; indeed, it is their activity which has, I will not say caused, but rather perpetuated, antisemitism, for antisemitism is but the successor of the anti-Judaism of the Middle Ages. Long ago, in Spain, the persecution of the Moriscoes and the Marranos was an attempt to eliminate a foreign element in the Spanish nation; and in the same way the Jews were regarded as a strange tribe, a horde of dei-cides, whose aim was by propaganda to infuse their spirit into the Christian peoples, and, in addition, to obtain possession of great wealth, the importance of which was becoming apparent even during the early years of the Mediaeval period. Antisemitism, at present, in Eastern Europe, at least, [337] finds different expression from that of former times; the charges brought against the Jew have

> [337] In Eastern Europe, in Persia and in Morocco, we have an approximately correct picture of the antisemitic movement of the Middle Ages. Social prejudice, restrictive legislation, in-sults, humiliations, riots, massacres, exile, nothing is wanting. This, I believe, I have proved for Russia and Roumania, in Chapter viii.

also varied, in that they are formulated after a different fashion and are given a basis of ethnologic and anthropologic theory; but the causes have not altered appreciably, and modern antisemitism differs from the anti-Judaism of former times only in that it is more self-conscious, more pragmatic, and more deliberate. At the bottom of the antisemitism of our own days, as at the bottom of the anti-Judaism of the thirteenth century are the fear of, and the hatred for, the stranger. This is the primal cause of all antisemitism, the never failing cause. It appears in Alexandria under the Ptolemies, in Borne during the lifetime of Cicero, in the Greek cities of Ionia, in Antioch, in Cyrenaica, in feudal Europe, and in the modern state whose soul is the spirit of nationality.

Let us leave now this old anti-Judaism and concern ourselves only with the antisemitism of modern times. A product of the spirit of national exclusiveness and of a reaction on the part of the conservative spirit against the tendencies set into motion by the Revolution, all the causes which have brought it about, or have served to maintain it, may be reduced to this one only: the Jews are not as yet assimilated; that is to say, they have not yet given up their belief in their own nationality. By the practice of circumcision, by the observation of their special rules of prayer and their dietary regulations, they still continue to differentiate themselves from those around them; they persist in being Jews. Not that they are incapable of the sentiment of patriotism—the Jews in certain countries, as in Germany, have contributed more than anybody else to the realization of national unity—but they seem to solve the apparently unsolvable problem of constituting an integral part of two nationalities; if they are Frenchmen, or if they are Germans, [338] they are also Jews, and if they succeed in gaining some slight appreciation as Germans or as Frechmen, their Judaism does not fail to invoke the liveliest reproach. Among all nations they are regarded as the Americans regard the Chinese, as an aggregation of strangers who have secured possession of the same privileges as the native-born, but who refuse to give up their separate identity. They are still considered as different from the rest, and the more the nations take on their peculiar characteristics,the more marked these differences become. In the great process of evolution which leads every people to assimilate harmoniously the various elements which compose it, the Jews are the refractory element. They are always the stiff-necked nation, against which the lawmaker launches his anathema. They still cling to forms of social life long since abolished and whose separate existence has long ago been destroyed. In a certain measure they are a nation which has survived its na-tionality, and for ages has been resisting death.

Why is this so? Because everything has contributed to maintain their peculiar characteristics as a people; because they have been the possessors of a religion which is national in character, and which had its perfect reason

[338] The German Antisemites accuse the Jews of entertaining sentiments hostile to Germany, and of partiality for the interests of France; but the French antisemites, in turn, reproach the Jews with entertaining a tender regard for Germany. This is merely a way of saying that the Jews are strangers, or, to put it in a better form, are not yet assimilated.

for existence while the Jews constituted a people, but which ceased to be of service after the Dispersion and now tends only to keep them apart from the rest of the world; because all over Europe they have established colonies jealous of their prerogatives, and clinging firmly to their customs, to their religions practices, to their manners of life; because they have been living for ages under the domination of a theological code, which has rendered them immobile; because the laws of the numerous countries in which they have made their abode, together with prejudice and persecution, have prevented them from mingling with the body of the people; be-cause since the second exodus, since their departure, that is, from Palestine, they have raised around themselves, and others have raised around them rigid and insurmountable barriers. Such as they are they are the result of a slow process of creation, on their own part, and on the part of others: their intellectual and moral life is what it is, because others made it their object to differentiate the Jews from the world, and the Jews themselves devoted themselves to the same object. They feared defilement through contact, and they were feared in turn as a source of defilement. Their doctors forbade them to unite with the Christians, and the Christian lawmakers forbade all union with the Jews. Of their own impulse they devoted themselves to the occupation of money-changing, and they were for hidden to exercise any other profession than that; of their own accord, they separated themselves from the world, and they were forced by others to remain in the Ghettoes.

In this manner did they remain different from those who lived beside them. Before their emancipation, however, they escaped the notice of man. They held themselves apart, and no one came into contact with them. Their portion was allotted to them; their territory was marked out for them, and they lived on the outskirts of society, without retarding in the least the general course of events, for they did not constitute a part of society. Once they were liberated, they scattered themselves everywhere, appearing before the eyes of men such as the ages had made them. They produced the same impression that would be experienced now, if of a sudden all the Gypsies of the world should rally to civilization, and demand their place in society. The environment in which the Jews had been living for so long a time had changed, but they themselves had not changed, and it required more than the decree of the National Assem-bly to accomplish such a feat. The product of a religion and of a law, the Jews could not alter unless that law and that religion were altered.

Here we find ourselves confronted with a most serious objection. The antisemites are not content with saying that the Jew belongs to a different race, and is therefore a stranger, but they declare that he is by nature an element which can never be assimilated; and even if some of them admit that the Jew may become a constituent part in the composition of nations, they would have it that such an amalgamation is only detrimental to that nation. The Semite, it is maintained, saps the strength of and destroys the Aryan, and this in spite of the antisemitic theory that the superior race is bound to overcome the inferior race without being in the least affected by it. Are the Jews then incapable of assimilation? Not the least in the world, and their entire history proves the contrary. It shows us [339] how large is the number of Jews who have become mixed with the other nations through baptism, how numerous were their conversions in the Middle Ages; how many Jews have been absorbed by the surrounding population, going over of their own free will to Christ, or driven to the baptismal font by the violence of monks and fanatical kings. Jews, in short, of whom we can no longer find any trace, just as we can no longer find any traces of the Goths, the Alamani and the Suevi, who with many other peoples united to form the French nation. At all times the Jew, like all Semites, has been in touch with the Aryan; at all times there has been intercommunication between the two races, and nothing can serve better to prove that their assimilation is possible. Besides, to demonstrate that the Jews cannot be assimilated, it is necessary to prove that they are incapable of change, for a human being incapable of adapting himself to his surroundings, can no more be merged into any social aggregation than a foreign element can enter into the economy of the human body. But as a matter of fact, the Jews have been constantly transformed by their surroundings. If we find certain resemblances between the Spanish Jew and the Jew of Russia [340] we find also marked differences, and these differences are due not only to the absorption of other races, attracted and converted by the Jew, but

[339] Chap. x.

[340] I am speaking, of course, of the Jews who have remained true to their faith.

are the result also of the Jew's natural environment, social, moral, and intellectual. The Jewish type has varied not only geographically, but has changed through time; it is a truism that the Jew of the Roman Ghetto was not the same as the Jew who fought under Bar-Cochba, just as the Jew of our great European cities does not resemble the Jew of the Middle Ages. Of course, the differences which I have pointed out as prevailing among Jews of different countries and of different times, are less striking than their resemblances; but that only proves that the artificial environment in which the Jew has been forced to live has proved more effective than his natural environment. This is always true in the history of Man, that he is less affected by climatic conditions against which he is always in reaction, than by his social surroundings. The Jew has been no exception to this law of human evolution, and it is not the snows of Poland, or the burning suns of Spain that have been the principal factors in his development. He has been reduced to a state of petrifaction by the hostile laws of the nations in which he lived, and by his religion, a puissant and fearful religion, like all non-metaphysical religions which are characterized predominantly by a ritual and a Law. For the Jew this religion and this Law have always been the same, in all times and all places. They have been constant forces in his development, both externally and internally.

But during the last hundred years, these seemingly constant factors have undoubtedly undergone a change. [341]

[341] I must repeat once more that I am speaking now only of the Jews of Western Europe, who have been admitted to the rights of citizenship in the countries where they live, and not of the Jews of the East, who are still

subject to discriminating laws, as in Roumania, in Russia, in Morocco, and in Persia,

There are no longer external legislative restrictions on the Jew; the special laws to which he was formerly subjective have been abolished, and henceforth, he is amenable only to the laws of the country of which he is a citizen (and these laws, let me remark, differing with every country constitute in themselves a factor of differentiation for the Jew). With the disappearance of discriminating laws, his own peculiar laws have also disappeared. The Jew no longer lives apart, but shares in the common life; is no longer a stranger to the civilization of the countries which have received him; has no longer a literature of his own; nor manners that mark him as different from others. In short, he has adapted himself to the mode of life of whatever nation he adheres to. And as these modes of life differ from nation to nation, they serve to create marked differences among the Jews themselves, with the progress of time creating more and more striking variety among them. Day by day they are departing from the class of occupations and the type of religion peculiar to the Jew. These, it is true, still exist, but they are maintained only by internal factors, by faith, by religious practices, and the manners of life which they impose, but which, necessarily, inevitably, indeed, must disappear.

At the presnt day, the religious practices of the Jews vary with the different countries. While in Galicia, for example, the utmost minutiae of religious observances are still maintained; in France, in England, and in Germany they are reduced to the minimum. If the study of the Talmud is still held in respect in Poland, in Russia, and in certain parts of Germany and Austria-Hungary, in other countries it has fallen into complete disrepute. The gulf betwen the emancipated Jew of France and the Talmudic Jew of Galicia widens day by day; and in this manner differences are created in the midst of Israel, differences which may be even observed between the reformed Jew and the orthodox.

Still more important, however, is the fact that the Talmudic spirit is slowly vanishing. Such schools of the Talmud as still exist in Western Europe are disappearing day by day: the modern Jew is not even able to read Hebrew; freed from the bonds of the rabbinical code, the synagogue of the present day professes at most a sort of ceremonial deism, and deism itself is losing its strength with the modern Jew, making every reformed Jew ready for rationalism. Nor is it only Tal-mudism that is dying, but the Jewish religion itself is in its death agony. It is the oldest of all existing religions, and it would seem right that it should be the first to dis-appear. Direct contact with the Christian world has started it upon its course of dissolution. For a long time it has endured as all bodies endure which are deprived of light and air: but once a breach is made in the cavern in Which it has been sleeping, the sun and the fresh breath of the outside air have entered and it has fallen apart Together with the Jewish religion, the Jewish spirit is vanishing. True it is that that was the spirit which animated Heine and Boerne, Marx and Lassalle, but they were still the products of the Jewry; they were cradled in traditions which the young Jews of to-day overlook or despise. At the present time, if there is still such a thing as Jewish personality, it tends to disappear. In this manner the Jews, made up as they are of several dissimilar strata, which similar conditions of external life, similar intellec-tual tendencies, similar religious, moral and social characteristics have united, are now resuming their heterogeneity. The constant factors in their evolution have become variable, and their artificial uniformity is disappearing for the reason that the Jewish faith, the Jewish practices, and the Jewish spirit, and with this faith, practices, and spirit, the Jews themselves, are disappearing. What religious persecu-tion could not bring about, the decline of religious faith, based upon national ideal has accomplished. The emancipated Jew, freed alike from hostile legislation and ob-scurant Talmudism, far from being an element to absorb others, has become an ele-ment that can be readily absorbed. In certain countries, as in the United States, the distinction between Jews and Christians is rapidly disappearing. [342] It is vanish-ing from day to day, because from day to day the Jews are abandoning their ancient prejudices, their peculiar modes of worship, the observance of their special laws of prayer and their dietary regulations. They no longer persist in the belief that they are destined always to remain a people; they no longer dream—a touching dream, perhaps, but ridiculous—that they have an eternal mission to fulfill. The time will come when they shall be completely eliminated; when they shall be

[342] Henry George, *Progress and Poverty.*

merged into the body of the nations, after the same manner as the Phoenicians, who, having planted their trading stations all over Europe disappeared without leaving a trace behind them. By that time, too, antisemitism will have run its course. The moment, to be sure, is not near; the number of orthodox Jews is still great, and as long as they exist it would seem that antisemitism must exist. Still antisemitism is not caused solely by Israel; it is the product of religious, ethnic, and economic causes which are independent of the Jew, and which are also capable of modification and of ultimate disappearance. In our own day we may say that their decline is a fact.

If Judaism, then, is in the process of dissolution, neither is Catholicism or Protestantism gaining in strength, and we may venture to say that every external form of religion is losing its influence. The contrary, of course, is maintained in the case of the Christian religion ; but in doing so, people are either the victims of an illusion, or else are guided by selfish interests. As Guyau has said, [343] "Religion has found defenders among the skeptics who support it partly out of regard for the poetry of life and the aesthetic beauty which lies in myths, and partly for its practical utility." This neo-mysticism is an outgrowth of that hunger for poetry and beauty, which believes that it can find satisfaction only in religious illusion. As for the practical value of religion we see it now sustained by that same capitalistic bourgeoisie which formerly attacked all religious belief in so far as it was the ally of the partisans of the ancient

[343] M. Guyau, *L'Irreligion de l'avenir;* Paris, 1893, p. xix.

regime, but who now call upon religion to strengthen their influence and defend their own privileges. These, however, are only artificial manifestations; religion itself in any positive or definitely prescribed form is rapidly disappearing. On the one hand, we are advancing towards a narrow and stupid materialism, opposed to all religious feeling; on the other, our way is towards a state of philosophic and moral un-religion which shall be "a degree higher than religion or civilization itself." [344] At the same time while these tendencies are increasing, religious prejudice is tending to disappear, and the prejudice of Christian against Jew, and of Jew against Christian, persistent, in its way, as the prejudice of the Catholic against the Protestant, cannot possibly be the only one to remain. Even now it is decreasing in intensity, and the time is near, no doubt, when every Jew will no longer be held responsible for the sufferings of Jesus on Calvary. With the steady extinction of religious animosities, one of the causes of antisemitism must disappear, and antisemitism itself must lose much of its violence, though exist it will, so long as the economic and ethnic causes which have made it, endure.

The spirit of national egotism and self-sufficiency, however strong it may be at present, is also showing signs of decay. Other ideas have arisen, which from day to day are gaining in influence; they enter into the spirits of men, they impress themselves upon their understanding, they engender new conceptions and new forms of thought. Though the principle of nationality is still a guiding force in international politics, brutal and un-

[344] M. Guyau, *loc. cit.,* page xv.

reasoning hatred against the foreigner is no longer upheld as a doctrine. [345] A new civilization is in the process of making, common to all enlightened nations—a civilization of humanity that shall be above the French civilization, or the German civilization, or the English civilization. Science, literature, and the arts are becoming international; not that they are losing those peculiar characteristics which constitute their charm and their value, nor that they are all aiming at the same deadly uniformity, but because they are animated by the same spirit. The brotherhood of nations which formerly was a mere chimera, may be dreamt of now, without transcending the limits of common sense. The sentiment of human solidarity is growing stronger; and the number of thinkers and writers who labor at furthering its growth is increasing from day to day. The nations are coming into closer touch, and are learning to know one another better, admire one another, love one another. Increased facilities of communication tend to favor the development of the cosmopolitan spirit, and this spirit of cosmopolitanism will unite one day the most diverse of races in a peaceful Federation of definite entities, substituting universal altruism for selfish patriotism. The Jews are bound to profit by this decline of national exclusiveness, in that it must coincide with the partial elimination of their own peculiar characteristics. The progress of internationalism must bring about the decay of antisemitism. Parallel with the decline of na-

> [345] Exceptions are the class of sublimated patriots, who, In France, for instance are Anglophobes and Germanophobes, on principle rather than for any ascertainable reason.

tional prejudices the Jews will witness the economic causes of antisemitism losing their force. At present the Jews are assailed as the representatives of foreign wealth. It is therefore just to suppose that when the animosity against things foreign shall have disappeared, Jewish capital will no longer be an object of attack for Christian capital. Competition will, of course, persist in spite of all this, and those Jews who persist in maintaining their national identity, will always remain the objects of an hostility based upon this competitive struggle.

Other events, however, and other changes may bring about the disappearance of these economic causes. In the struggle which is now on between the proletariat and the industrial and financial classes, we shall possibly see Jewish and Christian capitalists forgetting their dif-ferences to unite against a common enemy. If present social conditions persist, however, such a union of the Christian and Jewish bourgeoisie can only bring about a temporary truce. Prom the battle which must inevitably be fought out, the indications are that Capital cannot come out the victor. Pounded upon egoism, upon selfishness, upon injustice, upon lies, and upon theft, our present society is doomed to disappear. However brilliant it may appear, however resplendent, refined, luxurious, magnificent, it is stricken with death. It has been weighed morally and found wanting. The bourgeoisie which exercises all political power because it holds control of all economic agencies, will draw upon its resources in vain; in vain will it appeal to all the armies that defend it, to all the tribunals of justice that watch over it, to all the legal codes that protect it; it will not be able to withstand the inflexible laws which day by day are working towards the substitution of communal property for the capitalistic régime.

Everything is tending to bring about such a consummation. With its own hands the class of property owners is working destruction; for whenever a certain class of possessors enter into a struggle for the attainment of their selfish interests they are unconsciously fighting against themselves, and to the advantage of their enemies. Every intestine struggle within the capitalist class must redound to the benefit of the revolutionary cause. In proclaiming war against the Jewish capitalist, the Christian capitalists are warring upon themselves, and are helping to undermine the foundations of that state of society of which they are the most ardent cham-pions. Such is the irony of things that antisemitism which everywhere is the creed of the conservative class, of those who accuse the Jews of having worked hand in band with the Jacobins of 1789 and the Liberals and Revolutionists of the nineteenth century, this very anti-semitism is acting, in fact, as an ally of the Revolution. Drumont in Prance, Pattai in Hungary, Stoecker and von Boeckel in Germany are co-operating with the very demagogues and revolutionists whom they believe they are attacking. This antisemitic movement, in its origin reactionary, has become transformed and is acting now for the advantage of the revolutionary cause. Antisemitism stirs up the middle class, the small tradesmen, and sometimes the peasant, against the Jewish capitalist, but in doing so it gently leads them toward Socialism, prepares them for anarchy, infuses in them a hatred for all capitalists, and, more than that, for capital in the abstract.

And thus, unconsciously, antisemitism is working its own ruin, for it carries in itself the germ of destruction. Nor can it escape its fate. In preparing the way for Socialism and Communism, it is laboring at the elimination not only of the economic cause, but also of the religious and ethnic causes which have engendered it, and which will disappear with this society of ours of which they are the products.

Such, then, is the probable fate of modern antisemitism. I have tried to show how it may be traced back to the ancient hatred against the Jews; how it persisted after the emancipation of the Jews, how it has grown and what are its manifestations. I have attempted to discover the reasons for this existence, and having determined those, have ventured to predict its future on the basis of them. In every way I am led to believe that it must ultimately perish, and that it will perish for the various reasons which I have indicated, because the Jew is undergoing a process of change; because religious, political, social, and economic conditions are likewise changing; but above all, because antisemitism is one of the last, though most long lived, manifestations of that old spirit of reaction and narrow conservatism, which is vainly attempting to arrest the onward movement of the Revolution.

THE END.

www.bookjungle.com *email: sales@bookjungle.com fax: 630-214-0564 mail: Book Jungle PO Box 2226 Champaign, IL 61825*

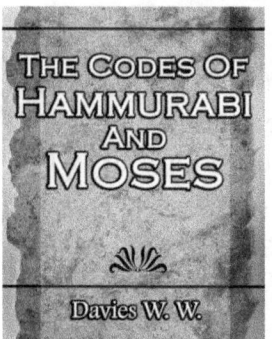

The Codes Of Hammurabi And Moses
W. W. Davies

QTY

The discovery of the Hammurabi Code is one of the greatest achievements of archaeology, and is of paramount interest, not only to the student of the Bible, but also to all those interested in ancient history...

Religion   **ISBN:** *1-59462-338-4*   **Pages:132**
MSRP $12.95

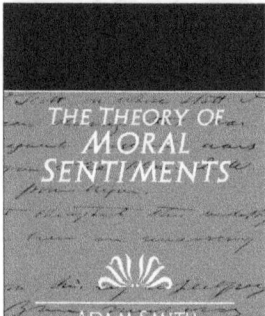

The Theory of Moral Sentiments
Adam Smith

QTY

This work from 1749. contains original theories of conscience amd moral judgment and it is the foundation for systemof morals.

Philosophy **ISBN:** *1-59462-777-0*   **Pages:536**
MSRP $19.95

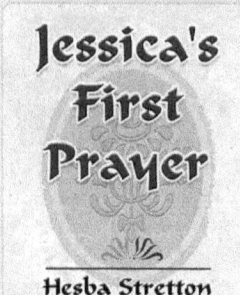

Jessica's First Prayer
Hesba Stretton

QTY

In a screened and secluded corner of one of the many railway-bridges which span the streets of London there could be seen a few years ago, from five o'clock every morning until half past eight, a tidily set-out coffee-stall, consisting of a trestle and board, upon which stood two large tin cans, with a small fire of charcoal burning under each so as to keep the coffee boiling during the early hours of the morning when the work-people were thronging into the city on their way to their daily toil...

Pages:84

Childrens   **ISBN:** *1-59462-373-2*   **MSRP $9.95**

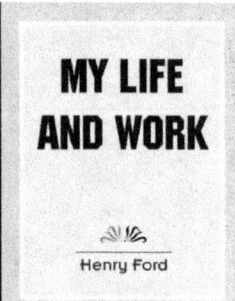

My Life and Work
Henry Ford

QTY

Henry Ford revolutionized the world with his implementation of mass production for the Model T automobile. Gain valuable business insight into his life and work with his own auto-biography... "We have only started on our development of our country we have not as yet, with all our talk of wonderful progress, done more than scratch the surface. The progress has been wonderful enough but..."

Pages:300

Biographies/   **ISBN:** *1-59462-198-5*   **MSRP $21.95**

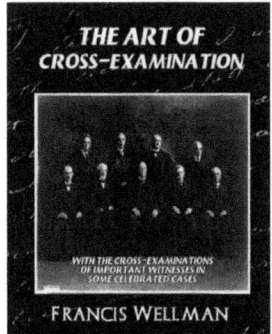

The Art of Cross-Examination
Francis Wellman

QTY

I presume it is the experience of every author, after his first book is published upon an important subject, to be almost overwhelmed with a wealth of ideas and illustrations which could readily have been included in his book, and which to his own mind, at least, seem to make a second edition inevitable. Such certainly was the case with me; and when the first edition had reached its sixth impression in five months, I rejoiced to learn that it seemed to my publishers that the book had met with a sufficiently favorable reception to justify a second and considerably enlarged edition. ..

Pages:412

Reference   ISBN: *1-59462-647-2*   *MSRP $19.95*

On the Duty of Civil Disobedience
Henry David Thoreau

QTY

Thoreau wrote his famous essay, On the Duty of Civil Disobedience, as a protest against an unjust but popular war and the immoral but popular institution of slave-owning. He did more than write—he declined to pay his taxes,   and was hauled off to gaol in consequence. Who can say how much this refusal of his hastened the end of the war and of slavery ?

Law   ISBN: *1-59462-747-9*   **Pages:48**

MSRP $7.45

Dream Psychology Psychoanalysis for Beginners
Sigmund Freud

QTY

Sigmund Freud, born Sigismund Schlomo Freud (May 6, 1856 - September 23, 1939), was a Jewish-Austrian neurologist and psychiatrist who co-founded the psychoanalytic school of psychology. Freud is best known for his theories of the unconscious mind, especially involving the mechanism of repression; his redefinition of sexual desire as mobile and directed towards a wide variety of objects; and his therapeutic techniques, especially his understanding of transference in the therapeutic relationship and the presumed value of dreams as sources of insight into unconscious desires.

Pages:196

Psychology   ISBN: *1-59462-905-6*   *MSRP $15.45*

The Miracle of Right Thought
Orison Swett Marden

QTY

Believe with all of your heart that you will do what you were made to do. When the mind has once formed the habit of holding cheerful, happy, prosperous pictures, it will not be easy to form the opposite habit. It does not matter how improbable or how far away this realization may see, or how dark the prospects may be, if we visualize them as best we can, as vividly as possible, hold tenaciously to them and vigorously struggle to attain them, they will gradually become actualized, realized in the life. But a desire, a longing without endeavor, a yearning abandoned or held indifferently will vanish without realization.

Pages:360

Self Help   ISBN: *1-59462-644-8*   *MSRP $25.45*

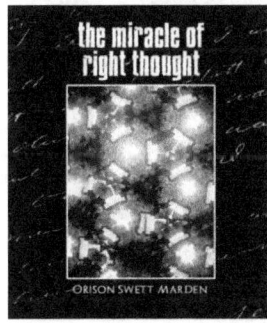

The Rosicrucian Cosmo-Conception Mystic Christianity *by Max Heindel*   ISBN: *1-59462-188-8* **$38.95**
The Rosicrucian Cosmo-conception is not dogmatic, neither does it appeal to any other authority than the reason of the student. It is; not controversial, but is: sent forth in the, hope that it may help to clear...   New Age/Religion Pages 646

Abandonment To Divine Providence *by Jean-Pierre de Caussade*   ISBN: *1-59462-228-0* **$25.95**
"The Rev. Jean Pierre de Caussade was one of the most remarkable spiritual writers of the Society of Jesus in France in the 18th Century. His death took place at Toulouse in 1751. His works have gone through many editions and have been republished...   Inspirational/Religion Pages 400

Mental Chemistry *by Charles Haanel*   ISBN: *1-59462-192-6* **$23.95**
Mental Chemistry allows the change of material conditions by combining and appropriately utilizing the power of the mind. Much like applied chemistry creates something new and unique out of careful combinations of chemicals the mastery of mental chemistry...   New Age Pages 354

The Letters of Robert Browning and Elizabeth Barret Barrett 1845-1846 vol II   ISBN: *1-59462-193-4* **$35.95**
by Robert Browning and Elizabeth Barrett   Biographies Pages 596

Gleanings In Genesis (volume I) *by Arthur W. Pink*   ISBN: *1-59462-130-6* **$27.45**
Appropriately has Genesis been termed "the seed plot of the Bible" for in it we have, in germ form, almost all of the great doctrines which are afterwards fully developed in the books of Scripture which follow...   Religion/Inspirational Pages 420

The Master Key *by L. W. de Laurence*   ISBN: *1-59462-001-6* **$30.95**
In no branch of human knowledge has there been a more lively increase of the spirit of research during the past few years than in the study of Psychology, Concentration and Mental Discipline. The requests for authentic lessons in Thought Control, Mental Discipline and...   New Age/Business Pages 422

The Lesser Key Of Solomon Goetia *by L. W. de Laurence*   ISBN: *1-59462-092-X* **$9.95**
This translation of the first book of the "Lernegton" which is now for the first time made accessible to students of Talismanic Magic was done, after careful collation and edition, from numerous Ancient Manuscripts in Hebrew, Latin, and French...   New Age/Occult Pages 92

Rubaiyat Of Omar Khayyam *by Edward Fitzgerald*   ISBN:*1-59462-332-5* **$13.95**
Edward Fitzgerald, whom the world has already learned, in spite of his own efforts to remain within the shadow of anonymity, to look upon as one of the rarest poets of the century, was born at Bredfield, in Suffolk, on the 31st of March, 1809. He was the third son of John Purcell...   Music Pages 172

Ancient Law *by Henry Maine*   ISBN: *1-59462-128-4* **$29.95**
The chief object of the following pages is to indicate some of the earliest ideas of mankind, as they are reflected in Ancient Law, and to point out the relation of those ideas to modern thought.   Religiom/History Pages 452

Far-Away Stories *by William J. Locke*   ISBN: *1-59462-129-2* **$19.45**
"Good wine needs no bush, but a collection of mixed vintages does. And this book is just such a collection. Some of the stories I do not want to remain buried for ever in the museum files of dead magazine-numbers an author's not unpardonable vanity..."   Fiction Pages 272

Life of David Crockett *by David Crockett*   ISBN: *1-59462-250-7* **$27.45**
"Colonel David Crockett was one of the most remarkable men of the times in which he lived. Born in humble life, but gifted with a strong will, an indomitable courage, and unremitting perseverance...   Biographies/New Age Pages 424

Lip-Reading *by Edward Nitchie*   ISBN: *1-59462-206-X* **$25.95**
Edward B. Nitchie, founder of the New York School for the Hard of Hearing, now the Nitchie School of Lip-Reading, Inc, wrote "LIP-READING Principles and Practice". The development and perfecting of this meritorious work on lip-reading was an undertaking...   How-to Pages 400

A Handbook of Suggestive Therapeutics, Applied Hypnotism, Psychic Science   ISBN: *1-59462-214-0* **$24.95**
by Henry Munro   Health/New Age/Health/Self-help Pages 376

A Doll's House: and Two Other Plays *by Henrik Ibsen*   ISBN: *1-59462-112-8* **$19.95**
Henrik Ibsen created this classic when in revolutionary 1848 Rome. Introducing some striking concepts in playwriting for the realist genre, this play has been studied the world over.   Fiction/Classics/Plays 308

The Light of Asia *by sir Edwin Arnold*   ISBN: *1-59462-204-3* **$13.95**
In this poetic masterpiece, Edwin Arnold describes the life and teachings of Buddha. The man who was to become known as Buddha to the world was born as Prince Gautama of India but he rejected the worldly riches and abandoned the reigns of power when...   Religion/History/Biographies Pages 170

The Complete Works of Guy de Maupassant *by Guy de Maupassant*   ISBN: *1-59462-157-8* **$16.95**
"For days and days, nights and nights, I had dreamed of that first kiss which was to consecrate our engagement, and I knew not on what spot I should put my lips..."   Fiction/Classics Pages 240

The Art of Cross-Examination *by Francis L. Wellman*   ISBN: *1-59462-309-0* **$26.95**
Written by a renowned trial lawyer, Wellman imparts his experience and uses case studies to explain how to use psychology to extract desired information through questioning.   How-to/Science/Reference Pages 408

Answered or Unanswered? *by Louisa Vaughan*   ISBN: *1-59462-248-5* **$10.95**
Miracles of Faith in China   Religion Pages 112

The Edinburgh Lectures on Mental Science (1909) *by Thomas*   ISBN: *1-59462-008-3* **$11.95**
This book contains the substance of a course of lectures recently given by the writer in the Queen Street Hall, Edinburgh. Its purpose is to indicate the Natural Principles governing the relation between Mental Action and Material Conditions...   New Age/Psychology Pages 148

Ayesha *by H. Rider Haggard*   ISBN: *1-59462-301-5* **$24.95**
Verily and indeed it is the unexpected that happens! Probably if there was one person upon the earth from whom the Editor of this, and of a certain previous history, did not expect to hear again...   Classics Pages 380

Ayala's Angel *by Anthony Trollope*   ISBN: *1-59462-352-X* **$29.95**
The two girls were both pretty, but Lucy who was twenty-one who supposed to be simple and comparatively unattractive, whereas Ayala was credited, as her Bombwhat romantic name might show, with poetic charm and a taste for romance. Ayala when her father died was nineteen...   Fiction Pages 484

The American Commonwealth *by James Bryce*   ISBN: *1-59462-286-8* **$34.45**
An interpretation of American democratic political theory. It examines political mechanics and society from the perspective of Scotsman James Bryce   Politics Pages 572

Stories of the Pilgrims *by Margaret P. Pumphrey*   ISBN: *1-59462-116-0* **$17.95**
This book explores pilgrims religious oppression in England as well as their escape to Holland and eventual crossing to America on the Mayflower, and their early days in New England...   History Pages 268

QTY

The Fasting Cure *by Sinclair Upton* ISBN: *1-59462-222-1* **$13.95**
In the Cosmopolitan Magazine for May, 1910, and in the Contemporary Review (London) for April, 1910, I published an article dealing with my experiences in fasting. I have written a great many magazine articles, but never one which attracted so much attention... New Age/Self Help/Health Pages 164

Hebrew Astrology *by Sepharial* ISBN: *1-59462-308-2* **$13.45**
In these days of advanced thinking it is a matter of common observation that we have left many of the old landmarks behind and that we are now pressing forward to greater heights and to a wider horizon than that which represented the mind-content of our progenitors... Astrology Pages 144

Thought Vibration or The Law of Attraction in the Thought World ISBN: *1-59462-127-6* **$12.95**
by William Walker Atkinson *Psychology/Religion Pages 144*

Optimism *by Helen Keller* ISBN: *1-59462-108-X* **$15.95**
Helen Keller was blind, deaf, and mute since 19 months old, yet famously learned how to overcome these handicaps, communicate with the world, and spread her lectures promoting optimism. An inspiring read for everyone... Biographies/Inspirational Pages 84

Sara Crewe *by Frances Burnett* ISBN: *1-59462-360-0* **$9.45**
In the first place, Miss Minchin lived in London. Her home was a large, dull, tall one, in a large, dull square, where all the houses were alike, and all the sparrows were alike, and where all the door-knockers made the same heavy sound... Childrens/Classic Pages 88

The Autobiography of Benjamin Franklin *by Benjamin Franklin* ISBN: *1-59462-135-7* **$24.95**
The Autobiography of Benjamin Franklin has probably been more extensively read than any other American historical work, and no other book of its kind has had such ups and downs of fortune. Franklin lived for many years in England, where he was agent... Biographies/History Pages 332

Name	
Email	
Telephone	
Address	
City, State ZIP	

☐ Credit Card   ☐ Check / Money Order

Credit Card Number	
Expiration Date	
Signature	

Please Mail to: Book Jungle
PO Box 2226
Champaign, IL 61825
or Fax to: 630-214-0564

ORDERING INFORMATION

web: *www.bookjungle.com*
email: *sales@bookjungle.com*
fax: *630-214-0564*
mail: *Book Jungle PO Box 2226 Champaign, IL 61825*
or PayPal *to sales@bookjungle.com*

Please contact us for bulk discounts

DIRECT-ORDER TERMS

20% Discount if You Order Two or More Books
Free Domestic Shipping!
Accepted: Master Card, Visa,
Discover, American Express